Eastern Hemisphere

Guided Reading Workbook

HOLT McDOUGAL
a division of Houghton Mifflin Harcourt

ISBN 978-0-547-51318-8

6 7 8 9 10   0982   15 14

4500467923   A B C D E F G

Contents

To the Student v

Introduction to Geography

A Geographer's World
Section 1.. 1
Section 2.. 4
Section 3.. 7

Planet Earth
Section 1.. 10
Section 2.. 13
Section 3.. 16

Climate, Environment, and Resources
Section 1.. 19
Section 2.. 22
Section 3.. 25
Section 4.. 28

The World's People
Section 1.. 31
Section 2.. 34
Section 3.. 37
Section 4.. 40

Southwest and Central Asia

History of the Fertile Crescent
Section 1.. 43
Section 2.. 46
Section 3.. 49
Section 4.. 52

Judaism and Christianity
Section 1.. 55
Section 2.. 58
Section 3.. 61

History of the Islamic World
Section 1.. 64
Section 2.. 67
Section 3.. 70
Section 4.. 73

The Eastern Mediterranean
Section 1.. 76
Section 2.. 79
Section 3.. 82
Section 4.. 85

The Arabian Peninsula, Iraq, and Iran
Section 1.. 88
Section 2.. 91
Section 3.. 94
Section 4.. 97

Central Asia
Section 1... 100
Section 2... 103
Section 3... 106

Africa

History of Ancient Egypt
Section 1... 109
Section 2... 112
Section 3... 115
Section 4... 118

History of Ancient Kush
Section 1... 121
Section 2... 124

History of West Africa
Section 1... 127
Section 2... 130
Section 3... 133

North Africa
Section 1... 136
Section 2... 139
Section 3... 142

West Africa
Section 1... 145
Section 2... 148
Section 3... 151

East Africa
Section 1... 154
Section 2... 157
Section 3... 160

Central Africa
Section 1... 163
Section 2... 166
Section 3... 169

Southern Africa
Section 1... 172
Section 2... 175
Section 3... 178

Guided Reading Workbook

South and East Asia and the Pacific

History of Ancient India
Section 1 181
Section 2 184
Section 3 187
Section 4 190
Section 5 193

History of Ancient China
Section 1 196
Section 2 199
Section 3 202
Section 4 205
Section 5 208

The Indian Subcontinent
Section 1 211
Section 2 214
Section 3 217
Section 4 220

China, Mongolia, and Taiwan
Section 1 223
Section 2 226
Section 3 229
Section 4 232

Japan and the Koreas
Section 1 235
Section 2 238
Section 3 241
Section 4 244

Southeast Asia
Section 1 247
Section 2 250
Section 3 253
Section 4 256

The Pacific World
Section 1 259
Section 2 262
Section 3 265

Europe and Russia

Early History of Europe
Section 1 268
Section 2 271
Section 3 274

History of Early Modern Europe
Section 1 277
Section 2 280
Section 3 283
Section 4 286

Modern European History
Section 1 289
Section 2 292
Section 3 295

Southern Europe
Section 1 298
Section 2 301
Section 3 304
Section 4 307

West-Central Europe
Section 1 310
Section 2 313
Section 3 316

Northern Europe
Section 1 319
Section 2 322
Section 3 325

Eastern Europe
Section 1 328
Section 2 331
Section 3 334
Section 4 337

Russia and the Caucasus
Section 1 340
Section 2 343
Section 3 346
Section 4 349

How to Use this Book

The *Guided Reading Workbook* was developed to help you get the most from your reading. Using this book will help you master geography content while developing your reading and vocabulary skills. Reviewing the next few pages before getting started will make you aware of the many useful features in this book.

Section summary pages allow you to interact with the content and key terms and places from each section of a chapter. The summaries explain each section of your textbook in a way that is easy to understand.

Section numbers make it easy to find your place in the workbook.

The main idea statements help focus your attention as you read the summaries.

Definitions for the key terms and places from your textbook are given.

Headings under each section summary match those of your textbook, which can help you find the material you need.

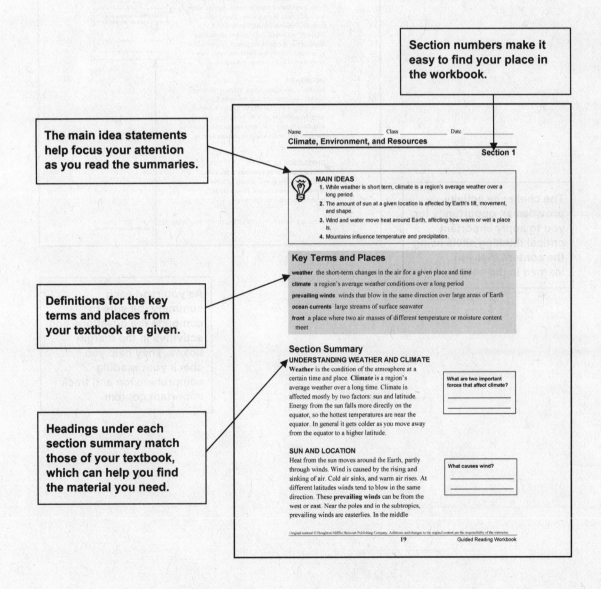

Name _____ Class _____ Date _____
Climate, Environment, and Resources
Section 1

MAIN IDEAS
1. While weather is short term, climate is a region's average weather over a long period.
2. The amount of sun at a given location is affected by Earth's tilt, movement, and shape.
3. Wind and water move heat around Earth, affecting how warm or wet a place is.
4. Mountains influence temperature and precipitation.

Key Terms and Places

weather the short-term changes in the air for a given place and time

climate a region's average weather conditions over a long period

prevailing winds winds that blow in the same direction over large areas of Earth

ocean currents large streams of surface seawater

front a place where two air masses of different temperature or moisture content meet

Section Summary
UNDERSTANDING WEATHER AND CLIMATE
Weather is the condition of the atmosphere at a certain time and place. **Climate** is a region's average weather over a long time. Climate is affected mostly by two factors: sun and latitude. Energy from the sun falls more directly on the equator, so the hottest temperatures are near the equator. In general it gets colder as you move away from the equator to a higher latitude.

SUN AND LOCATION
Heat from the sun moves around the Earth, partly through winds. Wind is caused by the rising and sinking of air. Cold air sinks, and warm air rises. At different latitudes winds tend to blow in the same direction. These **prevailing winds** can be from the west or east. Near the poles and in the subtropics, prevailing winds are easterlies. In the middle

What are two important forces that affect climate?
_____
_____

What causes wind?
_____
_____

Original content © Houghton Mifflin Harcourt Publishing Company. Additions and changes to the original content are the responsibility of the instructor.
19
Guided Reading Workbook

The key terms and places from your textbook have been boldfaced, allowing you to quickly find and study them.

The challenge activity provides an opportunity for you to apply important critical thinking skills using the content that you learned in the section.

Name _____ Class _____ Date _____

Section 1, *continued*

latitudes are the westerlies. Prevailing winds control an area's climate.

WIND AND WATER

Winds pick up moisture over oceans and dry out passing over land. At about 30° North and South latitude, dry winds cause many of the world's deserts.

Ocean currents—large streams of surface water—also move heat around. The Gulf Stream is a warm current that flows from the Gulf of Mexico across the Atlantic Ocean to western Europe.

Water heats and cools more slowly than land. Therefore, water helps to moderate the temperature of nearby land, keeping it from getting very hot or very cold.

A **front** is a place where two different air masses meet. In the United States and other regions, warm and cold air masses meet often, causing severe weather. These can include thunderstorms, blizzards, and tornadoes. Tornadoes are twisting funnels of air that touch the ground. Hurricanes are large tropical storms that form over water. They bring destructive high winds and heavy rain.

MOUNTAINS

Mountains also affect climate. Warm air blowing against a mountainside rises and cools. Clouds form, and precipitation falls on the side facing the wind. However, the air is dry by the time it goes over the mountain. This effect creates a rain shadow, a dry area on the side of the mountain facing land.

CHALLENGE ACTIVITY

Critical Thinking: Sequencing Write a short description of the process leading up to the formation of a rain shadow. Draw and label a picture to go with your description.

> Which heats and cools more slowly—land or water?
> _____
> _____

> What often happens when warm and cold air masses meet?
> _____
> _____

As you read each summary, be sure to complete the questions and activities in the margin boxes. They help you check your reading comprehension and track important content.

*The third page of each section allows you to demonstrate your understanding
of the key terms and places introduced in the section.*

**Some pages have a word
bank. You can use it to help
find answers or complete
writing activities.**

Name _____ Class _____ Date _____
Section 1, *continued*

| air mass | climate | front | ocean currents |
| precipitation | prevailing winds | rain shadow | weather |

DIRECTIONS On the line provided before each statement, write **T** if a
statement is true and **F** if a statement is false. If the statement is false,
write the correct term on the line after each sentence that makes the
sentence a true statement.

_____ 1. <u>Climate</u> describes the atmospheric conditions in a place at a specific time.
It changes rapidly.

_____ 2. Weather is the temperature and <u>wind</u> from hour to hour or day to day.

_____ 3. <u>Fronts</u> can cause severe weather. They may form when air masses of
different temperatures come together.

_____ 4. <u>Rain shadows</u> form on the side of a mountain away from the wind.

_____ 5. The Gulf Stream is an example of a/an <u>prevailing wind</u>.

**A variety of activities helps
you check your knowledge
of key terms and places.**

DIRECTIONS Choose five of the vocabulary words from the word
bank. Use these words to write a summary of what you learned in the
section.

_____
_____
_____
_____
_____
_____

**Writing activities require
you to include key words
and places in what you
write. Remember to check
to make sure that you are
using the terms and places
correctly.**

21   Guided Reading Workbook

A Geographer's World

MAIN IDEAS
1. Geography is the study of the world, its people, and the landscapes they create.
2. Geographers look at the world in many different ways.
3. Maps and other tools help geographers study the planet.

Key Terms and Places

geography the study of the world, its people, and the landscapes they create

landscape the human and physical features that make a place unique

social science a field that studies people and the relationships among them

region a part of the world with one or more common features distinguishing it from surrounding areas

map a flat drawing that shows part of Earth's surface

globe a spherical model of the entire planet

Section Summary

WHAT IS GEOGRAPHY?

For every place on Earth, you can ask questions to learn about it: What does the land look like? What is the weather like? What are people's lives like? Asking questions like these is how you study geography. **Geography** is the study of the world, its people, and the **landscapes** they create.

Geographers (people who study geography) ask questions about how the world works. For example, they may ask why a place gets tornadoes. To find answers, they gather data by observing and measuring. In this way, geography is like science.

Geography can also be like a social science. **Social science** studies people and how they relate to each other. This information cannot be measured in the same way. To study people, geographers may visit places and talk to the people about their lives.

> Underline the sentence that states how geography is like science.

LOOKING AT THE WORLD

Geographers must look carefully at the world around them. Depending on what they want to learn, they look at the world at different levels.

Geographers may study at the local level, such as a city or town. They may ask why people live there, what work they do, and how they travel. They can help a town or city plan improvements.

Geographers may also study at the regional level. A **region** is an area with common features. A region may be big or small. Its features make it different from areas around it. The features may be physical (such as mountains) or human (such as language).

Sometimes geographers study at the global level. They study how people interact all over the world. Geographers can help us learn how people's actions affect other people and places. For example, they may ask how one region influences other regions.

Circle the three levels that geographers study.

THE GEOGRAPHER'S TOOLS

Geographers need tools to do their work. Often, they use maps and globes. A **map** is a flat drawing that shows Earth's surface. A **globe** is a spherical (round) model of the whole planet.

Maps and globes both show what Earth looks like. Because a globe is round, it can show Earth as it really is. To show the round Earth on a flat map, some details have to change. For example, a place's shape may change a little. But maps have benefits. They are easier to work with. They can also show small areas, such as cities, better.

Geographers also use other tools, such as satellite images, computers, notebooks, and tape recorders.

In what way are maps and globes similar?
_____
_____

Underline two sentences that tell the benefits of using maps.

CHALLENGE ACTIVITY

Critical Thinking: Solving Problems Pick a foreign country you would like to study. You want to develop the most complete picture possible of this place and its people. Make a list of questions to ask and tools you would use to find the answers.

DIRECTIONS On the line provided before each statement, write **T** if the statement is true and **F** if the statement is false. If the statement is false, write the correct term on the line after each sentence that makes the sentence a true statement.

_____ 1. A <u>globe</u> is a flat drawing of Earth's surface.

_____

_____ 2. The study of the world, its people, and the landscapes they create is called <u>geography</u>.

_____

_____ 3. Geography is sometimes called a <u>social science</u> because it studies people and the relationships among them.

_____

_____ 4. An example of a small <u>region</u> that geographers might study is Chinatown in San Francisco.

_____

_____ 5. A <u>map</u> is a spherical model of the entire planet.

_____

_____ 6. The combination of human and physical features that make a place unique is called a <u>landscape</u>.

_____

_____ 7. <u>Satellite images</u> help geographers to create, update, and compare maps.

_____

A Geographer's World

 MAIN IDEAS
1. The five themes of geography help us organize our studies of the world.
2. The six essential elements of geography highlight some of the subject's most important ideas.

Key Terms and Places

absolute location a specific description of where a place is

relative location a general description of where a place is

environment an area's land, water, climate, plants and animals, and other physical features

Section Summary

THE FIVE THEMES OF GEOGRAPHY

Geographers use themes in their work. A theme is a topic that is common throughout a discussion or event. Many holidays have a theme, such as the flag and patriotism on the Fourth of July.

There are five major themes of geography: Location, Place, Human-Environment Interaction, Movement, and Regions. Geographers can use these themes in almost everything they study.

Location describes where a place is. This may be specific, such as an address. This is called an **absolute location.** It may also be general, such as saying the United States is north of Central America. This is called a **relative location.**

Place refers to an area's landscape. The landscape is made up of the physical and human features of a place. Together, these features give a place its own identity apart from other places.

Human-Environment Interaction studies how people and their environment affect each other. The **environment** includes an area's physical features, such as land, water, weather, and animals. Geographers study how people change their environment (by building, for example). They also

List the five major themes of geography:
_____
_____
_____
_____
_____

Guided Reading Workbook

study how the environment causes people to adapt (by dressing for the weather, for example).

Movement involves learning about why and how people move. Do they move for work or pleasure? Do they travel by roads or other routes?

Studying Regions helps geographers learn how places are alike and different. This also helps them learn why places developed the way they did.

> **Describe two ways that people and their environment affect each other.**
>
> _____
> _____
> _____
> _____
> _____

THE SIX ESSENTIAL ELEMENTS

It is important to organize how you study geography, so you get the most complete picture of a place. Using the five major themes can help you do this. Using the six essential elements can, also.

Geographers and teachers created the six elements from eighteen basic ideas, called standards. The standards say what everyone should understand about geography. Each element groups together the standards that are related to each other.

The six elements are: The World in Spatial Terms (spatial refers to where places are located); Places and Regions; Physical Systems; Human Systems; Environment and Society; Uses of Geography. The six elements build on the five themes, so some elements and themes are similar. Uses of Geography is not part of the five themes. It focuses on how people can use geography to learn about the past and present, and plan for the future.

> **What do the five themes and six elements of geography help you do? Underline the sentence that explains this.**

CHALLENGE ACTIVITY

Critical Thinking: Analyze Analyze a place you regularly visit, such as a vacation spot or a park in your neighborhood. Write a question about the place for each geography theme to help someone not familiar with the themes understand them.

absolute location	environment	element
interaction	relative location	

DIRECTIONS Write a word or phrase that has the same meaning as the term given.

1. absolute location _____

_____

2. element _____

_____

3. environment _____

_____

4. interaction _____

_____

5. relative location _____

_____

DIRECTIONS Choose at least four of the vocabulary words from the word bank. Use these words to write a story or poem that relates to the section.

_____

_____

_____

_____

_____

_____

_____

A Geographer's World

MAIN IDEAS

1. Physical geography is the study of landforms, water bodies, and other physical features.
2. Human geography focuses on people, their cultures, and the landscapes they create.
3. Other branches of geography examine specific aspects of the physical or human world.

Key Terms and Places

physical geography the study of the world's physical features, such as landforms, bodies of water, climates, soils, and plants

human geography the study of the world's people, communities, and landscapes

cartography the science of making maps

meteorology the study of weather and what causes it

Section Summary

PHYSICAL GEOGRAPHY

The field of geography has many branches, or divisions. Each branch has a certain focus. No branch alone gives us a picture of the whole world. When looked at together, the different branches help us understand Earth and its people better.

Geography has two main branches: physical geography and human geography. **Physical geography** is the study of the world's physical features, such as landforms, bodies of water, and weather.

Physical geographers ask questions about Earth's many physical features: Where are the mountains and flat areas? Why are some areas rainy and others dry? Why do rivers flow a certain way? To get their answers, physical geographers measure features— such as heights of mountains and temperatures of places.

> What do the different branches of geography help us do when they are looked at together? Underline the sentence that answers this.

> List the two main branches of geography:
>
> _____
>
> _____

Physical geography has important uses. It helps us understand how the world works. It also helps us predict and prepare for dangers, such as big storms.

HUMAN GEOGRAPHY

Human geography is the study of the world's people, communities, and landscapes. It is the other main branch of geography.

Human geographers study people in the past or present. They ask why more people live in some places than in others. They also ask other questions, such as what kinds of work people do.

People all over the world are very different, so human geographers often study a smaller topic. They might study people in one region, such as central Africa. They might study one part of people's lives in different regions, such as city life.

Human geography also has important uses. It helps us learn how people meet basic needs for food, water, and shelter. It helps people improve their lives. It can also help protect the environment.

OTHER FIELDS OF GEOGRAPHY

Other branches of geography study one aspect of the world. Some of these are smaller parts of physical geography or of human geography.

Here are a few other branches to know about. **Cartography** is the science of making maps. Hydrology is the study of water on Earth. **Meteorology** is the study of weather and what causes it.

CHALLENGE ACTIVITY

Critical Thinking: Drawing Inferences Examine a map of an unfamiliar city using a road atlas or an online map. Write a paragraph telling a visitor what physical and human features to look for in each quadrant (NE, SE, NW, SW).

Why do human geographers often study one smaller topic?
_____
_____

Circle three basic needs that people have to meet.

What is meteorology?
_____
_____

cartography	human geography	hydrology
meteorology	physical geography	

DIRECTIONS Read each sentence and fill in the blank with the word in the word pair that best completes the sentence.

1. _____ is the study of weather and what causes it. (cartography/meteorology)

2. Geographers might study _____ if they wanted to know how Victoria Falls formed. (physical geography/human geography)

3. Without _____, geographers would not be able to use maps to study where things are in the world. (cartography/meteorology)

4. The study of Earth's people, including their ways of life, homes, cities, beliefs, and customs is called _____. (physical geography/human geography)

5. Studying the world's river systems and how to protect the world's water supply are important parts of _____. (hydrology/meteorology)

DIRECTIONS Look up the vocabulary terms in the word bank in a dictionary. Write the dictionary definition of the word that is closest to the definition used in your textbook.

_____

_____

_____

_____

Planet Earth

Section 1

 MAIN IDEAS
1. Earth's movement affects the amount of energy we receive from the sun.
2. Earth's seasons are caused by the planet's tilt.

Key Terms

solar energy energy from the sun

rotation one complete spin of Earth on its axis

revolution one trip of Earth around the sun

latitude the distance north or south of Earth's equator

tropics regions close to the equator

Section Summary

EARTH'S MOVEMENT

Energy from the sun, or **solar energy,** is necessary for life on Earth. It helps plants grow and provides light and heat. Several factors affect the amount of solar energy Earth receives. These are rotation, revolution, tilt, and latitude.

Earth's axis is an imaginary rod running from the North Pole to the South Pole. Earth spins around on its axis. One complete **rotation** takes 24 hours, or one day. Solar energy reaches only half of the planet at a time. As Earth rotates, levels of solar energy change. The half that faces the sun receives light and heat and is warmer. The half that faces away from the sun is darker and cooler.

As Earth rotates, it also moves around the sun. Earth completes one **revolution** around the sun every year, in 365 1/4 days. Every four years an extra day is added to February. This makes up for the extra quarter of a day.

Earth's axis is tilted, not straight up and down. At different times of year, some locations tilt toward the sun. They get more solar energy than locations tilted away from the sun.

> **List the four factors that affect the amount of solar energy Earth receives.**
> _____
> _____

> **What would happen if Earth did not rotate?**
> _____
> _____

> **Underline the sentence that describes Earth's revolution around the sun.**

> **Where you live, does more solar energy reach Earth in winter or in summer?**
> _____

Latitude refers to imaginary lines that run east and west around the planet, north and south of the Earth's equator. Areas near the equator receive direct rays from the sun all year and have warm temperatures. Higher latitudes receive fewer direct rays and are cooler.

> Why are areas near the equator warmer than those in higher latitudes?
>
> _____

THE SEASONS

Many locations on Earth have four seasons: winter, spring, summer, and fall. These are based on temperature and how long the days are.

The seasons change because of the tilt of Earth's axis. In summer the Northern Hemisphere is tilted toward the sun. It receives more solar energy than during the winter, when it is tilted away from the sun.

Because Earth's axis is tilted, the hemispheres have opposite seasons. Winter in the Northern Hemisphere is summer in the Southern Hemisphere. During the fall and spring, the poles point neither toward nor away from the sun. In spring, temperatures rise and days become longer as summer approaches. In fall the opposite occurs.

> What would the seasons be like in the Northern and Southern hemispheres if Earth's axis weren't tilted?
>
> _____

In some regions, the seasons are tied to rainfall instead of temperature. One of these regions, close to the equator, is the **tropics.** There, winds bring heavy rains from June to October. The weather turns dry in the tropics from November to January.

> Circle the name of the warm region near the equator.

CHALLENGE ACTIVITY

Critical Thinking: Drawing Conclusions Imagine that you are a travel agent. One of your clients is planning a trip to Argentina in June, and another is planning a trip to Chicago in August. What kinds of clothing would you suggest they pack for their trips and why?

| latitude | revolution | rotation |
| solar energy | tropics | |

DIRECTIONS On the line provided before each statement, write **T** if a statement is true and **F** if a statement is false. If the statement is false, write the term from the word bank that would make the statement correct on the line after each sentence.

_____ 1. The hemisphere of Earth that is tilted away from the sun receives less direct <u>rainfall</u> than the other hemisphere receives.

_____

_____ 2. An umbrella might be more useful to a person in the <u>tropics</u> than a winter coat.

_____

_____ 3. Earth's path, or orbit, around the sun is its <u>rotation</u>.

_____

_____ 4. One <u>revolution</u> of Earth takes 24 hours.

_____

_____ 5. Plants in a high latitude receive less direct solar energy during the year than plants at a <u>lower latitude</u> because they are farther from the equator.

_____

Guided Reading Workbook

MAIN IDEAS

1. Salt water and freshwater make up Earth's water supply.
2. In the water cycle, water circulates from Earth's surface to the atmosphere and back again.
3. Water plays an important role in people's lives.

Key Terms

freshwater water without salt

glacier large area of slow-moving ice

surface water water that is stored in Earth's streams, rivers, and lakes

precipitation water that falls to Earth's surface as rain, snow, sleet, or hail

groundwater water found below Earth's surface

water vapor water that occurs in the air as an invisible gas

water cycle the circulation of water from Earth's surface to the atmosphere and back

drought a long period of lower-than-normal precipitation

Section Summary
EARTH'S WATER SUPPLY

Approximately three-quarters of Earth's surface is covered with water. There are two kinds of water—salt water and **freshwater.** About 97 percent of Earth's water is salt water. Most of it is in the oceans, seas, gulfs, bays, and straits. Some lakes, such as the Great Salt Lake in Utah, also contain salt water.

Salt water cannot be used for drinking. Only freshwater is safe to drink. Freshwater is found in lakes and rivers and stored underground. Much is frozen in **glaciers.** Freshwater is also found in the ice of the Arctic and Antarctic regions.

One form of freshwater is **surface water.** This is stored in streams, lakes, and rivers. Streams form when **precipitation** falls to Earth as rain, snow,

> Circle the places where we find salt water.

> Underline the places where we find freshwater.

sleet, or hail. These streams then flow into larger streams and rivers.

Most freshwater is stored underground. **Groundwater** bubbles to the surface in springs or can be reached by digging deep holes, or wells.

THE WATER CYCLE

Water can take the form of a liquid, gas, or solid. In its solid form, water is snow and ice. Liquid water is rain or water found in lakes and rivers. **Water vapor** is an invisible form of water in the air.

Water is always moving. When water on Earth's surface heats up, it evaporates and turns into water vapor. It then rises from Earth into the atmosphere. When it cools down, it changes from water vapor to liquid. Droplets of water form clouds. When they get heavier, these droplets fall to Earth as precipitation. This process of evaporation and precipitation is called the **water cycle.**

Some precipitation is absorbed into the soil as groundwater. The rest flows into streams, rivers, and oceans.

Underline the words that define water vapor.

What are the two main processes of the water cycle? _____ _____

WATER AND PEOPLE

Problems with water include shortages, pollution, and flooding. Shortages are caused by overuse and by **drought,** when there is little or no precipitation for a long time. Chemicals and waste can pollute water. Heavy rains can cause flooding.

Water quenches our thirst and allows us to have food to eat. Flowing water is an important source of energy. Water also provides recreation, making our lives richer and more enjoyable. Water is essential for life on Earth.

What water problems affect human beings? _____ _____

CHALLENGE ACTIVITY

Critical Thinking: Solving Problems You are campaigning for public office. Write a speech describing three actions you plan to take to protect supplies of freshwater.

Guided Reading Workbook

| drought | freshwater | glacier | groundwater |
| precipitation | surface water | water cycle | water vapor |

DIRECTIONS Read each sentence and fill in the blank with the word
in the word pair that best completes the sentence.

1. Some _____ is locked in Earth's glaciers.
   (drought/freshwater)

2. Less than one percent of Earth's water supply comes from

   _____ stored in streams, rivers, and lakes.

   (surface water/water vapor)

3. Water can be a solid (ice), a liquid, or a gas called _____.
   (precipitation/water vapor)

4. The water brought to the surface from deep holes dug in the ground is

   _____. (freshwater/groundwater)

5. _____ is water that falls from clouds as rain, snow, sleet, or
   hail. (Precipitation/Water cycle)

DIRECTIONS Use the terms from the word bank to write a summary
of what you learned in the section.

_____

_____

_____

_____

MAIN IDEAS
1. Earth's surface is covered by many different landforms.
2. Forces below Earth's surface build up our landforms.
3. Forces on the planet's surface shape Earth's landforms.
4. Landforms influence people's lives and culture.

Key Terms

landforms shapes on Earth's surface, such as hills or mountains

continents large landmasses

plate tectonics a theory suggesting that Earth's surface is divided into more than 12 slow-moving plates, or pieces of Earth's crust

lava magma, or liquid rock, that reaches Earth's surface

earthquake sudden, violent movement of Earth's crust

weathering the process of breaking rock into smaller pieces

erosion the movement of sediment from one location to another

Section Summary

LANDFORMS

Geographers study **landforms** such as mountains, valleys, plains, islands, and peninsulas. They study how landforms are made and how they influence people.

> **Give two examples of landforms.**
> _____
> _____

FORCES BELOW EARTH'S SURFACE

Below Earth's surface, or crust, is a layer of liquid and a solid core. The planet has seven **continents,** large landmasses made of Earth's crust. All of Earth's crust rests on 12 plates. These plates are constantly in motion. Geographers call the study of these moving pieces of crust **plate tectonics.**

All of these plates move at different speeds and in different directions. As they move, they shape Earth's landforms. Plates move in three ways: They collide, they separate, and they slide past each other.

> **Underline the sentence that lists the three different ways in which Earth's plates move.**

The energy of colliding plates creates new landforms. When two ocean plates collide, they may form deep valleys on the ocean's floor. When ocean plates collide with continental plates, mountain ranges are formed. Mountains are also created when two continental plates collide.

When plates separate, usually on the ocean floor, they cause gaps in the planet's crust. Magma, or liquid rock, rises through the cracks as **lava.** As it cools, it forms underwater mountains or ridges. Sometimes these mountains rise above the surface of the water and form islands.

Plates can also slide past each other. They grind along faults, causing **earthquakes.**

Underline what happens when two ocean plates collide with one another.

What causes earthquakes? _____ _____

FORCES ON EARTH'S SURFACE

As landforms are created, other forces work to wear them away. **Weathering** breaks larger rocks into smaller rocks. Changes in temperature can cause cracks in rocks. Water then gets into the cracks, expands as it freezes, and breaks the rocks. Rocks eventually break down into smaller pieces called sediment. Flowing water moves sediment to form new landforms, such as river deltas.

Another force that wears down landforms is **erosion.** Erosion takes place when sediment is moved by ice, water, and wind.

Circle the three forces that can cause erosion.

LANDFORMS INFLUENCE LIFE

Landforms influence where people live. For example, people might want to settle in an area with good soil and water. People change landforms in many ways. For example, engineers build tunnels through mountains to make roads. Farmers build terraces on steep hillsides.

CHALLENGE ACTIVITY

Critical Thinking: Drawing Inferences Find out about a landform in your area that was changed by people. Write a report explaining why and how it was changed.

continents	earthquake	erosion	landforms
lava	plate tectonics	weathering	

DIRECTIONS Look at each set of four vocabulary terms. On the line provided, write the letter of the term that does not relate to the others.

_____ 1. a. erosion   b. weathering   c. landform   d. continent

_____ 2. a. lava   b. erosion   c. earthquake   d. plate tectonics

DIRECTIONS Answer each question by writing a sentence that contains at least one word from the word bank.

3. What are two ways that the movement of tectonic plates affect the Earth?

_____

_____

_____

4. What is the most common cause of erosion?

_____

_____

_____

DIRECTIONS Choose four of the terms from the word bank. Look them up in a dictionary. Write the definition of the word that is closest to the definition that is used in your textbook.

_____

_____

_____

_____

Climate, Environment, and Resources

MAIN IDEAS

1. While weather is short term, climate is a region's average weather over a long period.
2. The amount of sun at a given location is affected by Earth's tilt, movement, and shape.
3. Wind and water move heat around Earth, affecting how warm or wet a place is.
4. Mountains influence temperature and precipitation.

Key Terms and Places

weather the short-term changes in the air for a given place and time

climate a region's average weather conditions over a long period

prevailing winds winds that blow in the same direction over large areas of Earth

ocean currents large streams of surface seawater

front a place where two air masses of different temperature or moisture content meet

Section Summary

UNDERSTANDING WEATHER AND CLIMATE

Weather is the condition of the atmosphere at a certain time and place. **Climate** is a region's average weather over a long time. Climate is affected mostly by two factors: sun and latitude. Energy from the sun falls more directly on the equator, so the hottest temperatures are near the equator. In general it gets colder as you move away from the equator to a higher latitude.

> **What are two important forces that affect climate?**
> _____
> _____

SUN AND LOCATION

Heat from the sun moves around the Earth, partly through winds. Wind is caused by the rising and sinking of air. Cold air sinks, and warm air rises. At different latitudes winds tend to blow in the same direction. These **prevailing winds** can be from the west or east. Near the poles and in the subtropics, prevailing winds are easterlies. In the middle

> **What causes wind?**
> _____
> _____

latitudes are the westerlies. Prevailing winds control an area's climate.

WIND AND WATER

Winds pick up moisture over oceans and dry out passing over land. At about 30° North and South latitude, dry winds cause many of the world's deserts.

Ocean currents—large streams of surface water—also move heat around. The Gulf Stream is a warm current that flows from the Gulf of Mexico across the Atlantic Ocean to western Europe.

Water heats and cools more slowly than land. Therefore, water helps to moderate the temperature of nearby land, keeping it from getting very hot or very cold.

A **front** is a place where two different air masses meet. In the United States and other regions, warm and cold air masses meet often, causing severe weather. These can include thunderstorms, blizzards, and tornadoes. Tornadoes are twisting funnels of air that touch the ground. Hurricanes are large tropical storms that form over water. They bring destructive high winds and heavy rain.

> **Which heats and cools more slowly—land or water?**
>
> _____

> **What often happens when warm and cold air masses meet?**
>
> _____

MOUNTAINS

Mountains also affect climate. Warm air blowing against a mountainside rises and cools. Clouds form, and precipitation falls on the side facing the wind. However, the air is dry by the time it goes over the mountain. This effect creates a rain shadow, a dry area on the side of the mountain facing land.

CHALLENGE ACTIVITY

Critical Thinking: Sequencing Write a short description of the process leading up to the formation of a rain shadow. Draw and label a picture to go with your description.

air mass	climate	front	ocean currents
precipitation	prevailing winds	rain shadow	weather

DIRECTIONS On the line provided before each statement, write **T** if a statement is true and **F** if a statement is false. If the statement is false, write the correct term on the line after each sentence that makes the sentence a true statement.

_____ 1. <u>Climate</u> describes the atmospheric conditions in a place at a specific time. It changes rapidly.

_____

_____ 2. Weather is the temperature and <u>wind</u> from hour to hour or day to day.

_____

_____ 3. <u>Fronts</u> can cause severe weather. They may form when air masses of different temperatures come together.

_____

_____ 4. <u>Rain shadows</u> form on the side of a mountain away from the wind.

_____

_____ 5. The Gulf Stream is an example of a/an <u>prevailing wind</u>.

_____

DIRECTIONS Choose five of the vocabulary words from the word bank. Use these words to write a summary of what you learned in the section.

_____

_____

_____

_____

_____

_____

Climate, Environment, and Resources

Section 2

> **MAIN IDEAS**
> 1. Geographers use temperature, precipitation, and plant life to identify climate zones.
> 2. Tropical climates are wet and warm, while dry climates receive little or no rain.
> 3. Temperate climates have the most seasonal change.
> 4. Polar climates are cold and dry, while highland climates change with elevation.

Key Terms and Places

monsoon winds that shift direction with the seasons and create wet and dry periods

savanna an area of tall grasses and scattered trees and shrubs

steppe a semi-dry grassland or prairie

permafrost permanently frozen layers of soil

Section Summary

MAJOR CLIMATE ZONES

We can divide Earth into five climate zones: tropical, temperate, polar, dry, and highland. Tropical climates appear near the equator, temperate climates are found in the middle latitudes, and polar climates occur near the poles. Dry and highland climates can appear at different latitudes.

> Underline the names of the five climate zones.

TROPICAL AND DRY CLIMATES

Humid tropical climates occur near the equator. Some are warm and rainy throughout the year. Others have **monsoons**—winds that shift directions and create wet and dry seasons. Rain forests need a humid climate to thrive and support thousands of species.

Moving away from the equator, we find tropical savanna climates. A **savanna** is an area of tall grasses and scattered trees and shrubs. A long, hot dry season is followed by short periods of rain.

> What happens when monsoon winds change direction?
> _____
> _____

Deserts are hot and dry. At night, the dry air cools quickly; desert nights can be cold. Only a few living things survive in a desert. Sometimes **steppes**—dry grasslands—are found near deserts.

TEMPERATE CLIMATES

Away from the ocean in the middle latitudes are humid continental climates. Most have four distinct seasons, with hot summers and cold winters. In this climate, weather often changes quickly when cold and warm air masses meet.

A Mediterranean climate has hot, sunny summers and mild, wet winters. They occur near the ocean, and the climate is mostly pleasant. People like to vacation in these climates. Only small, scattered trees survive in these areas.

East coasts near the tropics have humid subtropical climates, because of winds bringing in moisture from the ocean. They have hot, wet summers and mild winters. Marine west coast climates occur farther north and also get moisture from prevailing winds coming in from the ocean.

POLAR AND HIGHLAND CLIMATES

Subarctic climate occurs south of the Arctic Ocean. Winters are long and cold, and summers are cool. There is enough precipitation to support forests. At the same latitude near the coasts, tundra climate is also cold, but too dry for trees to survive. In parts of the tundra, soil is frozen as **permafrost.**

Ice cap climates are the coldest on Earth. There is little precipitation and little vegetation.

Highland, or mountain, climate changes with elevation. As you go up a mountain, the climate may go from tropical to polar.

CHALLENGE ACTIVITY

Critical Thinking: Comparing and Contrasting

Create a table showing the differences and similarities between any two types of climate.

> Underline the name of the climate that can have four distinct seasons.

> What do people typically like to do in Mediterranean climates?
> _____

> Can there be forests in subarctic climates? Explain.
> _____

DIRECTIONS Write three words or phrases that describe the term.

1. savanna _____

2. steppe _____

3. polar climate _____

4. monsoon _____

5. permafrost _____

DIRECTIONS Look at each set of four terms. On the line provided,
write the letter of the term that does not relate to the others.

_____ 6. a. coastal
      b. polar
      c. temperate
      d. tropical

_____ 7. a. humid continental
      b. marine west coast
      c. Mediterranean
      d. steppe

_____ 8. a. subarctic
      b. tundra
      c. desert
      d. ice cap

_____ 9. a. monsoon
      b. muggy
      c. prairies
      d. rain forest

_____ 10. a. forest
      b. tundra
      c. highland
      d. grassland

Climate, Environment, and Resources

MAIN IDEAS
1. The environment and life are interconnected and exist in a fragile balance.
2. Soils play an important role in the environment.

Key Terms and Places

environment a plant or animal's surroundings

ecosystem any place where plants and animals depend upon each other and their environment for survival

habitat the place where a plant or animal lives

extinct to die out completely

humus decayed plant or animal matter

desertification the slow process of losing soil fertility and plant life

Section Summary

THE ENVIRONMENT AND LIFE

Plants and animals cannot live just anywhere. They must have the right surroundings, or **environment.** Climate, land features, and water are all part of a living thing's environment. If an area has everything a living thing needs, it can be a **habitat** for that species.

Many plants and animals usually share a habitat. Many small animals eat plants, and then some large animals eat the small animals. Species are connected in many ways. A community of connected species is called an **ecosystem.** Ecosystems can be as small as a pond or as large as the entire Earth.

Geographers study how changes in environments affect living things. Natural events and human actions change environments. Natural events include forest fires, disease, and climate changes. Human actions include clearing land and polluting.

> How large can an ecosystem be?
> _____

> Underline two human actions that can cause changes in an environment.

If a change to the environment is extreme, a species might become **extinct,** or die out completely.

| What does it mean to become extinct? |
| _____ |
| _____ |

SOIL AND THE ENVIRONMENT

Without soil, much of our food would not exist. Soil forms in layers over hundreds or thousands of years. The most fertile layer, the topsoil, has the most humus. **Humus** is decayed plant or animal matter.

| Which has more humus— topsoil or subsoil? |
| _____ |

The next layer, the subsoil, has less humus and more material from rocks. Soil gets minerals from these rocks. Below the subsoil is mostly rock.

An environment's soil affects which plants can grow there. Fertile soils have lots of humus and minerals. Fertile soils also need to contain water and small air spaces.

| Underline four things found in fertile soil |

Soils can lose fertility from erosion by wind or water. Soil can also lose fertility from planting the same crops repeatedly. If soil becomes worn out and can no longer support plants, **desertification** can occur.

CHALLENGE ACTIVITY

Critical Thinking: Drawing Inferences Consider the interconnections in your environment. As you go through a normal day, keep a list of the sources you rely on for energy, food, and water.

broken rock	consequence	desertification	ecosystem
environment	erosion	extinct	fertile soils
habitat	humus	nutrients	topsoil

DIRECTIONS Read each sentence and fill in the blank with the word
in the word pair that best completes the sentence.

1. Organic material called _____ enriches the soil.
   (topsoil/humus)

2. When soil gets worn out, it may lead to _____.
   (erosion/desertification)

3. A prairie is a type of _____. A forest is another type.
   (ecosystem/environment)

4. If there are too many changes in conditions, a species may die out, or become

   _____. (consequence/extinct)

5. Most plant roots are found in the _____, or the uppermost
   layer of soil. (broken rock/topsoil)

6. A place where animals and plants live is called a/an _____.
   (environment/habitat)

7. All plants and animals are adapted to a certain _____, or
   surroundings. (environment/erosion)

DIRECTIONS Choose five of the words from the word bank. On a
separate sheet of paper, use these words to write a poem or story that
relates to the section.

Climate, Environment, and Resources

Section 4

MAIN IDEAS
1. Earth provides valuable resources for our use.
2. Energy resources provide fuel, heat, and electricity.
3. Mineral resources include metals, rocks, and salt.
4. Resources shape people's lives and countries' wealth.

Key Terms and Places

natural resource any material in nature that people use and value

renewable resources resources that can be replaced naturally

nonrenewable resources resources that cannot be replaced

deforestation the loss of forestland

reforestation planting trees to replace lost forestland

fossil fuels nonrenewable resources formed from the remains of ancient plants and animals

hydroelectric power the production of electricity by moving water

Section Summary
EARTH'S VALUABLE RESOURCES

Anything in nature that people use and value is a **natural resource.** These include such ordinary things as air, water, and soil. Resources such as trees are called **renewable resources** because Earth replaces them naturally. Those that cannot be replaced, such as oil, are called **nonrenewable resources.**

Air and water are renewable resources, but pollution can damage both. Some people get their water from underground wells, which can run out if too many people use them.

Soil is needed for all plant growth, including trees in forests. We get lumber, medicine, nuts, and rubber from forests. Soil and trees are renewable, but must be protected. The loss of forests is called **deforestation.** When we plant trees to replace lost forests, we call it **reforestation.**

> Are air and water renewable or nonrenewable resources?
> _____

> Underline the resources we can get from a forest.

ENERGY RESOURCES

Most of our energy comes from **fossil fuels,** which are formed from the remains of ancient living things. These include coal, oil, and natural gas.

We use coal mostly for electricity, but it causes air pollution. An advantage of coal is that Earth still has a large supply. Another fossil fuel is petroleum, or oil. It is used to make gasoline and heating oil. Oil can be turned into plastics and other products. Oil also causes pollution, but we depend on it for much of our energy. The cleanest fossil fuel is natural gas, which is used mainly for cooking and heating.

Renewable energy resources include **hydroelectric power**—the creation of electricity by moving water. This is accomplished mainly by building dams on rivers. Other renewable energy sources are wind, solar, and nuclear energy. Nuclear energy produces dangerous waste material that must be stored for thousands of years.

> **Where does gasoline come from?**
> _____

> **What is the cleanest-burning fossil fuel?**
> _____

MINERAL RESOURCES

Minerals are solid substances in the Earth's crust formed from nonliving matter. Like fossil fuels, minerals are nonrenewable. Types of minerals include metals, rocks and gemstones, and salt. Mineral uses include making steel from iron, making window glass from quartz, and using stone as a building material. We also use minerals to make jewelry, coins, and many other common objects.

> **List two uses of minerals.**
> _____
> _____

RESOURCES AND PEOPLE

Some places are rich in natural resources. Resources such as fertile farmland, forests, and oil have helped the United States become a powerful country with a strong economy.

CHALLENGE ACTIVITY

Critical Thinking: Drawing Inferences Write a short essay explaining why we still use coal, even though it causes pollution.

deforestation	electricity	fossil fuels
hydroelectric power	natural resources	nonrenewable resources
petroleum	reforestation	renewable resources

DIRECTIONS Answer each question by writing a sentence that
contains at least one word from the word list.

1. What problem is caused when trees are cut down faster than they can grow back?
   How can this problem be fixed?

   _____

   _____

   _____

2. What are some examples of alternatives to fossil fuels? List two types and
   explain how they work.

   _____

   _____

   _____

3. What may happen to a country that only has a few natural resources?

   _____

   _____

   _____

DIRECTIONS Write three examples of each term.

4. natural resources _____

5. renewable resources _____

6. fossil fuels _____

The World's People

Section 1

> **MAIN IDEAS**
> 1. Culture is the set of beliefs, goals, and practices that a group of people share.
> 2. The world includes many different culture groups.
> 3. New ideas and events lead to changes in culture.

Key Terms

culture the set of beliefs, values, and practices a group of people have in common

culture trait an activity or behavior in which people often take part

culture region an area in which people have many shared culture traits

ethnic group a group of people who share a common culture and ancestry

cultural diversity having a variety of cultures in the same area

cultural diffusion the spread of culture traits from one region to another

Section Summary

WHAT IS CULTURE?

Culture is the set of beliefs, values, and practices a group of people have in common. Everything in day-to-day life is part of culture, including language, religion, clothes, music, and foods. People everywhere share certain basic cultural features, such as forming a government, educating children, and creating art or music. However, people practice these things in different ways, making each culture unique.

Culture traits are activities or behaviors in which people often take part, such as language and popular sports. People share some culture traits, but not others. For example, people eat using forks, chopsticks, or their fingers in different areas.

> Underline the sentence which lists some parts of culture.

> What are some basic cultural features that people share?
>
> _____
>
> _____

CULTURE GROUPS

There are thousands of different cultures in the world. People who share a culture are part of a culture group that may be based on things like age or religion.

A **culture region** is an area in which people have many shared culture traits such as language, religion, or lifestyle. A country may have several different culture regions, or just a single region, such as Japan.

A culture region may be based on an **ethnic group,** a group of people who share the same religion, traditions, language, or foods. **Cultural diversity** is having a variety of cultures in the same area. It can create a variety of ideas and practices, but it can also lead to conflict.

> How can cultural diversity affect the people in an area?
> _____
> _____

CHANGES IN CULTURE

Cultures are constantly changing. They can change through the development of new ideas or contact with other societies. New ideas such as the development of electricity, motion pictures, and the Internet have changed what people do and how they communicate. When two cultures come in close contact, both usually change. For example, the Spanish and Native American cultures changed when the Spanish conquered parts of the Americas.

> Underline the sentences that describe how cultures change.

Cultural diffusion is the spread of culture traits from one part of the world to another. It can happen when people move and bring their culture with them. New ideas and customs, such as baseball or clothing styles, can spread from one place to another as people learn about them.

> What are two ways cultural diffusion occurs?
> _____

CHALLENGE ACTIVITY

Critical Thinking: Drawing Inferences Consider all of the parts of your culture that have been influenced by other cultures. During a normal day, keep a list of all the things you use or do that you think have been influenced by other cultures.

Guided Reading Workbook

| cultural diffusion | cultural diversity | culture trait |
| culture | culture region | ethnic group |

DIRECTIONS On the line provided before each statement, write **T** if a statement is true and **F** if a statement is false. If the statement is false, write the term that would make the statement correct on the line after each sentence.

_____ 1. The language you speak and the sports you play are examples of <u>culture traits</u>.

_____

_____ 2. <u>Cultural diversity</u> creates an interesting mix of ideas, but sometimes it can lead to conflict.

_____

_____ 3. When more than one cultural group lives in an area, this is called <u>cultural diffusion</u>.

_____

_____ 4. The spread of culture traits to different parts of the world is called <u>cultural diversity</u>.

_____

_____ 5. All aspects of your daily life are part of your <u>ethnic group</u>.

_____

DIRECTIONS Use all of the terms from the word bank to write a summary of what you learned in the section.

_____

_____

_____

_____

_____

Original content © Houghton Mifflin Harcourt Publishing Company. Additions and changes to the original content are the responsibility of the instructor.

The World's People

MAIN IDEAS

1. The study of population patterns helps geographers learn about the world.
2. Population statistics and trends are important measures of population change.

Key Terms

population the total number of people in a given area

population density a measure of the number of people living in an area, usually expressed as persons per square mile or square kilometer

birthrate the annual number of births per 1,000 people

migration the process of moving from one place to live in another

Section Summary

POPULATION PATTERNS

Population is the total number of people in a given area. Geographers study population patterns to learn about the world.

Some places are crowded with people, while others are almost empty. **Population density** is a measure of the number of people living in an area, usually expressed as persons per square mile or square kilometer. It describes how crowded a place is, which in turn affects how people live. In places with a high density, there is little open space, buildings are taller, and roads are more crowded than places with lower density. They also often have more products available for a variety of shoppers.

High density areas often have fertile soil, available water, and a favorable climate for agriculture. Areas that are less dense often have harsh land or climate that makes survival harder.

> Underline the two sentences that describe the effects of population density on a place.

> What is the land and climate often like in areas of high population density?
>
> _____
> _____

Guided Reading Workbook

POPULATION CHANGE

The number of people living in an area affects jobs, housing, schools, medical care, available food, and many other things. Geographers study population changes and world trends to understand how people live.

Three statistics are important to studying a country's population over time. **Birthrate** is the annual number of births per 1,000 people. Death rate is the annual number of deaths per 1,000 people. The rate of natural increase is found by subtracting the death rate from the birthrate.

> Underline the sentence that tells how to calculate the rate of natural increase.

Some areas have low rates of natural increase, such as Europe and North America. Some countries in Africa and Asia have very high rates of natural increase. High rates can make it hard for countries to develop economically because they need to provide jobs, education, and medical care for a growing population.

> How can high rates of natural increase make it hard for a country to develop economically?
>
> _____
> _____

Migration is the process of moving from one place to live in another. People may leave a place because of problems there, such as war, famine, drought, or lack of jobs. Other people may move to find political or religious freedom or economic opportunities in a new place.

The world's population has grown very rapidly in the last 200 years. Better health care and food supplies have helped more babies survive and eventually have children of their own. Many industrialized countries currently have slow population growth while other countries have very fast growth. Fast growth can put a strain on resources, housing, and government aid.

> How has the world's population changed during the last 200 years?
>
> _____
> _____

CHALLENGE ACTIVITY

Critical Thinking: Identify Cause and Effect

Find out the population density of your city or town. Write down ways that this density affects your life and the lives of others.

birthrate	migration	population
population density	population trends	sparse

DIRECTIONS Read each sentence and fill in the blank with the word
in the word pair that best completes the sentence.

1. The study of human _____ focuses on the total number of
   people in a given area. (population/migration)

2. Studying the _____ is one way to track the percentage of
   natural increase in the population. (population density/birthrate)

3. Calculating the _____ can tell us how crowded or sparse an
   area is. (population trends/population density)

4. _____ can cause one country's population to decline while it
   increases another country's population. (Birthrate/Migration)

5. One _____ shows that many of the world's industrialized
   nations have slow population growth. (birthrate/population trend)

DIRECTIONS Look up three terms from the word bank in a dictionary.
On a separate sheet of paper, write the dictionary definition of the term
that is closest to the definition used in your textbook. Then write a
sentence using each term correctly.

The World's People

Section 3

> **MAIN IDEAS**
> 1. The governments of the world include democracy, monarchy, dictatorship, and communism.
> 2. Different economic activities and systems exist throughout the world.
> 3. Geographers group the countries of the world based on their level of economic development.

Key Terms

democracy a form of government in which the people elect leaders and rule by majority

communism a political system in which the government owns all property and dominates all aspects of life in the country

market economy a system based on private ownership, free trade, and competition

command economy a system in which the central government makes all economic decisions

gross domestic product (GDP) the value of all goods and services produced within a country in a single year

developed countries countries with strong economies and a high quality of life

developing countries countries with less productive economies and a lower quality of life

Section Summary
GOVERNMENTS OF THE WORLD

People form governments to make laws, regulate business, and provide aid to people. A **democracy** is a form of government in which the people elect leaders and rule by majority. Most democracies protect people's rights to freedom of speech, religion, and a free press.

Monarchies are ruled directly by a king or queen who holds all the power. Dictatorships are also ruled by a single person. Dictators hold all the power and often rule by force. **Communism** is a system in which the government owns all property and dominates all aspects of life in the country. In most Communist states, the people have restricted rights and little freedom.

> **What rights are protected in most democracies?**
> _____
> _____

> **What types of government are ruled by a single person?**
> _____
> _____

Guided Reading Workbook

ECONOMIES OF THE WORLD

Primary industries provide natural resources to others through work such as farming, fishing, and mining. Secondary industries use raw materials to manufacture other products such as automobiles or furniture. Tertiary industries exchange goods and services through retail stores, health care and educational organizations, and so on. Quaternary industries involve workers such as architects, lawyers, and scientists who research and distribute information.

In a traditional economy, people make and use their own goods with little exchange of goods. A **market economy** is based on free trade and competition. People buy and sell as they wish and prices are determined by supply and demand. In a **command economy,** the government decides what to produce and what prices will be.

> **What are the four levels of industry in world economies?**
>
> _____
>
> _____

> **Underline the sentence that describes who controls a command economy.**

ECONOMIC DEVELOPMENT

One measure of economic development is **gross domestic product (GDP),** the value of all goods and services produced within a country in a single year. Other ways include the level of industrialization and the quality of life.

Developed countries have strong, wealthy economies and high standards of living. **Developing countries** have poorer economies and a lower quality of life. About two thirds of the world's people live in developing countries with poor education and little access to health care or telecommunications.

> **Which type of country is more industrialized?**
>
> _____
>
> _____

CHALLENGE ACTIVITY

Critical Thinking: Classify Select a family member or friend and ask them about their job. Classify it as one of the four basic types of industries and describe why it is important.

command economy	communism	democracy
developed countries	developing countries	
market economy	gross domestic product (GDP)	

DIRECTIONS Look at each set of four vocabulary terms. On the line provided, write the letter of the term that does not relate to the others.

_____ 1. a. communism
    b. dictatorship
    c. democracy
    d. command economy

_____ 2. a. market economy
    b. democracy
    c. traditional economy
    d. command economy

_____ 3. a. developed countries
    b. dictatorship
    c. developing countries
    d. economy

_____ 4. a. gross domestic product (GDP)
    b. manufacturing
    c. industrialization
    d. government

DIRECTIONS Write three words or phrases to describe each term.

5. democracy _____

6. communism _____

The World's People

Section 4

MAIN IDEAS
1. Globalization links the world's countries together through culture and trade.
2. The world community works together to solve global conflicts and crises.

Key Terms and Places

globalization the process in which countries are increasingly linked to each other through culture and trade

popular culture culture traits that are well known and widely accepted

interdependence the reliance of one country on the resources, goods, or services of another country

United Nations (UN) an organization of the world's countries that promotes peace and security around the globe

humanitarian aid assistance to people in distress

Section Summary

GLOBALIZATION

People around the world are more closely linked than ever before. **Globalization** is the process in which countries are increasingly linked to each other through culture and trade. Improvements in technology and communication have increased globalization.

> Underline the sentence which describes two ways countries are linked together.

Popular culture consists of culture traits that are well known and widely accepted. These traits can include food, sports, music, and movies. The United States has a great influence on popular culture through sales of American products and the use of English for business, science, and education around the world. It is also greatly influenced by other countries.

> What are four traits that can be considered part of popular culture?
> _____
> _____

World businesses are connected through trade. Companies may make products in many different countries or use products from around the world. **Interdependence** occurs when countries depend on each other for resources, goods, or services.

Companies and consumers depend on goods
produced elsewhere.

A WORLD COMMUNITY

Because places around the world are connected
closely, what happens in one place affects others.
The world community works together to promote
cooperation between countries.

When conflicts occur, countries from around the
world try to settle them. The **United Nations (UN)**
is an association of nearly 200 countries dedicated
to promoting peace and security.

Crises such as earthquakes, floods, droughts, or
tsunamis can leave people in great need. Groups
from around the world provide **humanitarian aid,**
or assistance to people in distress. Some groups
help refugees or provide medical care.

CHALLENGE ACTIVITY

Critical Thinking: Contrast Talk to a parent or
other adult about their knowledge of other countries
and their connections to them when they were
young. Write a short essay that contrasts their
global connections with yours.

| crisis | globalization | humanitarian aid |
| interdependence | popular culture | United Nations (UN) |

DIRECTIONS Read each sentence and fill in the blank with the word
in the word pair that best completes the sentence.

1. Groups from around the world come together to provide

   _____ in times of crisis. (humanitarian aid/globalization)

2. _____ occurs when countries depend on each other for
   resources, goods, or services. (Globalization /Interdependence)

DIRECTIONS On the line provided before each statement, write **T** if
the statement is true and **F** if the statement is false. If the statement is
false, write the correct term on the line after each sentence that makes
the sentence a true statement.

_____ 3. The process in which countries are linked to one another through culture
   and trade is called <u>popular culture</u>.

   _____

_____ 4. Culture traits such as food, music, movies, and sports are examples of
   <u>globalization</u>.

   _____

_____ 5. As a result of globalization, there is more <u>interdependence</u> among
   countries.

   _____

_____ 6. The <u>United Nations (UN)</u> promotes peace and security around the world.

   _____

History of the Fertile Crescent

MAIN IDEAS
1. The rivers of Southwest Asia supported the growth of civilization.
2. New farming techniques led to the growth of cities.

Key Terms

Fertile Crescent a large arc of rich farmland extending from the Persian Gulf to the Mediterranean Sea

silt a mix of rich soil and small rocks

irrigation a way of supplying water to an area of land

canals human-made waterways

surplus more of something than is needed

division of labor an arrangement in which people specialize in specific tasks

Section Summary

RIVERS SUPPORT THE GROWTH OF CIVILIZATION

Early people settled where crops would grow. Crops usually grew well near rivers, where water was available and regular floods made the soil rich.

Mesopotamia, part of the region known as the **Fertile Crescent** in Southwest Asia, lay between the Tigris and Euphrates rivers. Every year, floods on the rivers brought **silt**. The fertile silt made the land ideal for farming.

Hunter-gatherer groups first settled in Mesopotamia more than 12,000 years ago. Over time these people learned how to work together to control floods. They planted crops and grew their own food.

Farm settlements formed in Mesopotamia as early as 7000 BC. Farmers grew wheat, barley, and other grains. Livestock, birds, and fish were also sources of food. Plentiful food led to population growth and villages formed. Eventually, these early villages developed into the world's first civilization.

> Mesopotamia means "between the rivers" in Greek. To which two rivers does the name of the region refer?
>
> _____
> _____
> _____

> Name two grains grown by Mesopotamian farmers.
>
> _____
> _____
> _____

FARMING AND CITIES

Early farmers faced the challenge of learning how to control the flow of river water to their fields in both rainy and dry seasons. Flooding destroyed crops, killed livestock, and washed away homes. When water levels were too low, crops dried up.

To solve their problems, Mesopotamians used **irrigation**. They dug out large storage basins to hold water supplies. Then they dug **canals** that connected these basins to a network of ditches. These ditches brought water to the fields and watered grazing areas for cattle and sheep.

Because irrigation made farmers more productive, they produced a **surplus**. Some people became free to do other jobs. For the first time, people became craftspersons, religious leaders, and government workers. A **division of labor** developed.

Mesopotamian settlements grew in size and complexity. Most people continued to work in farming jobs. However, cities became important places. People traded goods in cities. Cities became the political, religious, cultural, and economic centers of Mesopotamian civilization.

> **Underline the sentence that lists some of the problems caused by flooding.**

> **What did Mesopotamians build to carry water from storage basins to irrigation ditches?**
> _____
> _____

> **Why were cities important to Mesopotamian civilization?**
> _____
> _____

CHALLENGE ACTIVITY

Critical Thinking: Drawing Inferences Use the information on this page to list six jobs that Mesopotamians might have had.

DIRECTIONS Write a word or phrase that has the same meaning as the term given.

1. surplus _____

2. irrigation _____

   _____

3. division of labor _____

   _____

4. Fertile Crescent _____

   _____

5. silt _____

   _____

6. canal _____

   _____

DIRECTIONS Look at each set of three terms following each number. On the line provided, write the letter of the term that does not relate to the others.

_____ 7. a. irrigation
          b. craftperson
          c. canal

_____ 8. a. surplus
          b. division of labor
          c. Fertile Crescent

_____ 9. a. hunter-gatherer
          b. Mesopotamia
          c. Fertile Crescent

History of the Fertile Crescent

MAIN IDEAS
1. The Sumerians created the world's first advanced society.
2. Religion played a major role in Sumerian society.

Key Terms and Places

Sumer area of Mesopotamia where the world's first civilization was developed

city-state a political unit consisting of a city and the surrounding countryside

empire land with different territories and people under a single rule

polytheism the worship of many gods

priests people who performed religious ceremonies

social hierarchy a division of society by rank or class

Section Summary

AN ADVANCED SOCIETY

In southern Mesopotamia about 3000 BC, people
known as the Sumerians (SOO-MER-ee-unz) created
a complex, advanced society. Most people in
Sumer (SOO-muhr) lived in rural areas, but they
were governed from urban areas that controlled the
surrounding countryside. The size of the
countryside controlled by each of these **city-states**
depended on its military strength. Stronger city-
states controlled larger areas. Individual city-states
gained and lost power over time.

> **When and where did the Sumerian society begin?**
> _____
> _____

Around 2300 BC Sargon was the leader of the
Akkadians (uh-KAY-dee-uhns), a people who lived
to the north of Sumer. Sargon built a large army and
defeated all the city-states of Sumer as well as all of
northern Mesopotamia. With these conquests,
Sargon established the world's first **empire**. It
stretched from the Persian Gulf to the
Mediterranean Sea. The Akkadian empire lasted
about 150 years.

> **Use a world atlas to determine the width of the Akkadian empire.**

RELIGION SHAPES SOCIETY

Religion played an important role in nearly every aspect of Sumerian public and private life. Sumerians practiced **polytheism**, the worship of many gods. They believed that their gods had enormous powers. Gods could bring a good harvest or a disastrous flood. The gods could bring illness or they could bring good health and wealth. The Sumerians believed that success in every area of life depended on pleasing the gods. Each city-state considered one god to be its special protector. People relied on **priests** to help them gain the gods' favor. Priests interpreted the wishes of the gods and made offerings to them.

A **social hierarchy** developed in Sumerian city-states. Kings were at the top. Below them were priests and nobles. The middle ranks included skilled craftspeople, and merchants. Farmers and laborers made up the large working class. Slaves were at the bottom of the social order. Although the role of most women was limited to the home and raising children, some upper-class women were educated and even became priestesses.

| **Why did Sumerians try to please the gods?** |
| _____ |
| _____ |
| _____ |
| _____ |

| **In Sumerian religious practice, what did priests do to try to please the gods?** |
| _____ |
| _____ |

| **Which two groups formed the Sumerian upper classes?** |
| _____ |
| _____ |
| _____ |

CHALLENGE ACTIVITY

Critical Thinking: Analyzing Information Make a chart or table to show the social hierarchy of Sumer.

| city-state | empire | polytheism | priests |
| social hierarchy | Sumer | | |

DIRECTIONS On the line provided before each statement, write **T** if a statement is true and **F** if a statement is false. If the statement is false, write the correct term on the line after each sentence that makes the sentence a true statement.

_____ 1. Land with different territories and peoples under a single rule is called a/an <u>city-state</u>.

_____

_____ 2. <u>Social hierarchy</u> is a division of society by rank or class.

_____

_____ 3. Kings in <u>Sargon</u> believed that the gods had chosen them to rule the people.

_____

_____ 4. A/n <u>empire</u> consists of a city, which is the political center, and the surrounding countryside.

_____

_____ 5. The practice of worshipping many gods is called <u>polytheism</u>.

_____

_____ 6. People relied on <u>priests</u> to help them gain the gods' favor.

_____

History of the Fertile Crescent

MAIN IDEAS
1. The Sumerians invented the world's first writing system.
2. Advances and inventions changed Sumerian lives.
3. Many types of art developed in Sumer.

Key Terms

cuneiform the Sumerian system of writing, which used symbols to represent basic parts of words

pictographs picture symbols that represented objects such as trees or animals

scribe writer

epics long poems that tell the story of a hero

architecture the science of building

ziggurat a pyramid-shaped temple tower

Section Summary

INVENTION OF WRITING

The Sumerians made one of the greatest cultural advances in history. They developed **cuneiform** (kyoo-NEE-uh-fohrm), the world's first system of writing. But Sumerians did not have pencils, pens, or paper. Instead, they used sharp reeds to make wedge-shaped symbols on clay tablets.

Sumerians first used cuneiform to keep records for business, government, and temples. As the use of cuneiform grew, simple **pictographs** evolved into more complex symbols that represented basic parts of words. Writing was taught in schools. Becoming a writer, or **scribe**, was a way to move up in social class. Scribes began to combine symbols to express complex ideas. In time, scribes wrote works on law, grammar, and mathematics. Sumerians also wrote stories, proverbs, songs, poems to celebrate military victories, and long poems called **epics**.

> Write the name of the world's first system of writing.
> _____
> _____

> What is a scribe?
> _____
> _____
> _____
> _____

ADVANCES AND INVENTIONS

The Sumerians were the first to build wheeled vehicles like carts and wagons. They invented the potter's wheel, a device that spins wet clay as a craftsperson shapes it into bowls. They invented the ox-drawn plow and greatly improved farm production. They built sewers under city streets. They learned to use bronze to make strong tools and weapons. They named thousands of animals, plants, and minerals, and used them to produce healing drugs. The clock and the calendar we use today are based on Sumerian methods of measuring time.

> **Which Sumerian invention greatly improved farm production?**
> _____
> _____

THE ARTS OF SUMER

Sumerian ruins reveal great skill in **architecture**. A pyramid-shaped **ziggurat** dominated each city. Most people lived in one-story houses with rooms arranged around a small courtyard.

Sumerian artists made sculpture and jewelry. Sculptors created statues of gods for the temples, and made small objects of ivory or rare woods. Jewelers worked with imported gold, silver, and fine stones. Earrings and other items found in the region show that Sumerian jewelers knew advanced methods for putting gold pieces together.

The Sumerians also developed a special art form called the cylinder seal. The cylinder seal was a small stone cylinder that was engraved with designs and could be rolled over wet clay to decorate containers or to "sign" documents.

Music played an important role in Sumerian society. Musicians played stringed instruments, reed pipes, drums, and tambourines both for entertainment and for special occasions.

> **Underline the sentence that describes the kind of houses in which most Sumerians lived.**

> **Name four types of musical instruments played by Sumerians.**
> _____
> _____
> _____
> _____

CHALLENGE ACTIVITY

Critical Thinking: Drawing Inferences Consider the inventions of writing and the wheel. As you go through a normal day keep a list of the things you do that rely on these two inventions.

Guided Reading Workbook

| architecture | cuneiform | epic |
| pictograph | scribe | ziggurat |

DIRECTIONS Read each sentence and fill in the blank with the word
in the word pair that best completes the sentence.

1. A _____ would be hired to keep track of the items people
   traded. (pictograph/scribe)

2. A pyramid-shaped tower that rose above each Sumerian city was called a

   _____. (cuneiform/ziggurat)

3. The Sumerians developed the world's first system of writing called

   _____. (cuneiform/ziggurat)

4. An _____ is a long poem that tells a story of a hero.
   (epic/architecture)

5. The _____ was the earliest form of written communication.
   (pictograph/scribe)

6. The science of building is known as _____.
   (epic/architecture)

DIRECTIONS Look at each set of three terms following each number.
On the line provided, write the letter of the term that does not relate to
the others.

_____ 7. a. pictograph   b. ziggurat   c. cuneiform

_____ 8. a. scribe   b. ziggurat   c. architecture

_____ 9. a. scribe   b. wheel   c. cuneiform

History of the Fertile Crescent

Section 4

MAIN IDEAS

1. The Babylonians conquered Mesopotamia and created a code of law.
2. Invasions of Mesopotamia changed the region's culture.
3. The Phoenicians built a trading society in the eastern Mediterranean region.

Key Terms and Places

Babylon important Mesopotamian city-state near present-day Baghdad

Hammurabi's Code the earliest known written collection of laws, comprising 282 laws that dealt with almost every part of life

chariot a wheeled, horse-drawn battle car

alphabet a set of letters that can be combined to form written words

Section Summary

THE BABYLONIANS CONQUER MESOPOTAMIA

By 1800 BC, a powerful city-state had arisen in **Babylon**, an old Sumerian city on the Euphrates. Babylon's greatest monarch (MAH-nark), Hammurabi, conquered all of Mesopotamia.

During his 42-year reign, Hammurabi oversaw many building and irrigation projects, improved the tax collection system, and brought prosperity through increased trade. He is most famous, however, for **Hammurabi's Code**, the earliest known written collection of laws. It contained laws on everything from trade, loans, and theft to injury, marriage, and murder. Some of its ideas are still found in laws today. The code was important not only for how thorough it was, but also because it was written down for all to see.

> **On what river was the city of Babylon located?**
> _____
> _____

> **What is Hammurabi's Code?**
> _____
> _____
> _____

INVASIONS OF MESOPOTAMIA

Several other civilizations developed in and around the Fertile Crescent. As their armies battled each other for Mesopotamia's fertile land, control of the region passed from one empire to another. The

Guided Reading Workbook

Hittites of Asia Minor captured Babylon in 1595 BC with strong iron weapons and the skillful use of the **chariot** on the battlefield. After the Hittite king was killed, the Kassites captured Babylon and ruled for almost 400 years.

The Assyrians were the next group to conquer all of Mesopotamia. They ruled from Nineveh, a city in the north. The Assyrians collected taxes, enforced laws, and raised troops through local leaders. The Assyrians also built roads to link distant parts of the empire. In 612 BC the Chaldeans, a group from the Syrian Desert, conquered the Assyrians.

Nebuchadnezzar (neb-uh-kuhd-NEZ-uhr), the most famous Chaldean king, rebuilt Babylon into a beautiful city. According to legend, his grand palace featured the famous Hanging Gardens. The Chaldeans revived Sumerian culture and made notable advances in astronomy and mathematics.

For about how long did the Babylonians rule Mesopotamia?
_____
_____

Which older Mesopotamian civilization did the Chaldeans admire and study?
_____
_____

THE PHOENICIANS

Phoenicia, at the western end of the Fertile Crescent along the Mediterranean Sea, created a wealthy trading society. Fleets of fast Phoenician trading ships sailed throughout the Mediterrranean and even into the Atlantic Ocean, building trade networks and founding new cities. The Phoenicians' most lasting achievement, however, was the **alphabet**, a major development that has had a huge impact on the ancient world and on our own.

On what body of water were most Phoenician colonies located?
_____
_____

CHALLENGE ACTIVITY

Critical Thinking: Drawing Inferences Make a time line with approximate dates showing the various empires and invasions that characterized the history of Mesopotamia up to the time of the Chaldeans.

Guided Reading Workbook

| alphabet | Babylon | Hammurabi's Code |
| chariot | Phoenicia | |

DIRECTIONS Read each sentence and fill in the blank with the word
in the word pair that best completes the sentence.

1. Nebuchadnezzar was the most famous Chaldean king who rebuilt a battle-

   damaged _____ into a beautiful city in which his palace was

   famous for the Hanging Gardens. (Phoenicia/Babylon)

2. A set of letters that can be combined together to form words is known as an

   _____, which was developed by the Phoenician traders.

   (alphabet/chariot)

3. _____ was a land with few resources other than cedar trees.
   (Babylon/Phoenicia)

4. The Hittites skillfully used the _____, a wheeled, horse-
   drawn battle car, to move quickly around the battlefield and fire arrows at their
   enemy. (chariot/alphabet)

5. _____ was a set of laws, that dealt with almost every part of
   daily life and was written down for all to see. (Babylon/Hammurabi's Code)

Judaism and Christianity

Section 1

MAIN IDEAS
1. The Hebrews' early history began in Canaan and ended when the Romans forced them out of Israel.
2. Jewish beliefs in God, justice, and law anchor their society.
3. Jewish sacred texts describe the laws and principles of Judaism.
4. Traditions and holy days celebrate the history and religion of the Jewish people.

Key Terms and Places

Judaism the Hebrews' religion

Canaan where Abraham settled on the Mediterranean Sea

Exodus a journey of the Hebrews out of Egypt, led by Moses

monotheism the belief in one and only one God

Torah the most sacred text of Judaism

rabbis religious teachers of Judaism

Section Summary

EARLY HISTORY

The Hebrews appeared in Southwest Asia sometime between 2000 and 1500 BC. Their religion was **Judaism.** According to the Hebrew Bible, the Hebrews are descended from Abraham. The Hebrew Bible says that God told Abraham to lead his family to **Canaan** on the Mediterranean Sea. Some of Abraham's decendents became known as Israelites.

According to the Hebrew Bible, some Hebrews moved to Egypt, where they were enslaved until a leader named Moses led them out of Egypt. During this journey, called the Exodus, God is said to have given Moses two stone tablets on a mountain called Sinai. A code of moral laws called the Ten Commandments was written on the tablets.

The Israelites reached Canaan, or Israel. Israel eventually split into two kingdoms—Israel and

> Circle the name of the man who the Bible says is the ancestor of the Hebrews.

Judah. The people of Judah became known as Jews. Invaders conquered Israel and Judah and sent the Jews out of Jerusalem as slaves. When the invaders were conquered, some Jews returned home. Some moved to other places. This scattering of Jews outside of Israel and Judah is called the Diaspora.

What is the Diaspora?
_____
_____

JEWISH BELIEFS

Jews share several central beliefs. One of these is **monotheism.** Jews believe that there is one and only one God. Ideas of justice and righteousness are also important. Justice means kindness and fairness toward all, even strangers and criminals. Righteousness means doing what is right. Jews value righteousness over rituals.

Underline the definition of monotheism.

Religious laws are also important. In addition to the Ten Commandments, many Jews follow laws that guide their daily lives.

JEWISH TEXTS

Judaism has several sacred texts. These contain the religion's basic laws and principles. The **Torah,** the first part of the Hebrew Bible, is the most sacred text. The Talmud is a set of laws, commentaries, stories and folklore. Jewish **rabbis,** or religious teachers, have studied these texts for centuries.

TRADITIONS AND HOLY DAYS

The two most sacred Jewish holidays are Rosh Hashanah and Yom Kippur. Rosh Hashanah celebrates the start of the new year. On Yom Kippur, Jews ask God to forgive their sins. This is the holiest day of the year for the Jews.

What is the holiest day of the year for Jews?
_____
_____
_____

CHALLENGE ACTIVITY

Critical Thinking: Drawing Conclusions Imagine you are helping to plan a museum of ancient Jewish history. Write a brief recommendation for three exhibits that you would like to include.

Guided Reading Workbook

Canaan	Exodus	Hebrews	Israelites
rabbis	Monotheism	plagues	principle
rabbis	Mount Sinai	Torah	Yom Kippur

DIRECTIONS Read each sentence and fill in the blank with the word in the word pair that best completes the sentence.

1. The Bible says that Abraham moved from his home in Mesopotamia to

   _____ on the Mediterranean Sea.

   (Mount Sinai/Canaan)

2. The moral laws Moses received on _____ are known as the Ten Commandments. (Mount Sinai/Yom Kippur)

3. Hebrew scribes recorded the Hebrews' early history and the laws of their religion, known as _____. (monotheism/Judaism)

4. The long journey of the Israelites away from slavery in Egypt is known as the _____. (Exodus/plagues)

5. The most sacred text of the Hebrews, the _____ is made up of five books. (Israelites/Torah)

DIRECTIONS Write a word or phrase that has the same meaning as the term given.

6. monotheism _____

7. rabbis _____

8. principle _____

Judaism and Christianity

Section 2

MAIN IDEAS
1. The life and death of Jesus of Nazareth inspired a new religion called Christianity.
2. Christians believe that Jesus's acts and teachings focused on love and salvation.
3. Jesus's followers taught others about Jesus's life and teachings.
4. Christianity spread throughout the Roman Empire by 400.

Key Terms and Places

Messiah a great leader the ancient Jews predicted would come to restore the greatness of Israel

Christianity a religion based on Jesus's life and teachings

Bible the holy book of Christianity

Bethlehem a small town where Jesus was born

Resurrection Jesus's rise from the dead

disciples followers

saint a person known and admired for his or her holiness

Section Summary

JESUS OF NAZARETH

Many people thought a Jewish teacher named Jesus was the **Messiah,** a leader who would bring back Israel's greatness. The life and teachings of Jesus of Nazareth are the basis of a religion called **Christianity.** Stories about Jesus's life are in the **Bible,** the holy book of Christianity.

Jesus was said to have been born in the town of **Bethlehem**. Jesus had many followers. But his teachings challenged the authority of political and religious leaders. Shortly after his arrest, the Romans tried and executed Jesus. According to the Bible, Jesus rose from the dead three days later. This event is known as the **Resurrection**. The Bible goes on to say that Jesus next appeared to his **disciples**, or followers. He gave them instructions

What did people think the Messiah would do?
_____
_____

According to the Bible, what happened after Jesus was executed?
_____
_____

about how to pass on his teachings. Then he rose up to heaven.

JESUS'S ACTS AND TEACHINGS

According to the Bible, Jesus performed miracles. He told many parables, stories that taught lessons about how people should live. Jesus taught people to love God and love other people. Jesus also taught about salvation, or the rescue of people from sin.

Since Jesus's death, people have interpreted his teachings in different ways. As a result, different denominations, or groups, of Christianity have developed.

> **Underline two of Jesus's major teachings.**

JESUS'S FOLLOWERS

After Jesus's death, his followers continued to spread his teachings. The New Testament books Matthew, Mark, Luke, and John tell the story of Jesus's life and teachings. Paul spread Jesus's teachings throughout the Mediterranean. Today, Christians regard Paul as a **saint.** A saint is a person known and admired for his or her holiness.

> **Why do you think Paul is important to Christians?**
> _____
> _____

THE SPREAD OF CHRISTIANITY

Christianity spread quickly. Roman leaders arrested and killed some Christians who refused to worship the gods of Rome. Some emperors banned Christianity. Christians often had to worship in secret. Local leaders called bishops led each community. The bishop of Rome, or the pope, came to be viewed as the head of the Christian Church.

Christianity continued to spread throughout Rome. Then the Roman emperor Constantine converted to Christianity. He lifted the bans against the practice of the religion. Christianity eventually spread from Rome all around the world.

> **What is another name for the bishop of Rome?**
> _____
> _____

CHALLENGE ACTIVITY

Critical Thinking: Understanding Cause and Effect What effect did Constantine's conversion have on the spread of Christianity?

Bethlehem	New Testament	Christianity	crucifixion
disciples	Gospels	ideals	Messiah
miracles	parables	Resurrection	saint

DIRECTIONS On the line provided before each statement, write a **T** if the statement is true and **F** if the statement is false. If the statement is false, write the correct term on the line after each sentence that makes the sentence a true statement.

_____ 1. Many people believed that Jesus of Nazareth was the <u>saint</u>.

_____

_____ 2. According to the New Testament, Jesus told his followers many <u>ideals</u> with lessons on how to live.

_____

_____ 3. The New Testament says that Jesus appeared to his <u>Gospels</u> after the Resurrection.

_____

_____ 4. Jesus's life and teachings form the basis of a religion called <u>Christianity</u>.

_____

DIRECTIONS Choose four of the words from the word bank. Use these words to write a summary of what you learned in the section.

_____

_____

_____

_____

_____

_____

Judaism and Christianity

MAIN IDEAS

1. Eastern emperors ruled from Constantinople and tried but failed to reunite the whole Roman Empire.

2. The people of the eastern empire created a new society that was very different from society in the west.

3. Byzantine Christianity was different from religion in the west.

Key Terms and Places

Constantinople the eastern capital of the Roman Empire

Byzantine Empire the society that developed in the eastern Roman Empire after the west fell

mosaics pictures made with pieces of colored stone or glass

Section Summary

EMPERORS RULE FROM CONSTANTINOPLE

The capital of the eastern Roman Empire was **Constantinople.** The city was located between two seas. It controlled trade between Asia and Europe. After the fall of Rome in 476, this city was the center of Roman power.

The emperor Justinian ruled from 527 to 565. He tried to conquer lands to reunite the old Roman empire. Justinian made other changes as well. He simplified Roman laws and organized them into a legal system called Justinian's Code. The code helped guarantee fairer treatment for all.

Justinian had many successes, but he also made enemies. These enemies tried to overthrow him in 532. His wife Theodora convinced Justinian to stay in Constantinople and fight. With her advice, he found a way to end the riots.

The eastern empire began to decline after Justinian died. Invaders took away all the land he had gained. Nearly 900 years after Justinian died, the eastern Roman Empire finally ended. In 1453 invaders captured Constantinople. With this defeat

> What was Justinian's Code?
> _____
> _____

> Circle the name of Justinian's wife.

> Circle the date when the Roman Empire ended. Why did it end?
> _____
> _____

the 1,000-year history of the eastern Roman Empire came to an end.

A NEW SOCIETY

After Justinian's death, non-Roman influences took hold throughout the empire. Many people spoke Greek, and scholars studied Greek philosophy. A new society developed. This society is called the **Byzantine Empire.** The Byzantines interacted with many groups, largely because of trade.

The eastern empire was different from the western empire in another way. Byzantine emperors had more power than western emperors did. They were the heads of the church as well as political rulers. The leaders of the church in the west were bishops and popes. The western emperors had only political power.

> What were two ways that the Byzantine Empire was different from the western empire?
>
> _____
>
> _____
>
> _____
>
> _____

BYZANTINE CHRISTIANITY

Christianity was central to the lives of nearly all Byzantines. Artists created beautiful works of religious art. Many Byzantine artists made **mosaics.** These were pictures made with pieces of colored stone or glass. Some were made of gold, silver, and jewels. Magnificent churches also were built.

> Underline the description of mosaics.

Over time, eastern and western Christianity became very different. People had different ideas about how to interpret and practice the religion. By the 1000s the church split in two. Eastern Christians formed the Orthodox Church.

CHALLENGE ACTIVITY

Critical Thinking: Comparing and Contrasting

Create a Venn diagram illustrating the similarities and differences between the eastern and western empires. Conduct library or Internet research to find interesting details for your diagram.

Guided Reading Workbook

Section 3, *continued*

Byzantine Empire	Constantinople	Hagia Sofia
Justinian	mosaics	Theodora

DIRECTIONS Answer each question by writing a sentence that contains at least one word from the word bank.

1. What city was the capital of the eastern Roman empire? What was important about this city?

   _____

   _____

   _____

2. Who is considered the last Roman emperor of the eastern empire? What changes occurred after his death?

   _____

   _____

   _____

3. What new society developed in the eastern Roman Empire after the fall of the Roman Empire in the west? Name two ways this new society was different from the Roman Empire in the west.

   _____

   _____

   _____

4. What kind of religious art was popular with Byzantine artists? Describe this type of art.

   _____

   _____

   _____

History of the Islamic World

MAIN IDEAS
1. Arabia is a mostly a desert land, where two ways of life, nomadic and sedentary, developed.
2. A new religion called Islam, founded by the prophet Muhammad, spread throughout Arabia in the 600s.

Key Terms and Places

Mecca birthplace of Muhammad

Islam religion based on messages Muhammad received from God

Muslim a person who follows Islam

Qur'an the holy book of Islam

Medina city that Muhammad and his followers moved to from Mecca in 622

mosque a building for Muslim prayer

Section Summary

LIFE IN A DESERT LAND

Arabia, in the southwest corner of Asia, is the crossroads for Africa, Europe, and Asia. Arabia is a mostly hot and dry desert of scorching temperatures and little water. Water is scarce and exists mainly in oases, or wet, fertile areas in the desert. Oases are key stops along Arabia's trade routes.

People developed two ways to live in the desert. Nomads moved from place to place. Nomads lived in tents and raised goats, sheep, and camels. They traveled with their herds to find food and water for their animals. They traveled in tribes, or groups of people. Tribe membership provided protection from danger and reduced competition for grazing lands.

Others led a settled life. Towns sprang up in oases along the trade routes. Merchants and craftspeople traded with groups of traders who traveled together in caravans. Most towns had a market or bazaar. Both nomads and caravans used these centers of trade.

> **Arabia was the trading crossroads for what three continents?**
>
> _____
> _____
> _____

> **Why would a nomad prefer to travel in a tribe?**
>
> _____
> _____
> _____
> _____

Guided Reading Workbook

A NEW RELIGION

A man named Muhammad brought a new religion to Arabia. Much of what we know about him comes from religious writings. Muhammad was born in the city of **Mecca** around 570. As a child, he traveled with his uncle's caravans. As an adult, Muhammad managed a caravan business.

Muhammad was upset that rich people did not help the poor. He often went to a cave to meditate on this problem. According to Islamic belief, when Muhammad was 40, an angel spoke to him. These messages form the basis of a religion called **Islam**. A follower of Islam is called a **Muslim**. The messages were written in the **Qur´an** (kuh-RAN), the holy book of Islam.

Muhammad taught that there was only one God, Allah. The belief in one God was a new idea for many Arabs. Before this time, Arabs prayed to many gods at shrines. The most important shrine was in Mecca. Many people traveled to Mecca every year on a pilgrimage. Muhammad also taught that the rich should give money to the poor. But rich merchants in Mecca rejected this idea.

Slowly, Muhammad's message began to influence people. The rulers in Mecca felt threatened by him. Muhammed left and went to **Medina**. His house there became the first **mosque**, or building for Muslim prayer. After years of conflict, the people of Mecca finally gave in and accepted Islam.

| Circle the name of the city where Muhammed was born. |

| What problem troubled Muhammed? _____ _____ |

| Why do you think the rich merchants disliked being told they should give money to the poor? _____ _____ _____ _____ |

CHALLENGE ACTIVITY

Critical Thinking: Drawing Inferences If you lived in Arabia, would you choose a nomadic or more settled, sedentary life? Write a one-page description of what your life would be like.

Guided Reading Workbook

DIRECTIONS Write two words or phrases that describe the term.

1. Islam _____

_____

2. Mecca _____

_____

3. Medina _____

_____

4. mosque _____

_____

5. Muslim _____

_____

6. Qur´an _____

MAIN IDEAS
1. The Qur'an guides Muslims' lives.
2. The Sunnah tells Muslims of important duties expected of them.
3. Islamic law is based on the Qur'an and the Sunnah.

Key Terms

jihad literally means "to make an effort" or "to struggle"

Sunnah a collection of actions or sayings by Muhammad

Five Pillars of Islam the five acts of worship required of all Muslims

Section Summary

THE QUR'AN

After Muhammad died, his followers wrote down all of the messages he received from Allah. This collection of teachings became known as the Qur'an. Muslims believe that the Qur'an is the exact word of God as it was told to Muhammad. Like the Jewish and Christian bibles, the Qur'an says there is one God (Allah). Islam teaches that there is a definite beginning and end to the world. On that final day, Muslims believe, God will judge all people. Those who have obeyed God's orders will be granted life in paradise. Those who have not obeyed God will be punished.

Muslims believe that God wishes them to follow many rules in order to be judged a good person. These rules affect the everyday life of Muslims. In the early days of Islam, these rules led to great changes in Arabian society. For example, owning slaves was forbidden.

Jihad (ji-HAHD) is an important Islamic concept. Literally, jihad means "to make an effort" or "to struggle." It refers to the internal struggle of a Muslim trying to follow Islamic beliefs. It can also mean the struggle to defend the Muslim community

> Circle the name of the collection of messages that Muhammed received from Allah.

> What did Islam tell followers about slavery?
>
> _____
> _____
> _____
> _____

or convert people to Islam. The word has also been translated as "holy war."

THE SUNNAH

Another important holy book in Islam is the **Sunnah** (SOOH-nuh), a collection of Muhammad's words and actions. The Sunnah spells out the main duties for Muslims. These are known as the **Five Pillars of Islam**. The first pillar is a statement of faith. The second pillar says a Muslim must pray five times daily. The third pillar is a yearly donation to charity. The fourth pillar is fasting during the holy month of Ramadan (RAH-muh-dahn). The fifth pillar is the hajj (HAJ), a pilgrimage to Mecca. The hajj must be made at least once in a lifetime.

The Sunnah also preaches moral duties that must be met in daily life, in business, and in government. For example, it is considered immoral to owe someone money or to disobey a leader.

> Circle the name of the book that spells out the Five Pillars of Islam.

> What is the third pillar of Islam?
> _____
> _____
> _____

ISLAMIC LAW

The Qur´an and the Sunnah form the basis of Islamic law, or Shariah (shuh-REE-uh). Shariah lists rewards or punishments for obeying or disobeying laws. Shariah punishments can be severe. Shariah makes no distinction between religious and secular life. Most Islamic countries today blend Islamic law with a legal system much like that in the United States.

> Describe the system of laws used in most Islamic nations today.
> _____
> _____
> _____
> _____

CHALLENGE ACTIVITY

Critical Thinking: Drawing Inferences Why would it be helpful to have Five Pillars, or main duties to perform?

Guided Reading Workbook

Allah	explicit	Five Pillars of Islam
Sunnah	implicit	jihad
hadith		

DIRECTIONS Read each sentence and choose the correct term from the word bank to replace the underlined phrase. Write the term in the space provided and then define the term in your own words.

1. The first duties of a Muslim are known as the <u>hadith</u>. _____

   Your definition: _____

   _____

2. The inner struggle people go through in their effort to obey God and behave

   according to Islamic ways is known as <u>Sunnah</u>. _____

   Your definition: _____

   _____

3. The <u>Five Pillars of Islam</u> describes Muhammed's words and actions and provides

   a model for the duties and the way of life expected of Muslims.

   _____

   Your definition: _____

   _____

4. Some guidelines for life are <u>implicit</u>, or stated directly in the Qur'an.

   _____

   Your definition: _____

   _____

History of the Islamic World

MAIN IDEAS

1. Muslim armies conquered many lands into which Islam slowly spread.
2. Trade helped Islam spread into new areas.
3. Three Muslim empires controlled much of Europe, Asia, and Africa from the 1400s to the 1800s.

Key Terms and Places

caliph title of the highest Islamic leader

tolerance acceptance

Baghdad city that became the capital of the Islamic Empire in 762

Córdoba Muslim city in Spain that became the largest and most advanced city in western Europe in the early 900s

janissaries slave boys converted to Islam and trained as soldiers

Istanbul capital of the Ottoman Empire; formerly Constantinople

Esfahan capital of the Safavid Empire

Section Summary

MUSLIM ARMIES CONQUER MANY LANDS

After Muhammad's death Abu Bakr (UH-boo BAK-uhr) was the leader of Islam. He was the first **caliph** (KAY-luhf). This title was used for the highest Islamic leader. Abu Bakr unified Arabia. The Arab army conquered the Persian and Byzantine empires.

Later caliphs conquered lands in Central Asia, northern India, and North Africa. They controlled eastern Mediterranean trade routes. After many years of fighting, the Berbers of North Africa converted to Islam. A combined Arab and Berber army conquered Spain and ruled for 700 years.

TRADE HELPS ISLAM SPREAD

Arab merchants took Islamic beliefs and practices with them to new lands. Coastal trading cities developed into large Muslim communities.

> **What present-day countries mark the eastern and western boundaries of the Islamic empire?**
> _____
> _____
> _____

> **Why do you think trade flourishes in coastal cities?**
> _____
> _____
> _____
> _____

Muslims generally practiced **tolerance**, or acceptance. They did not ban all other religions in their lands. More people began speaking Arabic and practicing Islam. The Arabs also took on non-Muslim customs. Cultural blending changed Islam into a religion of many cultures. The development of Muslim cities like **Baghdad** and **Córdoba** reflected this blending of cultures.

THREE MUSLIM EMPIRES

In the 1200s, Muslim Turks known as Ottomans attacked the Byzantine Empire. They trained **janissaries**, boys from conquered towns who were enslaved and converted to Islam. The janissaries fought fiercely. In 1453 the Ottomans took Constantinople, which they called **Istanbul**. This ended the Byzantine Empire. By 1566 the Ottomans took control of the eastern Mediterranean and parts of Europe.

> Underline the phrase that tells where the Ottomans found fierce soldiers to fight in their armies.

> What date signifies the end of the Byzantine Empire?
> _____
> _____

The Safavids (sah-FAH-vuhds) gained power in the east. They soon came into conflict with the Ottomans. The conflict stemmed from an old disagreement about who should be caliph. In the mid-600s, Islam had split into two groups—the Sunni and the Shia. The Ottomans were Sunni, and the Safavids were Shia. The Safavid Empire conquered Persia in 1501 and soon grew wealthy, building glorious mosques in **Esfahan**, their capital.

East of the Safavid Empire, in India, lay the Mughal (MOO-guhl) Empire. The Mughals united many diverse peoples and were known for their architecture—particularly the Taj Mahal. Under the leader Akbar, the Mughal Empire was known for its religious tolerance. But more restrictive policies after his death led to the end of the empire.

> What empire built the Taj Mahal in India?
> _____
> _____

CHALLENGE ACTIVITY

Critical Thinking: Analyzing Information Make a map showing the location and largest size of the Ottoman, Safavid, and Mughal empires.

DIRECTIONS Write a word or phrase that describes the term.

1. Baghdad _____

_____

2. caliph_____

_____

3. Córdoba_____

_____

4. Damascus _____

_____

5. Esfahan _____

_____

6. Istanbul _____

_____

7. janissaries _____

_____

8. tolerance _____

_____

History of the Islamic World

Section 4

MAIN IDEAS

1. Muslim scholars made lasting contributions to the fields of science and philosophy.

2. In literature and the arts, Muslim achievements included beautiful poetry, memorable short stories, and splendid architecture.

Key Terms and Places

Sufism a movement of Islam, based on the belief that one must have a personal relationship with God

minarets tall towers on mosques from which Muslims are called to prayer

calligraphy decorative writing

Section Summary

SCIENCE AND PHILOSOPHY

Islamic scholars made great advances in many fields. These included astronomy, geography, math, and science. At Baghdad and Córdoba, Greek and other writings were translated into Arabic. A common language helped scholars share research.

Muslim scientists built observatories to study the stars. They also improved the astrolabe. The Greeks had invented this tool to chart the position of the stars. The astrolabe would later be used in sea exploration.

It was a Muslim mathematician who invented algebra. Muslims found better ways to calculate distance and make precise maps. They also used the stars to navigate. Muslim merchants and explorers traveled far and wide. One great explorer was Ibn Battutah. He traveled to Africa, India, China, and Spain.

Muslims were also known in medicine. They added greatly to Greek and Indian medicine. Muslims also started the first school of pharmacy. A doctor in Baghdad found out how to detect and treat the disease smallpox. Another doctor, known in the West as Avicenna (av-uh-SEN-uh), wrote a medical

What two Islamic cities were centers of research and scholarship?
_____
_____

Why do you think the astrolabe would be useful in sea exploration?
_____
_____

What were two medical achievements made by Muslim doctors?
_____
_____
_____
_____

encyclopedia. It was used widely in Europe for centuries.

A new philosophy developed. It was called **Sufism** (SOO-fi-zuhm). People who practice Sufism are Sufis (SOO -feez). Sufis seek a personal relationship with God. Sufism has brought many followers to Islam.

LITERATURE AND THE ARTS

Poetry and short stories were popular among Muslims. The collection of stories called *The Thousand and One Nights* is still one of the best-loved books in the world. Sufi poets were popular, including the famous Omar Khayyám (OH-mahr ky-AHM).

There were many achievements in architecture. Rulers liked to be patrons. Patrons helped fund the design and construction of beautiful mosques. The main part of a mosque is a huge hall where thousands of people gather to pray. Often mosques have large domes and **minarets**.

Islam does not allow artists to show animals or humans in religious art. Muslims believe only Allah can create humans and animals or their images. In part for this reason, Muslim artists turned to **calligraphy**. This decorative writing became an art form.

> **What is the name of the collection of traditional Muslim stories?**
> _____
> _____
> _____

> **Underline the sentence that helps to explain why Muslim artists developed calligraphy as a fine art.**

CHALLENGE ACTIVITY

Critical Thinking: Drawing Inferences Islamic culture made many advances in science, medicine, and art that still affect us today. Pick the advance that you think is the most interesting, and write a one-page paper explaining why.

| calligraphy | classical | minarets |
| mosques | *Rubáiyát* | Sufism |

DIRECTIONS Use the words in the word bank to write a summary of what you learned in this section.

_____

_____

_____

_____

_____

_____

_____

_____

_____

_____

The Eastern Mediterranean

Section 1

MAIN IDEAS

1. The Eastern Mediterranean's physical features include the Bosporus, the Dead Sea, rivers, mountains, deserts, and plains.

2. The region's climate is mostly dry with little vegetation.

3. Important natural resources in the Eastern Mediterranean include valuable minerals and the availability of water.

Key Terms and Places

Dardanelles body of water that connects the Sea of Marmara and the Mediterranean Sea; part of the narrow waterway that separates Europe and Asia

Bosporus body of water that connects the Black Sea and the Sea of Marmara; part of the narrow waterway that separates Europe and Asia

Jordan River river that begins in Syria and flows south through Israel and Jordan, finally emptying into the Dead Sea

Dead Sea lowest point on any continent and the world's saltiest body of water

Syrian Desert a desert of rock and gravel covering much of Syria and Jordan

Section Summary

PHYSICAL FEATURES

The Eastern Mediterranean is part of a larger region called Southwest Asia, or the Middle East. The **Dardanelles**, the **Bosporus**, and the Sea of Marmara separate Europe from Asia. A small part of Turkey lies in Europe. The larger Asian part of Turkey is called Anatolia.

The **Jordan River** flows from Syria to Israel and Jordan, then empties into the **Dead Sea**, the world's saltiest body of water.

Two mountain systems stretch across Turkey. The Pontic Mountains lie in the north, and the Taurus Mountains lie in the south. A narrow plain runs from Turkey into Syria. The Euphrates River flows south-east through this plain. Hills, valleys, and plateaus are located farther inland. Two mountain ridges run north-south. One runs from

> **What three bodies of water separate Europe and Asia?**
>
> _____
> _____
> _____

> **Which two mountain systems stretch across Turkey?**
>
> _____
> _____

Guided Reading Workbook

Syria through western Jordan. The other runs through Lebanon and Israel.

CLIMATE AND VEGETATION

The Eastern Mediterranean is a mostly dry region. However, there are important variations. Turkey's Black Sea coast and the Mediterranean coast to northern Israel have a Mediterranean climate. Central Syria and lands farther south have a desert climate. Much of Turkey has a steppe climate, and a small area in the northeast has a humid subtropical climate.

The driest areas are the deserts. The **Syrian Desert** covers much of Syria and Jordan. The Negev Desert lies in southern Israel.

> Circle the four words and phrases that describe climates in the eastern Mediterranean.

NATURAL RESOURCES

Because the region is so dry, water is a valuable resource. Commercial farming relies on irrigation. Subsistence farming and herding takes place in drier areas.

Many minerals, including sulfur, mercury, and copper, are found in the region. Phosphates are produced in Syria, Jordan, and Israel. They are used to make fertilizers. The area also exports asphalt, the dark tarlike material used to pave streets.

> What mineral resources are found in the region?
> _____
> _____
> _____
> _____

CHALLENGE ACTIVITY

Critical Thinking: Drawing Inferences Based on what you've learned about the climates in the Eastern Mediterranean region, write an essay describing which location you think would be best for farming. What crops would you expect to grow well there?

| Bosporus | Dardanelles | Dead Sea | Jordan River |
| Negev Desert | phosphates | Sea of Marmara | Syrian Desert |

DIRECTIONS On the line provided before each statement, write **T** if a statement is true and **F** if a statement is false. If the statement is false, write the correct term on the line after each sentence that makes the sentence a true statement.

_____ 1. The Sea of Marmara, the Bosporus, and the <u>Negev</u> separate the European and Asian parts of Turkey.

_____

_____ 2. <u>Phosphates</u> are produced in Syria, Israel, and Jordan.

_____

_____ 3. The <u>Syrian Desert</u> is the lowest point on any continent.

_____

_____ 4. The strategic location of the <u>Bosporus</u> makes it a prized area.

_____

_____ 5. The <u>Dardanelles</u> empties into the Dead Sea.

_____

DIRECTIONS Choose four terms from the word bank. Include these words in a written summary of what you learned in the section.

_____

_____

_____

_____

_____

_____

MAIN IDEAS
1. Turkey's history includes invasion by the Romans, rule by the Ottomans, and a twentieth-century democracy.
2. Turkey's people are mostly ethnic Turks, and its culture is a mixture of modern and traditional.
3. Today, Turkey is a democratic nation seeking economic opportunities as a future member of the European Union.

Key Terms and Places

Ankara the capital of Turkey

Istanbul Turkey's largest city

secular religion is kept separate from government

Section Summary

HISTORY

About 8,000 years ago the area that is now Turkey was home to the world's earliest farming villages.

Turkey has been invaded by powerful empires for centuries. The Romans were the first empire to invade the area. They captured Byzantium, located between Europe and Asia, and renamed it Constantinople. After the fall of Rome, Constantinople became the capital of the Byzantine Empire.

Seljuk Turks, a nomadic people from Central Asia, invaded the area in the AD 1000s. In 1453 the Ottoman Turks captured Constantinople and made it the capital of the Islamic Empire. The Ottoman Empire was very powerful during the 1500s and 1600s, controlling territory in northern Africa, southwestern Asia, and southeastern Europe. The Ottomans fought on the losing side of World War I, and lost most of their territory at the end of the war.

Military officers took over the government after World War I, led by Mustafa Kemal. He later adopted the name Kemal Atatürk, which means

> **What did the Romans rename Byzantium?**
>
> _____
>
> _____

> **Who were the Seljuk Turks?**
>
> _____
>
> _____

> **Who was the leader of Turkey after World War I?**
>
> _____

Father of Turks. Atatürk created the democratic nation of Turkey and moved the capital to **Ankara** from Constantinople, which was renamed **Istanbul**.

Atatürk believed in modernizing Turkey, mainly by adopting some Western methods. He banned certain types of traditional clothing of both men and women, made new laws allowing women to vote and hold office, replaced the Arabic alphabet with the Latin alphabet, and adopted the metric system.

> **Why did Atatürk make so many changes and laws?**
> _____
> _____

PEOPLE AND CULTURE

Most of the people living in Turkey are ethnic Turks. Kurds are the largest minority, making up 20 percent of the population.

Turkey's culture today reflects Kemal Atatürk's changes. He created a cultural split between the urban middle class and rural villagers. In general, middle-class lifestyle and attitude reflect middle-class Europeans, while rural Turks are more traditional and reflect Islamic influences.

> **What is the largest minority living in Turkey today?**
> _____
> _____
> _____

TURKEY TODAY

Istanbul is Turkey's largest city, but the government meets in the capital of Ankara. Turkey has a legislature called the National Assembly. A president and prime minister share executive power. Although most of the people living in Turkey are Muslim, Turkey is a **secular** state.

The economy in Turkey is based on important industries, including textiles and clothing, cement, and electronics, as well as agriculture.

> **What is the National Assembly?**
> _____
> _____

CHALLENGE ACTIVITY

Critical Thinking: Drawing Inferences Kemal Atatürk is the founder of modern Turkey. Do you think he had a greater influence on people living in cities or in the countryside? Explain your reasoning.

Ankara	Constantinople	fez	Istanbul
modernize	Ottoman Empire	secular	shish kebab

DIRECTIONS Answer each question by writing a sentence that contains at least one term from the word bank. You should use all the terms.

1. What role did Constantinople have in Turkey's past? What role does the city of Istanbul have now?

   _____

   _____

   _____

2. Describe some of the changes made by Kemal Atatürk.

   _____

   _____

   _____

3. Who controlled Turkey during the 1500s and 1600s? What happened to this power?

   _____

   _____

   _____

4. What Turkish foods do you think you would like or dislike?

   _____

   _____

   _____

5. What is Turkey's government like today? Where does Turkey's government meet?

   _____

   _____

   _____

MAIN IDEAS
1. Israel's history includes the ancient Hebrews and the creation of the nation of Israel.
2. In Israel today, Jewish culture is a major part of daily life.
3. The Palestinian Territories are areas within Israel controlled partly by Palestinian Arabs.

Key Terms and Places

Diaspora the scattering of the Jewish population

Jerusalem the capital of Israel

Zionism a movement that called for Jews to establish a Jewish state in Palestine

kosher the term used for food allowed under Jewish dietary laws

kibbutz a large farm where people share everything in common

Gaza a small, crowded piece of coastal land disputed over by Jews and Arabs

West Bank a largely populated, rural piece of land disputed over by Jews and Arabs

Section Summary
HISTORY

Israel is often referred to as the Holy Land. It is home to sacred sites for Jews, Muslims, and Christians. The Israelites established the kingdom of Israel about 1000 BC. In the 60s BC the Roman Empire conquered the region, calling it Palestine, and forced most Jews to leave the region. This was known as the **Diaspora**. Arabs then conquered the land, but it was later invaded by Christian Crusaders, who captured the city of **Jerusalem**, but were eventually driven out. Palestine was part of the Ottoman Empire until it came under British control after World War I.

In the late 1800s European Jews began a movement called **Zionism** that called for Jews to establish a Jewish state in their ancient homeland. In 1947 the United Nations voted to divide Palestine into Jewish and Arab states. Arab countries rejected this plan. Israel and Arab countries have fought in

> **Why is Israel often referred to as the Holy Land?**
> _____
> _____

> **When did the Roman Empire conquer the region?**
> _____

several wars over this issue, and disputes between the two sides continue today.

ISRAEL TODAY

Israel is a modern, democratic country with a diverse economy. About 75 percent of Israel's population is Jewish. The rest of the population is mostly Arab. Tel Aviv is Israel's largest city.

Jewish holidays and traditions are an important aspect of Israeli Jewish culture. Many Jews follow a **kosher** diet based on ancient religious laws. About 100,000 Israeli Jews live in **kibbutzim**, large farms where people share everything in common.

> **What percentage of Israel's population is Jewish?**
> _____

> **What are kibbutzim?**
> _____
> _____

THE PALESTINIAN TERRITORIES

In 1967 Israel captured land occupied by Palestinian Arabs—**Gaza**, the **West Bank**, and East Jerusalem. Since then Jews and Arabs have fought over the right to live in these two regions.

In the 1990s Israel agreed to turn over parts of the territories to Palestinians if the Palestinian leadership—the Palestinian Authority—agreed to work for peace. In 2005, Israelis transferred Gaza to the Palestinian Authority. The future of the peace process remains uncertain.

> **Which areas of land have been the source of the greatest conflict between Arabs and Israelis?**
> _____
> _____

CHALLENGE ACTIVITY

Critical Thinking: Drawing Inferences In what areas of Israel do you think most Arabs live? Draw an outline map of Israel, locating major cities and the areas with the largest Arab populations.

Arabic	Diaspora	Gaza	Hebrew
Jerusalem	kibbutz	Knesset	kosher
Palestinian	West Bank	Yom Kippur	Zionism

DIRECTIONS Read each sentence and fill in the blank with the term in the word bank that best completes the sentence.

1. Arabic and _____ are both official languages of Israel. (Zionism/Hebrew)

2. The movement that called Jewish people to start a country in Palestine is called _____. (Zionism/Hebrew)

3. If you lived on a _____ you would work on the farm and share everything with other people. (kibbutz/kosher)

4. _____ is an important Jewish holiday celebrated in October. (Diaspora/Yom Kippur)

5. Ramallah is a city in the disputed land of the _____. (Gaza/West Bank)

6. _____ is a holy city to Jews, Christians, and Muslims. (Gaza/Jerusalem)

7. The _____ is the name of Israel's parliament, which is part of the government. (Knesset/Diaspora)

8. The forced removal of Jewish people from Palestine by the Romans is called the _____. (Knesset/Diaspora)

MAIN IDEAS
1. Syria, once part of the Ottoman Empire, is an Arab country ruled by a powerful family.
2. Lebanon is recovering from civil war and its people are divided by religion.
3. Jordan has few resources and is home to Bedouins and Palestinian refugees.

Key Terms and Places

Damascus the capital of Syria

Beirut the capital of Lebanon

Bedouins Arab-speaking nomads who mostly live in the deserts of Southwest Asia

Amman the capital of Jordan

Section Summary

SYRIA

The capital of Syria, **Damascus**, is believed to be the oldest continuously inhabited city in the world. Syria became part of the Ottoman Empire in the 1500s. After World War I, France controlled Syria. Syria gained independence in the 1940s.

The Syrian government was led by Hafiz al-Assad from 1971 to 2000. Assad's son, Bashar, was elected president after his father's death in 2000. Syria's government owns the country's oil refineries, larger electrical plants, railroads, and some factories.

More than 20 million people live in Syria. About 90 percent of the population is Arab, and the remaining 10 percent include Kurds and Armenians. About 74 percent of Syrians are Sunni Muslim, about 16 percent are Alawites and Druze, and about 10 percent are Christian. There are also small Jewish communities in some Syrian cities.

Which country controlled Syria after World War I?

_____

Underline the sentence that describes Syria's main industries and who owns them.

LEBANON

Lebanon is a small, mountainous country. Many ethnic minority groups settled in Lebanon during the Ottoman Empire. After World War I it was controlled by France. Lebanon finally gained its independence in the 1940s.

Most Lebanese people are Arab, but they are divided by religion. The main religions in Lebanon are Islam and Christianity, with each of these groups divided into smaller groups. Muslims are divided into Sunni, Shia, and Druze. The Maronites are the largest Christian group.

After gaining independence, Christian and Muslim politicians shared power. However, over time this cooperation broke down and tensions mounted. Warfare between the groups lasted until 1990. The capital, **Beirut**, was badly damaged.

> When did Lebanon gain its independence?
> _____

> What are the two main religious groups in Lebanon?
> _____
> _____

JORDAN

The country of Jordan was created after World War I. The British controlled the area until the 1940s, when the country gained full independence. King Hussein ruled Jordan from 1952 to 1999. He enacted some democratic reforms in the 1990s.

Jordan is a poor country with limited resources. Many people in Jordan are **Bedouins**, or Arab-speaking nomads who live mainly in the deserts of Southwest Asia. **Amman**, the capital, is Jordan's largest city. The country's resources include phosphates, cement, and potash. In addition, the tourism and banking industries are growing. Jordan depends on economic aid from oil-rich Arab nations and the United States.

> When was Jordan created?
> _____
> _____

> Underline the sentences that describe Jordan's economy.

CHALLENGE ACTIVITY

Critical Thinking: Analyzing Information Make a table with a column for each country in this section. List information about the people of each country in the appropriate column. Based on your table, which of these nations has the greatest diversity?

Amman	Bedouins	Beirut
Damascus	Palmyra	

DIRECTIONS Read each sentence and fill in the blank with the word in the word pair that best completes the sentence.

1. _____ is the capital of Syria and is thought to be the oldest continuously inhabited city in the world. (Damascus/Beirut)

2. _____, the capital of Lebanon, was badly damaged during a civil war. (Damascus/Beirut)

3. The Romans called this ancient trading center in Syria _____, meaning "city of palm trees." (Bedouins/Palmyra)

4. _____, who mostly live in the deserts of Southwest Asia, are Arabic-speaking nomads. (Bedouins/Palmyra)

5. The capital of Jordan, _____, is also the country's largest city. (Beirut/Amman)

DIRECTIONS On a separate piece of paper create a crossword puzzle using the words in the word bank. Use the definition or description of each term as a clue. If you wish, you may add other words from the section to create a bigger puzzle.

The Arabian Peninsula, Iraq, and Iran

Section 1

MAIN IDEAS

1. Major physical features of the Arabian Peninsula, Iraq, and Iran are desert plains and mountains.
2. The region has a dry climate and little vegetation.
3. Most of the world is dependent on oil, a resource that is exported from this region.

Key Terms and Places

Arabian Peninsula region of the world that has the largest sand desert in the world

Persian Gulf body of water surrounded by the Arabian Peninsula, Iran, and Iraq

Tigris River river that flows across a low, flat plain in Iraq and joins the Euphrates River

Euphrates River river that flows across a low, flat plain in Iraq and joins the Tigris River

oasis a wet, fertile area in a desert that forms where underground water bubbles to the surface

wadis dry streambeds

fossil water water that is not being replaced by rainfall

Section Summary

PHYSICAL FEATURES

The region of the **Arabian Peninsula**, Iraq, and Iran has huge deserts. Not all deserts are sand. Some are bare rock or gravel. The region forms a semicircle, with the **Persian Gulf** at the center.

The region's main landforms are rivers, plains, plateaus, and mountains. The two major rivers are the **Tigris** and **Euphrates** in Iraq. They make a narrow area good for crops. This area was called Mesopotamia in ancient times.

The Arabian Peninsula has flat, open plains in the east. In the south, desert plains are covered with sand. Deserts in the north are covered with volcanic rock. The peninsula rises slowly towards the Red Sea. This makes a high landscape of mountains and

> Underline the words that tell you what deserts can be made of.

> List the four main landforms of this region.
>
> _____
> _____
> _____
> _____

flat plateaus. The highest point is in the mountains in Yemen. Plateaus and mountains also cover most of Iran.

CLIMATE AND VEGETATION

This region has a desert climate. It can get very hot in the day and very cold at night. The Rub' al-Khali desert in Saudi Arabia is the world's largest sand desert. Its name means "Empty Quarter," because it has so little life.

Some areas with plateaus and mountains get rain or snow in winter. Some mountain peaks get more than 50 inches of rain a year. Trees grow in these areas. They also grow in **oases** in the desert. At an oasis, underground water bubbles up. Some plants also grow in parts of the desert. Their roots either go very deep or spread out very far to get as much water as they can.

> **Is the desert always hot? Explain your answer.**
> _____
> _____
> _____
> _____

> **Underline the sentence that explains how desert plants get water.**

RESOURCES

Water is one of this region's two most valuable resources. But water is scarce. Some places in the desert have springs that give water. Wells also provide water. Some wells are dug into dry streambeds called **wadis**. Other wells go very deep underground. These often get **fossil water**. This is water that is not replaced by rain, so these wells will run dry over time.

Oil is the region's other important resource. This resource is plentiful. Oil has brought wealth to the countries that have oil fields. But oil cannot be replaced once it is taken. Too much drilling for oil may cause problems in the future.

> **Circle two important resources in this region.**

CHALLENGE ACTIVITY

Critical Thinking: Designing Design an illustrated poster using the term *Persian Gulf*. For each letter, write a word containing that letter that tells something about the region.

| Arabian Peninsula | Euphrates River | fossil water | oasis |
| Persian Gulf | Tigris River | wadis | |

DIRECTIONS Read each sentence and fill in the blank with the word in the word pair that best completes the sentence.

1. The countries of the _____ form a semicircle.
   (Persian Gulf/Arabian Peninsula)

2. The _____ begins in a humid region and flows through a dry area. (Tigris River/fossil water)

3. The _____ joins with the Tigris River before reaching the Persian Gulf. (oasis/Euphrates River)

4. The _____ is in the center of this region.
   (Persian Gulf/Arabian Peninsula)

5. One water resource for this region is the wells that are dug into

   _____, or dry streambeds. (fossil water/wadis)

DIRECTIONS Use all of the terms from the word bank to write a summary of what you learned in the section.

_____

_____

_____

_____

_____

_____

_____

_____

The Arabian Peninsula, Iraq, and Iran

Section 2

MAIN IDEAS

1. Islamic culture and an economy greatly based on oil influence life in Saudi Arabia.

2. Most other Arabian Peninsula countries are monarchies influenced by Islamic culture and oil resources.

Key Terms

Shia branch of Islam in which Muslims believe that true interpretations of Islamic teachings can only come from certain religious and political leaders

Sunni branch of Islam in which Muslims believe in the ability of the majority of the community to interpret Islamic teachings

OPEC Organization of Petroleum Exporting Countries, an international organization whose members work to influence the price of oil on world markets by controlling the supply

Section Summary
SAUDI ARABIA

Saudi Arabia is the largest country on the Arabian Peninsula. It is a major center of religion and culture. Its economy is one of the strongest in this region.

Most Saudis speak Arabic. Islam is a strong influence on their culture and customs. This religion was started in Saudi Arabia by Muhammad. Most Saudis follow one of two branches of Islam—**Shia** or **Sunni**. About 85 percent of Saudi Muslims are Sunni.

Islam influences Saudi culture in many ways. It teaches modesty, so traditional clothing is long and loose, covering the arms and legs. Women rarely go out in public without a husband or male relative. But women can own and run businesses.

The country's government is a monarchy. There are also local officials. Only men can vote.

Saudi Arabia is an important member of **OPEC**, an organization with members from different

What branch of Islam do most Saudis follow?

_____

_____

Guided Reading Workbook

countries. OPEC works to control oil supplies to influence world oil prices.

Saudi Arabia also has challenges. It has very little freshwater to grow crops, so it has to import most of its food. There is high unemployment, especially among young people.

> **Underline two challenges Saudi Arabia faces.**

OTHER COUNTRIES OF THE ARABIAN PENINSULA

There are six smaller countries of this region: Kuwait, Bahrain, Qatar, the United Arab Emirates (UAE), Oman, and Yemen. Like Saudi Arabia, they are all influenced by Islam and most have monarchies and depend on oil.

> **List the six smaller countries on the Arabian Peninsula.**
> _____
> _____
> _____
> _____
> _____

Most of these countries are rich. Yemen is the poorest. Oil was only discovered there in the 1980s.

Most of these countries have a monarchy. Some also have elected officials. Yemen's government is elected, but political corruption has been a problem.

Some of these countries support their economy in other ways besides oil. Bahrain's oil began to run out in the 1990s. Banking and tourism are now important. Qatar and the UAE also have natural gas. Oman does not have as much oil as other countries, so it is trying to create new industries.

> **Circle three ways besides oil that countries in this region are supporting their economies.**

The Persian Gulf War started in 1990 when Iraq invaded Kuwait. The United States and other countries helped Kuwait defeat Iraq. Many of Kuwait's oilfields were destroyed during the war.

CHALLENGE ACTIVITY

Critical Thinking: Compare and Contrast Use a Venn diagram or a Features Chart to compare and contrast Saudi Arabia with at least two other countries of the Arabian Peninsula. Consider features such as religious influences, resources, governments, and economies.

| OPEC | procedure | reserves |
| Shia | Sunni | desalination |

DIRECTIONS Use a word from the word bank to fill in the blank in each sentence below.

1. The majority of Saudis are _____ Muslims.

2. A _____ is a series of steps taken to accomplish a task.

3. _____ Muslims believe that only imams can interpret Islamic teachings.

4. _____ is an international organization that controls the supply of oil to influence prices on world markets.

5. Saudi Arabia uses _____ plants to remove salt from sea water.

6. Saudi Arabia has the world's largest _____, or supplies, of oil.

The Arabian Peninsula, Iraq, and Iran

Section 3

MAIN IDEAS

1. Iraq's history includes rule by many conquerors and cultures, as well as recent conflicts and wars.

2. Most people in Iraq are Arabs, but Kurds live in the north.

3. Iraq today must rebuild its government and economy, which have suffered years of conflict.

Key Terms and Places

embargo limit on trade

Baghdad capital of Iraq

Section Summary

HISTORY

The world's first civilization was in Iraq, in the area called Mesopotamia. Throughout history, many cultures and empires conquered Mesopotamia, including Great Britain in World War I. In the 1950s, Iraqi army officers overthrew British rule.

| Circle the location of the world's first civilization. |

Iraq's recent history includes wars and a harsh, corrupt leader. In 1968, the Ba'ath Party took power. In 1979 the party's leader, Saddam Hussein, became president. He restricted the press and people's freedoms. He killed an unknown number of political enemies.

| Why was Saddam Hussein considered a harsh leader? |

Saddam led Iraq into two wars. In 1980, Iraq invaded Iran. The Iran-Iraq War lasted until 1988. In 1990, Iraq invaded Kuwait. Western leaders worried about Iraq controlling too much oil and having weapons of mass destruction. An alliance of countries led by the United States forced Iraq from Kuwait. After the war, Saddam Hussein did not accept all the terms of peace, so the United Nations placed an **embargo** on Iraq. This hurt the economy.

| Underline the word that means a limit on trade. |

Guided Reading Workbook

In March 2003, the United States invaded Iraq.
Saddam Hussein went into hiding and Iraq's
government fell. Saddam Hussein was later found
and arrested.

When did the United States invade Iraq? _____

PEOPLE AND CULTURE

Most of Iraq's people belong to two ethnic groups.
The majority are Arab, who speak Arabic. The
others are Kurd, who speak Kurdish in addition to
Arabic. Kurds live in a large region in the north of
Iraq.

Most people of Iraq are Muslim. About 60
percent are Shia Muslims and live in the south.
About one third are Sunni Muslims and live in the
north.

Circle the ethnic group that most people in Iraq belong to.

IRAQ TODAY

Today Iraq is slowly recovering from war.
Baghdad, Iraq's capital of 6 million people, was
badly damaged. People lost electricity and running
water. After the war, the U.S. military and private
companies helped to restore water and electricity,
and to rebuild homes, businesses, and schools.

In January 2005 the people of Iraq took part in
democracy for the first time. They voted for
members of the National Assembly. This group's
main task was to write Iraq's new constitution.

Iraq is trying to rebuild a strong economy. Oil
and crops are important resources. It may take years
for Iraq to rebuild structures such as schools,
hospitals, and roads. It may be even harder to create
a free society and strong economy.

The U.S. census for the year 2000 reports that about 3,700,000 people live in the city of Los Angeles. How does the population of Baghdad compare with this?

Underline the main task of Iraq's National Assembly.

CHALLENGE ACTIVITY

Critical Thinking: Analyzing On a separate piece
of paper, create a time line of events in Iraq since
1968.

alliance	Baghdad	embargo
Kurds	Saddam Hussein	uprising

DIRECTIONS Read each sentence and fill in the blank with the word
in the word pair that best completes the sentence.

1. The United Nations placed an _____, or limit on trade, on
   Iraq after the 1991 war. (embargo/alliance)

2. _____ is Iraq's capital. (Kurds/Baghdad)

3. _____ was the ruler of Iraq for many years.
   (Saddam Hussein/Kurds)

4. The _____ are mostly farmers and live in northern Iraq.
   (Kurds/Baghdad)

5. When Shia Muslims attempted an _____, Saddam Hussein's
   response was brutal. (alliance/uprising)

DIRECTIONS Use at least four of the words from the word bank to
write a summary of what you learned in the section.

_____

_____

_____

_____

_____

_____

_____

_____

_____

The Arabian Peninsula, Iraq, and Iran

Section 4

 MAIN IDEAS
1. Iran's history includes great empires and an Islamic republic.
2. In Iran today, Islamic religious leaders restrict the rights of most Iranians.

Key Terms and Places

shah king

revolution a drastic change in a country's government and way of life

Tehran capital of Iran

theocracy a government ruled by religious leaders

Section Summary

HISTORY

Iran today is an Islamic republic. In the past, the region was ruled by the Persian Empire and a series of Muslim empires.

The Persian Empire was a great center of art and learning. It was known for architecture and many other arts, including carpets. The capital, Persepolis, had walls and statues that glittered with gold, silver, and jewels. When Muslims conquered the region, they converted the Persians to Islam. But most people kept their Persian culture.

In 1921 an Iranian military officer took charge. He claimed the Persian title of **shah**, or king. In 1941 his son took control. This shah was an ally of the United States and Britain. He tried to make Iran more modern, but his programs were not popular.

In 1979 Iranians began a **revolution**. They overthrew the shah. The new government set up an Islamic republic that follows strict Islamic law.

Soon after the revolution began, Iran's relations with the United States broke down. A mob of students attacked the U.S. Embassy in **Tehran**. Over 50 Americans were held hostage for a year.

> **Name and describe the capital of the Persian Empire.**
> _____
> _____
> _____
> _____

> **Underline the phrase that explains what an Islamic republic does.**

IRAN TODAY

Iran is unique in Southwest Asia, where most people are Arabs and speak Arabic. In Iran, more than half the people are Persian. They speak Farsi, the Persian language.

Iran has one of Southwest Asia's largest populations. It has about 66 million people, and the average age is about 27.

Iran is very diverse. Along with Persians, Iranian ethnic groups include Azerbaijanis, Kurds, Arabs, and Turks. Most Iranians are Shia Muslim. About 10 percent are Sunni Muslim. Others practice Christianity, Judaism, and other religions.

Persian culture influences life in Iran in many ways. People celebrate the Persian New Year, Nowruz. Persian food is an important part of most family gatherings.

Iran's economy is based on oil. There are also other industries, including carpet production and agriculture.

Iran's government is a **theocracy**. Its rulers, or *ayatollahs*, are religious leaders. The country also has an elected president and parliament.

Iran's government has supported many hard-line policies, such as terrorism. Today, the United States and other nations are concerned about Iran's nuclear program as a threat to world security.

Estimate the number of Iranians under age 27.

Circle two ways that Persian culture is part of people's lives today.

CHALLENGE ACTIVITY

Critical Thinking: Analyzing Information Create a table about Saudi Arabia, Iraq, and Iran. For each nation, list information about religion, government, language, ethnic groups, and economy. After you complete your chart, write one or two sentences to summarize the ways these nations are alike and different.

Farsi	Nowruz	revolution
shah	Tehran	theocracy

DIRECTIONS Write three words or phrases related to the term.

1. Nowruz _____

2. revolution _____

3. shah _____

4. Tehran _____

5. theocracy _____

6. Farsi _____

DIRECTIONS Choose three of the words from the word bank. On a separate sheet of paper, use the words to write a paragraph about Iran.

MAIN IDEAS
1. Key physical features of landlocked Central Asia include rugged mountains.
2. Central Asia has a harsh, dry climate that makes it difficult for vegetation to grow.
3. Key natural resources in Central Asia include water, oil and gas, and minerals.

Key Terms and Places

landlocked completely surrounded by land with no direct access to the ocean

Pamirs some of Central Asia's high mountains

Fergana Valley large fertile valley in the plains region of Central Asia

Kara-Kum desert in Turkmenistan

Kyzyl Kum desert in Uzbekistan and Kazakhstan

Aral Sea sea that is actually a large lake, which is shrinking due to irrigation

Section Summary
PHYSICAL FEATURES

Central Asia, the middle part of the continent, is **landlocked**. In the region's east, there are rugged, high mountains. Large glaciers are common in the high mountains. One area of high mountains is called the **Pamirs**.

Because it is landlocked and has such rugged land, Central Asia is isolated. Communication and travel are difficult. The area also has many earthquakes.

From the mountains, the land slowly slopes down to the Caspian Sea in the west. Some land there is 95 feet (29 m) below sea level. The land between the sea and mountains is plains and plateaus. The fertile **Fergana Valley** is in the plains.

Central Asia also has some rivers and lakes. Two important rivers are the Syr Darya (sir durh-YAH) and the Amu Darya (uh-MOO duhr-YAH).

> What two factors make Central Asia isolated?
> _____
> _____

> Underline the sentence that names two important rivers in Central Asia.

They make the Fergana Valley fertile. The rivers flow into the Aral Sea, which is really a large lake. Lake Balkhash is also an important lake. It has freshwater at one end and salty water at the other.

> Circle the name of the sea that is really a large lake.

CLIMATE AND VEGETATION

Most of Central Asia has a harsh, dry climate. Temperatures range from very cold to very hot, and there is not much rain. It is hard for plants to grow.

The mountain peaks are cold, dry, and windy. There are harsh desert areas between the mountains and sea. Two major deserts are the **Kara-Kum** and **Kyzyl Kum**. The deserts do have some sources of water. Some areas have rivers crossing them, which lets people live there. People use rivers to irrigate, or supply water to the land.

Only the far north of Central Asia has a milder climate. Grasses and trees are able to grow there.

> Underline the names of two major deserts in Central Asia.

NATURAL RESOURCES

Some of Central Asia's natural resources are water, oil, and gas. There is also a supply of minerals, such as gold, lead, and copper.

People use the Syr Darya and Amu Darya rivers to irrigate and make electricity. But water is limited. This has led to conflicts over how to use it. Also, irrigation has kept the rivers from flowing into the **Aral Sea**. As a result, the sea has lost much of its water.

Oil and gas can only help the region if the countries can sell it. There are no ocean ports to transport it, so they need to build and maintain pipelines. But this is hard because of the rugged land, as well as economic and political problems.

> List some of Central Asia's natural resources:
> _____
> _____
> _____

CHALLENGE ACTIVITY

Critical Thinking: Analyzing Information Write a fact sheet called *Central Asia: Tips for Hikers*. Include key facts that hikers to the region should know and a list of supplies they should bring.

| Aral Sea | Caspian Sea | Fergana Valley | Lake Balkhash |
| Kara-Kum | Kyzyl Kum | landlocked | Pamirs |

DIRECTIONS Read each sentence and fill in the blank with the word in the word pair that best completes the sentence.

1. The _____ receives very little rainfall.
   (Kara-Kum/Fergana Valley)

2. Large glaciers can be found in the _____.
   (Kyzyl Kum/Pamirs)

3. The _____ is a major farming area in Central Asia.
   (Kara-Kum/Fergana Valley)

4. The _____ is located in Uzbekistan and Kazakhstan.
   (Caspian Sea/Kyzyl Kum)

5. The _____ has been devastated by the irrigation practices in Central Asia. (Aral Sea/Caspian Sea)

DIRECTIONS Use at least four of the terms from the word bank to write a summary of what you learned in the section.

_____

_____

_____

_____

_____

Section 2

MAIN IDEAS
1. Throughout history, many different groups have conquered Central Asia.
2. Many different ethnic groups and their traditions influence culture in Central Asia.

Key Terms and Places

Samarqand city along the Silk Road that grew rich from trade

nomads people who move often from place to place

yurt moveable round house made of wool felt mats hung over a wood frame

Section Summary

HISTORY

For hundreds of years, many groups of people came through Central Asia. They left lasting influences.

At one time, there were two trade routes through Central Asia. One route went between Europe and India, through Afghanistan. The other route went through the rest of Central Asia. It was called the Silk Road, because traders from Europe traveled it to get silk and spices from China. **Samarqand** and other cities on the Silk Road grew rich.

By 1500, Europeans stopped using these roads. They discovered they could sail to East Asia on the Indian Ocean. The region became isolated and poor.

The Silk Road brought many people into Central Asia. In AD 500, Turkic-speaking nomads came from northern Asia. From the 700s to 1200s, Arabs ruled. They brought their religion, Islam. Then the Mongols conquered Central Asia. After the Mongols, groups such as the Uzbeks, Kazaks, and Turkmen came in.

In the mid-1800s, Russia conquered this region. Russians built railroads. They also increased oil and cotton production. But people began to resist Russia's rule. After the Soviets took power in Russia, they wanted to weaken resistance to their

What places did the two trade routes in Central Asia connect?
_____
_____

Underline the reason that Europeans stopped using the trade routes.

Circle the dates that the Arabs ruled Central Asia.

rule. So they divided Central Asia into republics. They also encouraged ethnic Russians to move in. The Soviets also built huge irrigation projects for more cotton production. In 1991, the Soviet government collapsed. Central Asia's republics became independent countries.

> **What happened to Asia's republics when the Soviet government collapsed in 1991?**
>
> _____
>
> _____

CULTURE

The people who came through Central Asia brought new languages, religions, and ways of life. These mixed with traditional ways.

For centuries, Central Asians raised herds of horses, cattle, goats, and sheep. Many lived as **nomads**. They moved their herds to different pastures in summer and winter. They also moved their houses. The Central Asian nomad's moveable house is called a **yurt**. It is an important symbol today. Even people in cities put up yurts for special events. Nomads are still common in Kyrgyzstan.

> **Unscramble these letters to identify a feature of nomad life: *tury*. Write your answer:**
>
> _____

Today, most of the region's ethnic groups are part of the larger Turkic group. There are ethnic Russians, also. Each group speaks its own language. Some countries have many languages. In some countries Russian is still the official language, because of earlier Russian rule. The Russians also brought Cyrillic, their alphabet. Now most countries use the Latin alphabet, the one for writing English.

> **Circle the name of the Russian alphabet.**

The region's main religion is Islam, but there are also others. Some people are Russian Orthodox, a Christian religion. Today, many religious buildings that were closed by the Soviets have opened again.

CHALLENGE ACTIVITY

Critical Thinking: Drawing Conclusions Central Asia has always been a crossroads for people. Using the dates in the summary, make a timeline of the people who have ruled the region. Which group do you think had the most lasting influence on Central Asia? Why do you think so?

| Cyrillic | nomads | Pashto |
| Samarqand | Silk Road | yurt |

DIRECTIONS On the line provided before each statement, write **T** if the statement is true and **F** if the statement is false. If the statement is false, write the term that makes the sentence a true statement on the line after each sentence.

_____ 1. <u>Yurts</u> are people who move around often.

_____

_____ 2. A <u>nomad</u> is a movable, round house.

_____

_____ 3. The city of <u>Samarqand</u> was along the Silk Road.

_____

_____ 4. The Russians introduced the <u>Pashto</u> alphabet in Central Asia.

_____

_____ 5. <u>Cyrillic</u> is one of the official languages of Afghanistan.

_____

Central Asia

MAIN IDEAS
1. The countries of Central Asia are working to develop their economies and to improve political stability in the region.
2. The countries of Central Asia face issues and challenges related to the environment, the economy, and politics.

Key Terms and Places

Taliban radical Muslim group that arose in Afghanistan in the mid-1990s

Kabul capital of Afghanistan

dryland farming farming that relies on rainfall instead of irrigation

arable suitable for growing crops

Section Summary
CENTRAL ASIA TODAY

Central Asia is working to recover from a history of invasions and foreign rulers. The region is trying to build more stable governments and stronger economies.

During the 1980s, Afghanistan was at war with the Soviet Union. In the mid-1990s, the **Taliban** took power. This was a radical Muslim group. It ruled most of the country, including **Kabul**, the capital. It based its laws on strict Islamic teachings. Most people disagreed with the Taliban. A terrorist group based in Afghanistan attacked the United States on September 11, 2001. As a result, U.S. and British forces toppled the Taliban government. Now people in Afghanistan have a constitution and more freedom. But some groups still threaten violence.

Kazakhstan was the first area in Central Asia that Russia conquered. It still has many Russian influences. Its economy suffered when the Soviet Union fell. But it is growing again, because of oil reserves and a free market. Kazakhstan has a stable democratic government. People elect a president and parliament.

> **What group ruled Afghanistan from the mid-1990s to 2001?**
> _____

> **Underline the sentence that explains why Kazakhstan's economy is growing.**

In Kyrgystan, many people farm. They irrigate or
use **dryland farming**. This does not bring much
money, but tourism may help the economy. In
recent years, there have been government protests.

Tajikistan now has a more stable government,
after ending conflicts between different groups.
Today, the economy relies on cotton farming. But
only about 7 percent of the land is **arable**.

Turkmenistan's president is elected for life and
has all the power. The economy is based on oil, gas,
and cotton farming. The country is a desert, but it
has the longest irrigation channel in the world.

Uzbekistan's president is also elected and has all
the power. The economy is based on oil and cotton.
The economy is stable, but not really growing.

> **Why should Tajikistan look for other ways to support its economy?**
>
> _____
>
> _____

ISSUES AND CHALLENGES

Central Asia faces challenges in three areas today:
environment, economy, and politics.

The shrinking Aral Sea is a serious problem for
Central Asia's environment. The seafloor is dry.
Dust, salt, and pesticides blow out of it. Its
environment also has leftover radiation from Soviet
nuclear testing. People's health is a concern. Crop
chemicals are also a problem for the environment,
harming farmlands.

> **Underline the main challenges that Central Asia's environment faces.**

Central Asia's economy relies on cotton. This has
hurt many of their economies. Oil and gas reserves
may bring in more money one day. Today there are
still challenges, such as old equipment, that need to
be overcome for Central Asia's economy to grow.

Central Asia does not have widespread political
stability. In some countries, people do not agree on
the best kind of government. Some turn to violence
or terrorism as a result.

CHALLENGE ACTIVITY

Critical Thinking: Analyzing Information If you
were asked to plan a meeting about protecting the
environment in Central Asia, what topics would you
put on the agenda? What topic would you want to
spend the most time discussing?

DIRECTIONS Look at each set of four vocabulary terms following
each number. On the line provided, write the letter of the term that does
not relate to the others.

_____ 1. a. Kabul   b. Astana   c. Tashkent   d. Taliban

_____ 2. a. dryland farming b. nomads   c. crops   d. arable

_____ 3. a. Issyk-Kul   b. Kazakhs   c. Afghans   d. Kyrgyz

_____ 4. a. Turkmenistan b. Kabul   c. Uzbekistan   d. Afghanistan

DIRECTIONS Write three words or phrases that describe each term.

5. dryland farming _____

6. arable _____

7. Taliban _____

8. Kabul _____

MAIN IDEAS
1. Egypt was called the gift of the Nile because the Nile River was so important.
2. Civilization developed after people began farming along the Nile River.
3. Strong kings unified all of ancient Egypt.

Key Terms and Places

Nile River important river in Egypt

Upper Egypt southern part of Egypt

Lower Egypt northern part of Egypt

cataracts river rapids

delta triangle-shaped area of land made from soil deposited by a river

pharaoh ruler of ancient Egypt, literally means "great house"

dynasty series of rulers from the same family

Section Summary

THE GIFT OF THE NILE

The existence of Egypt was based solely around the **Nile River**, the world's longest river. The Nile carries water from central Africa through a vast stretch of desert land. The river was so important to people that Egypt was called the gift of the Nile.

Ancient Egypt developed along a 750-mile stretch of the Nile, and was originally organized into two kingdoms—**Upper Egypt** and **Lower Egypt**. Upper Egypt was located upriver in relation to the Nile's flow. Lower Egypt was the northern region and was located downriver.

Cataracts, or rapids, marked the southern border of Upper Egypt. Lower Egypt was centered in the river **delta**, a triangle-shaped area of land made of soil deposited by the river. In midsummer, the Nile would flood Upper Egypt and in the fall the river would flood Lower Egypt. This made sure that the farmland would stay moist and fertile. As the land surrounding the Nile Valley was arid desert, this

Why is a river a gift to a desert land?

_____

_____

watered area was the lifeline for everyone who lived in the region.

CIVILIZATION DEVELOPS IN EGYPT

With dry desert all around, it is no wonder that ancient settlers were attracted to this abundant and protected area of fertile farmland. Hunter-gatherers first moved to the area around 12,000 years ago and found plenty of meat and fish to hunt and eat. By 4500 BC farmers were living in villages and growing wheat and barley. They were also raising cattle and sheep.

Around 3200 BC the Egyptian villages became organized into two kingdoms. The capital of Lower Egypt was located in the northwest Nile Delta at a town called Pe. The capital city of Upper Egypt was called Nekhen. It was located on the west bank of the Nile.

KINGS UNIFY EGYPT

Around 3100 BC Menes (MEE-neez), the king of Upper Egypt, invaded Lower Egypt. He married a princess there in order to unite the two kingdoms under his rule. Menes was the first **pharaoh,** which literally means ruler of a "great house." He also started the first Egyptian **dynasty,** or series of rulers from the same family. He built a new capital city, Memphis, which became a popular cultural center. His dynasty ruled for nearly 200 years.

> **Why do you think Menes wanted to unite the two kingdoms?**
>
> _____
>
> _____
>
> _____
>
> _____

CHALLENGE ACTIVITY

Critical Thinking: Drawing Inferences Villages did not develop until people could stop being hunter-gatherers and start growing their own food. From villages came powerful leaders who united larger territories and people under one organization. Imagine that you are an ancient Egyptian interested in becoming a leader. Write a speech explaining what would make you a powerful person fit for ruling a large village.

Guided Reading Workbook

| cataract | delta | dynasty | Lower Egypt |
| Upper Egypt | Nile River | pharaoh | |

DIRECTIONS Write a word or phrase that has the same meaning as
the term given.

1. Upper Egypt _____

2. dynasty _____

3. cataract _____

4. pharaoh _____

5. delta _____

6. Nile River _____

7. Lower Egypt _____

DIRECTIONS Look at each set of three vocabulary terms following
each number. On the line provided, write the letter of the term that does
not relate to the others.

_____ 8. a. cataract   10. a. delta
           b. pharaoh   b. Lower Egypt
           c. Nile River   c. dynasty

_____ 9. a. delta
           b. dynasty
           c. pharaoh

History of Ancient Egypt

MAIN IDEAS
1. Life in the Old Kingdom was influenced by pharaohs, roles in society, and trade.
2. Religion shaped Egyptian life.
3. The pyramids were built as tombs for Egypt's pharaohs.

Key Terms and Places

Old Kingdom a period in Egyptian history that lasted from about 2700 to 2200 BC

nobles people from rich and powerful families

afterlife life after death, a widely held ancient Egyptian belief

mummies specially treated bodies wrapped in cloth

elite people of wealth and power

pyramids huge, stone tombs with four triangle-shaped walls that meet at a top point

engineering application of scientific knowledge for practical purposes

Section Summary

LIFE IN THE OLD KINGDOM

Around 2700 BC the Third Dynasty began a period in Egyptian history known as the **Old Kingdom**. During the next 500 years, the Egyptians developed a political system based on the belief that the pharaoh was both a king and a god. The most famous pharaoh of the Old Kingdom was Khufu, in whose honor the largest of the pyramids was built.

Although the pharaoh owned everything, he was also held personally responsible if anything went wrong. He was expected to make trade profitable and prevent war. To manage these duties, he appointed government officials, mostly from his family. Social classes developed, with the pharaoh at the top and **nobles** from rich and powerful families making up the upper class. The middle class included some government officials, scribes, and rich craftspeople. Most people, including

> Would you say that there was any distinction between religion and politics in Egypt's Old Kingdom? Why or why not?
>
> _____
> _____
> _____
> _____

farmers, belonged to the lower class. Lower-class people were often used by the pharaoh as labor.

Trade also developed during the Old Kingdom. Traders sailed on the Mediterranean and south on the Nile and the Red Sea to acquire gold, copper, ivory, slaves, wood, and stone.

> **Of the upper, middle, and lower classes, which was the largest in ancient Egypt?**
>
> _____
>
> _____

RELIGION AND EGYPTIAN LIFE

The Old Kingdom formalized a religious structure that everyone was expected to follow. Over time, certain cities built temples and were associated with particular gods.

Much of Egyptian religion focused on the **afterlife**. Each person's *ka* (KAH), or life force, existed after death, but remained linked to the body. To keep the *ka* from suffering, the Egyptians developed a method called embalming to preserve bodies. Royalty had their bodies preserved as **mummies**, specially treated bodies wrapped in cloth. Other members of the **elite** also had their bodies preserved.

> **What is the *ka*?**
>
> _____
>
> _____

THE PYRAMIDS

Pyramids, spectacular stone monuments, were built to house dead rulers. Many pyramids are still standing today, amazing reminders of Egyptian engineering.

CHALLENGE ACTIVITY

Critical Thinking: Drawing Inferences Think about the way in which Egyptians viewed the pharaoh. Then think about how we view our current U.S. President. In what ways are these views similar? In what ways are they different? Write a one-page essay considering whether people would accept a god-king pharaoh today.

afterlife	elite	engineering	Khufu
mummies	nobles	Old Kingdom	pyramids

DIRECTIONS Read each sentence and fill in the blank with the word
in the word pair that best completes the sentence.

1. Most Egyptians focused on the _____ because they believed
   it was a happy place. (pyramids/afterlife)

2. Only royalty and other members of Egypt's _____ could
   afford to have mummies made. (elite/Old Kingdom)

3. _____ is the application of scientific knowledge for practical
   purposes. (Khufu/Engineering)

4. _____ was the most famous pharaoh of the Old Kingdom
   and was best known for the monuments built to him. (Pyramids/Khufu)

5. Specially treated bodies wrapped in cloth are called _____.
   (afterlife/mummies)

6. The upper classes of Egypt consisted of priests and key government officials

   called _____. (nobles/engineering)

7. Huge stone tombs with four triangle-shaped walls that meet in a point on top are

   called _____. (mummies/pyramids)

8. During the _____ the Egyptians continued to develop their
   political system, a system that was based on the belief that the pharaoh was both
   a king and a god. (Khufu/Old Kingdom)

9. Paintings from Egyptian tombs show the _____ as an ideal
   world where the people are young and healthy. (Old Kingdom/afterlife)

10. The _____ were built as royal tombs. (mummies/pyramids)

History of Ancient Egypt

MAIN IDEAS

1. The Middle Kingdom was a period of stable government between periods of disorder.
2. The New Kingdom was the peak of Egyptian trade and military power, but its greatness did not last.
3. Work and daily life differed among Egypt's social classes.

Key Terms and Places

Middle Kingdom period of stability and order in ancient Egypt between about 2050 and 1750 BC

New Kingdom the height of Egypt's power and glory, between 1550 and 1050 BC

Kush kingdom south of Egypt

trade routes paths followed by traders

Section Summary

THE MIDDLE KINGDOM

The Old Kingdom ended with the pharaohs in debt. Ambitious nobles serving in government positions managed to take power from the pharaohs and rule Egypt for nearly 160 years. Finally, a powerful pharaoh regained control of Egypt around 2050 BC and started a peaceful period of rule. This era was called the **Middle Kingdom** and lasted until Southwest Asian invaders conquered Lower Egypt around 1750 BC.

> From where did the raiders who ended the Middle Kingdom come?
> _____
> _____

THE NEW KINGDOM

When an Egyptian named Ahmose (AHM-ohs) drove away the invaders and declared himself king of Egypt in 1550 BC, he ushered in Egypt's eighteenth dynasty and the start of the **New Kingdom**. Responding to invasions, Egypt took control of possible invasion routes by taking over areas such as Syria and **Kush**, and quickly became the leading military power in the region, with an empire extending from the Euphrates River in the northeast

to Nubia in the south. These conquests also made
Egypt rich, through gifts and vastly expanded **trade
routes**. One ruler in particular, Queen Hatshepsut,
was active in establishing new paths for traders.

Despite the strong leadership of Ramses the
Great, a tide of invasions from Southwest Asia and
from the west eventually reduced Egypt to violence
and disorder.

> Which direction would you go from Egypt to reach Nubia?
> _____
> _____

WORK AND DAILY LIFE

During the Middle and New Kingdoms, Egypt's
population continued to grow and become more
complex. Professional and skilled workers like
scribes, artisans, artists, and architects were
honored. These roles in society were usually passed
on in families, with young boys learning a trade
from their fathers.

For farmers and peasants, who made up the vast
majority of the population, life never changed. In
addition to hard work on the land, they were
required to pay taxes and were subject to special
labor duty at any time. Only slaves were beneath
them in social status.

> Who had a higher place in Egyptian society, farmers or artisans?
> _____
> _____

Most Egyptian families lived in their own homes.
Boys were expected to marry young and start their
own families. Women focused on the home, but
many also had jobs outside the home. Egyptian
women had the legal rights to own property, make
contracts, and divorce their husbands.

> What legal rights did women have in the Middle and New Kingdoms?
> _____
> _____
> _____

CHALLENGE ACTIVITY

Critical Thinking: Drawing Inferences Design a
"want ad" for a position held in ancient Egyptian
society. Then write a letter to a potential employer
explaining why you should be hired.

Kush	Middle Kingdom	New Kingdom
Queen Hatshepsut	Ramses	the Great trade routes

DIRECTIONS On the line provided before each statement, write **T** if a statement is true and **F** if a statement is false. If the statement is false, write the correct term on the line after each sentence that makes the sentence a true statement.

_____ 1. <u>Trade routes</u> were paths followed by traders that brought Egyptian merchants into contact with more distant lands.

_____

_____ 2. The pharaoh <u>Ramses the Great</u> fought the Hittites for many years, but neither could defeat the other.

_____

_____ 3. The <u>Middle Kingdom</u> began when a powerful pharaoh defeated his rivals, which began a period of order and stability.

_____

_____ 4. <u>Kush</u> worked to increase Egyptian trade by sending ships south to trade with the kingdom of Punt on the Red Sea and north to trade with Asia Minor and Greece.

_____

_____ 5. During the <u>New Kingdom</u> Egypt reached the height of its power and glory as conquest and trade brought tremendous wealth to the pharaohs.

_____

_____ 6. <u>Queen Hatshepsut</u> is remembered for the many impressive monuments and temples built during her reign.

_____

_____ 7. When Ahmose drove the Hyksos out of Egypt, it was the beginning of the <u>Middle Kingdom</u>.

_____

MAIN IDEAS
1. Egyptian writing used symbols called hieroglyphics.
2. Egypt's great temples were lavishly decorated.
3. Egyptian art filled tombs.

Key Terms and Places

hieroglyphics Egyptian writing system, one of the world's first, which used symbols

papyrus long-lasting, paper-like substance made from reeds

Rosetta Stone a stone slab discovered in 1799, that was inscribed with hieroglyphics and their Greek meanings

sphinxes imaginary creatures with the bodies of lions and the heads of other animals or humans

obelisk a tall, four-sided pillar that is pointed on top

Section Summary

EGYPTIAN WRITING

Egyptians invented one of the world's first writing systems, using a series of images, symbols, and pictures called **hieroglyphics** (hy-ruh-GLIH-fiks). Each symbol represented one or more sounds in the Egyptian language.

At first hieroglyphics were carved in stone. Later, they were written with brushes and ink on **papyrus** (puh-PY-ruhs). Because papyrus didn't decay, many ancient Egyptian texts still survive, including government records, historical records, science texts, medical manuals, and literary works such as *The Book of the Dead*. The discovery of the **Rosetta Stone** in 1799 provided the key to reading Egyptian writing, as its text was inscribed both in hieroglyphics and in Greek.

> **What language helped scholars to understand the meaning of hieroglyphics on the Rosetta Stone?**
>
> _____
> _____

EGYPT'S GREAT TEMPLES

Egyptian architects are known not only for the pyramids but also for their magnificent temples.

The temples were lavishly designed with numerous statues and beautifully painted walls and pillars. **Sphinxes** and **obelisks** were usually found near the entrances to the temples.

EGYPTIAN ART

Ancient Egyptians were masterful artists and many of their greatest works are found in either the temples or the tombs of the pharaohs. Most Egyptians, however, never saw these paintings, because only kings, priests, or other important people could enter these places.

Egyptian paintings depict a variety of subjects, from crowning kings to illustrating religious rituals to showing scenes from daily life. The paintings also have a particular style, with people drawn as if they were twisting as they walked, and in different sizes depending upon their stature in society. In contrast, animals appear more realistically. The Egyptians were also skilled stone and metal workers, creating beautiful statues and jewelry.

Much of what we know about Egyptian art and burial practices comes from the tomb of King Tutankhamen, one of the few Egyptian tombs that was left untouched by raiders looking for valuables. The tomb was discovered in 1922.

> **Who was allowed to see ancient Egyptian sculpture and painting?**
>
> _____
>
> _____
>
> _____

> **Why is King Tutankhamen's tomb so important for the study of Egyptian history?**
>
> _____
>
> _____
>
> _____
>
> _____

CHALLENGE ACTIVITY

Critical Thinking: Drawing Inferences Using the library or an online resource, find a key to translate Egyptian hieroglyphics into English. Write a message using hieroglyphics and trade with another student to see if you can read each other's messages. Then write a paragraph about the advantages and disadvantages of hieroglyphics in comparison to the Roman alphabet. Be sure to provide your paragraph along with a copy of your message and the translation to your teacher.

| hieroglyphics | King Tutankhamen | obelisk |
| papyrus | Rosetta Stone | sphinxes |

DIRECTIONS Answer each question by writing a sentence that
contains at least one word from the word bank.

1. What discovery was the key needed to read ancient Egyptian writing?

_____

_____

2. Which pharaoh's tomb provided information about Egyptian burial practices and
beliefs?

_____

_____

3. What is the name of the ancient Egyptian writing system?

_____

_____

4. What object stands on either side of the gate at the entrance of many Egyptian
temples? Describe this object.

_____

_____

5. What paper-like material did the Egyptians make and use to write on?

_____

_____

6. What statues of imaginary creatures are found along the path leading to the
entrance of many Egyptian temples?

_____

_____

MAIN IDEAS

1. Geography helped early Kush civilization develop in Nubia.
2. Egypt controlled Kush for about 450 years.
3. After winning its independence, Kush ruled Egypt and set up a new dynasty there.

Key Terms and Places

Nubia a region in northeast Africa where the kingdom of Kush developed

ebony a type of dark, heavy wood

ivory a white material taken from elephant tusks

Section Summary

GEOGRAPHY AND EARLY KUSH

The kingdom of Kush developed south of Egypt along the Nile, in the region we now call **Nubia**. Every year, floods provided a rich layer of fertile soil. Farming villages thrived. The area was also rich in minerals such as gold, copper, and stone. These resources contributed to the region's wealth.

Over time some rich farmers became leaders of their villages. Around 2000 BC, one of these leaders took control of other villages and made himself king of Kush.

The kings of Kush ruled from their capital at Kerma (KAR-muh). The city was located on the Nile just south of a cataract, or stretch of rapids. Because the Nile's cataracts made parts of the river hard to pass through, they were natural barriers against invaders.

As time passed Kushite society became more complex. In addition to farmers and herders, some people of Kush became priests or artisans.

EGYPT CONTROLS KUSH

Kush and Egypt were neighbors and trading partners. The Kushites sent slaves to Egypt. They

> **What valuable minerals were important to Kush's prosperity?**
>
> _____
> _____
> _____

> **Around what year did the first king of Kush appear?**
>
> _____
> _____

also sent gold, copper, and stone, as well as the prized materials **ebony** and **ivory**.

Relations between Kush and Egypt were not always peaceful, however. Around 1500 BC Egyptian armies under the pharaoh Thutmose I invaded and conquered most of Nubia, including all of Kush. The Kushite palace at Kerma was destroyed. Kush remained an Egyptian territory until the mid-1000s BC, when the Kushite leaders regained control.

For about how many years was Kush under Egyptian control?

_____

_____

KUSH RULES EGYPT

By around 850 BC, Kush was once again as strong as it had been before it was conquered by Egypt. During the 700s, under the king Kashta, the Kushites began to invade Egypt. Kashta's son, Piankhi (PYANG-kee), believed that the gods wanted him to rule all of Egypt. By the time he died in 716 BC, Piankhi had accomplished this task. His kingdom extended north from Napata all the way to the Nile Delta.

Piankhi's brother, Shabaka (SHAB-uh-kuh), declared himself pharaoh and began the Twenty-fifth, or Kushite, Dynasty in Egypt. Egyptian culture thrived during the Twenty-fifth Dynasty. In the 670s BC, however, the powerful army of the Assyrians from Mesopotamia invaded Egypt. The Assyrians' iron weapons were better than the Kushites' bronze weapons. The Kushites were slowly pushed out of Egypt.

What metals did the Assyrians and Kushites use to make weapons?

_____

_____

CHALLENGE ACTIVITY

Critical Thinking: Drawing Conclusions Kush invaded Egypt during the 700s. Why do you think Kashta and his son Piankhi wanted to control Egypt? What advantages would control of Egypt give to Kush?

ebony	ivory	Piankhi
Kush	Nubia	Kerma
Kashta	Nile	Shabaka

DIRECTIONS On the line provided before each statement, write **T** if a statement is true and **F** if a statement is false. If the statement is false, write the correct term from the word bank on the line after each sentence that makes the sentence a true statement.

_____ 1. The Kushites sent <u>ivory</u>, a white material made from elephant tusks, to Egypt for their use.

_____

_____ 2. A fierce warrior on the battlefield but also deeply religious, <u>Piankhi</u> continued to attack Egypt after the death of his father.

_____

_____ 3. <u>Ivory</u> is a dark, heavy wood.

_____

_____ 4. The kingdom of <u>Kerma</u> was established in the region we now call Nubia.

_____

_____ 5. <u>Kashta</u> was the capital city of Kush.

_____

_____ 6. <u>Shabaka</u> took control of the territory his brother Piankhi had conquered.

_____

_____ 7. <u>Nubia</u> is a region in northeast Africa that lies on the Nile River south of Egypt.

_____

_____ 8. <u>Nile</u> was the son of Kashta and brother of Shabaka.

_____

MAIN IDEAS
1. Kush's economy grew because of its iron industry and trade network.
2. Some elements of Kushite society and culture were borrowed from other cultures while others were unique to Kush.
3. The decline and defeat of Kush was caused by both internal and external factors.

Key Terms and Places

Meroë economic center of Kush, new Kushite capital

trade network a system of people in different lands who trade goods back and forth

merchants traders

exports items sent to other regions for trade

imports goods brought in from other regions

Section Summary

KUSH'S ECONOMY GROWS

After they lost control of Egypt, the people of Kush devoted themselves to increasing agriculture and trade, hoping to make their country rich again. The economic center of Kush during this period was **Meroë** (MER-oh-wee). Gold could be found nearby, as could forests of ebony and other wood. In this rich location the Kushites developed Africa's first iron industry. Iron ore and wood for furnaces were easily available, so the iron industry grew quickly.

In time, Meroë became the center of a large **trade network**. The Kushites sent goods down the Nile to Egypt. From there, Egyptian and Greek **merchants** carried goods to ports on the Mediterranean and Red seas, and to southern Africa. These goods may have eventually reached India and perhaps China. Kush's **exports** included gold, pottery, iron tools, ivory, leopard skins, ostrich feathers, elephants, and slaves. **Imports** included fine jewelry and luxury

> What industry helped make Kush a rich and successful kingdom again?
>
> _____
>
> _____

> What direction is "down the Nile?"
>
> _____
>
> _____

items from Egypt, Asia, and lands along the
Mediterranean.

SOCIETY AND CULTURE

The most obvious influence on Kush during this
period was Egyptian, but many elements of Kushite
culture were not borrowed from anywhere else. The
people of Kush worshipped their own gods and
even developed their own written language. Women
were expected to be active in their society. Some
women rose to positions of great authority,
especially in religion. A few women, such as Queen
Shanakhdakheto (shah-nahk-dah-KEE-toh), even
ruled the empire alone.

> How was the position of women in Kushite society different than that of women in most other ancient civilizations?
>
> _____
> _____
> _____
> _____

DECLINE AND DEFEAT

Kushite civilization centered at Meroë reached its
height in the first century BC. Eventually it fell due
to both external and internal factors. The stores of
iron and other metals dwindled, and the overgrazing
of cattle caused a deterioration of farmland. Another
powerful trading center, Aksum (AHK-soom),
located in modern-day Ethiopia and Eritrea, began
competing with Kush. Soon trade routes were
bypassing Meroë for Aksum. After Aksum had
decimated Kush economically, the Aksumite leader
King Ezana (AY-zah-nah) sent an invading army
and conquered the once-powerful Kush.

> Circle the name and kingdom of the ruler who eventually defeated Kush.

CHALLENGE ACTIVITY

Critical Thinking: Drawing Inferences You are a
Kushite leader in the 600s BC. Write a short essay
explaining your plan to make the kingdom of Kush
rich and powerful again.

trade network	merchants	exports
imports	Queen Shanakhdakheto	King Ezana
Meroë	Meroitic	authority

DIRECTIONS Write a word or phrase that has the same meaning as the term given.

1. exports _____

_____

2. King Ezana _____

_____

3. merchants _____

_____

4. imports _____

_____

5. Queen Shanakhdakheto _____

_____

6. trade networks _____

_____

7. Meroë _____

_____

8. Meroitic _____

_____

9. authority _____

_____

History of West Africa

MAIN IDEAS
1. Ghana controlled trade and became wealthy.
2. Through its control of trade, Ghana built an empire.
3. Attacking invaders, overgrazing, and the loss of trade caused Ghana's decline.

Key Terms

silent barter a process in which people exchange goods without ever contacting each other directly

Section Summary

GHANA CONTROLS TRADE

The empire of Ghana (GAH-nuh) became powerful by controlling Saharan trade routes. Ghana lay between the Niger and Senegal rivers in sub-Saharan Africa, northwest of the nation now called Ghana.

Historians think the first people in Ghana were farmers. Starting around 300, these farmers were threatened by nomadic herders. The herders wanted the water and pastures. For protection, small groups began to band together. These groups grew stronger with the introduction of farming tools and weapons made of iron.

Ghana's territory lay between the desert and the forests. These were areas rich with salt and gold. The gold and salt trade sometimes followed a process called **silent barter**. In this process people exchange goods without contacting each other directly. This ensured peaceful business and kept the location of the gold mines secret.

As populations grew and trade increased, the rulers of Ghana grew stronger. Their armies used iron weapons. They took control of the trade routes that had been run by North African merchants.

> **What helped Ghana become a powerful empire?**
>
> _____
>
> _____

> **Which do you think was more valuable, salt or gold? Why do you think so?**
>
> _____
>
> _____
>
> _____
>
> _____

GHANA BUILDS AN EMPIRE

By 800, Ghana was firmly in control of West Africa's trade routes. As a result, trade became safer and Ghana's influence increased. Traders were charged a tax to enter or leave Ghana. The kings made it illegal for anyone other than themselves to own gold. They also taxed the people of Ghana.

The kings increased the size of Ghana by conquering other tribes. However, Ghana's kings allowed former rulers to keep much of their own power. These kings acted as governors of their territories. The empire of Ghana reached its peak under Tunka Manin (TOOHN-kah MAH-nin).

> **What caused Ghana's influence to increase?**
> _____
> _____
> _____

GHANA'S DECLINE

By the end of the 1200s, Ghana had collapsed. Three major factors contributed to its decline. A group of Muslim Berbers called the Almoravids invaded and weakened the empire. These Berbers were herders. Their animals overgrazed and ruined the farmland. Many farmers left. At the same time, internal rebellions led to loss of order in Ghana.

> **List two reasons for the decline of Ghana's empire.**
> _____
> _____
> _____

CHALLENGE ACTIVITY

Critical Thinking: Drawing Inferences Recreate the silent barter system in the classroom. Divide students into groups of gold and salt traders. Each group of "traders" should write a one-page paper detailing the advantages and disadvantages of silent barter.

| Ghana Empire | process | resources |
| silent barter | trade route | Tunka Manin |

DIRECTIONS Use the terms from the word bank to write a letter that relates to the section.

_____

_____

_____

_____

_____

_____

_____

_____

_____

_____

_____

_____

_____

_____

_____

_____

_____

_____

_____

History of West Africa

Section 2

MAIN IDEAS
1. The empire of Mali reached its height under the ruler Mansa Musa, but the empire fell to invaders in the 1400s.
2. The Songhai built a new Islamic empire in West Africa, conquering many of the lands that were once part of Mali.

Key Terms and Places

Niger River river that went through Ghana and Mali

Timbuktu important trade city in Mali

mosque building for Muslim prayer

Gao capital of Songhai

Djenné center of learning in Songhai

Section Summary

MALI

Like Ghana, Mali (MAH-lee) lay along the upper **Niger River.** Mali's location on the Niger River allowed its people to control trade on the river. Mali's rise to power began under a ruler named Sundiata (soohn-JAHT-ah).

A cruel ruler conquered Mali when Sundiata was a boy. When Sundiata grew older, he raised an army and won Mali's independence. Sundiata conquered nearby kingdoms, including Ghana, and took over the salt and gold trades. He also took over religious and political authority held by local leaders.

Mali's greatest and most famous ruler was a Muslim named Mansa Musa (MAHN-sah moo-SAH). Under his leadership, Mali reached its peak. Musa ruled Mali for about 25 years and captured many important trading cities, including **Timbuktu**. He also made the Islamic world aware of Mali on his pilgrimage to Mecca.

> **What river flowed through both Ghana and Mali?**
>
> _____
>
> _____

Mansa Musa stressed the importance of learning Arabic in order to read the Qur´an. He spread Islam through West Africa by building **mosques** in cities.

After Mansa Musa died, invaders destroyed the schools and mosques of Timbuktu. Nomads from the Sahara seized the city. By 1500 nearly all of the lands the empire had once ruled were lost.

Name three important things Mansa Musa did as leader of Mali.
_____
_____
_____
_____

SONGHAI

As Mali was reaching its height, the neighboring Songhai (SAHNG-hy) kingdom was also growing in strength. In the 1300s, the Songhai lands, including **Gao**, its capital, lay within the empire of Mali. As Mali weakened, the Songhai broke free. Songhai leader Sunni Ali (SOOH-nee ah-LEE) strengthened and enlarged the Songhai empire.

After Sunni Ali died, his son Sunni Baru became ruler. He was not Muslim. The Songhai people feared that if Sunni Baru did not support Islam they would lose trade, so they rebelled. After overthrowing Sunni Baru, the leader of that rebellion became known as Askia the Great.

Why was Sunni Baru overthrown?
_____
_____
_____
_____

Muslim culture and education thrived during Askia's reign. Timbuktu's universities, schools, libraries, and mosques attracted thousands. **Djenné** was also an important center of learning.

Morocco invaded Songhai and destroyed Gao and Timbuktu. Songhai never recovered and trade declined. Other trade centers north and south of the old empire became more important. The period of great West African empires came to an end.

Name two cities that were important centers of learning in the Songhai empire.
_____
_____

CHALLENGE ACTIVITY

Critical Thinking: Drawing Inferences You are a reporter in West Africa. You have just met the ruler of Mali or Songhai. Write an article about this person.

| Djenné | Gao | Niger River |
| Timbuktu | mosque | |

DIRECTIONS Answer each question by writing a sentence that
contains at least one word from the word bank.

1. What city was home to the University of Sankore?

_____

_____

_____

2. Where was the capital of Songhai located?

_____

_____

_____

3. Along what geographical feature were several cities in Mali and Songhia located?

_____

_____

_____

4. What city was southwest of Timbuktu and was known as a center of learning?

_____

_____

_____

5. What was one way that Mansa Musa spread Islam throughout West Africa?

_____

_____

_____

MAIN IDEAS
1. West Africans have preserved their history through storytelling and the written accounts of visitors.
2. Through art, music, and dance, West Africans have expressed their creativity and kept alive their cultural traditions.

Key Terms

oral history a spoken record of past events

griots West African storytellers responsible for reciting oral history

proverbs short sayings of wisdom or truth

kente handwoven, brightly colored cloth made in West Africa

Section Summary
PRESERVING HISTORY

Writing was not common in West Africa. None of the major early civilizations of West Africa developed a written language. Arabic was the only written language used. Instead of writing their history, West Africans passed along information about their civilization through **oral history** in their native languages.

The task of remembering and telling West Africa's history was entrusted to storytellers called **griots** (GREE-ohz). Griots tried to make their stories entertaining. They also told **proverbs**, or short sayings of wisdom or truth. The griots had to memorize hundreds of names and dates. Some griots confused names and events in their heads, so some facts became distorted. Still, much knowledge could be gained by listening to a griot.

Some griot poems are epics, long poems about kingdoms and heroes. Many of these poems were collected in the *Dausi* (DAW-zee) and the *Sundiata*. The *Dausi* tells the history of Ghana, but it also includes myths and legends. The *Sundiata* tells the story of Mali's great ruler. A conqueror killed his

Did Arabic replace the native languages of the West Africans? How do you know your answer is correct?

_____
_____
_____
_____

Why might the history of the griots not be perfectly accurate?

_____
_____
_____
_____

family, but the boy was spared because he was sick. He grew up to be a great warrior and overthrew the conqueror.

Though the West Africans left no written histories, visitors from other parts of the world did write about the region. Much of what we know about early West Africa comes from the writings of travelers and scholars from Muslim lands such as Spain and Arabia. Ibn Battutah was the most famous visitor to write about West Africa.

ART, MUSIC, AND DANCE

Besides storytelling, West African cultures considered other art forms, including sculpture, mask-making, cloth-making, music, and dance just as important. West African artists made sculptures of people from wood, brass, clay, ivory, stone, and other materials. Some of these images have inspired modern artists like Henri Matisse and Pablo Picasso.

West Africans are also known for distinctive mask-making and textiles. Particularly prized is the brightly colored **kente** (ken-TAY), a hand-woven cloth that was worn by kings and queens on special occasions.

In many West African societies, music and dance were as important as the visual arts. Singing, dancing, and drumming were great entertainment, but they also helped people celebrate their history and were central to many religious celebrations.

> Circle the names of the modern artists inspired by the images crafted by West African sculptors.

> List three ways in which music had a place in West African culture.
>
> _____
>
> _____
>
> _____
>
> _____

CHALLENGE ACTIVITY

Critical Thinking: Drawing Inferences Much of what we know about West Africa comes from oral traditions or accounts by visitors to the land. Write a short essay evaluating the accuracy of these sources. Consider how much a visitor who was not raised in a culture can really understand about that culture.

DIRECTIONS Look at each set of four terms. On the line provided, write the letter of the term that does not relate to the others.

_____ 1. a. spoken record
        b. oral history
        c. griots
        d. kente

_____ 4. a. kente
        b. oral history
        c. proverbs
        d. griots

_____ 2. a. kente
        b. bright colors
        c. hand-woven
        d. oral history

_____ 5. a. masks
        b. oral history
        c. kente
        d. sculptures

_____ 3. a. storyteller
        b. colored fabric
        c. griots
        d. proverbs

North Africa

Section 1

MAIN IDEAS
1. Major physical features of North Africa include the Nile River, the Sahara, and the Atlas Mountains.
2. The climate of North Africa is hot and dry, and water is the region's most important resource.

Key Terms and Places

Sahara world's largest desert, covering most of North Africa

Nile River the world's longest river, located in Egypt

silt finely ground, fertile soil good for growing crops

Suez Canal strategic waterway connecting the Mediterranean and Red Seas

oasis wet, fertile area in a desert where a natural spring or well provides water

Atlas Mountains mountain range on the northwestern side of the Sahara

Section Summary

PHYSICAL FEATURES

Morocco, Algeria, Tunisia, Libya, and Egypt are the five countries of North Africa. All five countries have northern coastlines on the Mediterranean Sea. The largest desert in the world, the **Sahara**, covers most of North Africa.

The **Nile River**, the world's longest, flows northward through the eastern Sahara. Near its end, it becomes a large river delta that empties into the Mediterranean Sea. The river's water irrigates the farmland along its banks. In the past, flooding along the Nile left finely ground fertile soil, called **silt**, in the surrounding fields. Today, the Aswan High Dam controls flooding and prevents silt from being deposited in the nearby fields. As a result, farmers must use fertilizer to aid the growth of crops. East of the Nile River is the Sinai Peninsula, which is made up of rocky mountains and desert. The Sinai is separated from the rest of Egypt by the **Suez**

Name the five countries of North Africa.
_____
_____

Describe the Nile River.
_____
_____
_____

Canal, a strategic waterway that connects the Mediterranean Sea with the Red Sea.

The Sahara has a huge impact on all of North Africa. It is made up of sand dunes, gravel plains, and rocky, barren mountains. Because of the Sahara's harsh environment, few people live there. Small settlements of farmers are located by **oases**— wet, fertile areas in the desert that are fed by natural springs. The Ahaggar Mountains are located in central North Africa. The **Atlas Mountains** are in the northwestern part of North Africa.

> **Why would an oasis be valuable to someone traveling in the desert?**
> _____
> _____

CLIMATE AND RESOURCES

Most of North Africa has a desert climate. It is hot and dry during the day, and cool or cold during the night. There is very little rain. Most of the northern coast west of Egypt has a Mediterranean climate. There it is hot and dry in the summer, and cool and moist in the winter. Areas between the coast and the Sahara have a steppe climate.

> **What kind of climate covers most of North Africa?**
> _____

Important resources include oil and gas, particularly for Libya, Algeria, and Egypt. In Morocco, iron ore and minerals are important. Coal, oil, and natural gas are found in the Sahara.

CHALLENGE ACTIVITY

Critical Thinking: Evaluating Why do you think almost all of Egypt's population lives along the Nile River? Write a brief paragraph that explains your answer.

Aswan High Dam	Atlas Mountains	delta
Nile River	oasis	Sahara
silt	Sinai Mountains	Suez Canal

DIRECTIONS On the line provided before each statement, write **T** if a statement is true and **F** if a statement is false. If the statement is false, write the term from the word bank that would make the sentence a true statement on the line provided below the sentence.

_____ 1. Built by the French in the 1860s, the <u>Aswan High Dam</u> connects the Mediterranean Sea with the Red Sea.

_____

_____ 2. Flowing for 4,132 miles, the <u>Nile River</u> is the world's longest river.

_____

_____ 3. Annual floods along the northern Nile River left fertile soil called <u>silt</u> in the surrounding fields.

_____

_____ 4. The <u>Sinai Mountains</u>, located on the northwestern side of the Sahara, rise as high as 13,671 feet (4,167 m).

_____

_____ 5. In a desert such as the Sahara, a(an) <u>delta</u> is a wet, fertile area where a natural spring or well provides water.

_____

DIRECTIONS Write three words or phrases that describe each term.

6. Sahara _____

7. Nile River _____

8. silt _____

9. oasis _____

10. Suez Canal _____

MAIN IDEAS
1. North Africa's history includes ancient Egyptian civilization.
2. Islam influences the cultures of North Africa and most people speak Arabic.

Key Terms and Places

Alexandria city in Egypt founded by Alexander the Great in 332 BC

Berbers an ethnic group who are native to North Africa and speak Berber languages

Section Summary

NORTH AFRICA'S HISTORY

Around 3200 BC people along the northern Nile united into a single Egyptian Kingdom. The ancient Egyptians participated in trade, developed a writing system, and built pyramids in which to bury their pharaohs, or kings. The pyramids were made of large blocks of stone that were probably rolled on logs to the Nile and then moved by barge to the building site. The Great Pyramid of Egypt took about twenty years to finish.

Hieroglyphs, pictures and symbols that stand for ideas and words, formed the basis for Egypt's first writing system. Each symbol stood for one or more sounds in the Egyptian language. Many writings recorded the achievements of pharaohs.

Invaders of North Africa included people from the eastern Mediterranean, Greeks, and Romans. Alexander the Great, the Macedonian king, founded the city of **Alexandria** in Egypt in 332 BC. It became an important port of trade and a great center of learning. Arab armies from Southwest Asia started invading North Africa in the AD 600s. They ruled most or all of North Africa until the 1800s, bringing the Arabic language and Islam to the region.

> **Where did ancient Egyptians bury their kings?**
> _____
> _____

> **What are hieroglyphs?**
> _____
> _____
> _____

> **How long did Arabs from Southwest Asia rule North Africa?**
> _____

In the 1800s European countries began invading North Africa. By 1912 Spain and France controlled Morocco, France also controlled Tunisia and Algeria, Italy controlled Libya, and the British controlled Egypt. The countries gradually gained independence in the mid-1900s. Algeria was the last country to win independence in 1962. Today the countries of North Africa are trying to build stronger ties to other Arab countries.

> **What European countries ruled North Africa in the early 1900s?**
> _____
> _____

CULTURES OF NORTH AFRICA

Egyptians, **Berbers**, and Bedouins make up almost all of Egypt's population. People west of Egypt are mostly of mixed Arab and Berber ancestry. Most North Africans speak Arabic and are Muslims.

> **What language do most North Africans speak? What religion do they practice?**
> _____
> _____

Grains, vegetables, fruits, and nuts are common foods. Couscous, a pellet-like pasta made from wheat, is served steamed with vegetables or meat. Another favorite dish is *fuul*, made from fava beans.

Two important holidays are Muhammad's birthday and Ramadan, a holy month during which Muslims fast. Traditional clothing is long and loose. Many women cover their entire body except for the face and hands.

> **Name two important North African holidays.**
> _____
> _____

North Africa is known for its beautiful architecture, wood carving, carpets, and hand-painted tiles. The region has produced important writers, including Egypt's Nobel Prize winner Naguib Mahfouz. Egypt also has a thriving film industry. North African music is based on a scale containing more notes than the one common in Western music, which creates a wailing or wavering sound. The three-stringed sintir of Morocco is a popular instrument.

CHALLENGE ACTIVITY

Critical Thinking: Evaluating Imagine that you are spending your summer vacation traveling throughout North Africa. Write a letter to a friend at home that describes the people you meet and the places you visit.

Alexandria	Arabic	Berbers	couscous
fuul	harissa	hieroglyphics	pharaohs

DIRECTIONS Look at each set of four terms. On the line provided,
write the letter of the term that does not relate to the others.

_____ 1. a. pharaohs   b. pyramids   c. Egyptians   d. Muslims

_____ 2. a. couscous   b. fuul   c. Cleopatra   d. harissa

_____ 3. a. King Tut   b. Berbers   c. herders   d. tribes

_____ 4. a. writing   b. couscous   c. hieroglyphics   d. pictures

_____ 5. a. trade   b. Alexandria   c. Morocco   d. seaport

DIRECTIONS Answer each question by writing a sentence that
contains at least one word from the word bank.

6. What languages do North Africans speak?

_____

_____

7. What are some common foods served in North Africa?

_____

_____

MAIN IDEAS
1. Many of Egypt's people are farmers and live along the Nile River.
2. People in the other countries of North Africa are mostly pastoral nomads or farmers, and oil is an important resource in the region.

Key Terms and Places

Cairo capital of Egypt, located in the Nile Delta

Maghreb collective name for Western Libya, Tunisia, Algeria, and Morocco

souks large marketplaces

free port a city in which almost no taxes are placed on goods sold there

dictator someone who rules a country with complete power

Section Summary

EGYPT

More than half of all Egyptians live in rural areas. Most rural Egyptians own small farms or work on large ones owned by powerful families. **Cairo,** Egypt's capital and largest city, is located in the Nile Delta. Overcrowding, limited housing, and pollution are serious problems in Cairo. Alexandria, Egypt's second-largest city, is a major seaport and industrial center. Oil and tourism are important industries in Egypt. Revenue from the Suez Canal provides another source of income. Cotton is an important crop in the Nile Delta. Vegetables, grain, and fruit are grown along the Nile River.

Egypt faces important challenges today. Fertilizing farmland is expensive. Poverty, illiteracy, disease, and pollution are other problems. Still another is the role of Islam. Egyptians disagree on the extent to which Muslim beliefs should influence government. These disagreements have led to violence at times.

> **Name two important industries in Egypt.**
> _____
> _____
> _____

> **What are some challenges that Egypt faces today?**
> _____
> _____
> _____

OTHER COUNTRIES OF NORTH AFRICA

Western Libya, Tunisia, Algeria, and Morocco are known as the **Maghreb**. The Sahara covers most of this region. The major cities and most of the farm-land lie along the Mediterranean coast.

Algeria's capital, Algiers, includes an old district called the Casbah. Marketplaces called **souks** jam the narrow streets of this district. In Algeria, as in Egypt, disagreement over the role of Islam in society has led to violence at times.

Tunisia's capital and largest city is Tunis. Tunisia, like other North African countries, has close economic ties to Europe. About two thirds of its imports are from the European Union.

The largest city in Morocco is Casablanca. Tangier, overlooking the Strait of Gibraltar to Spain, is a **free port**. Almost no taxes are charged on goods sold there. Morocco has little oil, but it is an important producer of fertilizer.

More than 77 percent of Libya's population lives in cities. The two largest cities are Benghazi and the capital, Tripoli. The **dictator**, Muammar al-Gadhafi, rules Libya. Because of his support of terrorist activities, Libya's economic relationship with other countries has been hurt.

Oil is the most important industry in North Africa. Mining and tourism are important too. The region's farmers grow and export grains, olives, fruits, and nuts.

> **Why is Europe important to the economies of North Africa?**
> _____
> _____
> _____

> **What is the most important industry in North Africa?**
> _____

CHALLENGE ACTIVITY

Critical Thinking: Making Judgments Create a chart that lists four cities in North Africa and include facts about each one. Which city would you most like to visit? Write a paragraph explaining your choice.

Guided Reading Workbook

Algiers	Cairo	dictator	free port
Maghreb	souks	Tripoli	Tunis

DIRECTIONS Read each sentence and fill issn the blank with the word
in the word pair that best completes the sentence.

1. With a population of more than 10 million, _____ is Egypt's
   capital and largest city. (Cairo/Tripoli)

2. Western Libya, Tunisia, Algeria, and Morocco make up the

   _____. (Algiers/Maghreb)

3. In the Casbah, _____ sell spices, carpets, copper tea pots,
   and other goods. (free ports/souks)

4. Tangier is known as a _____, a city in which almost no taxes
   are placed on the goods it sells. (free port/souk)

5. Most of Libya's people live in cities, including its capital,

   _____. (Tripoli/Tunis)

DIRECTIONS Choose five of the terms from the word bank. Use these
words to write a summary of what you learned in the section.

_____

_____

_____

_____

_____

_____

_____

_____

_____

West Africa

Section 1

MAIN IDEAS
1. West Africa's key physical features include plains and the Niger River.
2. West Africa has distinct climate and vegetation zones that go from arid in the north to tropical in the south.
3. West Africa has good agricultural and mineral resources that may one day help the economies in the region.

Key Terms and Places

Niger River most important river in West Africa

zonal organized by zone

Sahel a strip of land that divides the desert from wetter areas

desertification the spread of desert-like conditions

savanna an area of tall grasses and scattered trees and shrubs

Section Summary
PHYSICAL FEATURES

The main physical features in West Africa are plains and rivers. Most of the region is covered by plains. Plains along the coast have most of the region's cities. People on inland plains usually farm or raise animals. There are a few highlands in the southwest and northeast of the region.

The **Niger River** is the most important river in the region. It brings water to the people of the region for farming and fishing. It also provides a transportation route. It has an inland delta hundreds of miles from the coast where it divides into a network of channels, swamps, and lakes.

> Underline the sentences that describe the importance of the Niger River to the region.

CLIMATE AND VEGETATION

West Africa has four climate regions, which are **zonal**, or organized by zone. They stretch from east to west. The zone farthest north is part of the largest desert in the world, the Sahara.

> Circle the name of the largest desert in the world.

Guided Reading Workbook

Just to the south of the Sahara is a region called
the **Sahel**. It is a strip of land that divides the desert
from wetter areas. It has a steppe climate where
rainfall varies greatly from year to year. Although it
is very dry, enough plants grow there to support
some grazing animals.

Because animals have overgrazed the Sahel and
people have cut trees for firewood, the wind blows
soil away. There has also been drought in the area.
This has caused **desertification**, or the spread of
desert-like conditions.

To the south of the Sahel is **savanna**, an area of
tall grasses and scattered trees and shrubs. When
rain falls regularly, it is a good area for farming.

The coasts of the Atlantic Ocean and the Gulf of
Guinea have a humid tropical climate. Much rain
there supports tropical forests. Many trees have
been cut to make room for the growing population.

What are two causes of desertification?
_____
_____

Why have many trees been cut from tropical rain forests?
_____
_____

RESOURCES

Because of the good farmland and climate in some
areas, agricultural products are an important
resource. These include coffee, coconuts, peanuts,
and cacao, which is used to make chocolate. West
Africa also has minerals such as diamonds, gold,
iron ore, and bauxite, which is the source of
aluminum. Oil is the region's most valuable
resource. Nigeria is a major exporter of oil, which is
found near its coast.

List four mineral resources found in West Africa.
_____
_____

CHALLENGE ACTIVITY

Critical Thinking: Identifying Cause and Effect

Why do you think fewer people live in the northern
portion of the region than in the southern portion?
Write a paragraph to explain your reasoning.

delta	desertification	Gulf of Guinea	Niger River
Sahara	Sahel	savanna	zonal

DIRECTIONS Read each sentence and fill in the blank with the word
in the word pair that best completes the sentence.

1. Geographers describe West Africa's climates as _____
   because they stretch from east to west in bands. (savanna/zonal)

2. Desertification in the _____ is causing the expansion of the
   Sahara. (Gulf of Guinea/Sahel)

3. The _____ brings life-giving water to West Africa.
   (Niger River/Gulf of Guinea)

4. Hundreds of miles from the coast in Mali, the Niger River divides into a network

   of channels called the inland _____. (Sahara/delta)

5. Very little vegetation grows in the _____, and few people live
   there. (savanna/Sahara)

DIRECTIONS Write three words or phrases that describe each term.

6. savanna _____

_____

7. Niger River _____

_____

8. zonal _____

_____

West Africa

Section 2

MAIN IDEAS
1. In West Africa's history, trade made great kingdoms rich, but this greatness declined as Europeans began to control trade routes.
2. The culture of West Africa includes many different ethnic groups, languages, religions, and housing styles.

Key Terms

Timbuktu the cultural center of the Songhai Empire in the 1500s

animism the belief that bodies of water, animals, trees, and other natural objects have spirits

extended family a group of family members that includes the father, mother, children, and close relatives in one household

Section Summary

HISTORY

One of the earliest kingdoms in West Africa was Ghana, which became rich and powerful by about 800. It controlled trade in gold and salt across the Sahara. In about 1300, the empire of Mali took over. It controlled the trade routes and supported artists and scholars. The empire of Songhai took control in the 1500s. Its cultural center was **Timbuktu**. It had a university, mosques, and many schools. But invasions weakened it, and trade decreased.

Europeans began the Atlantic slave trade in the 1500s. Europeans who owned large plantations in the Americas wanted cheap labor. European traders sold enslaved Africans to colonists. Families were split up, and many people died. By the time the slave trade ended in the 1800s, millions of Africans had been taken from their homes.

European countries claimed colonies in the late 1800s so they could have access to West African resources. Europeans built schools, roads, and railroads, but they also created problems for West

> **Underline the sentence describing Timbuktu.**

> **When did the Atlantic slave trade begin? When did it end?**
> _____
> _____

Africans. All the countries in West Africa became independent by 1974.

CULTURE

The societies in West Africa have been influenced by African cultures, European culture, and Islam. There are hundreds of ethnic groups in the region. European colonizers drew borders for countries that put different ethnic groups in one country or separated one group into different countries. Many West Africans are more loyal to their own ethnic groups than to their country. The groups speak hundreds of languages. The use of colonial languages or West African languages that many people share helps with communication.

> **Circle three influences on West African societies.**

West African religions include Islam in the north and Christianity in the south. Both were introduced by traders coming to the area. Traditional religions are forms of **animism**. Animism is the belief that bodies of water, animals, trees, and other natural objects have spirits.

> **What religions did traders introduce in West Africa?**
> _____
> _____

Some people in the region wear Western-style clothing. Others wear traditional cotton clothing which is loose and flowing. Rural homes are small and often circular. They are made from mud or straw and have straw or tin roofs. Extended families often live close together in a village. An **extended family** includes parents, children, and other relatives. West Africa's cities have modern buildings. Extended families may live together in houses or high-rise apartments.

> **What is an extended family?**
> _____
> _____
> _____
> _____

CHALLENGE ACTIVITY

Critical Thinking: Drawing Inferences Write a letter to a newspaper to explain the problems that could arise from creating borders that put different ethnic groups in one country or separating ethnic groups into different countries.

| ancestors | animism | archaeology | extended family |
| Hausa | oral history | Songhai | Timbuktu |

DIRECTIONS On the line provided before each statement, write **T** if a statement is true and **F** if a statement is false. If the statement is false, write the correct term on the line after each sentence that makes the sentence a true statement.

_____ 1. Much of our knowledge about early West Africa is based on <u>animism</u>.

_____

_____ 2. The city of <u>Songhai</u> served as a cultural center as Mali declined.

_____

_____ 3. The belief that bodies of water, animals, trees, and other natural objects have spirits is called <u>animism</u>.

_____

_____ 4. Family members—father, mother, children, and close relatives—living in one household are known as <u>ancestors</u>.

_____

_____ 5. <u>Hausa</u> is one of the largest ethnic groups in West Africa as well as a common language people use to communicate.

_____

DIRECTIONS Choose five of the terms from the word bank. Use these words to write a summary of what you learned in this section on a separate piece of paper.

MAIN IDEAS

1. Nigeria has many different ethnic groups, an oil-based economy, and one of the world's largest cities.

2. Most coastal countries of West Africa have struggling economies and weak or unstable governments.

3. Lack of resources in the Sahel countries is a main challenge to economic development.

Key Terms and Places

secede break away from the main country

Lagos the former capital of Nigeria and the most populous city in West Africa

famine an extreme shortage of food

Section Summary

NIGERIA

Nigeria is the second largest country in West Africa. It has the largest population in Africa and the region's strongest economy. The Igbo ethnic group unsuccessfully tried to **secede**, or break away from the main country, in the 1960s. Leaders moved the capital to Abuja where there are few people, partly to avoid ethnic conflicts. The government is now a democracy after the military ruled for many years.

> Underline the name of the capital of Nigeria.

Nigeria's most important resource is oil. It accounts for 95 percent of the country's export earnings. The main industrial center is **Lagos**, which is the most populous city in West Africa and the former capital of Nigeria. Although Nigeria has many resources, many people are poor. It has a very high birthrate and cannot produce enough food. Corrupt government has also contributed to the country's poverty.

> What are two causes of poverty in Nigeria?
>
> _____
> _____
> _____
> _____

OTHER COASTAL COUNTRIES

Small countries along the coast struggle to develop their economies and stabilize their governments. Senegal and Gambia produce peanuts and offer tourism sites. Guinea has some bauxite reserves. Guinea-Bissau has undeveloped mineral resources. Cape Verde is an island country with a democratic government.

| Circle the type of government Cape Verde has. |

Liberia was founded in the 1820s by Americans for freed slaves. A long civil war there ended in 2003. Civil war in Sierra Leone helped destroy the economies in the area and killed thousands. Ghana and Côte d'Ivoire have rich natural resources including gold, timber, and agricultural products, but these countries have also experienced civil war. Unstable governments and poor farming economies have hurt Togo and Benin.

| Underline three natural resources found in Ghana and Côte d'Ivoire. |

SAHEL COUNTRIES

Drought and the expanding desert challenge the Sahel countries to feed their own people. Former nomads in Mauritania are now crowded into cities. Ethnic tensions continue to cause problems there. Niger has a very small amount of farmland where people grow staple, or main, crops. Drought and locusts created **famine**, or an extreme shortage of food, there in the early 2000s. Chad depends on farming and fishing in Lake Chad, although much of its water has evaporated in recent years. It began to export oil in 2004.

| Underline the causes of famine in Niger. |

Much of Mali is desert with some farming in the south. It is one of the poorest countries in the world, but its economy is improving. Burkina Faso is also very poor and has few resources. Conflicts in the region have hurt its economy.

CHALLENGE ACTIVITY

Critical Thinking: Comparing and Contrasting

Write an essay that compares and contrasts the government, resources, and economy of Nigeria with the other countries in the region.

Guided Reading Workbook

| Abuja | Cape Verde | civil war | distribute |
| famine | Lagos | secede | Togo |

DIRECTIONS Read each sentence and fill in the blank with the word
in the word pair that best completes the sentence.

1. _____ is West Africa's only island country.
   (Cape Verde/Togo)

2. Locusts and drought destroy crops, causing widespread _____.
   (famine/civil war)

3. Palm products, cacao, and coffee are the main crops in Benin and

   _____, where people depend on farming and herding for

   their income. (Cape Verde/Togo)

4. The most populous city in West Africa is _____.
   (Abuja/Lagos)

5. The Igbo tried to _____ from Nigeria due to ethnic conflicts.
   (distribute/secede)

East Africa

MAIN IDEAS

1. East Africa's physical features range from rift valleys to plains.
2. East Africa's climate is influenced by its location and elevation, and the region's vegetation includes savannas and forests.

Key Terms and Places

rift valley places on Earth's surface where the crust stretches until it breaks

Great Rift Valley the largest rift on Earth, made up of two rifts—the eastern rift and the western rift

Mount Kilimanjaro the highest mountain in Africa

Serengeti Plain one of Tanzania's largest plains, home to abundant wildlife

Lake Victoria Africa's largest lake and the source of the White Nile

drought period when little rain falls, and crops are damaged

Section Summary

PHYSICAL FEATURES

The landscape of East Africa is varied and a home to diverse and abundant wildlife. **Rift valleys** cut from north to south across the region. Rift walls are often steep cliffs that can rise as much as 6,000 feet. The **Great Rift Valley** is made up of two rifts.

East Africa has many volcanic mountains. The tallest of these is **Mount Kilimanjaro**. Although the mountain is located near the equator, its peak is covered with ice and snow. Another area of high elevation is the Ethiopian Highlands.

Some areas of East Africa are flat plains. The **Serengeti Plain** in Tanzania is one of the largest. Many kinds of wildlife live here, including elephants, giraffes, lions, and zebras. Tanzania established much of the plain as a national park.

A number of rivers and lakes are found in East Africa. The Nile is the world's longest river. It begins in East Africa. Then it flows north to the Mediterranean Sea. The source of the White Nile is **Lake Victoria**. The Blue Nile begins in the

> What is surprising about Mount Kilimanjaro?
> _____
> _____
> _____
> _____

> Underline examples of wildlife that can be found on the Serengeti Plain.

> Circle the name of the world's longest river.

Ethiopian Highlands. Both rivers meet in Sudan to form the Nile.

Lake Victoria is Africa's largest lake, but many other lakes also lie along the rift valleys. Some of these lakes are extremely hot or salty.

Underline the name of Africa's largest lake.

CLIMATE AND VEGETATION

East Africa has a variety of climate and vegetation. Latitude and elevation affect climate. For example, areas near the equator receive heavy rains. Farther from the equator, the weather is drier. When little rain falls, **droughts** can occur. During a drought, crops fail, cattle die, and people begin to starve. There have been severe droughts in East Africa.

What happens during a drought?
_____
_____
_____

The climate south of the equator is tropical savanna. In savannas, plants include tall grasses and scattered trees. The rift floors have grasslands and thorn shrubs.

Plateaus and mountains are found north of the equator. They have a highland climate and thick forests. The highlands receive a lot of rainfall. The mild climate makes farming possible. Many people live in the highlands. Forests are found at higher elevations.

Circle the reasons that farming is possible in the highlands.

East of the highlands and on the Indian Ocean coast, the elevation is lower. Desert and steppe climates are found here. Vegetation is limited to shrubs and grasses.

CHALLENGE ACTIVITY

Critical Thinking: Making Generalizations Write a booklet for tourists to read before they embark on a helicopter tour of East Africa. What might they find most interesting about the region?

Guided Reading Workbook

Blue Nile	drought	Ethiopian Highlands
Great Rift Valley	White Nile	Lake Victoria
Mount Kilimanjaro	rift valley	savanna
Serengeti Plain		

DIRECTIONS Read each sentence and fill in the blank with the word
in the word pair that best completes the sentence.

1. _____ are formed when two tectonic plates move away from
   each other, stretching and breaking Earth's crust. (Savannas/Rift valleys)

2. The _____ receives water from the Ethiopian Highlands.
   (Blue Nile/White Nile)

3. _____ is the highest point in Africa.
   (Lake Victoria/Mount Kilimanjaro)

4. The _____ in Tanzania is home to a great variety of wildlife.
   (Serengeti Plain/Great Rift Valley)

5. During a _____, little rain falls, and crops and animals die as
   a result. (savanna/drought)

DIRECTIONS Look up the words in the word bank in a dictionary.
Write the dictionary definition of the word that is closest to the
definition used in your textbook.

_____

_____

_____

_____

_____

_____

East Africa

MAIN IDEAS
1. The history of East Africa is one of religion, trade, and European influence.
2. East Africans speak many different languages and practice several different religions.

Key Terms and Places

Nubia part of Egypt and Sudan, an early center of Christianity in Africa

Zanzibar an East African island that became an international slave trading center in the late 1700s

imperialism a practice that tries to dominate other countries' government, trade, and culture

Section Summary

HISTORY

Early civilizations in East Africa were highly developed. Later, Christianity and Islam were brought to the region.

Ethiopia was an early center of Christianity. From there, Christianity spread to **Nubia**, in present-day Egypt and Sudan. An early Christian emperor in Ethiopia was Lalibela. He built 11 rock churches in the early 1200s.

> Circle the names of the two early centers for Christianity.

Muslim Arabs from Egypt brought Islam into northern Sudan. Islam also spread to the Indian Ocean coast of present-day Somalia.

> Who brought Islam to East Africa?
> _____
> _____

The East African slave trade dates back more than 1,000 years. In the 1500s the Portuguese built forts and towns on the coast. The island of **Zanzibar** became a center of the international slave trade. Later, Europeans forced enslaved people to work on plantations in the interior.

Most European nations ended slavery in the early 1800s, and shifted their focus to trading goods such as gold, ivory, and rubber. In the 1880s, European powers divided up most of Africa. They used **imperialism** to keep power. This is a policy of

> How did most European nations control their colonies?
> _____
> _____

taking over other countries' governments, trade, and culture. The British controlled much of East Africa. Ethiopia, however, was the one country of East Africa that was never colonized.

Large numbers of Europeans settled in Kenya. But most colonial rulers used African deputies to control the countries. Many deputies were traditional chiefs. They often favored their own peoples. This caused conflict between ethnic groups. These conflicts have made it hard for governments to encourage feelings of national identity.

Most East African countries gained independence in the early 1960s. New challenges faced the newly independent countries.

> Underline the name of the only East African country that was never colonized.

CULTURE

East Africa has a diversity of people and cultures. For example, people speak many different languages. French is the official language in Rwanda, Burundi, and Djibouti. English is spoken in Uganda, Kenya, and Tanzania. Swahili is an African language spoken by about 80 million East Africans. Other languages include Amharic, Somali, and Arabic.

> Circle the three main languages spoken in East Africa.

Religion and family traditions are important in East Africa. Religions vary within and among ethnic groups. Most of the cultures honor ancestors.

Many East Africans are followers of animist religions. They believe the natural world contains spirits. Some Africans also combine ancient forms of worship with Christianity and Islam.

CHALLENGE ACTIVITY

Critical Thinking: Analyzing Information Choose a country in East Africa. Imagine you are a student who has been asked to speak at your country's one-year anniversary celebration. Write a speech that describes the strengths of your country and the challenges that await.

animist	Arabic	imperialism	Lalibela
Nubia	Swahili	Zanzibar	

DIRECTIONS Write three words or phrases that describe each term.

1. imperialism _____

2. Zanzibar _____

3. Lalibela _____

4. Swahili _____

5. Nubia _____

DIRECTIONS Read each sentence and fill in the blank with the word
in the word pair that best completes the sentence.

6. In East Africa, many people are followers of _____ religions
and believe that the natural world contains spirits. (Swahili/animist)

7. The English practiced _____ in East Africa as they tried to
dominate countries' governments, trade, and cultures. (Swahili/imperialism)

8. The island of _____ was once a slave-trading center.
(Zanzibar/Nubia)

9. Christianity spread into _____ in the AD 500s, about 200
years later than Ethiopia. (Lalibela/Nubia)

10. The word *Swahili* comes from the _____ word meaning
"on the coast." (Arabic/Zanzibar)

East Africa

Section 3

MAIN IDEAS

1. National parks are a major source of income for Tanzania and Kenya.
2. Rwanda and Burundi are densely populated rural countries with a history of ethnic conflict.
3. Both Sudan and Uganda have economies based on agriculture, but Sudan has suffered from years of war.
4. The countries of the Horn of Africa are among the poorest in the world.

Key Terms and Places

safari an overland journey to view African wildlife

geothermal energy energy produced from the heat of Earth's interior

genocide the intentional destruction of a people

Darfur a region of Sudan

Mogadishu port city in Somalia

Section Summary

TANZANIA AND KENYA TODAY

Tanzania and Kenya rely on agriculture and tourism. Tourists come to see wildlife on **safaris**. Much of Kenya has been set aside as national parkland to protect wildlife.

Tanzania is rich in gold and diamonds. But most of its people are farmers. The mountains of Kenya provide rich soils for coffee and tea. **Geothermal energy**, another important resource, rises up through cracks in the rift valleys.

Dar es Salaam was once Tanzania's capital. Today the capital is Dodoma. Kenya's capital is Nairobi. In 1998, al Qaeda terrorists bombed the U.S. embassies in Dar es Salaam and Nairobi.

> Circle the capital cities of Tanzania and Kenya.

RWANDA AND BURUNDI TODAY

Rwanda and Burundi were once German colonies. Both have experienced conflicts between ethnic groups—the Tutsi and Hutu. This conflict led to **genocide** in Rwanda. Genocide is the intentional

> Underline the names of two ethnic groups in Rwanda and Burundi.

destruction of a people. Rwanda and Burundi are
densely populated. They export tea and coffee.

SUDAN AND UGANDA TODAY

Sudan is Africa's largest country. During the last
several decades Muslims and Christians have fought
a civil war. An Arab militia group has killed tens of
thousands in a region of Sudan called **Darfur**.

Uganda was a military dictatorship for several
decades. The country has become more democratic
since 1986. Economic progress has been slow,
however. About 80 percent of Ugandans work in
agriculture. Coffee is the country's main export.

> Circle the names of the
> groups fighting a civil war
> in Sudan.

THE HORN OF AFRICA

The Horn of Africa is made up of four countries—
Ethiopia, Eritrea, Somalia, and Djibouti.

Ethiopia has always been independent. Its people
are mostly Christian and Muslim. Agriculture is the
main economic activity. Severe droughts during the
1980s led to starvation. Plenty of rain has fallen in
recent years, however.

Eritrea was once an Italian colony. Then it
became part of Ethiopia. It broke away in 1993.
Today tourism and farming are important to the
growing economy.

Most Somalis are nomadic herders. Clans have
fought over grazing rights. They have fought for
control of port cities such as **Mogadishu**. Civil war
and drought led to starvation in the 1990s.

Djibouti is a small desert country. It lies on a
strait between the Red Sea and the Indian Ocean. Its
port is a major source of income. Djibouti was once
a French colony. Its people include the Issa and the
Afar. They fought a civil war that ended in 2001.

> What four countries make
> up the Horn of Africa?
> _____
> _____
> _____

> Underline important
> industries in Eritrea.

CHALLENGE ACTIVITY

Critical Thinking: Drawing Conclusions

Suppose you joined a United Nations delegation in
East Africa. Propose ways the UN could help
people in the region.

DIRECTIONS Look at each set of four terms following each number. On the line provided, write the letter of the term in each set that does not relate to the others.

_____ 1. a. safari   b. wildebeest   c. Mogadishu   d.Serengeti Plain

_____ 2. a. Hutu   b. Tutsi   c. genocide   d. Kenya

_____ 3. a. Darfur   b. Rwanda   c. Burundi   d. Uganda

_____ 4. a. Somalia   b. Eritrea   c. Rwanda   d. Djibouti

_____ 5. a. Amharic   b. Ethiopia   c. coastline   d. drought

affect	Darfur	genocide
geothermal energy	Mogadishu	safari

DIRECTIONS On the line provided before each statement, write **T** if a statement is true and **F** if a statement is false. If the statement is false, write the correct term on the line after each sentence that makes it a true statement.

_____ 6. Different clans have fought for control of the port city of <u>Mogadishu</u>.

_____

_____ 7. Energy that is produced from the heat of Earth's interior is called <u>geothermal energy</u>.

_____

_____ 8. A <u>safari</u> occurred in a region of Sudan, causing millions to flee the area.

_____

_____ 9. Using national parkland as farmland would <u>affect</u> Kenya's economy and tourism industry.

_____

_____ 10. Ethnic conflict in <u>Tanzania</u> led to thousands of people being killed by an Arab militia group.

_____

Central Africa

MAIN IDEAS
1. Central Africa's major physical features include the Congo Basin and plateaus surrounding the basin.
2. Central Africa has a humid tropical climate and dense forest vegetation.
3. Central Africa's resources include forest products and valuable minerals such as diamonds and copper.

Key Terms and Places

Congo Basin the basin near the middle of Central Africa

basin a generally flat region surrounded by higher land such as mountains and plateaus

Congo River river that drains the Congo Basin and empties into the Atlantic Ocean

Zambezi River river in the southern part of the region that flows eastward toward the Indian Ocean

periodic market open-air trading market that is set up once or twice a week

copper belt area where copper is found that runs through northern Zambia and southern Democratic Republic of the Congo

Section Summary
PHYSICAL FEATURES

Central Africa lies between the Atlantic Ocean and the Western Rift Valley. Near the middle of the region is the **Congo Basin**. Plateaus and low hills surround the **basin**. The highest mountains in Central Africa are east of the basin along the Western Rift Valley. Lake Nyasa, also called Lake Malawi, and Lake Tanganyika lie along the rift. The **Congo River** is an important transportation route. It drains the Congo Basin and has hundreds of smaller rivers flowing into it. The many rapids and waterfalls prevent ships from traveling from the interior of the region all the way to the Atlantic. The **Zambezi River** flows toward the Indian Ocean. Many rivers in Angola and Zambia and from Lake Nyasa flow into the Zambezi. It also has many waterfalls, including Victoria Falls.

> Where are the tallest mountains in the region found?
>
> _____
>
> _____

CLIMATE, VEGETATION, AND ANIMALS

Because of its position along the equator, the Congo Basin and much of the Atlantic coast have a humid tropical climate with warm temperatures and plenty of rainfall all year. The warm, wet climate has led to the growth of dense tropical forests. These forests are home to such animals as gorillas, elephants, and okapis—relatives of the giraffe. However, large areas of these forests are now being cleared for farming and logging. To protect the forests and the animals that live there, some Central African governments have set up national park areas.

The climate north and south of the Congo Basin is a tropical savanna climate with warm weather all year but with distinct dry and wet seasons. Grasslands, scattered trees, and shrubs are the main vegetation. In the east, the high mountains have a highland climate. The far southern part of the region has dry steppe and desert climates.

> How has the warm and rainy climate of the Congo Basin affected the vegetation?
> _____
> _____

RESOURCES

The tropical climate is good for farming. Most people are subsistence farmers. Many grow crops for sale. In rural areas people sell goods at a **periodic market**. Other natural resources include timber from forests and rivers, which are important to travel, trade, and production of hydroelectricity. Some countries have oil, natural gas, and coal and valuable minerals such as copper, uranium, tin, zinc, diamonds, gold, and cobalt. Most of Africa's copper is in the **copper belt**. However, political problems and poor transportation have kept these resources from being fully developed.

> Name three kinds of natural resources in Central Africa.
> _____
> _____

> Circle the area where most of the copper is mined.

CHALLENGE ACTIVITY

Critical Thinking: Making Inferences Why might the Congo River be important to the development of the region's mineral resources? Write your answer in a sentence.

Guided Reading Workbook

basin	Congo Basin	Congo River	copper belt
Lake Tanganyika	periodic market	Victoria Falls	Zambezi River

DIRECTIONS On the line provided before each statement, write **T** if the statement is true and **F** if the statement is false. If the statement is false, write the correct term on the line after each sentence to make the sentence a true statement.

_____ 1. A <u>copper belt</u> is generally a flat region surrounded by higher land such as mountains and plateaus.

_____

_____ 2. The <u>Congo River</u> is fed by hundreds of smaller rivers.

_____

_____ 3. The <u>Zambia River</u> flows eastward toward the Indian Ocean.

_____

_____ 4. A <u>periodic market</u> is an open-air trading market that is set up once or twice a week.

_____

_____ 5. Most of Africa's copper is found in the <u>Congo Basin</u>, which stretches through northern Zambia and the southern Democratic Republic of the Congo.

_____

DIRECTIONS Write two words or phrases that describe each term.

6. Congo Basin: _____

7. Lake Tanganyika: _____

8. Victoria Falls: _____

Central Africa

MAIN IDEAS
1. Great African kingdoms and European colonizers have influenced the history of Central Africa.
2. The culture of Central Africa includes many ethnic groups and languages, but it has also been influenced by European colonization.

Key Terms and Places

Kongo Kingdom one of the most important kingdoms in Central Africa, founded in the 1300s near the mouth of the Congo River

dialects regional varieties of a language

Section Summary

HISTORY

Early humans have lived in Central Africa for many thousands of years. About 2,000 years ago people from outside the region began to migrate into the region. They formed kingdoms. The **Kongo Kingdom** was one of the most important. Its people grew rich from trade in animal skins, shells, slaves, and ivory. They set up trade routes to western and eastern Africa.

> **How did the Kongo Kingdom become rich?**
> _____
> _____

The arrival of Europeans in the 1400s changed the region. The Europeans first came looking for trade goods. They wanted the region's forest products and other natural resources. Europeans also traded with some Central African kingdoms for slaves. The slave trade lasted about 300 years, with tragic effects for millions of enslaved Africans. They were forced to go to colonies in the Americas. At first some African kingdoms became richer by trading with Europeans, but in time these kingdoms were weakened by the Europeans.

> **Underline the sentence that tells why the Europeans first came to the region.**

> **How did the slave trade affect the people of the region?**
> _____
> _____
> _____
> _____

In the late 1800s France, the United Kingdom, Belgium, Germany, Spain, and Portugal divided all of Central Africa into colonies. The colonial borders ignored the homelands of different groups and put groups with different languages and customs together. This led to serious problems and conflicts after these colonies became independent nations.

Central African colonies gained independence after World War II. In some cases they fought bloody wars to do so. Angola was the last colony to win independence. It did not become an independent country until 1975. After independence, fighting continued among ethnic groups within new countries. The Cold War led to more fighting. Both the Soviet Union and the United States supported different groups in small wars that killed many people.

> **What problems did colonial borders create for the people of the region?**
> _____
> _____

> **How did the United States and the Soviet Union add to the conflicts in Africa?**
> _____
> _____

CULTURE

People in Central Africa speak different languages. Many speak different **dialects** of Bantu languages. Most countries also have official languages such as French, English, Portuguese, or Spanish because of the influence of the European colonial powers. The region's colonial history also influenced religion. Many people in former French, Spanish, and Portuguese colonies are Roman Catholics. In former British colonies, many people are Protestants. The northern part of the region near the Sahel has many Muslims. Many Muslims and Hindus live in Zambia.

The traditional cultures of Central Africa's ethnic groups have influenced the arts. The region is famous for sculpture, carved wooden masks, and colorful cotton gowns. The region is also the birthplace of a popular musical instrument called the *likembe*, or thumb piano, and a type of dance music called *makossa*.

> **List four types of Central African arts.**
> _____
> _____
> _____
> _____

CHALLENGE ACTIVITY

Critical Thinking: Evaluating Information Do you think colonial rule helped or hurt the people of Central Africa? Explain your answer in a brief essay.

dialects	interact	ivory
Kongo Kingdom	likembe	makossa

DIRECTIONS Read each sentence and fill in the blank with the word
in the word pair that best completes the sentence.

1. _____ is considered one of the most important kingdoms
formed in Central Africa. Founded in the 1300s, it was located near the mouth of
the Congo River. (Makossa/Kongo Kingdom)

2. _____ is a cream-colored material that comes from
elephant tusks. (Ivory/Likembe)

3. _____ are regional varieties of a language.
(Dialects/Makossa)

4. The _____, or thumb piano, was invented in the Congo
region. (ivory/likembe)

5. A type of dance music called _____ originated in Cameroon
and has become popular throughout Africa. (interact/makossa)

Central Africa

MAIN IDEAS
1. The countries of Central Africa are mostly poor, and many are trying to recover from years of civil war.
2. Challenges to peace, health, and the environment slow economic development in Central Africa.

Key Terms and Places

Kinshasa capital of the Democratic Republic of the Congo

inflation the rise in prices that occurs when currency loses its buying power

malaria a disease spread by mosquitoes that causes fever and pain

malnutrition the condition of not getting enough nutrients from food

Section Summary

COUNTRIES OF CENTRAL AFRICA

Most Central African countries are very poor. Because of colonial rule and civil wars, they have had problems building stable governments and strong economies. Before independence, the Democratic Republic of the Congo was a Belgian colony. After the Belgians left, the country had few teachers or doctors. Ethnic groups fought for power. For several decades a corrupt dictator, Mobutu Sese Seko, ran the country. The economy collapsed, but Mobutu became very rich. In 1997 a civil war ended his rule. Although the country has resources such as minerals and forest products, civil war, bad government, and crime have scared away foreign businesses. Most people live in rural areas, but many are moving to the capital, **Kinshasa**.

Since independence, other Central African countries have had similar problems. Central African Republic has had military coups, corrupt leaders, and improper elections. Civil wars in the Republic of the Congo and Angola have hurt their governments and economies. In Angola land mines left from its civil war, high **inflation**, and corrupt officials have caused problems.

> Underline two reasons why Central African countries have had trouble building stable governments and strong economies.

> Circle the problems that have stopped foreign businesses from investing in the Democratic Republic of the Congo.

In most countries the majority of people are subsistence farmers. The economies of many countries depend heavily on the sale of natural resources like oil, copper, or diamonds or on export crops like coffee or cocoa. The Republic of the Congo has oil and forest products. Angola has diamonds and large oil deposits. Zambia's economy depends on copper mining. Malawi relies on farming and foreign aid. Oil discoveries in Equatorial Guinea and São Tomé and Príncipe may help their economies improve. Most nations need better railroads or ports for shipping goods to develop their natural resources.

Cameroon's stable government has helped its economy grow. It has good roads and railways. Gabon also has a stable government. Its economy is the strongest in the region. Half of its income comes from oil.

What kind of work do most people in Central African countries do?
_____
_____

What would help the countries of the region get more out of their natural resources?
_____
_____

ISSUES AND CHALLENGES

The region faces serious challenges from wars, diseases such as **malaria** and AIDS, and threats to the environment. Wars are one cause of the poor economies in the region. Deaths from wars and disease have resulted in fewer older, more skilled workers. Health officials and some national governments are trying to control malaria by teaching people ways to protect themselves. Other issues include rapid population growth, food shortages, and **malnutrition**. Because so many people die of disease, the region has a very young population. Farmers can't meet the demand for food, so food shortages occur. Other threats are the destruction of tropical forests and open-pit mining of diamonds and copper, which destroys the land.

What diseases are a problem in Central Africa?
_____
_____

CHALLENGE ACTIVITY

Critical Thinking: Cause and Effect List one challenge facing the region today. Write a sentence describing one effect of this problem on the people or land of the region.

Guided Reading Workbook

| Cabinda | inflation | Kinshasa |
| malaria | malnutrition | political |

DIRECTIONS Read each sentence and fill in the blank with the word in the word pair that best completes the sentence.

1. The capital of the Democratic Republic of the Congo is

   _____. (Kinshasa/Cabinda)

2. A rise in prices that occurs when currency loses its buying power is

   _____. (inflation/political)

3. _____ is a disease spread by mosquitoes that causes fever and pain. (Malnutrition/Malaria)

4. The condition of not getting enough nutrients from food is called

   _____. (malnutrition/inflation)

5. The word _____ means relating to politics. (political/inflation)

MAIN IDEAS
1. Southern Africa's main physical feature is a large plateau with plains, rivers, and mountains.
2. The climate and vegetation of Southern Africa is mostly savanna and desert.
3. Southern Africa has valuable mineral resources.

Key Terms and Places

escarpment the steep face at the edge of a plateau or other raised area

veld open grassland areas of South Africa

Namib Desert a desert located on the Atlantic coast, the driest place in the region

pans low, flat areas into which ancient streams drained and later evaporated

Section Summary
PHYSICAL FEATURES

Southern Africa is covered with grassy plains, steamy swamps, mighty rivers, rocky waterfalls, and steep mountains and plateaus.

Most of Southern Africa lies on a large plateau. The steep face at the edge of a plateau or other raised area is called an **escarpment**. In eastern South Africa, part of the escarpment is made up of a mountain range called the Drakensberg. Farther north, the Inyanga Mountains separate Zimbabwe and Mozambique.

Many large rivers cross Southern Africa's plains. The Okavango flows from Angola into a huge basin in Botswana. The Orange River passes through the Augrabies Falls and flows into the Atlantic Ocean.

CLIMATE AND VEGETATION

Southern Africa's climates change from east to west. The east coast of the island of Madagascar is the wettest place in the region. In contrast to the eastern part of Africa, the west is very dry. Deserts along the Atlantic coast give way to plains with semiarid and steppe climates. Much of Southern

> **What is an escarpment?**
> _____
> _____

> **Name two major rivers of Southern Africa.**
> _____
> _____

Africa is covered by a large savanna region. On this grassland plain, shrubs and short trees grow. These grassland areas are known as the **veld** in South Africa.

The **Namib Desert** on the Atlantic Coast is the driest area in the region. The Kalahari Desert covers most of Botswana. Here ancient streams have drained into low, flat areas, or **pans**. On these pans, a glittering white layer forms when the streams dry up and leave minerals behind.

While the mainland is mostly dry, Madagascar has lush vegetation and tropical forests. Many animals, such as lemurs, are found here and nowhere else in the world. Unfortunately, rain forest destruction has endangered many of Madagascar's animals.

Which desert covers most of Botswana?
_____

RESOURCES

Rich in natural resources, Southern Africa has useful rivers, forests, and minerals. Its rivers provide a source of hydroelectric power and irrigation for farming. Forests are a source of timber. Mineral resources include gold, diamonds, platinum, copper, uranium, coal, and iron ore. Mining is very important to Southern Africa's economy. However, mining can harm the surrounding natural environments.

What are some of Southern Africa's mineral resources?
_____
_____
_____
_____
_____

CHALLENGE ACTIVITY

Critical Thinking: Summarizing Based on what you've read so far, write a one-sentence summary to go with each of the following headings.

    a. Physical Features of Southern Africa

    b. Climates of Southern Africa

    c. Vegetation of Southern Africa

    d. Resources of Southern Africa

                     Guided Reading Workbook

Augrabies Falls	Drakensberg	escarpment	Inyanga Mountains
Limpopo River	Namib Desert	Orange River	Okavango River
pans	veld		

DIRECTIONS Read each sentence and fill in the blank with the word
in the word pair that best completes the sentence.

1. The _____, Botswana's major river, flows into a huge basin
and forms a swampy inland delta that is home to many animals.
(Okavango River/Limpopo River)

2. The open grassland areas of South Africa are known as the

_____. (veld/pans)

3. In the Kalahari, low, flat areas covered with mineral deposits are called

_____. (veld/pans)

4. The _____ makes up much of Southern Africa's Atlantic
coast. (Namib Desert/Drakensberg)

5. The _____ passes through the Augrabies Falls as it flows to
the Atlantic Ocean. (Okavango River/Orange River)

DIRECTIONS Choose five of the terms from the word bank. Use these
terms to write a summary of what you learned in the section.

_____
_____
_____
_____
_____
_____
_____
_____

MAIN IDEAS
1. Southern Africa's history began with hunter-gatherers, followed by great empires and European settlements.
2. The cultures of Southern Africa are rich in different languages, religions, customs, and art.

Key Terms and Places

Great Zimbabwe the stone-walled capital built by the Shona in the late 1000s

Cape of Good Hope area at the tip of Africa near where a trade station was set up by the Dutch in 1652

Afrikaners Dutch, French, and German settlers and their descendants living in South Africa

Boers Afrikaner frontier farmers who had spread out from the original Cape colony

apartheid the policy of racial separation set up by South Africa's government

township the separate areas where blacks had to live under apartheid

Section Summary
HISTORY

The Khoisan peoples lived in Southern Africa for centuries. They were hunter-gatherers and herders. Bantu farmers moved from West Africa to Southern Africa about 2,000 years ago. The Bantu brought new languages and iron tools.

A Bantu group, the Shona, built an empire that reached its peak in the 1400s. The Shona farmed, raised cattle, and traded gold. They also built **Great Zimbabwe**, a stone-walled capital made of huge granite boulders and stone blocks. The city became a large trading center until the gold trade slowed.

In the late 1400s Portuguese traders set up bases on the Southern African coast. In 1652 the Dutch set up a trade station in a natural harbor near the **Cape of Good Hope**. The Cape sits at the tip of Africa.

> **What group built an empire in Southern Africa?**
> _____
> _____

> **What was the Great Zimbabwe?**
> _____
> _____
> _____

Other Europeans settled on the Cape. In South Africa, the Dutch, French, and German settlers and their descendants were called **Afrikaners**.

The British took over the Cape area in the early 1800s. The **Boers**, Afrikaner frontier farmers, tried to stop the British, but lost. At about this time, the Zulu became a powerful force in the region. The Zulu were a Bantu-speaking group. However, the British defeated them and took over this land, too. Diamonds and gold were found in South Africa in the 1860s.

South Africa was ruled by white Afrikaners and became more racist in the 1900s. Black South Africans who opposed them formed the African National Congress (ANC). The white government set up a policy called **apartheid**, which divided people into four groups: whites, blacks, Coloureds, and Asians. Coloureds and Asians could only live in certain areas. Blacks had to live in separate areas called **townships**. They had few rights.

Who were the Boers?
_____
_____

What resources were found in South Africa in the 1860s?
_____
_____

What were townships?
_____
_____

CULTURE

Southern Africa has a rich and diverse culture. Its people belong to hundreds of different ethnic groups. They speak many languages, most of which are related to Khoisan or Bantu. They practice different religions, including Christianity and traditional African religions. Its arts reflect its many cultures, using traditional ethnic designs and crafts.

CHALLENGE ACTIVITY

Critical Thinking: Drawing Inferences What do you think the culture of Southern Africa would be like today if Europe still ruled over the region?

Afrikaners	apartheid	Boers
Cape of Good Hope	Great Zimbabwe	townships

DIRECTIONS On the line provided before each statement, write **T** if a statement is true and **F** if a statement is false. If the statement is false, write the correct term on the line after each sentence to make the sentence a true statement.

_____ 1. In 1652 the Dutch set up a trading colony near the <u>Boers</u>.

_____

_____ 2. The Shona built a large empire and constructed stone-walled towns, including <u>Mozambique</u>, the Shona capital.

_____

_____ 3. Dutch, French, and German settlers and their descendants in South Africa were called <u>Afrikaners</u>.

_____

_____ 4. The <u>Zulu</u> were Afrikaner frontier farmers who resisted British authority in the Cape area.

_____

_____ 5. During apartheid, many blacks were forced to live in separate, crowded areas called <u>colonies</u>.

_____

Section 3

MAIN IDEAS

1. South Africa ended apartheid and now has a stable government and strong economy.

2. Some countries of Southern Africa have good resources and economies, but several are still struggling.

3. Southern African governments are responding to issues and challenges such as drought, disease, and environmental destruction.

Key Terms and Places

sanctions economic or political penalties imposed by one country on another to force a change in policy

Cape Town city in South Africa that attracts many tourists

enclave a small territory surrounded by a foreign territory

Section Summary

SOUTH AFRICA

Today South Africa has made great progress, but challenges remain. Perhaps South Africa's biggest challenge has been ending apartheid. Many people objected to apartheid. As a result, some countries put **sanctions** —penalties to force a change in policy—on South Africa. Protest within the country increased as well. In response, the government outlawed the African National Congress (ANC), a group defending the rights of black South Africans.

In the late 1980s, South Africa moved away from apartheid. In 1990 the government released its political prisoners, including Nelson Mandela. He was elected South Africa's president in 1994. South Africa's new government is a republic. Its constitution stresses equality and human rights.

South Africa has the region's strongest economy, with more resources and industry than most African countries. Large cities such as Johannesburg and **Cape Town** contribute to the economy.

What are sanctions?
_____
_____
_____
_____

What is the ANC?
_____
_____
_____
_____

Who was elected president of South Africa in 1994?
_____
_____

OTHER COUNTRIES OF SOUTHERN AFRICA

Surrounded by South Africa, Lesotho and Swaziland are both **enclaves**. An enclave is a small territory surrounded by a foreign territory.

Namibia gained independence in 1990. It is a republic. Most of its income comes from mineral resources. Fishing and ranching are also important.

Botswana is rich in mineral resources and has a stable, democratic government. Cattle ranching and diamond mining are its main economic activities.

Zimbabwe is politically unstable. In 2000, the president began a land reform program, taking land from white farmers and giving it to black residents. However, food shortages resulted.

Mozambique is one of the world's poorest countries. The economy was hurt by a civil war. It relies on taxes collected on products shipped out of its ports from the interior of Africa.

> **What does Mozambique's economy rely on?**
> _____
> _____

Madagascar has an elected president, but the economy is struggling. The country is popular with tourists because of its unique plants and animals. Comoros is made up of four tiny islands. It is poor and politically unstable. However, the government hopes to improve education and promote tourism.

> **What makes Madagascar a tourist destination?**
> _____
> _____

ISSUES AND CHALLENGES

Southern Africa faces many challenges, especially poverty, disease, and environmental destruction. The African Union (AU) is working to promote cooperation among African countries to try to solve these problems.

> **What is the AU?**
> _____
> _____

CHALLENGE ACTIVITY

Critical Thinking: Comparing and Contrasting
Contrast the economies and governments of Botswana and Zimbabwe. Write a couple of sentences to explain how they are different from one another.

| African National Congress | Cape Town | enclave |
| execute | Johannesburg | sanctions |

DIRECTIONS Answer each question by writing a sentence or two that contains at least one term from the word bank.

1. How did other countries pressure South Africa to end apartheid?

_____

_____

_____

_____

2. How did South Africa respond to antiapartheid protests within its country?

_____

_____

_____

3. How do South Africa's large cities contribute to its economy?

_____

_____

_____

_____

4. Why are Lesotho and Swaziland influenced by South Africa?

_____

_____

_____

_____

History of Ancient India

MAIN IDEAS
1. Located on the Indus River, the Harappan civilization also had contact with people far from India.
2. Harappan achievements included a writing system, city planning, and art.
3. The Aryan invasion changed India's civilization.

Key Terms and Places

Indus River major river in India along which the Harappan civilization developed

Harappa city in ancient India

Mohenjo Daro city in ancient India

Sanskrit the most important language of ancient India

Section Summary

HARAPPAN CIVILIZATION

India's first civilization was the Harappan civilization, which developed along the **Indus River**. Archaeologists believe Harappan civilization thrived between 2300 and 1700 BC. Harappan settlements were scattered over a huge area, but most lay next to rivers. The largest settlements were **Harappa** and **Mohenjo Daro**. The Harappans may have traded with people as far away as southern India and Mesopotamia.

HARAPPAN ACHIEVEMENTS

The Harappans developed India's first writing system. Although archaeologists have found examples of their writing, scholars have not been able to read it. Most information about Harappans comes from studying the ruins of cities, especially Harappa and Mohenjo Daro. These cities were well-planned and advanced. Each city was built in the shadow of a fortress that could easily oversee the city streets. The streets themselves were built at right angles and had drainage systems.The

> Why do you think we know so little about the Harappans?
>
> _____
>
> _____
>
> _____

Harappans also developed beautiful artisan crafts, some of which have helped historians draw conclusions about Harappan society. Harappan civilization collapsed by the early 1700s BC, possibly due to invasions or natural disasters.

ARYAN MIGRATION

Originally from Central Asia, the Aryans first reached India in the 2000s BC. Over time they spread south and east into central India and eventually into the Ganges River Valley. Much of what is known about the Aryans comes from a collection of religious writings called the Vedas.

Unlike the Harappans, Aryans lived in small communities run by a local leader, or raja. Aryan groups fought each other as often as they fought outsiders.

The Aryans spoke **Sanskrit** and memorized poems and hymns that survived by word of mouth. People later figured out how to write in Sanskrit. Sanskrit records are a major source of information about Aryan society. Today Sanskrit is the root of many modern South Asian languages.

CHALLENGE ACTIVITY

Critical Thinking: Drawing Inferences Do you think we know more about the Harappans or the Aryans? Explain your answer.

> **What were two features of city streets in Harappa and Mohenjo Dara?**
> _____
> _____
> _____
> _____

> **The early Aryans had a rich and expressive language, but they did not write. How did they preserve their poems and their history without writing?**
> _____
> _____
> _____
> _____

DIRECTIONS Write a word or phrase that has the same meaning as
the term given.

1. raja _____

2. Sanskrit _____

3. Vedas _____

DIRECTIONS Read each sentence and fill in the blank with the word
in the word pair that best completes the sentence.

4. The _____ civilization along the Indus River was India's
first civilization. (Aryan/Harappan)

5. Ancient writings known as the _____ are collections of
poems, hymns, myths, and rituals. (Vedas/Sanskrit)

6. The leader of each village was given the title of _____.
(Vedas/raja)

7. The _____ were invaders from Central Asia who may have

helped end the _____ civilization. (Aryans/Harappans);

(Aryan/Harappan)

8. _____ was the language of the _____.
(Veda/Sanskrit); (Aryans/Harappans)

9. Mohenjo Daro and _____ were the largest ancient
settlements along the Indus River. (Harappa/Delhi)

MAIN IDEAS
1. Indian society divided into distinct groups.
2. The Aryans formed a religion known as Brahmanism.
3. Hinduism developed out of Brahmanism and influences from other cultures.
4. The Jains reacted to Hinduism by breaking away.

Key Terms

caste system a division of Indian society into groups based on a person's birth, wealth, or occupation

reincarnation the belief that the soul, once a person dies, is reborn in a new body

karma the effects that good or bad actions have on a person's soul

nonviolence the avoidance of violent actions

Section Summary

INDIAN SOCIETY DIVIDES

Aryan society was divided into social classes. There were four main groups, called *varnas*. The Brahmins (BRAH-muhns) were priests and were the highest ranking varna. The Kshatriyas (KSHA-tree-uhs) were rulers or warriors. The Vaisyas (VYSH-yuhs) were commoners, including farmers, craftspeople, and traders. The Sudras (SOO-drahs) were laborers and servants.

What role did Brahmins play in Aryan society?
_____
_____

Eventually a more complex **caste system** developed, dividing Indian society into many groups based on birth, wealth, or occupation. Castes were family based. If you were born into a caste, you would probably stay in it for your whole life. Life for the lower castes was difficult, but those who had no caste, called untouchables, were ostracized.

What determined a person's caste in Indian society?
_____
_____

BRAHMANISM

Because Aryan priests were called Brahmins, the Aryan religion became known as Brahmanism. Brahmanism was perhaps the most important part of

ancient Indian life, as shown by the high status of
the priest caste. The religion was based on the four
Vedas, writings that contained ancient sacred hymns
and poems. Over time, Aryan Brahmins and scholars
wrote their thoughts about the Vedas. These
thoughts were compiled into Vedic texts. The texts
described rituals, such as how to perform sacrifices,
and offered reflections from religious scholars.

HINDUISM DEVELOPS

Hinduism is India's largest religion today. It
developed from Brahmanism and other influences.
Hindus believe that there are many gods, but all
gods are part of a universal spirit called Brahman.
Hindus believe everyone has a soul, or atman, and
the soul will eventually join Brahman. This happens
when the soul recognizes that the world we live in is
an illusion. Hindus believe this understanding takes
several lifetimes, so **reincarnation**, or rebirth, is
necessary. How you are reborn depends upon your
karma, or the effects of good or bad actions on
your soul. In the caste system, those who have good
karma are born to higher castes. Those with bad
karma are born into lower castes or maybe even
an animal.

> **What is the Hindu name for the soul?**
> _____

> **According to Hindu belief, what is the effect of good karma?**
> _____
> _____

JAINS REACT TO HINDUISM

The religion of Jainism developed in reaction to
Hinduism. Jains believe in injuring no life, telling
the truth, not stealing, and not owning property.
Jains also practice **nonviolence**, or *ahimsa*. This
emphasis on nonviolence comes from the belief that
everything in nature is part of the cycle of rebirth.

CHALLENGE ACTIVITY

Critical Thinking: Organizing Information Create
a glossary of at least 10 terms from this section.
Place the words in alphabetical order and write a
definition.

Guided Reading Workbook

| atman | Brahman | caste system | Hinduism |
| Jainism | karma | nonviolence | reincarnation |

DIRECTIONS On the line provided before each statement, write **T** if a statement is true and **F** if a statement is false. If the statement is false, write the correct term on the line after each sentence that makes the sentence a true statement.

_____ 1. The <u>Jainism</u> divided the Indian society into groups based on rank, wealth, and occupation.

_____

_____ 2. <u>Hinduism</u> is based on four major principles: Injure no life, tell the truth, do not steal, and own no property.

_____

_____ 3. Brahma the Creator, Siva the Destroyer, and Vishnu the Preserver are the three major gods of <u>Hinduism</u>, the largest religion in Indian society.

_____

_____ 4. <u>Nonviolence</u> is the avoidance of violent actions, which was practiced by the Jains.

_____

_____ 5. Hindus believe that souls are born and reborn many times, each time into a new body, which is a process called <u>reincarnation</u>.

_____

_____ 6. According to Hindu teachings, everyone has a soul, or <u>atman</u>, inside them.

_____

_____ 7. Hindus believe that a person's ultimate goal should be to reunite their soul with <u>karma</u>, the universal spirit.

_____

MAIN IDEAS
1. Siddhartha Gautama searched for wisdom in many ways.
2. The teachings of Buddhism deal with finding peace.
3. Buddhism spread far from where it began in India.

Key Terms

fasting going without food

meditation the focusing of the mind on spiritual ideas

nirvana a state of perfect peace

missionaries people who work to spread their religious beliefs

Section Summary

SIDDHARTHA'S SEARCH FOR WISDOM

Not everyone in India accepted Hinduism. In the late 500s BC, a major new religion began to develop from questions posed by a young prince named Siddhartha Gautama (si-DAHR-tuh GAU-tuh-muh). Siddhartha was born to a wealthy family and led a life of comfort, but he wondered at the pain and suffering he saw all around him. By the age of 30, Siddharta left his home and family to look for answers about the meaning of life. He talked to many priests and wise men, but he was not satisfied with their answers.

Siddhartha did not give up. He wandered for years through the forests trying to free himself from daily concerns by **fasting** and **meditating**. After six years, Siddhartha sat down under a tree and meditated for seven weeks. He came up with an answer to what causes human suffering. Suffering is caused by wanting what one does not have, wanting to keep what one likes and already has, and not wanting what one dislikes but has. He began to travel and teach his ideas, and was soon called the Buddha, or "Enlightened One." From his teachings sprang the religion Buddhism.

> **Why did Siddhartha leave his life of luxury?**
> _____
> _____
> _____
> _____

> **What was Siddharta called after he attained wisdom?**
> _____

TEACHINGS OF BUDDHISM

Buddhism is based upon the Four Noble Truths.
These truths are: Suffering and unhappiness are part
of life; suffering stems from our desire for pleasure
and material goods; people can overcome their
desires and reach **nirvana**, a state of perfect peace,
which ends the cycle of reincarnation; and people
can follow an eightfold path to nirvana, overcoming
desire and ignorance.

> What are the central
> teachings of Buddhism
> called?
> _____
> _____

These teachings were similar to some Hindu
concepts, but went against some traditional Hindu
ideas. Buddhism questioned the need for animal
sacrifice. It also challenged the authority of the
Brahmins. The Buddha said that each individual
could reach salvation on his or her own. Buddhism
also opposed the caste system.

> What traditional Hindu
> ideas did Buddhism
> challenge?
> _____
> _____
> _____

BUDDHISM SPREADS

Buddhism spread quickly throughout India. With
the help of Indian king Asoka, Buddhist
missionaries were sent to other countries to teach
their religious beliefs. Missionaries introduced
Buddhism to Sri Lanka and other parts of Southeast
Asia, as well as Central Asia and Persia. It
eventually spread to China, Japan, and Korea. In
modern times, Buddhism has become a major
global religion.

CHALLENGE ACTIVITY

Critical Thinking: Cause and Effect Compare
and contrast the roles of Constantine and Asoka in
spreading Christianity and Buddhism. Write a
paragraph to explain how they were alike and
different.

Guided Reading Workbook

| the Buddha | Buddhism | fasting |
| meditation | missionaries | nirvana |

DIRECTIONS Answer each question by writing a sentence that contains at least one term from the word bank.

1. According to Buddhist teachings, if people can overcome their desire and ignorance, they will reach what?

_____

_____

_____

2. What did Siddhartha do to free his mind from daily concerns?

_____

_____

_____

3. Who did the king send to spread the religious beliefs of Buddhism?

_____

_____

_____

4. What is the term that means "Enlightened One?"

_____

_____

_____

5. What is the religion based on the teachings of Siddhartha?

_____

_____

_____

History of Ancient India

MAIN IDEAS
1. The Mauryan Empire unified most of India.
2. Gupta rulers promoted Hinduism in their empire.

Key Terms

mercenaries hired soldiers

edicts laws

Section Summary

MAURYAN EMPIRE UNIFIES INDIA

Under Aryan rule, India was divided into several states with no central leader. Then, during the 300s BC, Alexander the Great brought much of India into his empire. An Indian military leader named Candragupta Maurya followed Alexander's example and seized control of the entire northern part of India, using an army of **mercenaries**, or hired soldiers. The Mauryan Empire lasted for about 150 years.

Candragupta's complex government included a huge army and a network of spies. He taxed the population heavily for the protection he offered. Eventually, Candragupta became a Jainist monk and gave up his throne to his son. His family continued to expand the Indian empire.

Candragupta's grandson, Asoka, was the strongest ruler of the Mauryan dynasty. The empire thrived under his rule. But at last, tired of killing and war, Asoka converted to Buddhism. He sent Buddhist missionaries to other countries and devoted the rest of his rule to improving the lives of his people. He had workers build wells, tree-shaded roads, and rest houses, and raised large stone pillars carved with Buddhist **edicts**, or laws. When Asoka died, however, his sons struggled for power and foreign invaders threatened the country. The

> Who inspired Indian leader Candragupta Maurya to unify India for the first time?
>
> _____
> _____

> Underline the sentence that describes Candragupta's government.

> How did Asoka's conversion to Buddhism affect his philosophy of leadership?
>
> _____
> _____
> _____
> _____

Mauryan Empire fell in 184 BC, and India remained divided for about 500 years. The spread of Buddhism steadily increased, while Hinduism declined.

GUPTA RULERS PROMOTE HINDUISM

A new dynasty was established in India. During the 300s AD, the Gupta Dynasty once again rose to unite and build the prosperity of India. Not only did the Guptas control India's military, they were devout Hindus and encouraged the revival of Hindu traditions and writings. The Guptas, however, also supported Jainism and Buddhism.

Indian civilization reached a high point under Candra Gupta II. He poured money and resources into strengthening the country's borders, as well as promoting the arts, literature, and religion.

The Guptas believed the caste system supported stability. This was not good for women, whose role under the empire was very restricted. Women were expected to marry, in weddings arranged by their parents, and raise children. A woman had to obey her husband and had few rights.

The Gupta Dynasty lasted until fierce attacks by the Huns from Central Asia during the 400s drained the empire of its resources. India broke up once again into a patchwork of small states.

> **What religions did the Gupta rulers encourage and support?**
> _____
> _____
> _____

> **How was the role of women restricted during the Gupta empire?**
> _____
> _____
> _____
> _____

CHALLENGE ACTIVITY

Critical Thinking: Drawing Inferences Why do you think unification often leads to prosperity? Write a paragraph to explain.

Guided Reading Workbook

Asoka	Candra Gupta II	Candragupta Maurya
edicts	mercenaries	Gupta Dynasty
Huns		

DIRECTIONS Read each sentence and fill in the blank with the word in the word pair that best completes the sentence.

1. The Mauryan Empire began after an army of _____ seized control of northern India. (edicts/mercenaries)

2. _____ was a strong ruler who conquered other kingdoms and made his own empire both stronger and richer. Later, he converted to Buddhism and swore that he would not fight any more wars. (Asoka/Candra Gupta II)

3. The Mauryan Empire was founded by _____ who ruled with a complex government that included a network of spies and a huge army. (Candra Gupta II/Candragupta Maurya)

4. When the _____ from Central Asia invaded India, it led to the end of the Gupta Dynasty. (edicts/Huns)

5. Under the _____, Hinduism became popular again, but the rulers also supported Buddhism and Jainism. (Gupta Dynasty/Huns)

6. Asoka had stone pillars carved with Buddhist _____ built. (edicts/mercenaries)

7. Under Emperor _____, the Gupta empire stretched all the way across northern India. The empire's economy strengthened and people prospered. (Candra Gupta II/Candragupta Maurya)

Guided Reading Workbook

History of Ancient India

MAIN IDEAS

1. Indian artists created great works of religious art.
2. Sanskrit literature flourished during the Gupta period.
3. The Indians made scientific advances in metalworking, medicine, and other sciences.

Key Terms

metallurgy the science of working with metals

alloys mixtures of two or more metals

Hindu-Arabic numerals the numbering system invented by Indian mathematicians and brought to Europe by Arabs; the numbers we use today

inoculation a method of injecting a person with a small dose of a virus to help him or her build up defenses to a disease

astronomy the study of stars and planets

Section Summary

RELIGIOUS ART

Both the Mauryan and Gupta empires unified India and created a stable environment where artists, writers, scholars, and scientists could thrive. Their works are still admired today. Much of the Indian art from this period was religious, inspired by both Hindu and Buddhist teachings. Many beautiful temples were built during this time and decorated with elaborate wood and stone carvings.

> What was the main inspiration for art and literature during the Mauryan and Gupta empires?
>
> _____
>
> _____

SANSKRIT LITERATURE

Great works of literature were written in Sanskrit, the ancient Aryan language, during the Gupta Dynasty. The best-known works are the *Mahabharata* (muh-HAH-BAH-ruh-tuh) and the *Ramayana* (rah-MAH-yuh-nuh). The *Mahabharata*, a long story about the struggle between good and evil, is considered a classic Hindu text. The most famous passage is called the *Bhagavad Gita* (BUG-uh-vuhd GEE-tah). The *Ramayana* is the story of the

> Sanskrit literature had a long tradition before it was written down. How were these early works first preserved?
>
> _____
>
> _____

Prince Rama, a human incarnation of one of the three major Hindu gods, Vishnu, who fights demons and marries the beautiful princess Sita.

SCIENTIFIC ADVANCES

Scientific and scholarly work also blossomed during the early Indian empires. Most prominent was the development of **metallurgy**, the science of working with metals. Indian technicians and engineers made strong tools and weapons. They also used processes for creating **alloys**, or mixtures of metals. For example, they made an iron alloy that did not rust as easily as most iron.

The numbers we use today, called **Hindu-Arabic numerals**, were first developed by Indian mathematicians. They also created the concept of zero, upon which all modern math is based.

Other sciences also benefited from this period of Indian history. In medicine, Indians developed the technique of **inoculation**, which is injecting a person with a small dose of a virus to help him or her build up defenses to a disease. Doctors could even perform certain surgeries. India's fascination with **astronomy**, the study of stars and planets, led to the discovery of seven of the planets in our solar system.

> How did Indian technicians improve iron?
> _____
> _____

> What are two ways that early Indian mathematicians influenced modern mathematics?
> _____
> _____

> How many planets did ancient Indian astronomers discover?
> _____

CHALLENGE ACTIVITY

Critical Thinking: Drawing Inferences Why do you think so much of the art and literature from this period is religious?

DIRECTIONS Write a word or phrase that has the same meaning as the term given.

1. alloy _____

2. astronomy _____

3. Hindu-Arabic numerals _____

4. inoculation _____

5. metallurgy _____

DIRECTIONS Read each sentence and fill in the blank with the word in the word pair that best completes the sentence.

6. Identifying seven of the nine planets in our solar system is one accomplishment

   India made in the field of _____. (astronomy/metallurgy)

7. Indian doctors knew how to protect people against disease through

   _____. (alloy/inoculation)

8. Ancient Indians were masters of _____ and knew processes

   for mixing metals to create _____.

   (astronomy/metallurgy); (alloys/inoculations)

9. The _____ is one of Hinduism's most sacred texts.
   (*Bhagavad Gita*/metallurgy)

10. The numbers we use today are called _____ because they
    were created by Indian scholars and brought to Europe by the Arabs.
    (Sanskrit/Hindu-Arabic numerals)

History of Ancient China

MAIN IDEAS
1. Chinese civilization began along two rivers.
2. The Shang dynasty was the first known dynasty to rule China.
3. The Zhou and Qin dynasties changed Chinese society and made great advances.

Key Terms and Places

Chang Jiang a river in China

Huang He a river in China

mandate of heaven the idea that heaven chose China's ruler and gave him or her power

Xi'an present name of the capital city of the Qin dynasty

Great Wall a barrier that linked earlier walls that stood near China's northern border

Section Summary

CHINESE CIVILIZATION BEGINS

Like other ancient peoples, people in China first settled along rivers. By 7000 BC farmers grew rice in the **Chang Jiang** Valley. Along the **Huang He**, they grew millet and wheat. Some villages along the Huang He grew into large towns. Many artifacts were left in these towns, including pottery and tools. As Chinese culture became more advanced, people started to use potter's wheels and dig wells for water. Population continued to grow and villages spread into northern and southeastern China.

> **Where did the Chinese first grow rice?**
> _____
> _____

SHANG DYNASTY

Societies along the Huang He grew larger and more complex. The first dynasty for which we have clear evidence is the Shang. It was firmly established by the 1500s BC. The Shang made many advances, including China's first writing system. The Chinese symbols that are used today are based on those of the Shang period.

> **Which dynasty provided the basis for China's writing system?**
> _____
> _____

Shang artisans made beautiful bronze containers for cooking and religious ceremonies. They also made ornaments, knives, and axes from jade. Shang astrologers developed a calendar based on the cycles of the moon.

ZHOU AND QIN DYNASTIES

The Zhou overthrew the Shang dynasty during the 1100s BC. The Zhou believed in the **mandate of heaven**, or the idea that they had been chosen by heaven to rule China. A new political order was established under the Zhou, with the emperor granting lands to lords in return for loyalty and military assistance. Peasants were below the lords, and owned little land. In 771 BC, the emperor was overthrown and China broke apart into many kingdoms, entering an era called the Warring States period.

The Warring States period ended when one state, the Qin, defeated the other states. In 221 BC the Qin king was able to unify China. He gave himself the title Shi Huangdi, which means "first emperor."

Shi Huangdi greatly expanded the size of China. He took land away from the lords and forced noble families to move to his capital, present-day **Xi'an**. Qin rule brought other changes to China. Shi Huangdi set up a uniform system of law. He also standardized the written language, and a new monetary system. The completion of the **Great Wall** was a major Qin achievement. The Qin built the wall to protect China from northern invaders.

Although Shi Huangdi unified China, no strong rulers took his place. China began to break apart once again within a few years of his death.

> **Who was at the top of the Zhou political system? Who was at the bottom?**
>
> _____
>
> _____

> **List three ways that Shi Huangdi unified China.**
>
> _____
>
> _____

CHALLENGE ACTIVITY

Critical Thinking: Analyzing Information Create a time line to show the events and eras discussed in this section. If you do not have an exact date, just show the century when an event took place.

Guided Reading Workbook

DIRECTIONS Read each sentence and fill in the blank with the word in the word pair that best completes the sentence.

1. The land along the _____ was good for growing cereals such as millet and wheat. (Chang Jiang/Huang He)

2. The _____ dynasty lasted longer than any other dynasty in Chinese history. (Shang/Zhou)

3. Shi Huangdi ordered nobles to move to the capital city of

    _____. (Xi'an/Qin)

4. The breaking down of the Zhou political system resulted in the

    _____. (Warring States period/mandate of heaven)

5. Around 3,000 BC, people started to use _____ and dig water wells. (bronze containers/potter's wheels)

6. During the _____ dynasty, systems of laws, money, and writing were developed. (Qin/Zhou)

7. The _____ was built because Shi Huangdi wanted to keep invaders out of China. (Chang Jiang/Great Wall)

DIRECTIONS Look at each set of three terms. On the line provided, write the letter of the term that does not relate to the others.

_____ 8. a. Chang Jiang   b. Huang He   c. Great Wall

_____ 9. a. jade   b. bronze   c. dynasty

_____ 10. a. mandate of heaven   b. Zhou   c. Shang

       Guided Reading Workbook

History of Ancient China

MAIN IDEAS

1. Han dynasty government was largely based on the ideas of Confucius.
2. Han China supported and strengthened family life.
3. The Han made many achievements in art, literature, and learning.

Key Terms

sundial a device that uses the position of shadows cast by the sun to tell the time of day

seismograph a device that measures the strength of earthquakes

acupuncture the practice of inserting fine needles through the skin at specific points to cure disease or relieve pain

Section Summary

HAN DYNASTY GOVERNMENT

Liu Bang (lee-OO bang), a peasant, won control of China and became the first emperor of the Han dynasty. He earned the people's loyalty and trust. He lowered taxes for farmers and made punishments less severe. He set up a government that built on the foundation begun by the Qin. Liu Bang's successor, Wudi (WOO-dee), made Confucianism the official government philosophy of China. To get a government job, a person had to pass a test based on Confucian teachings. However, wealthy and influential families still controlled the government.

> What did Liu Bang do to win the people's loyalty and trust?
>
> _____
> _____
> _____

FAMILY LIFE

A firm social order took hold during Han rule. In the Confucian view, peasants made up the second-highest class. Merchants occupied the lowest class because they merely bought and sold what others had made. However, this social division did not indicate wealth or power. Peasants were still poor and merchants were still rich.

> Why did Confucian thinking devalue merchants?
>
> _____
> _____
> _____

During Wudi's reign, Confucian teachings about the family were also honored. Children were taught from birth to respect their elders. Within the family, the father had absolute power. Han officials believed that if the family was strong and people obeyed the father, then people would obey the emperor, too. Chinese parents valued boys more highly than girls. Some women, however, still gained power. They could influence their sons' families. An older widow could even become the head of the family.

> **Who had absolute power in the family under the Han?**
> _____
> _____

> **Circle the sentence that explains which women could become heads of families.**

HAN ACHIEVEMENTS

The Han dynasty was a time of great accomplishments. Art and literature thrived, and inventors developed many useful devices. Han artists painted portraits and realistic scenes that showed everyday life. Poets developed new styles of verse. Historian Sima Qian wrote a complete history of China until the Han dynasty.

The Han Chinese invented paper. They made it by grinding plant fibers into a paste and then letting it dry in sheets. They made "books" by pasting sheets together into a long sheet that was rolled into a scroll.

Other Han innovations included the **sundial** and the **seismograph**. They developed the distinctive Chinese medical practice of **acupuncture** (AK-yoo-punk-cher). These and other Han inventions and advances are still used today.

> **Explain how the Han Chinese made "books."**
> _____
> _____
> _____
> _____

CHALLENGE ACTIVITY

Critical Thinking: Drawing Inferences Which invention of the Han Chinese has the greatest impact on your daily life? Explain your answer.

DIRECTIONS Write a word or phrase that has the same meaning as the term given.

1. acupuncture _____

2. seismograph _____

3. sundial _____

DIRECTIONS Read each sentence and fill in the blank with the word in the word pair that best completes the sentence.

4. Under Emperor _____, Confucianism became China's official government policy. (Wudi/Liu Bang)

5. _____ was born a peasant, but he became emperor after his army won control of China after the fall of the Qin dynasty. (Wudi/Liu Bang)

6. Under the _____ dynasty, the Chinese made several advances in art, literature, medicine, and science. (Qin/Han)

7. A _____ is a device that measures the strength of an earthquake. (seismograph/sundial)

8. The practice of inserting fine needles through the skin at specific points to cure disease or relieve pain is called _____.
(seismograph/acupuncture)

9. A _____ is an early type of clock. (seismograph/sundial)

10. The _____ dynasty rose after the collapse of the _____ dynasty. (Qin/Han); (Qin/Han)

DIRECTIONS Look at each set of three terms. On the line provided, write the letter of the term that does not relate to the others.

_____ 11. a. acupuncture   b. paper   c. Great Wall

_____ 12. a. Shi Huangdi   b. Han dynasty   c. Wudi

_____ 13. a. peasants   b. military   c. artisans

History of Ancient China

MAIN IDEAS

1. After the Han dynasty, China fell into disorder but was reunified by new dynasties.
2. Cities and trade grew during the Tang and Song dynasties.
3. The Tang and Song dynasties produced fine arts and inventions.

Key Terms and Places

Grand Canal a canal linking northern and southern China

Kaifeng capital of the Song dynasty

porcelain a thin, beautiful pottery invented by the Chinese

woodblock printing a form of printing in which an entire page is carved into a block of wood that is covered with ink and then pressed against paper to make a copy of the page

gunpowder a mixture of powders used in guns and explosives

compass an instrument that uses the earth's magnetic field to indicate direction

Section Summary

DISORDER AND REUNIFICATION

China broke apart into several kingdoms after the fall of the Han dynasty. This time period, sometimes known as the Period of Disunion, ended with the rise of the Sui dynasty in 589. Around this time, work was soon started on the **Grand Canal**, a system of waterways linking northern and southern China. The Sui dynasty, which did not last long, was followed by the Tang dynasty, which lasted nearly 300 years. This period was considered a golden age for China, with military reform, new law codes, and advances in art. The Song dynasty followed the Tang dynasty after a short period of disorder. The Song, like the Tang, ruled for about 300 years, and brought about many great achievements.

> Under what dynasty was work on the Grand Canal begun?
>
> _____
>
> _____

CITIES AND TRADE

Chinese cities grew and flourished as the trade centers of the Tang and Song dynasties. Chang'an (chahng-AHN), with a population of more than a million people, was by far the largest city in the world at the time. Several other cities, including **Kaifeng**, the Song capital, had about a million people. Traders used the Grand Canal, a series of waterways that linked major cities, to ship goods and agricultural products throughout China.

Foreign trade used both land routes and sea routes. China's Pacific ports were open to foreign traders. Chinese exports included tea, rice, spices, and jade. Especially prized by foreigners, however, were silk and **porcelain**. The method of making silk was kept secret for centuries.

> **Why do you think the Chinese kept the method for making silk a secret?**
>
> _____
>
> _____
>
> _____
>
> _____

ARTS AND INVENTIONS

The Tang dynasty produced some of China's greatest artists and writers, including the poets Li Bo and Du Fu, and the Buddhist painter Wu Daozi (DOW-tzee). The Song dynasty produced Li Qingzhao (ching-ZHOW), perhaps China's greatest female poet. Artists of the Tang and Song dynasties created exquisite objects in clay, particularly porcelain items with a pale green glaze called celadon (SEL-uh-duhn).

The Tang and Song dynasties produced some of the most remarkable—and important—inventions in human history. The world's oldest-known printed book, using **woodblock printing**, was printed in China in 868. Later, during the Song dynasty, the Chinese invented movable type for printing. The Song dynasty also introduced the world's first paper money. Two other inventions include **gunpowder** and the **compass**.

> **What printing technology replaced woodblock printing?**
>
> _____
>
> _____

CHALLENGE ACTIVITY

Critical Thinking: Drawing Inferences In what ways might large cities lead to new inventions?

DIRECTIONS Write a word or phrase that has the same meaning as the term given.

1. compass _____

_____

2. gunpowder _____

_____

3. porcelain _____

_____

4. woodblock printing _____

_____

5. Grand Canal _____

_____

6. movable type _____

_____

7. celadon _____

_____

8. merchant class _____

_____

9. Kaifeng _____

_____

DIRECTIONS Look at each set of four terms. On the line provided, write the letter of the term that does not relate to the others.

_____ 10. a. compass   b. Li Po   c. gunpowder   d. movable type

_____ 11. a. tea   b. porcelain   c. silk   d. Li Qingzhao

_____ 12. a. compass   b. paper money   c. movable type   d. Li Qingzhao

        Guided Reading Workbook

History of Ancient China

MAIN IDEAS
1. Confucianism, based on Confucius's teachings about proper behavior, dramatically influenced the Song system of government.
2. Scholar-officials ran China's government during the Song dynasty.

Key Terms

bureaucracy body of unelected government officials

civil service service as a government official

scholar-official an educated member of the government

Section Summary

CONFUCIANISM

Confucianism is the name given to the ideas of the Chinese philosopher Confucius. Confucius's teachings focused on ethics, or proper behavior, of individuals and governments. He argued that society would function best if everyone followed two principles, *ren* and *li*. *Ren* means concern for others, and *li* means appropriate behavior. Order in society is maintained when people know their place and behave appropriately.

For a thousand years after his death, Confucius's ideas went in and out of favor several times. Early in the Song dynasty, however, a new version of Confucianism, known as Neo-Confucianism, was adopted as official government policy. In addition to teaching proper behavior, Neo-Confucian scholars and officials discussed spiritual questions like what made human beings do bad things even if their basic nature was good.

> **What two principles did Confucius emphasize in his teachings?**
>
> _____
>
> _____
>
> _____
>
> _____

> **What was the name of the version of Confucianism adopted as official policy by the Song dynasty?**
>
> _____
>
> _____

SCHOLAR-OFFICIALS

The Song dynasty took another major step that would affect the Chinese imperial state for centuries to come. The Song improved the system by which people went to work for the government. These workers formed a large **bureaucracy** by passing a series of written **civil service** examinations.

The tests covered both the traditional teachings of Confucius and related ideas. Because the tests were extremely difficult, students spent years preparing for them. Candidates had a strong incentive for studying hard. Passing the tests meant life as a **scholar-official**, whose benefits included considerable respect and reduced penalties for breaking the law.

The civil service examination system helped ensure that talented, intelligent people became scholar-officials. This system was a major factor in the stability of the Song government.

What did people have to do to get a government job during the Song dynasty?
_____
_____

What were the benefits of becoming a scholar-official in the Song dynasty?
_____
_____
_____
_____

CHALLENGE ACTIVITY

Critical Thinking: Evaluating Information Would you prefer a government that gave people jobs based on test scores or one that gave people jobs based on their family connections? Explain your answer.

bureaucacy	civil service	Confucius
ethics	Neo-Confucianism	scholar-official

DIRECTIONS Read each sentence and fill in the blank with the word in the word pair that best completes the sentence.

1. _____ means service as a government official. (bureaucracy/civil service)

2. People who went to work for the government formed a large _____, a body of government officials. (bureaucracy/scholar-official)

3. _____ followed the teachings of Confucius, but also emphasized spiritual matters. (civil service/Neo-Confucianism)

4. Confucius's teachings focused on _____, proper behavior, instead of religious beliefs. (civil service/ethics)

5. In order to become a government official, a person had to pass a series of exams

   that tested students' knowledge of the teachings of _____

   and spiritual questions. (bureaucracy/Confucius)

6. A _____ was an elite member of society who received considerable respect, a good salary, and reduced penalties for breaking the law. (scholar-official/bureaucracy)

DIRECTIONS On the line provided before each statement, write **T** if a statement is true and **F** if a statement is false. If the statement is false, write the correct term on the line after each sentence that makes the sentence a true statement.

_____ 7. <u>Ethics</u> taught that people should conduct their lives according to two basic principles, *ren* and *li*.

_____

_____ 8. Often, only 1 in 20 students passed the <u>civil service</u> examinations.

_____

Guided Reading Workbook

History of Ancient China

 MAIN IDEAS
1. The Mongol Empire included China, and the Mongols ruled China as the Yuan dynasty.
2. The Ming dynasty was a time of stability and prosperity.
3. The Ming brought great changes in government and relations with other countries.

Key Terms and Places

Beijing present-day city near the capital of the Yuan dynasty

Forbidden City a huge palace complex that included hundreds of imperial residences, temples, and other government buildings

isolationism a policy of avoiding contact with other countries

Section Summary

THE MONGOL EMPIRE

In 1206, a powerful Mongol leader known as Genghis Khan (jeng-uhs KAHN) led huge armies through much of Asia and Eastern Europe. He first led his armies into northern China in 1211, then headed south. By the time of Genghis Khan's death in 1227, all of northern China was under Mongol control.

Genghis Khan's grandson, Kublai Khan (KOO-bluh KAHN), completed the conquest of China and declared himself emperor in 1279. This began the Yuan dynasty, a period also known as the Mongol Ascendancy.

Kublai Khan did not force the Chinese to accept Mongol customs, but he did try to control them. One way was by having the Chinese pay heavy taxes, which were used to pay for building projects. One such project was the building of a new capital, Dadu, near the present-day city of **Beijing**.

Kublai Khan's regime preserved much of the structure of the Song dynasty, including the civil service and trade routes. The Italian merchant

> How many years did it take for the Mongol armies to conquer all of China?
>
> _____
> _____

> Which two aspects of Song dynasty structure did Kublai Khan preserve?
>
> _____
> _____
> _____
> _____
> _____

Guided Reading Workbook

Marco Polo, who traveled in China between 1271 and 1295, wrote of his travels and sparked Europeans' interest in China.

Two failed campaigns against Japan and expensive public works projects weakened the Yuan dynasty. Many Chinese groups rebelled, and in 1368, Zhu Yuanzhang (JOO yoo-ahn-JAHNG) took control and founded the Ming dynasty.

THE MING DYNASTY

The Ming dynasty lasted nearly 300 years, from 1368 to 1644. Ming China proved to be one of the most stable and prosperous times in Chinese history. Great Ming achievements include the remarkable ships and voyages of Zheng He (juhng HUH), the Great Wall of China, and the **Forbidden City** in Beijing. The Forbidden City was a massive palace of residences, temples, and government buildings. Common people were not allowed to enter the Forbidden City.

> Who was not allowed to enter the Forbidden City?
>
> _____
>
> _____
>
> _____

CHINA UNDER THE MING

Emperors during the Ming dynasty worked to eliminate foreign influences from Chinese society. China entered a period of **isolationism**. Ironically, the consequences of this policy included a weakness that allowed opportunistic Westerners to seize considerable power in some parts of China as China's imperial glory faded.

> What did Ming emperors try to eliminate from Chinese society?
>
> _____
>
> _____

CHALLENGE ACTIVITY

Critical Thinking: Analyzing Information Create a graphic organizer to compare the causes for the downfall of the Yuan and Ming dynasties.

Beijing	Forbidden City	Kublai Khan
isolationism	Zheng He	

DIRECTIONS Answer each question by writing a sentence that contains at least one word from the word bank.

1. Who was considered one of the greatest sailors during the history of early China?

_____

_____

_____

2. What huge palace complex was a symbol of China's glory for centuries?

_____

_____

_____

3. In the 1430s, what policy did China follow in terms of contact with other countries?

_____

_____

_____

4. Who became the ruler of the Mongol Empire and completed his grandfather's conquest of China?

_____

_____

_____

5. Near what modern-day city was the Yuan capital built?

_____

_____

_____

MAIN IDEAS
1. Towering mountains, large rivers, and broad plains are the key physical features of the Indian Subcontinent.
2. The Indian Subcontinent has a great variety of climate regions and resources.

Key Terms and Places

subcontinent a large landmass that is smaller than a continent

Mount Everest world's highest mountain, located between Nepal and China

Ganges River India's most important river, flows across northern India into Bangladesh

delta a landform at the mouth of a river created by sediment deposits

Indus River river in Pakistan that creates a fertile plain known as the Indus River Valley

monsoons seasonal winds that bring either moist or dry air to an area

Section Summary
PHYSICAL FEATURES

The Indian Subcontinent is made up of the countries Bangladesh, Bhutan, India, Maldives, Nepal, Pakistan, and Sri Lanka. This subcontinent is also known as South Asia. A **subcontinent** is a large landmass that is smaller than a continent. Huge mountains separate the Indian Subcontinent from the rest of Asia—the Hindu Kush in the northwest and the Himalayas along the north. Lower mountains, called the Ghats, run along India's eastern and western coasts. The Himalayas stretch about 1,500 miles across and are the highest mountains in the world. The highest peak, **Mount Everest**, rises 29,035 feet (8,850 m) above sea level. Pakistan's K2 is the world's second tallest peak. Two major river systems originate in the Himalayas. They have flooded the surrounding land, creating fertile plains. The **Ganges River** flows across northern India. The area along the

Circle the names of the seven countries in South Asia.

Underline the world's two highest mountain peaks.

Ganges is called the Ganges Plain. It is India's farming heartland. In Bangladesh the Ganges River joins other rivers to form a huge **delta**, a landform created by sediment deposits. Pakistan's **Indus River** also forms a fertile plain, the Indus River Valley. This region was once home to the earliest Indian civilizations. Now, it is the most heavily populated area in Pakistan.

Other features include a hilly plateau south of the Ganges Plain called the Deccan. East of the Indus Valley is the Thar, or Great Indian Desert. In southern Nepal, the Tarai region is known for its fertile farmland and tropical jungles.

Which river forms a fertile plain in Pakistan?
_____

CLIMATES AND RESOURCES

Nepal and Bhutan, located in the Himalayas, have a highland climate which brings cool temperatures. In the plains south of the Himalayas, the climate is humid subtropical. The rest of the subcontinent has mainly tropical climates. Central India and Sri Lanka have a tropical savanna climate, with warm temperatures year round. Bangladesh, Sri Lanka, Maldives, and parts of southwest India have a humid tropical climate, with warm temperatures and heavy rains. Southern and western India and most of Pakistan have desert and steppe climates. **Monsoons**—winds that bring either dry or moist air—greatly affect the subcontinent's climate. From June to October, summer monsoons from the Indian Ocean bring heavy rains. In winter, monsoons change direction and bring in dry air from the north.

The subcontinent's fertile soil is a vital resource for the region. It allows farmers to produce tea, rice, nuts, and jute. Other important resources are timber, livestock, iron ore, coal, natural gas, and gemstones.

Underline the type of climate found in Nepal and Bhutan.

Define monsoon in your own words on the lines below.
_____
_____

Circle the resources of the Indian Subcontinent.

CHALLENGE ACTIVITY

Critical Thinking: Organizing Information Make a table with two columns to show major mountain ranges and river valleys of the Indian subcontinent.

delta	Ganges River	Himalayas	Hindu Kush
Indus River	monsoons	Mount Everest	subcontinent

DIRECTIONS Read each sentence and fill in the blank with the word
in the word pair that best completes the sentence.

1. A _____ is a large landmass that is smaller than a continent.
   (delta/subcontinent)

2. The _____ creates a fertile plain, which is Pakistan's most
   densely populated region. (Indus River/Ganges River)

3. Summer _____ bring moist air up from the Indian Ocean,
   causing heavy rains. (monsoons/Himalayas)

4. The most important river in India is the _____.
   (Indus River/Ganges River)

5. The world's highest mountain is _____.
   (Hindu Kush/Mount Everest)

DIRECTIONS Use five of the terms from the word bank to write a
summary of what you learned in the section. Use another piece of paper
if you need more space.

_____

_____

_____

_____

_____

_____

_____

_____

The Indian Subcontinent

MAIN IDEAS

1. Advanced civilizations and powerful empires shaped the early history of India.
2. Powerful empires controlled India for hundreds of years.
3. Independence from Great Britain led to the division of India into several countries.
4. Religion and the caste system are two important parts of Indian culture.

Key Terms and Places

Delhi site of former Muslim kingdom in northern India

colony territory inhabited and controlled by people from a foreign land

partition division

Hinduism one of the world's oldest religions, the dominant religion of India

Buddhism religion based on the teaching of Siddhartha Gautama, the Buddha

caste system divides Indian society into groups based on birth or occupation

Section Summary

EARLY CIVILIZATIONS AND EMPIRES

The Indian Subcontinent's first urban civilization—the Harappan—was in the Indus Valley. Later the Aryans moved from Central Asia into the Indian Subcontinent. They settled along the Indus and Ganges rivers. An Aryan language, Sanskrit, became the basis for many languages, including Hindi. Aryan customs mixed with those of other people, forming much of India's culture.

> Circle the Aryan language that is the basis for Hindi.

The Mauryan people then conquered most of the subcontinent by about 320 BC. However, after the death of Asoka, one of the greatest Mauryan rulers, the empire split up. In the AD 300s the Gupta Empire united most of northern India. Trade and culture thrived under Gupta rulers until around 550.

> Underline the name of one of the greatest Mauryan emperors.

POWERFUL EMPIRES

In the late 600s Muslim armies invaded India. They set up a kingdom at **Delhi** in northern India and formed the Mughal Empire. Trade and culture flourished during this period, especially under Akbar, one of India's greatest rulers.

In the 1600s, as the Mughal Empire declined, the British East India Company gained valuable trading rights. India eventually became a British **colony**, a territory controlled by people from a foreign land. Many Indians rebelled against the British company. The British government crushed the rebellion and began ruling India directly.

> Underline the sentence that explains what a colony is.

INDEPENDENCE AND DIVISION

By the late 1800s many Indians were upset at British rule. One group formed the Indian National Congress to gain more rights. Later, Mohandas Gandhi led nonviolent protests to gain Indian independence. However, Muslims feared having little say in the new India. To avoid civil war, the British agreed to the **partition**, or division of India. As a result, two independent countries, India and Pakistan, were formed in 1947. Later Sri Lanka and Maldives gained independence. Bangladesh broke away from Pakistan to form a new nation in 1971.

> Why was India divided into two independent countries?
> _____
> _____

INDIAN CULTURE

India is the birthplace of **Hinduism**, one of the world's oldest religions. Hindus believe everything in the universe is part of one spirit called Brahman. The goal of Hindus is to reunite their souls with Brahman. Another religion, **Buddhism**, is based on the teachings of the Buddha, Siddhartha Gautama. It also began in India. The Buddha taught that people can achieve a state of peace called nirvana.

> Circle the two religions that began in India.

Indian society was organized into a **caste system**, which divides people into different classes. A person's caste was based on his or her birth or occupation.

> Explain the caste system in your own words on the lines below.
> _____
> _____

CHALLENGE ACTIVITY

Critical Thinking: Comparing and Contrasting

Write a paragraph that explains how Mughal and British rule were alike and different.

| Buddhism | caste system | colony | Delhi |
| Hinduism | influence | partition | tolerance |

DIRECTIONS Write two words or phrases that describe the term.

1. tolerance _____

2. influence _____

3. colony _____

4. partition _____

5. caste system _____

DIRECTIONS Choose five of the terms from the word bank. Use these terms to write a summary of the section.

_____

_____

_____

_____

_____

_____

_____

_____

_____

_____

_____

_____

_____

_____

_____

Section 3

MAIN IDEAS
1. Daily life in India is centered around cities, villages, and religion.
2. Today India faces many challenges, including a growing population and economic development.

Key Terms and Places

Mumbai (Bombay) one of India's largest cities

Kolkata (Calcutta) one of India's largest cities

urbanization increase in the percentage of people who live in cities

green revolution program that encouraged farmers to adopt modern agricultural methods

Section Summary

DAILY LIFE IN INDIA

Nearly 1.2 billion people live in India. India has many different ethnic groups, religions, and lifestyles. City life, village life, and religion help unite India's people.

India's three largest cities, **Mumbai (Bombay)**, **Delhi**, and **Kolkata (Calcutta)**, are among the world's most populous. Cities such as Mumbai and Bangalore have universities, research centers, and high-tech businesses. But most city-dwellers have a hard time making a living. Many live in shacks, with no plumbing and little clean water.

More than 70 percent of India's population lives in villages. Most work on farms and live with extended families in simple homes. In many areas paved roads and electricity have only recently been provided.

Religion plays a key role in Indian villages and cities. Most people practice Hinduism, while others practice Islam, Buddhism, Jainism and Sikhism. Diwali, the festival of lights, is one of India's most popular religious events. Diwali celebrates Hindu, Sikh, and Jain beliefs.

> Circle the number of people who live in India.

> Underline the sentence that describes the living conditions of many city-dwellers.

> Circle the names of religions practiced in India.

INDIA'S CHALLENGES

Only China has more people than India. India's population has doubled since 1947. This great increase in population has strained India's environment and resources such as food, housing, and schools. **Urbanization**—an increase in the percentage of a country's people who live in cities—has greatly affected India's cities. In search of jobs, millions of people moved to India's cities.

Since gaining independence, India's leaders have improved its government and economy. India is now one of the strongest nations in Asia—and the world's largest democracy. India faces two main challenges. The first is how to provide resources for its growing population. The second is how to resolve conflicts with its neighbor, Pakistan.

India's gross domestic product (GDP) makes it one of the world's top five industrial nations. However, GDP per capita (per person) is only $3,700, so millions of Indians live in poverty. To help address this problem, India's government began a program called the **green revolution**, which encouraged farmers to use more modern farming methods. Recently, the government has worked to bring high-tech businesses to India.

> Why have millions of Indians moved to cities?
>
> _____
>
> _____

> Circle India's per capita gross domestic product (GDP).

CHALLENGE ACTIVITY

Critical Thinking: Making Inferences If India is one of the world's top five industrial nations, why do so many of its people live in poverty? Write a short paragraph to explain your answer.

| Bollywood | Diwali | green revolution |
| Kolkata (Calcutta) | Mumbai (Bombay) | urbanization |

DIRECTIONS On the line provided before each statement, write **T** if a statement is true and **F** if a statement is false. If the statement is false, write the correct term on the line after each sentence that makes the sentence a true statement.

_____ 1. <u>Diwali</u> is the festival of lights, celebrating Hindu, Jain, and Sikh beliefs.

_____

_____ 2. The <u>urbanization</u> was a program of the Indian government to encourage modern agricultural methods.

_____

_____ 3. India's movie industry is also known as <u>Bollywood</u>.

_____

_____ 4. Rapid <u>industrialization</u> has taken place in India as people have moved to cities seeking jobs.

_____

_____ 5. <u>New Delhi</u> and Kolkata (Calcutta) are India's two largest cities.

_____

DIRECTIONS Choose four of the terms from the word bank. On a separate piece of paper, use these terms to write a summary of what you learned in the section.

The Indian Subcontinent

MAIN IDEAS
1. Many different ethnic groups and religions influence the culture of India's neighbors.
2. Rapid population growth, ethnic conflicts, and environmental threats are major challenges to the region today.

Key Terms and Places

Sherpas ethnic group from the mountains of Nepal

Kashmir a region which both India and Pakistan claim control over

Dhaka capital of Bangladesh and its largest city

Kathmandu capital of Nepal and its largest city

Section Summary

CULTURE

India's neighbors have different ways of life. Their cultures reflect the customs of many ethnic groups. For example, the **Sherpas** in Nepal often serve as guides through the Himalayas. Many of the Tamil in Sri Lanka came from India to work on plantations.

People of the region also have different religious beliefs. Like India, most of its neighbors have one major religion. For example, most people in Pakistan and Bangladesh practice Islam. Hinduism is the major religion in Nepal while Buddhism is the major religion in Sri Lanka and Bhutan.

> **Circle the countries of the Indian subcontinent where most people practice Islam.**

THE REGION TODAY

Since its creation in 1947, Pakistan has not had a stable government. Rebellions and assassinations have hurt the country. Pakistan also faces the challenges of overpopulation and poverty. These challenges could cause even more instability. Pakistan has also clashed with India over control of the territory of **Kashmir**. Pakistan controls western Kashmir and India controls the east. However, both countries claim control over this region.

> **What challenges does Pakistan face?**
> _____
> _____

Since 2001 Pakistan has helped the United States fight terrorism. Many people, though, think terrorists still remain in Pakistan.

Bangladesh is a small country, but one of the world's most densely populated. It has about 2,734 people per square mile (1,055 per square km). More than 13 million people live in Bangladesh's capital, **Dhaka**. One of the country's main challenges is flooding from rivers and monsoons, which often causes heavy damage. For example, one flood left over 25 million people homeless.

> Underline the sentence that tells one of Bangladesh's main challenges.

Nepal's population is growing rapidly. Its largest city and capital, **Kathmandu**, is poor and overcrowded. Nepal also faces environmental threats. Land cleared to grow food causes deforestation, leading to soil erosion and harming wildlife. Tourists also harm its environment by leaving trash behind and using valuable resources.

> What are two causes of damage to Nepal's environment?
>
> _____
> _____
> _____

Bhutan is a small, isolated mountain kingdom between India and China. After years of isolation, Bhutan formed ties with Great Britain and India in the 1900s. Bhutan has begun to modernize, building new roads, schools, and hospitals. Most of its people are farmers, growing rice, potatoes, and corn. To protect its environment and way of life, Bhutan limits the number of tourists who may visit.

> Underline the crops Bhutan's farmers grow.

Sri Lanka has been greatly influenced by its close neighbor, India. Two of Sri Lanka's main ethnic groups—the Tamil and the Sinhalese—have Indian roots. The Tamil minority has fought for years to create a separate state. The fighting ended in 2009 when the government defeated the Tamils. In 2004, an Indian Ocean tsunami struck Sri Lanka, killing thousands. More than 500,000 were left homeless. Sri Lanka is still trying to rebuild its fishing and agricultural industries.

> Circle the two main ethnic groups in Sri Lanka.

CHALLENGE ACTIVITY

Critical Thinking: Analyzing Information Make a chart to compare the challenges faced by Nepal, Bhutan, and Sri Lanka.

Guided Reading Workbook

| circumstances | Dhaka | Kashmir |
| Kathmandu | Sherpas | Tamils |

DIRECTIONS Read each sentence and choose the correct term from the word bank to replace the underlined phrase. Write the term in the space provided and then define the term in your own words.

1. <u>They</u> have provided many guides for Himalayan expeditions.

_____

Your definition: _____

_____

2. <u>This city</u> is the capital of Nepal.

_____

Your definition: _____

_____

3. <u>This region</u> is the source of conflict between India and Pakistan.

_____

Your definition: _____

_____

4. <u>They</u> came from India to work on Sri Lanka's plantations.

_____

Your definition: _____

_____

5. Flooding in Bangladesh results from many <u>conditions</u> such as monsoons.

_____

Your definition: _____

_____

China, Mongolia, and Taiwan

MAIN IDEAS
1. Physical features of China, Mongolia, and Taiwan include mountains, plateaus and basins, plains, and rivers.
2. China, Mongolia, and Taiwan have a range of climates and natural resources.

Key Terms and Places

Himalayas the world's tallest mountain range

Plateau of Tibet the world's highest plateau, located in southwest China

Gobi located in Mongolia, the world's coldest desert

North China Plain fertile plain in east China

Huang He the Yellow River, a river in northern China that often floods

loess fertile, yellowish soil

Chang Jiang the Yangzi River, Asia's longest river, flows across central China

Section Summary
PHYSICAL FEATURES

China has a range of physical features. These include the world's tallest mountains, as well as some of the world's driest deserts and longest rivers. Mongolia and Taiwan are two of China's neighbors. Mongolia is a dry, landlocked country. Taiwan is a green tropical island.

Mountains are found in much of the region. The **Himalayas** run along the border of southwest China. They are the highest mountains in the world. The highest plateau in the world—the **Plateau of Tibet**—is also located in southwest China. Many of the region's mountain ranges are separated by plateaus, basins, and deserts.

The Taklimakan Desert is located in western China. Swirling sandstorms are frequent here. Another desert, the **Gobi**, is located in Mongolia. It is the world's coldest desert.

> **How are Mongolia and Taiwan different?**
> _____
> _____
> _____

> **Where in China are the Himalayas and the Plateau of Tibet located?**
> _____

Most Chinese live in the eastern **North China Plain**. This region is made up of low plains and river valleys. In Taiwan most people live on a plain on the west coast.

Two long rivers run west to east across China. One of these, the **Huang He**, or the Yellow River, picks up a yellowish, fertile soil called **loess**. When the river floods, it deposits the loess, enriching the farmland along the banks. But many people are killed by these floods. Another river, the **Chang Jiang**, or the Yangzi River, flows across central China. It is Asia's longest river and a major transportation route.

| Underline the region where most Chinese live. |

| How does the Huang He both help and harm people? |

CLIMATE AND RESOURCES

Climate varies widely across the region. The tropical southeast is warm to hot. There, monsoons bring heavy rains in the summer. Violent storms called typhoons bring heavy winds and rain in the summer and fall. The climate in the north and west is mainly dry. Temperatures across this area vary. The climate in the northeast is quite different. It is drier and colder. In the winter, temperatures can drop below 0°F (–18°C).

The region has a variety of natural resources. Farmland is an important resource in both China and Taiwan. Taiwan grows a variety of crops, including sugarcane, tea, and bananas. China also has many mineral, metal, and forest resources. Mongolia's natural resources include minerals and livestock.

| What is a typhoon? |

| Circle an important resource in both China and Taiwan. |

CHALLENGE ACTIVITY

Critical Thinking: Making Generalizations Write a journal entry describing your travels through a part of the region, such as hiking in the Himalayas, traveling with nomads across the Gobi desert, or visiting a city. What are your general impressions?

Guided Reading Workbook

Gobi	Himalayas	Chang Jiang (Yangzi River)
loess	North China Plain	Huang He (Yellow River)
Plateau of Tibet		

DIRECTIONS Read each sentence and fill in the blank with the word
in the word pair that best completes the sentence.

1. Asia's longest river, the _____, flows through Central China.
   (Chang Jiang/Huang He)

2. The _____ is the world's coldest desert.
   (North China Plain/Gobi)

3. The Roof of the World is another name for the _____.
   (Plateau of Tibet/Himalayas)

4. The Yellow River picks up large amounts of fertile, yellowish soil called

   _____. (loess/Gobi)

5. Mount Everest, the world's highest mountain, is located in the

   _____. (Himalayas/North China Plain)

DIRECTIONS Answer each question by writing a sentence that
contains at least one word from the word bank.

6. Where are China's main population centers?

   _____

   _____

   _____

7. How do China's rivers both help and hurt the country's people?

   _____

   _____

   _____

MAIN IDEAS

1. Family lines of emperors ruled China for most of its early history.
2. In China's modern history, revolution and civil war led to a Communist government.
3. China has the world's most people as well as a rich culture shaped by ancient traditions.

Key Terms

dynasty a series of rulers from the same family line

dialect a regional version of a language

Daoism belief system that stresses living simply and in harmony with nature

Confucianism a philosophy based on the ideas and teachings of Confucius

pagodas Buddhist temples that have multi-storied towers with an upward curving roof at each floor

Section Summary

CHINA'S EARLY HISTORY

China's civilization has lasted for about 4,000 years. For most of its long history, China was ruled by dynasties. A **dynasty** is a series of rulers from the same family line.

China limited contact with the outside world for much of its history. But many people wanted Chinese goods, such as silk and tea. Some European powers forced China to open up trade in the 1800s.

> Underline the definition of *dynasty*.

CHINA'S MODERN HISTORY

Rebels forced out China's last emperor in 1911. Over time, the Nationalists and the Communists fought a long civil war. The Communists won in 1949, and the Nationalists fled to Taiwan.

Mao Zedong led the new Communist government in China. Some people's lives improved. But people who criticized the government were punished, and freedoms were limited. Some economic programs failed, causing famine and other problems.

> Who won China's civil war? When did the war end?
>
> _____
>
> _____

Mao died in 1976. China's next leader was Deng Xiaoping. Deng worked to modernize and improve the economy. The economy began growing rapidly. Later leaders continued economic reforms.

CHINA'S PEOPLE AND CULTURE

China has 1.3 billion people. Most are crowded in the east, on the Manchurian and North China plains. The majority belong to the Han ethnic group. Many speak Mandarin, China's official language. Others speak a **dialect**, a regional version of a language.

Modern China is influenced by many values and beliefs. The main belief systems are Buddhism and Daoism. **Daoism** stresses living simply and in harmony with nature. Buddhists believe moral behavior, kindness, and meditation can lead to peace.

Many Chinese blend elements of these religions with **Confucianism**. This philosophy is based on the ideas and teachings of Confucius. It stresses family, moral values, and respect for one's elders.

The Chinese have rich artistic traditions. Crafts are made from materials such as bronze, jade, ivory, silk, wood, and porcelain. Paintings on silk paper, calligraphy, poetry, and opera are also common. Traditional architecture features wooden buildings with upward-curving roofs. Buddhist temples called **pagodas** have multi-storied towers with roofs that curve upward at each floor. Popular culture includes sports such as martial arts and activities such as visiting karaoke clubs.

CHALLENGE ACTIVITY

Critical Thinking: Making Judgments Imagine that you are a Chinese emperor and that Europeans want to begin trading with China. Would you allow such contact with the outside world? Why or why not? Explain your answer in a brief essay.

> How did China's economy change under Deng Xiaoping?
> _____
> _____

> Circle the name of China's official language.

> What is Confucianism?
> _____
> _____

Confucianism	Daoism	dialect
dynasty	pagodas	

DIRECTIONS On the line provided before each statement, write **T** if a statement is true and **F** if a statement is false. If the statement is false, write the correct term from the word bank on the line after each sentence that makes the sentence a true statement.

_____ 1. Confucianism stresses living simply and in harmony with nature.

_____

_____ 2. The Qin dialect was the first to unify China under one empire.

_____

_____ 3. Many pagodas, or Buddhist temples, can be seen throughout China.

_____

DIRECTIONS Look at each set of four vocabulary terms. On the line provided, write the letter of the term that does not relate to the others.

_____ 4. a. Daoism   b. Buddhism   c. Communism   d. Confucianism

_____ 5. a. dialect   b. dynasty   c. Qin   d. Qing

_____ 6. a. Han   b. Hui   c. Zhuang   d. Mandarin

_____ 7. a. Great Wall   b. civil war   c. Shi Huangdi   d. terra-cotta soldiers

China, Mongolia, and Taiwan

MAIN IDEAS

1. China's booming economy is based on agriculture, but industry is growing rapidly.
2. China's government controls many aspects of life and limits political freedom.
3. China is mainly rural, but urban areas are growing.
4. China's environment faces a number of serious problems.

Key Terms and Places

command economy an economic system in which the government owns all businesses and makes all decisions

Beijing China's capital

Tibet the Buddhist region in southwest China

Shanghai China's largest city

Hong Kong important center of trade and tourism in southern China

Section Summary

CHINA'S ECONOMY

Communist China used to have a **command economy**, in which the government owns all the businesses and makes all decisions. Because it had major economic problems, China began allowing some aspects of a market economy in the 1970s. In a market economy people can make their own decisions and keep the profits they earn.

China's mixed economic approach has helped its economy boom. Today it is the world's second-largest economy.

More than half of all Chinese workers are farmers. They are able to produce a lot of food. However, industry and manufacturing are the most profitable part of China's economy. Economic growth has improved wages and living standards in China. Still, many rural Chinese remain poor. Many do not have work.

> How is a command economy different from a market economy?
> _____
> _____

> Underline the reason why China is able to grow a lot of food.

Guided Reading Workbook

CHINA'S GOVERNMENT

China's citizens have little political freedom. In 1989, a huge protest took place in China's capital, **Beijing**. About 100,000 people gathered in Tiananmen Square to demand more political rights and freedoms. The government crushed the protest.

China has also put down ethnic rebellions. One revolt took place in 1959 in **Tibet**, a Buddhist region. China has since restricted Tibetans' rights.

Other nations have criticized these actions. They have considered stopping or limiting trade with China until it shows more respect for human rights.

> **How have some countries responded to China's actions against human rights?**
> _____
> _____
> _____
> _____

RURAL AND URBAN CHINA

Most of China's people live in small rural villages. But many people are moving to China's growing cities. The country's largest city is **Shanghai**. China's second-largest city is Beijing. Beijing is an important cultural and political center. Two important cities on the southern coast are **Hong Kong** and Macau. These were once under European control but have recently been returned to China.

> **Circle the names of two of China's cities that were under European control until recently.**

CHINA'S ENVIRONMENT

China's growth has created environmental problems. These include air and water pollution. Forestland and farmland have been lost. China is working to solve these problems.

CHALLENGE ACTIVITY

Critical Thinking: Drawing Conclusions Imagine that you are living in China and that you have a new pen pal who is curious about what it is like to live in your country. Write a brief letter describing life in China.

Guided Reading Workbook

Beijing	command economy	free enterprise
Hong Kong	Shanghai	Tibet
most-favored-nation status		

DIRECTIONS On the line provided before each statement, write **T** if a statement is true and **F** if a statement is false. If the statement is false, write the correct term from the word bank on the line after each sentence that makes the sentence a true statement.

_____ 1. A <u>free enterprise</u> is a system in which the government owns most businesses and makes most economic decisions.

_____

_____ 2. In 1997 the United Kingdom returned control of <u>Hong Kong</u> to China.

_____

_____ 3. Controlled by China since 1950, <u>Tibet</u> is a Buddhist region located in southwest China.

_____

_____ 4. China's government will not allow <u>most-favored nation status</u>, an economic system in which people can choose their own careers, decide what to make or sell, and keep the profits they earn.

_____

_____ 5. The United States has threatened to cancel China's <u>command economy</u>, which would hurt China's trade benefits.

_____

DIRECTIONS Write three words or phrases that describe each term.

6. Shanghai _____

7. Beijing _____

Section 4

MAIN IDEAS
1. Mongolia is a sparsely populated country where many people live as nomads.
2. Taiwan is a small island with a dense population and a highly industrialized economy.

Key Terms and Places

gers large, circular, felt tents that are easy to put up, take down, and move

Ulaanbaatar Mongolia's capital and only large city

Taipei Taiwan's capital and main financial center

Kao-hsiung Taiwan's main seaport and a center of heavy industry

Section Summary

MONGOLIA

The people of Mongolia have a proud and fascinating history. In the late 1200s, Mongolia was perhaps the greatest power in the world. The Mongol Empire stretched from Europe to the Pacific Ocean. Over time, the empire declined. China conquered Mongolia in the late 1600s.

Mongolia declared independence from China in 1911. The Communists gained control 13 years later. The Soviet Union was a strong influence in Mongolia. But in the early 1990s, the Soviet Union collapsed. Since then, Mongolians have worked for democracy and a free-market economy.

> Circle the name of the country that had a strong influence in Mongolia for much of the 1900s.

Many Mongolians have a traditional way of life. Nearly half live as nomads, herding livestock. Many live in **gers**. These large, circular, felt tents are easy to put up, take down, and move. Horses play an important role in the lives of the nomads.

> How do many Mongolians live?
> _____

Mongolia has a small population. Only about 2.7 million people live in the entire country. Mongolia's capital and only large city is **Ulaanbaatar**. One in four Mongolians lives there. The country's main industries include textiles, carpets, coal, copper, and

> Circle the name of Mongolia's capital city.

oil. Mongolia produces livestock but very little
other food. The country faces both food and water
shortages.

TAIWAN

Both China and Japan controlled Taiwan at
different times. In 1949 the Chinese Nationalists
took over the island. They had left the Chinese
mainland after the Communists took over. The
Nationalists ruled Taiwan under martial law, or
military rule, for 38 years. Today, Taiwan's
government is a multiparty democracy.

Tension remains between China and Taiwan.
China claims that Taiwan is a rebel part of China.
Taiwan claims to be China's true government.

Taiwan's history is reflected in its culture. Most
Taiwanese are descendants of people from China.
As a result, Chinese ways are an important part of
Taiwan's culture. Japan's influence is also seen.
European and American practices and customs are
beginning to be seen in Taiwan's cities.

Taiwan is a modern country with about
23 million people. Most Taiwanese live in cities on
the island's western coastal plain. The rest of the
country is mountainous. The two largest cities are
Taipei and **Kao-hsiung**. Taipei is Taiwan's capital.
It is a main financial center. Kao-hsiung is a center
of heavy industry and Taiwan's main seaport.

What group came to Taiwan after the Communists took over mainland China?
_____

What are some cultural influences on Taiwanese culture? Which is the major influence?
_____
_____
_____

Underline the place where most Taiwanese live. What is the rest of the country like?
_____

CHALLENGE ACTIVITY

Critical Thinking: Making Judgments Imagine
that you are a government official from Taiwan
visiting Mongolia. Write a report explaining why
Mongolia and Taiwan should or should not become
trade partners.

| Chang Kai-shek | gers | Ghengis Khan | Kao-hsiung |
| Nationalists | nomads | Taipei | Ulaanbaatar |

DIRECTIONS Read each sentence and fill in the blank with the word
in the word pair that best completes the sentence.

1. _____ is Taiwan's capital and main financial center.
   (Taipei/Chang Kei-shek)

2. A powerful warrior and ruler, _____ built up a huge
   Mongolian Empire. (Kao-hsiung/Genghis Khan)

3. The coastal city of _____ is Taiwan's main seaport.
   (Kao-hsiung/Taipei)

4. The capital city of _____ is home to more than a quarter of
   Mongolia's population. (Ulaanbaatar/Kao-hsiung)

5. _____ served as leader of the Chinese Nationalists in 1949.
   (Ghengis Khan/Chang Kai-shek)

DIRECTIONS Look up the vocabulary terms below in a dictionary.
Write the dictionary definition of the word that is closest to the
definition used in your textbook.

6. gers _____

   _____

7. nomads _____

   _____

Japan and the Koreas

Section 1

MAIN IDEAS
1. The main physical features of Japan and the Koreas are rugged mountains.
2. The climates and resources of Japan and the Koreas vary from north to south.

Key Terms and Places

Fuji Japan's highest mountain

Korean Peninsula Asian peninsula that includes both North Korea and South Korea

tsunamis destructive waves caused by large underwater earthquakes

fishery place where lots of fish and other seafood can be caught

Section Summary
PHYSICAL FEATURES

Japan is made up of four large islands and more than 3,000 smaller ones. They stretch across 1,500 miles of ocean, about the length of the Eastern United States coastline. But they include only about as much land area as California. Most people live on the four largest islands, which are Hokkaido, Honshu, Shikoku, and Kyushu. Mountains cover about 75 percent of Japan. The Japanese Alps are Japan's largest mountain range. Japan's highest mountain, **Fuji**, is not in any mountain range, but is an isolated volcanic peak in eastern Honshu. It has become a symbol of Japan, and is considered sacred by some people. Many shrines and temples have been built around it.

The **Korean Peninsula** juts south from the Asian mainland, and is divided between North and South Korea. Rugged mountains run along the eastern coast, and plains can be found on the western coast and in the river valleys. Korea has more rivers than Japan. Most of them flow westward and empty in the Yellow Sea.

> **Circle the names of Japan's four largest islands.**

> **Where on the Korean Peninsula are the mountains located?**
> _____
> _____

Japan is subject to volcanic eruptions, earthquakes, and **tsunamis**, which are destructive waves
caused by underwater earthquakes. Korea does not
have many earthquakes or volcanoes. Like Japan,
Korea is subject to huge storms, called typhoons,
that sweep in from the Pacific Ocean.

> **Underline the sentence that explains what a tsunami is.**

CLIMATE AND RESOURCES

Just as Japan and the Koreas have many similar
physical features, they also have similar climates. In
both places, climate varies from north to south. The
northern regions have a humid continental climate
with cool summers, long, cold winters, and a short
growing season. In the south, a humid subtropical
climate brings mild winters and as much as 80
inches of rain each year. Most of the rain falls
during the hot, humid summers, which is also when
typhoons occur.

> **In a humid subtropical climate, when does most of the rain fall?**
>
> _____

Unlike the rest of the region, North Korea is rich
in mineral resources such as iron and coal. Both of
the Koreas use their quick-flowing rivers to
generate hydroelectric power. Japan has one of the
world's strongest fishing economies. The islands lie
near one of the world's most productive **fisheries**,
which are areas where lots of fish and seafood can
be caught. Huge fishing nets are used to catch the
large number of fish needed to serve Japan's busy
fish markets.

> **Which country on the Korean Peninsula has mineral deposits?**
>
> _____

CHALLENGE ACTIVITY

Critical Thinking: Analyzing Write a paragraph
describing the physical features and climate of
Japan.

| fishery | Fuji | humid continental |
| humid subtropical | Korean Peninsula | tsunamis |

DIRECTIONS Read each sentence and fill in the blank with the word in the word pair that best completes the sentence.

1. The northern parts of the region have a _____ climate, in which the summers are cool, but the winters are long and cold. (humid continental/humid subtropical)

2. The _____ is covered with rugged mountains. (fishery/Korean Peninsula)

3. A _____ can be brought on by underwater earthquakes. (tsunami/fishery)

4. Due to the swift ocean currents near Japan, it has one of the world's most

   productive _____. (fisheries/tsunamis)

5. Many Japanese consider _____ a sacred place. (Fuji/the Korean Peninsula)

DIRECTIONS Choose four of the vocabulary terms from the word bank. Use these words to write a summary of what you learned in the section.

_____

_____

_____

_____

_____

Japan and the Koreas

MAIN IDEAS

1. The early histories of Japan and Korea were closely linked, but the countries developed very differently.

2. Japanese culture blends traditional customs with modern innovations.

3. Though they share a common culture, life is very different in North and South Korea.

Key Terms and Places

Kyoto Japan's imperial capital, known before as Heian

shoguns powerful military leaders of imperial Japan

samurai highly trained warriors

kimonos traditional Japanese robes

kimchi Korean dish made from pickled cabbage and spices

Section Summary

HISTORY

China has had much influence on both Japan and the Koreas. One example is Buddhism, which was once the main religion in both countries. Japan's first government was modeled after China's. Japan's emperors made their capital Heian (now called **Kyoto**) a center for the arts. Some of them paid so much attention to the arts that they allowed generals called **shoguns** to take control. Shoguns had armies of warriors called **samurai** who helped them rule Japan until 1868, when a group of samurai gave power back to the emperor. During World War II, the Japanese brought the United States into the war by bombing its naval base at Pearl Harbor. To end the war, the Americans dropped atomic bombs on the Japanese cities of Hiroshima and Nagasaki.

China ruled the Korean Peninsula for centuries. Later, the Japanese invaded. After World War II, Korea became independent. However, the Soviet Union helped Communists take control in the north

> Underline the sentence that explains how the shoguns gained power.

> Which country helped Communists take control in North Korea?
>
> _____

while the United States helped to form a democratic government in the south. In 1950 North Korea invaded the south, wanting to unite Korea. The United States and other countries helped the South Koreans remain separate.

JAPANESE CULTURE

The Japanese system of writing uses two types of characters. Some characters, called kanji, each represent a single word. Others, called kana, each stand for a part of a word. Most Japanese people combine elements of Shinto and Buddhism in their religious practices. In the Shinto tradition—native to Japan—everything in nature is believed to have a spirit, or *kami*, which protects people. Through Buddhism, people in Japan have learned to seek enlightenment and peace. Most people in Japan wear Western style clothing, but many also wear the traditional **kimono** on special occasions. Traditional forms of art include Noh and Kabuki plays.

> Circle the names of the kinds of characters used to write Japanese.

> What do Japanese people wear most of the time?
> _____

KOREAN CULTURE

People in both North and South Korea speak Korean. Unlike Japanese, written Korean uses an alphabet. In the past, most Koreans were Buddhist or Confucianist. Today, about one fourth of South Koreans are Christian. Communist North Korea discourages people from practicing any religion.

The people of Korea have kept many old traditions, such as **kimchi**, a dish made from pickled cabbage. Traditional Korean art forms remain, especially in North Korea, where the Communists think Korean culture is the best in the world. In the south, people have adopted new ways of life and forgotten some of their traditions.

> Underline the names of religions practiced in Korea.

CHALLENGE ACTIVITY

Critical Thinking: Sequencing Write a paragraph describing three periods or events in Japan's history.

abstract	Buddhism	Kabuki	kana
kanji	kimchi	kimonos	Kyoto
Noh	samurai	Shinto	shoguns

DIRECTIONS On the line provided before each statement, write **T** if the statement is true and **F** if the statement is false. If the statement is false, write the correct term on the line after each sentence to make the sentence a true statement.

_____ 1. The imperial capital at Heian, now called <u>Shinto</u>, was a Japanese center of art, literature, and learning for many centuries.

_____

_____ 2. Many Japanese wear traditional robes called <u>kimonos</u> on special occasions, just as samurai did long ago.

_____

_____ 3. <u>Kanji</u> plays tell stories, but often teach lessons about duty and other abstract lessons as well.

_____

_____ 4. Most texts written in Japanese use a combination of <u>kimchi</u> and kana characters.

_____

_____ 5. In the past, most Koreans practiced <u>kami</u> and Confucianism.

_____

DIRECTIONS Write three words or phrases that describe the term.

6. shoguns _____

7. samurai _____

8. kimchi _____

Japan and the Koreas

MAIN IDEAS

1. Since World War II, Japan has developed a democratic government and one of the world's strongest economies.

2. A shortage of open space shapes daily life in Japan.

3. Crowding, competition, and pollution are among Japan's main issues and challenges.

Key Terms and Places

Diet Japan's elected legislature

Tokyo capital of Japan

work ethic belief that work in itself is worthwhile

trade surplus exists when a country exports more goods than it imports

tariff fee a country charges for exports or imports

Osaka Japan's second largest city

Section Summary
GOVERNMENT AND ECONOMY

Although Japan's emperor is the country's official leader, he has little power and his main role is to act as a symbol. In Japan today power rests with an elected prime minister and a legislature, called the **Diet**, that govern from the capital of **Tokyo**. Starting in the 1950s, Japan has become an economic powerhouse. Japanese companies use the latest manufacturing techniques to make goods such as cars, televisions, and DVD players. The government has helped Japanese companies succeed by controlling production and planning for the future. The strong **work ethic** of Japan's workers has also helped. They are very well-trained and loyal. Most goods made in Japan are for export to places like the United States. Japan exports much more than it imports, causing a huge **trade surplus**, which has added to Japan's wealth. The amount of imported goods is kept low through high **tariffs**, or fees, which are added to their cost.

> Circle the terms that explain who has power in Japan.

> What happens to most goods manufactured in Japan?
>
> _____
>
> _____

Japan's economic success is due to its manufacturing techniques, not natural resources. Japan must import most of the raw materials it uses to make goods, and much of its food.

DAILY LIFE

Japan is densely populated, and cities such as Tokyo are very crowded. Almost 36 million people live near Tokyo, making land scarce and expensive. Therefore, Tokyo has many tall buildings to get the most from scarce land. They also locate shops underground. Some hotels save space by housing guests in tiny sleeping chambers. Crowded commuter trains bring many people to work in Tokyo every day. For fun, people visit parks, museums, baseball stadiums, an indoor beach, and a ski resort filled with artificial snow.

> **About how many people live in the Tokyo area?**
> _____

> **Underline the places people in Tokyo visit for fun.**

Other cities include Osaka, Japan's second largest city, and Kyoto, the former capital. Japan's major cities are linked by efficient, high-speed trains, which can travel at more than 160 miles per hour.

Most people live in cities, but some live in villages or on farms. The average farm in Japan is only 2.5 acres, too small for most farmers to make a living, forcing many to look for jobs in the city.

ISSUES AND CHALLENGES

Despite its success, Japan is faced with several challenges. The lack of space due to dense population is a growing problem. In recent years, countries such as China and South Korea have taken business from Japanese companies. Pollution is another problem of growing concern.

> **Underline Japan's issues and challenges.**

CHALLENGE ACTIVITY

Critical Thinking: Evaluating Information Write a paragraph about which of Japan's issues and challenges you think is the most serious. Support your choice with details from the text.

Guided Reading Workbook

| Diet | Osaka | tariff |
| Tokyo | trade surplus | work ethic |

DIRECTIONS On the line provided before each statement, write **T** if the statement is true and **F** if the statement is false. If the statement is false, write the correct term on the line after each sentence to make the sentence a true statement.

_____ 1. Because Japan exports more than it imports, it has a large <u>tariff</u>.

_____

_____ 2. Japanese companies are successful partly because of their employees' loyalty and strong <u>work ethic</u>.

_____

_____ 3. <u>Osaka</u> is Japan's capital city.

_____

_____ 4. Located in western Honshu, <u>Tokyo</u> is Japan's second-largest city.

_____

_____ 5. In Japan, the <u>Diet</u> and the prime minister make the laws.

_____

DIRECTIONS Look up three vocabulary terms in the word bank in a dictionary. Write the dictionary definition of the word that is closest to the definition used in your textbook.

_____

_____

_____

_____

_____

Japan and the Koreas

Section 4

MAIN IDEAS

1. The people of South Korea today have freedom and economic opportunities.
2. The people of North Korea today have little freedom or economic opportunity.
3. Some people in both South and North Korea support the idea of Korean reunification.

Key Terms and Places

Seoul the capital of South Korea

demilitarized zone an empty buffer zone created to keep two countries from fighting

Pyongyang the capital of North Korea

Section Summary

SOUTH KOREA TODAY

The official name of South Korea is the Republic of Korea. It is headed by a president and assembly elected by the people. The United States helped create South Korea's government after World War II.

Like Japan, South Korea is densely populated. Its capital, **Seoul**, is a prosperous and modern city with some 40,000 people per square mile. Many people live near the western coastal plain, preferring it to the mountainous interior. In the cities, people live in small apartments and enjoy an extensive subway system. In the country, many South Koreans live on small farms, grow rice, beans, and cabbage, and follow traditional ways of life.

Although South Korea has a strong economy, in the past, the country's industry was controlled by only four families, and some members of these families were corrupt. New laws and greater foreign investment have brought reforms. South Korea is also challenged by its relationship with North Korea. Since the end of the Korean War in the 1950s, the countries have been separated by a **demilitarized** zone, a buffer zone patrolled by soldiers on both sides.

> What is the population density of Seoul?
> _____
> _____

> Underline the sentence that explains what a demilitarized zone is.

Guided Reading Workbook

NORTH KOREA TODAY

North Korea's official name, the Democratic People's Republic of Korea, is misleading. The country is a totalitarian state controlled by the Communist Party. From 1948 until 1994 it was led by the dictator Kim Il Sung. Since then his son Kim Jong Il has ruled. North Korea has a command economy in which the government makes all economic decisions. North Korea uses much of its rich mineral resources to make machinery and military supplies in out-of-date factories. Farms are run as cooperatives, but there is little good farmland and some food must be imported.

Although most North Koreans live in cities, such as the capital **Pyongyang**, their life is different from that of their neighbors to the south. Most people are poor and they are denied the rights of freedom of the press, speech, and religion.

Communist North Korea has been very isolated since the fall of the Soviet Union. Its economy has caused shortages and poverty. Also, many countries worry about North Korea's ability to make and use nuclear weapons. Negotiations are underway to resolve this issue.

> **What years did Kim Il Sung rule North Korea?**
> _____

> **Circle the rights that are denied to North Koreans.**

KOREAN REUNIFICATION

Both North and South Korean governments have expressed support for reunification. In 2000, leaders met for the first time since the Korean War. They agreed to build a road connecting the two Koreas. However, they don't agree on the type of government the reunified country would have. South Korea prefers democracy, and North Korea prefers communism.

> **Underline the sentence that explains the greatest obstacle to the reunification of Korea.**

CHALLENGE ACTIVITY

Critical Thinking: Comparing and Contrasting

Draw a Venn diagram to compare and contrast South Korea and North Korea.

cooperative	demilitarized zone	policy
Pyongyang	Seoul	

DIRECTIONS Read each sentence and choose the correct term from the word bank to replace the underlined phrase. Write the term in the space provided and then define the term in your own words.

1. North Korea is mostly farmed by <u>these</u> groups who work the

   land together. _____

   Your definition: _____

   _____

   _____

2. <u>This densely populated city</u> is the capital of South Korea. _____

   Your definition: _____

   _____

   _____

3. <u>This area</u> lies between North and South Korea to keep the two countries from

   fighting. _____

   Your definition: _____

   _____

   _____

4. Few people in <u>this crowded city</u> own private cars because the North Korean

   government allows only top Communist officials to own cars. _____

   Your definition: _____

   _____

   _____

Southeast Asia

MAIN IDEAS
1. Southeast Asia's physical features include peninsulas, islands, rivers, and many seas, straits, and gulfs.
2. The tropical climate of Southeast Asia supports a wide range of plants and animals.
3. Southeast Asia is rich in natural resources such as wood, rubber, and fossil fuels.

Key Terms and Places

Indochina Peninsula peninsula that makes up part of Mainland Southeast Asia

Malay Peninsula peninsula that makes up part of Mainland Southeast Asia

Malay Archipelago island group that makes up part of Island Southeast Asia

archipelago a large group of islands

New Guinea Earth's second largest island

Borneo Earth's third largest island

Mekong River most important river in Southeast Asia

Section Summary
PHYSICAL FEATURES

Two peninsulas and two large island groups make up the Southeast Asia region. Mainland Southeast Asia is made up of the **Indochina Peninsula** and the **Malay Peninsula**. Island Southeast Asia is made up of the many islands of the Philippines and the **Malay Archipelago**. A large group of islands is called an **archipelago**.

Mainland Southeast Asia has rugged mountains, low plateaus, and river floodplains. Island Southeast Asia has more than 20,000 islands, including **New Guinea**, the world's second largest island, and **Borneo**, the world's third largest island. Island Southeast Asia is part of the Ring of Fire, where earthquakes and volcanoes often occur.

For all of Southeast Asia, water is of great importance. The region's fertile river valleys and

> Underline the two peninsulas that make up Mainland Southeast Asia.

> Circle the two island groups that make up Island Southeast Asia.

deltas support farming and are home to many people. The **Mekong River** is the region's most important river.

CLIMATE, PLANTS, AND ANIMALS

Southeast Asia is in the tropics, the area on and around the equator. This region is generally warm all year round.

The climate on the mainland is mostly tropical savanna. Monsoon winds bring heavy rain in summer and drier air in winter there. Savannas—areas of tall grasses and some trees and shrubs—grow here.

The islands and the Malay Peninsula have a mostly humid tropical climate. Here, it's hot, muggy, and rainy all year. This climate supports tropical rain forests. These forests are home to many different plants and animals. Some animals are only found here, such as orangutans and Komodo dragons. Many plants and animals are endangered, however, due to the cutting down of the rain forest.

> **What kinds of plants grow in the region's tropical savanna climate?**
> _____
> _____

> **Why are the plants and animals of the rain forest endangered?**
> _____
> _____

NATURAL RESOURCES

Southeast Asia is rich in natural resources. Farming is very productive here thanks to the region's climate and rich soil. Rice is a major crop. Rubber tree plantations are found on Indonesia and Malaysia. The rain forests supply hardwoods and medicines. The region also has fisheries, minerals, and fossil fuels.

CHALLENGE ACTIVITY

Critical Thinking: Drawing Inferences Write an essay explaining the advantages and disadvantages of Southeast Asia's water resources for its people.

Guided Reading Workbook

archipelago	Borneo	Indochina Peninsula
Malay Archipelago	Malay Peninsula	Mekong River
New Guinea	tropics	

DIRECTIONS On the line provided before each statement, write **T** if the statement is true and **F** if the statement is false. If the statement is false, write the correct term on the line after each sentence that makes the sentence a true statement.

_____ 1. New Guinea and the Philippines are the world's second- and third-largest islands respectively.

_____

_____ 2. The most important river in Southeast Asia is the Mekong River.

_____

_____ 3. Mainland Southeast Asia is made up of two peninsulas—the Borneo Peninsula and the Indochina Peninsula.

_____

_____ 4. The two large island groups in Southeast Asia are the Philippines and the New Guinea Archipelago.

_____

_____ 5. Southeast Asia lies in the floodplains, the area on and around the equator.

_____

DIRECTIONS Choose four of the terms from the word bank. On a separate piece of paper, use these terms to write a summary of what you learned in the section.

Southeast Asia

MAIN IDEAS

1. Southeast Asia's early history includes empires, colonial rule, and independence.
2. The modern history of Southeast Asia involves struggles with war and communism.
3. Southeast Asia's culture reflects its Chinese, Indian, and European heritage.

Key Terms and Places

Timor small island that Portugal kept control of after Dutch traders drove them out of the rest of the region

domino theory idea that if one country fell to communism, other countries nearby would follow like falling dominoes

wats Buddhist temples that also serve as monasteries

Section Summary

EARLY HISTORY

The most advanced early civilization was the Khmer Empire in what is now Cambodia. The Khmer built a huge temple, Angkor Wat. This temple showed their advanced civilization and Hindu religion. Later, the Thai settled in the Khmer area. Buddhism began to replace Hinduism in the region.

In the 1500s European countries set up colonies. Led by Portugal, they came to colonize, trade, and spread their religion. Spain claimed the Philippines and spread Roman Catholicism there. Later, the Dutch drove Portugal out of much of the region. **Timor**, a small island, was all that stayed under Portugal's control.

In the 1800s the British and French set up colonies and spread Christianity. The United States came into the region in 1898, when it won the Philippines from Spain in the Spanish-American War. Colonial powers ruled all of the area, except for Siam (now Thailand) by the early 1900s.

> **Why did European countries come to this region?**
> _____
> _____

> **Circle the year the United States entered the region.**

After World War II, the United States granted the Philippines independence. Other people in the region started to fight for freedom, too. The French left in 1954 after a bloody war in Indochina. The independent countries of Cambodia, Laos, and Vietnam were formed from this area. By 1970, most of Southeast Asia was free from colonial rule.

> **Name the three countries formed out of Indochina.**
> _____
> _____
> _____

MODERN HISTORY

In Vietnam, the fighting against the French divided the country into North and South Vietnam. In South Vietnam, a civil war started. In the 1960s, the U.S. decided to send troops to South Vietnam based on the **domino theory**—the idea that if one country fell to communism, other nearby countries would fall, too. After years of fighting, North and South Vietnam became one Communist country.

> **Restate the domino theory in your own words.**
> _____
> _____
> _____

In Laos and Cambodia civil wars broke out, too. Fighting lasted in Cambodia until the mid-1990s, when the United Nations helped restore peace.

CULTURE

The many different ethnic groups in this region mean that many different languages are spoken here. The main religions are Buddhism, Christianity, Hinduism, and Islam. Many grand Buddhist temples, or **wats**, which also serve as monasteries, are found in Southeast Asia. Traditonal customs are still popular, especially in rural areas. Also, many people still wear traditional clothing such as sarongs, strips of cloth worn wrapped around the body.

CHALLENGE ACTIVITY

Critical Thinking: Understanding Cause and Effect Several European countries had colonies in Southeast Asia for hundreds of years. Make a two-column chart of cultural effects and political effects of colonization on the region.

criterion	domino theory	Dutch East Indies	Khmer
Siam	Timor	wats	

DIRECTIONS Read each sentence and fill in the blank with the word in the word pair that best completes the sentence.

1. The _____ had the most developed society in early Southeast Asian history. (Dutch East Indies/Khmer)

2. _____ is now called Thailand. (Timor/Siam)

3. The _____ are now called Indonesia. (Khmer/Dutch East Indies)

4. The region has many _____, or Buddhist temples. (criterion/wats)

5. The United States sent troops to South Vietnam to prevent the spread of

   communism based on the _____. (domino theory/criterion)

DIRECTIONS Choose four of the terms from the word bank. On a separate piece of paper, use these terms to write a poem or short story that relates to the section.

Section 3

MAIN IDEAS

1. The area today is largely rural and agricultural, but cities are growing rapidly.
2. Myanmar is poor with a harsh military government, while Thailand is a democracy with a strong economy.
3. The countries of Indochina are poor and struggling to rebuild after years of war.

Key Terms and Places

Yangon Myanmar's capital and major seaport

human rights rights that all people deserve, such as rights to equality and justice

Bangkok capital and largest city of Thailand

klongs canals

Phnom Penh Cambodia's capital and chief city

Hanoi capital of Vietnam, located in the north

Section Summary

THE AREA TODAY

Mainland Southeast Asia includes the countries of Myanmar, Thailand, Cambodia, Laos, and Vietnam. Because of war, harsh governments, and other problems, progress has slowed in much of this area. However, in an effort to promote political, economic, and social cooperation throughout the region, most of the countries of Southeast Asia have joined the Association of Southeast Asian Nations.

Most people in the region are farmers, living in small villages and growing rice. This area also has several big cities. They are growing rapidly as people move to them in search of work. Rapid growth, however, has led to crowding and pollution.

> Circle the countries of Mainland Southeast Asia.

> What are the effects of the rapid growth on the area's cities?
> _____
> _____

MYANMAR AND THAILAND

Although Myanmar, also called Burma, has many resources, it is a poor country. **Yangon**, or Rangoon, is its capital and a major port city. A harsh military government rules Myanmar. This government abuses **human rights**—rights that all people deserve. One woman, Aung San Suu Kyi, is working to reform Myanmar so people have more rights. Suu Kyi and others have been repeatedly arrested, however. Because of Myanmar's poor record on human rights, many countries will not trade with it. As a result, Myanmar's economy has suffered.

Thailand, once called Siam, has a strong economy. Its capital and largest city is **Bangkok**, a city famous for its **klongs**, or canals. Bangkok's klongs are used for trade and travel, and to drain floodwater. Thailand has a democratically elected government and rich resources. These factors have helped its economy grow.

Why won't some countries trade with Myanmar?
_____
_____

THE COUNTRIES OF INDOCHINA

After decades of war, the countries of Indochina—Cambodia, Laos, and Vietnam—are working hard to improve their economies.

The capital and chief city of Cambodia, **Phnom Penh**, is a center of trade. However, years of war have left the country with little industry. Although farming has improved, many landmines still remain buried.

Laos is the area's poorest country. It is landlocked, with few roads, no railroads, and little electricity. Most people are subsistence farmers, just growing enough food to support their families.

Vietnam's main cities include its capital in the north, **Hanoi**, and Ho Chi Minh City in the south. Although still a Communist country, Vietnam's government has been allowing more economic freedoms. Industry and services are growing, but most people still farm.

How has war affected the countries of Indochina?
_____
_____

CHALLENGE ACTIVITY

Critical Thinking: Summarizing Summarize the information about the countries of Mainland Southeast Asia, using a graphic organizer.

Guided Reading Workbook

Bangkok	Burma	Hanoi
Ho Chi Minh City	human rights	klongs
pedicabs	Phnom Penh	Yangon

DIRECTIONS Read each sentence and fill in the blank with the word
in the word pair that best completes the sentence.

1. _____ is the capital and largest city of Cambodia.
   (Phnom Penh/Yangon)

2. The capital of Myanmar is _____. (Phnom Penh/Yangon)

3. In Thailand _____ are used for transportation, trade, and draining
   floodwaters. (pedicabs/klongs)

4. Vietnam's largest city, _____, is in the south, in the Mekong delta.
   (Hanoi/Ho Chi Minh City)

5. _____ lies near the mouth of the Chao Phraya River.
   (Bangkok/Burma)

DIRECTIONS Write two words or phrases that describe the term.

6. Bangkok _____

7. Hanoi _____

8. human rights _____

9. klongs _____

10. Yangon _____

MAIN IDEAS

1. The area today has rich resources and growing cities but faces challenges.

2. Malaysia and its neighbors have strong economies but differ in many ways.

3. Indonesia is big and diverse with a growing economy, and East Timor is small and poor.

4. The Philippines has less ethnic diversity, and its economy is improving.

Key Terms and Places

kampong village or city district with traditional houses built on stilts; slums around cities

Jakarta capital of Indonesia

Kuala Lumpur Malaysia's capital and a cultural and economic center

free ports ports that place few if any taxes on goods

sultan supreme ruler of a Muslim country

Java Indonesia's main island

Manila capital of the Philippines

Section Summary

THE AREA TODAY

The countries of Southeast Asia are Malaysia, Singapore, Brunei, Indonesia, Timor-Leste, and the Philippines. Like the mainland countries, these island countries face challenges, too, such as ethnic conflicts, poverty, and environmental problems.

As on the mainland, many people in Island Southeast Asia live in rural areas. They fish or farm. Rice is the main crop. Also like the mainland, many people here are moving to cities for work. In some areas, people live in **kampongs**, places with traditional houses on stilts. The term *kampong* also refers to slums around **Jakarta**, Indonesia's capital, and around other cities of Island Southeast Asia.

> Underline the challenges facing Island Southeast Asia.

> Circle the main crop of this area.

MALAYSIA AND ITS NEIGHBORS

Malaysia has two parts. One is on the Malay Peninsula, where most Malaysians live. Its capital, **Kuala Lumpur**, is there as well. The other part is on Borneo. Malaysia is ethnically diverse, with a strong economy. It has a constitutional monarchy, with a prime minister and elected legislature.

Singapore is located on a tiny island that lies on a major shipping route. It is one of the world's busiest **free ports**—ports with few or no taxes on goods. Singapore is modern, wealthy, and clean. It has a strict government. Brunei is on the island of Borneo. A **sultan**, the supreme ruler of a Muslim country, governs this tiny country. As a result of oil and gas deposits, Brunei has grown wealthy.

> How does Singapore's location help its economy?
> _____
> _____

INDONESIA AND TIMOR-LESTE

Indonesia is the world's largest archipelago. It has the world's largest Muslim population and is ethnically diverse. **Java** is Indonesia's main island. More than half its people live there. Indonesia has rich resources, such as rubber, oil, gas, and timber, but religious and ethnic conflicts have led to violence.

Years of fighting for independence from Indonesia have left tiny Timor-Leste poor. Most people there farm.

> What are some of Indonesia's resources?
> _____
> _____

THE PHILIPPINES

The Philippines has less ethnic diversity than other island countries. **Manila** is its capital. Most Filipinos are poor farmers who do not own any land. The country is mainly Roman Catholic.

CHALLENGE ACTIVITY

Critical Thinking: Drawing Inferences Choose two island countries of Southeast Asia and write an essay that compares two of the following categories: geography, people, government, economy.

concrete	free ports	Jakarta
Java	kampongs	Kuala Lumpur
Manila	sultan	

DIRECTIONS On the line provided before each statement, write **T** if the statement is true and **F** if the statement is false. If the statement is false, write the correct term on the line after each sentence that makes the sentence a true statement.

_____ 1. Singapore is one of the world's busiest kampongs.

_____

_____ 2. Malaysia's capital, Java, is also a cultural and economic center.

_____

_____ 3. The Philippines has many islands, including Luzon, which is where the capital city of Manila is located.

_____

_____ 4. More than half of Indonesia's people live in its capital, Kuala Lampur.

_____

_____ 5. The supreme ruler of Brunei, a Muslim country, is a sultan.

_____

DIRECTIONS Choose four of the terms from the word bank. On a separate piece of paper, use these terms to write a summary of what you learned in the section.

MAIN IDEAS

1. The physical geography of Australia and New Zealand is diverse and unusual.
2. Native peoples and British settlers shaped the history of Australia and New Zealand.
3. Australia and New Zealand today are wealthy and culturally diverse countries.

Key Terms and Places

Great Barrier Reef largest coral reef in the world, off Australia's northeastern coast

coral reef a collection of rocky material found in shallow, tropical waters

Aborigines first humans to live in Australia

Maori New Zealand's first settlers

Outback Australia's interior

Section Summary

PHYSICAL GEOGRAPHY

Australia has wide, flat stretches of dry land. Low mountains, valleys, and a major river system make up the eastern part of the country. The **Great Barrier Reef**, the world's largest **coral reef**, is located off of Australia's northeastern coast.

New Zealand is made up of North Island and South Island. A large mountain range called the Southern Alps is a key feature of South Island. New Zealand also has green hills, volcanoes, hot springs, dense forests, deep lakes, and fertile plains.

Most of Australia has warm, dry desert and steppe climates. The coastal areas are milder and wetter. New Zealand has a marine climate with plenty of rainfall and mild temperatures. Native animals include Australia's kangaroo and koala and New Zealand's kiwi, a flightless bird. Australia has many valuable mineral resources, and farms raise wheat, cotton, and sheep despite the poor soil. New

> Underline the two islands that make up New Zealand.

> Circle the region's native animals.

Zealand has few mineral resources, but plenty of rich soil.

HISTORY

Aborigines, the first humans in Australia, came from Southeast Asia more than 40,000 years ago. Early Aborigines were nomads who gathered plants, hunted animals, and fished. The **Maori**, New Zealand's first settlers, came from other Pacific islands about 1,200 years ago. They hunted, fished, and farmed. Captain James Cook visited New Zealand in 1769. British settlers began arriving in Australia and New Zealand in the late 1700s and early 1800s. Australia and New Zealand gained independence in the early 1900s. Both countries are in the British Commonwealth and close allies of the United Kingdom.

> Who were the first humans to settle in Australia and New Zealand?
>
> _____
>
> _____

AUSTRALIA AND NEW ZEALAND TODAY

Most people in both countries are of British ancestry. Sydney and Melbourne are Australia's two largest cities. Auckland is New Zealand's largest city. Both countries produce wool, meat, and dairy products. Mining is important throughout the **Outback**. Other industries include steel, heavy machines, and computers. Manufacturing, banking, and tourism are important in New Zealand.

Today, Australia and New Zealand face the challenge of improving the political and economic status of their native populations.

> Circle the name of New Zealand's largest city.

CHALLENGE ACTIVITY

Critical Thinking: Making Judgments Why do you think the Aboriginal and Maori populations of Australia and New Zealand declined after British settlers arrived? Explain your answer in a short paragraph.

Aborigines	Aukland	coral reef	fjord
Great Barrier Reef	kiwi	koala	Maori
Melbourne	Outback	Sydney	Uluru

DIRECTIONS Read each sentence and fill in the blank with the word
in the word pair that best completes the sentence.

1. The _____ were the first people to inhabit Australia.
   (Aborigines/Maori)

2. Melbourne and _____ are two large cities in Australia.
   (Aukland/Sydney)

3. A _____ is a collection of rocky materials found in shallow,
   tropic waters. (coral reef/fjord)

4. The _____ is a flightless bird unique to New Zealand.
   (koala/kiwi)

5. The _____ is a well-known rock formation in Australia.
   (Outback/Uluru)

DIRECTIONS Choose five of the terms from the word bank. Use these
terms to write a summary of what you learned in this section.

_____

_____

_____

_____

_____

_____

_____

_____

The Pacific World

MAIN IDEAS

1. Unique physical features, tropical climates, and limited resources shape the physical geography of the Pacific Islands.
2. Native customs and contact with the western world have influenced the history and culture of the Pacific Islands.
3. Pacific Islanders today are working to improve their economies and protect the environment.

Key Terms and Places

Micronesia region of Pacific Islands located east of the Philippines

Melanesia region of Pacific Islands stretching from New Guinea to Fiji

Polynesia largest region of Pacific Islands, east of Melanesia

atoll small, ring-shaped coral island surrounding a lagoons

territory an area that is under the control of another government

Section Summary

PHYSICAL GEOGRAPHY

There are three regions of islands in the Pacific. **Micronesia**, consisting of about 2,000 small islands, is east of the Philippines. **Melanesia**, the most heavily populated region, stretches from New Guinea to Fiji. **Polynesia**, the largest region, is located east of Melanesia.

There are two kinds of islands in the Pacific: high islands and low islands. High islands are formed from volcanoes or continental rock. They tend to be mountainous and rocky. They have dense forests, rich soil, and many mineral resources. Low islands are much smaller; they have thin soil, little vegetation, few resources, and low elevations. Many low islands are **atolls**, small ring-shaped coral islands surrounding lagoons.

Most high and low islands have a humid tropical climate. Temperatures are warm and rain falls all year.

> **What three regions make up the Pacific Islands?**
> _____
> _____
> _____

> **Circle the type of climate that most high and low islands have.**

HISTORY AND CULTURE

People began settling the Pacific more than 40,000 years ago. They arrived in Melanesia first. Polynesia was the last region to be settled. Europeans first encountered the Pacific Islands in the 1500s. John Cook, a captain in the British Navy visited all the main regions in the 1700s. By the late 1800s, Britain, Spain, France, and other European nations gained control of most of the islands. When the United States defeated Spain in the Spanish-American War, it took Guam as a **territory**, which is an area that is under the authority of another government. After World War I, Japan gained control of many islands. After World War II, the United Nations placed some islands under the control of the United States and its Allies.

Nearly 8 million people of many cultures and ethnic groups live in the Pacific Islands. Most are descended from the original settlers. Some are ethnic Europeans and Asians. Most islanders are now Christian. Many, however, continue to practice traditional customs ranging from building constructions to art styles and various ceremonies.

> Circle the name of the Pacific Island region that was first to be settled.

> What country took Guam as a territory after the Spanish-American war?
> _____

> About how many people live in the Pacific Islands?
> _____

THE PACIFIC ISLANDS TODAY

The Pacific Islands face important challenges today. They are trying to build stronger economies through tourism, agriculture, and fishing. Some countries, including Papua New Guinea, export gold, copper, and oil. The islands also must cope with the potentially damaging effects of past nuclear testing in the area and global warming.

> Underline three ways the Pacific Islands are trying to improve their economies.

CHALLENGE ACTIVITY

Critical Thinking: Drawing Conclusions Which island countries probably have stronger economies: those occupying high islands or those occupying low islands? Support your answer using details from the summary.

atoll	Melanesia	Micronesia
Polynesia	territory	

DIRECTIONS On the line provided before each statement, write **T** if a statement is true and **F** if a statement is false. If the statement is false, write the correct term on the line after each sentence that makes the sentence a true statement.

_____ 1. Melanesia, which means "tiny islands," is a group of 2,000 small islands in the Pacific.

_____

_____ 2. Tonga and Hawaii are part of Polynesia.

_____

_____ 3. Micronesia is the most heavily populated of the three Pacific island groups.

_____

DIRECTIONS Read each sentence and choose the correct term from the word bank to replace the underlined phrase. Write the term in the space provided and then define the term in your own words.

4. Wake Island, located west of the Hawaiian islands is an unusual physical feature.

_____

Your definition: _____

_____

5. When the United States defeated Spain in the Spanish-American War, Guam became a U.S. political unit. _____

Your definition: _____

_____

Guided Reading Workbook

MAIN IDEAS
1. Freezing temperatures, ice, and snow dominate Antarctica's physical geography.
2. Explorations in the 1800s and 1900s led to Antarctica's use for scientific research.
3. Research and protecting the environment are key issues in Antarctica today.

Key Terms and Places

ice shelf ledge of ice that extends over the water

icebergs floating masses of ice that have broken off a glacier

Antarctic Peninsula peninsula that extends north of the Antarctic Circle

polar desert a high-latitude region that receives very little precipitation

ozone layer layer of Earth's atmosphere that protects living things from the harmful effects of the sun's ultraviolet rays

Section Summary

PHYSICAL GEOGRAPHY

Ice covers more than 98 percent of Antarctica. Ice flows slowly toward the coasts of Antarctica. At the coast it forms a ledge over the water called an **ice shelf**. Antarctica's largest ice shelf is the Ross Ice Shelf. Floating masses of ice that break off from ice shelves are called **icebergs**. The **Antarctic Peninsula** is on the western side of the continent.

Antarctica has a freezing ice cap climate. It is a **polar desert**, a high-latitude region that receives little precipitation. It is bitterly cold during the dark winter. Summer temperatures reach near freezing.

Tundra plant life grows in ice-free areas. Insects are the only animals on the land. Penguins, seals, and whales live in the nearby waters. Antarctica has many mineral resources.

> How is an iceberg related to an ice shelf?
> _____
> _____
> _____

EARLY EXPLORATIONS

Antarctica was first sighted in 1775. European explorations investigated Antarctica throughout the

1800s. A team of Norwegian explorers became the first people to reach the South Pole in 1911.

Several countries have claimed parts of Antarctica. In 1959, several countries signed the Antarctic Treaty, which bans military activity on the continent and sets it aside for scientific research.

What are the terms of the Antarctic Treaty of 1959?
_____
_____
_____

ANTARCTICA TODAY

Antarctica is the only continent with no permanent human population. Scientists use Antarctica to conduct research and study the environment. Several countries, including the United States, have bases there.

Antarctic research includes studies of plant and animal life, analyzing weather conditions and patterns, and examining issues affecting Earth's environment. Scientists are concerned about the thinning of the **ozone layer**—the layer of Earth's atmosphere that protects living things from the harmful effects of the sun's ultraviolet rays.

Tourism, oil spills, and mining are real and potential threats to Antarctica's environment. An agreement reached in 1991 bans mining and drilling and limits tourism.

Underline three activities that threaten Antarctica's environment.

CHALLENGE ACTIVITY

Critical Thinking: Making Judgments What do you think is the greatest threat to Antarctica's environment? Why? Explain your answer.

| Antarctic Peninsula | Antarctic Treaty | glacier | ice shelf |
| icebergs | motive | ozone layer | polar desert |

DIRECTIONS Answer each question by writing a sentence that contains at least one word from the word bank.

1. Describe the physical geography of Antarctica.

_____

_____

_____

2. What kinds of things are scientists studying in Antarctica?

_____

_____

DIRECTIONS Write three words or phrases that describe the term.

3. icebergs _____

_____

4. polar desert _____

_____

5. Antarctic Peninsula _____

_____

6. ozone layer _____

_____

Early History of Europe

MAIN IDEAS
1. Early Greek culture saw the rise of the city-state and the creation of colonies.
2. The golden age of Greece saw advances in government, art, and philosophy.
3. Alexander the Great formed a huge empire and spread Greek culture into new areas.

Key Terms and Places

city-states political units made up of a city and all the surrounding lands

golden age a period in a society's history marked by great achievements

Athens a city-state in eastern Greece

Sparta a rival city-state to Athens

Hellenistic Greek-like

Section Summary

EARLY GREEK CULTURE

To protect against invaders, early Greeks joined together. Over time, they developed into **city-states**, political units made up of a city and its surrounding lands. As populations grew, city-states formed colonies, or new cities—and Greek culture spread.

> **What was an effect of city-states forming new colonies?**
> _____
> _____

THE GOLDEN AGE OF GREECE

Greece is famous for its many contributions to world culture, especially during a period of great achievements called the **golden age**. Greece's golden age took place between 400 and 300 BC, after **Athens** and other city-states defeated a powerful Persian army around 500 BC. The defeat of the Persians increased the confidence of the Greeks, and they began to make many advances.

Athens became the cultural center of Greece during the golden age. Leaders such as Pericles supported the arts and other great works. But these leaders did not rule Athens, which became the world's first democracy. Instead, power was in the

> **Briefly define "golden age."**
> _____
> _____

> **How did the defeat of the Persians contribute to the rise of Greece's golden age?**
> _____
> _____
> _____
> _____

hands of the people, who voted in an assembly, which made the laws.

Many accomplishments in art, architecture, literature, philosophy, and science took place during Greece's golden age. Drama, or plays, became an important part of Greek literature. Greek philosophers such as Socrates, Plato, and Aristotle continue to shape how we think today.

> **Underline the areas of accomplishment during the golden age.**

Greece's golden age would not last. It came to an end when Athens and its rival **Sparta** went to war. Sparta had a strong army and was jealous of Athens's influence in Greece. The war raged for years, with other city-states joining in. Sparta finally won, but Greece overall had been weakened. It lay open to a foreign conqueror to take over.

THE EMPIRE OF ALEXANDER

That conqueror was Alexander the Great, who took over Greece in the 330s BC. He conquered not only Greece, but also huge areas of the rest of the world from Greece to India, and most of central Asia. He dreamed of conquering more territory, but his tired and homesick troops refused to continue. Alexander died on his return home, at the age of 33.

> **Do you think Alexander could have taken over Greece if Sparta and Athens had not gone to war? Why or why not?**
>
> _____
>
> _____
>
> _____

Alexander admired Greek culture and wanted it to spread throughout his empire. He urged Greek people to move to new cities. Many Greeks did move. Greek culture then blended with other cultures. These blended cultures are referred to as **Hellenistic**, or Greek-like.

> **What was Alexander's attitude toward Greek culture?**
>
> _____
>
> _____

CHALLENGE ACTIVITY
Critical Thinking: Analyzing Information

Imagine that you are a newspaper reporter from a Greek city-state, and your assignment is to write about Athens. Write a brief article describing what you have seen on your visit. In your article include information about the many accomplishments during Greece's golden age.

city-states	golden age	Athens	empire
Sparta	Hellenistic	colonies	

DIRECTIONS On the line provided before each statement, write **T** if the statement is true and **F** if the statement is false. If the statement is false, write the correct term from the word bank on the line after each sentence that makes the sentence a true statement.

_____ 1. <u>City-states</u> are political units made up of a city and all the surrounding lands.

_____

_____ 2. A period in a society's history marked by great achievements is called a/an <u>empire</u>.

_____

_____ 3. <u>Sparta</u> was a city-state in eastern Greece that led the fight against the invading Persians around 500 BC.

_____

_____ 4. A Greek-like blended culture is also called <u>Sparta</u>.

_____

_____ 5. Because of overcrowding, Greek city-states set up <u>colonies</u>, or new cities, around the Mediterranean and Black Seas.

_____

Guided Reading Workbook

MAIN IDEAS
1. The Roman Republic was governed by elected leaders.
2. The Roman Empire was a time of great achievements.
3. The spread of Christianity began during the empire.
4. Various factors helped bring about the decline of Rome.

Key Terms and Places

Rome a city in Italy

republic a type of government in which people elect leaders to make laws for them

Senate a council of rich and powerful Romans who helped run the city

citizens people who could take part in the Roman government

Carthage a city in North Africa

empire a land that includes many different peoples and lands under one rule

aqueducts channels used to carry water over long distances

Section Summary
THE ROMAN REPUBLIC

Rome began as a small city in Italy. It was ruled by a series of kings, some of whom were cruel rulers. Over time the Romans formed a **republic**, in which elected leaders made all government decisions. The leaders worked with the **Senate**, a group of powerful men. **Citizens** voted and ran for office.

Before long, Rome began to expand its territory. It took over much of the Mediterranean world, including the city of **Carthage** in North Africa. A general named Julius Caesar conquered many new lands. Afraid of his power, a group of Senators killed him in 44 BC.

What is a republic?
_____
_____

THE ROMAN EMPIRE

Caesar's adopted nephew Octavian became Rome's first emperor, ruling a huge **empire**. This far-flung land contained many different people. Octavian was also called Augustus, or "honored one," because of

Circle the name of Rome's first emperor.

his many accomplishments. Augustus conquered many new lands. He built monuments and roads.

The Romans had a long period of peace and achievement called the Pax Romana. Their many building projects included **aqueducts**—channels used to carry water over long distances. The Romans also wrote literature and built legal systems that have had a worldwide influence. The founders of the United States used the Roman government as a model.

> In what way does the Roman government affect the United States today?
> _____
> _____
> _____

THE SPREAD OF CHRISTIANITY

Christianity first appeared in the Roman Empire. The religion was based on the teachings of Jesus of Nazareth. Jesus's followers preached throughout the Roman world. For many years, Rome tried unsuccessfully to stop the spread of Christianity. Then in the 300s an emperor named Constantine became a Christian. Christianity soon became Rome's official religion. By the end of the 300s it had become a powerful force in the Roman world.

> Underline the name of the Roman emperor who converted to Christianity.

THE DECLINE OF ROME

Rome's decline had several causes. A number of bad emperors ignored their duties and the needs of the Roman people. Military leaders tried to take over, but many of them were poor rulers as well.

The emperor Constantine created a new capital in a central location. But this change was not enough. The empire, weakened by its internal problems, was vulnerable to invaders the Romans called barbarians. In 476 they attacked Rome and removed its emperor. The Roman Empire was no more.

> Why is the year 476 considered the end of the Roman Empire?
> _____

CHALLENGE ACTIVITY
Critical Thinking: Analyzing Information

Imagine that you are a Roman citizen. Write a letter to either Constantine or Augustus, asking him to take an important action to improve the Roman Empire. Include reasons why this action is needed, based on details in the section.

aqueducts	Carthage	citizens	Colosseum
empire	facilitate	Pax Romana	republic
Rome	Senate		

DIRECTIONS Read each sentence and fill in the blank with the word in the word pair that best completes the sentence.

1. The city of _____ is thought to have been set up in 753 BC by a group called the Latins. (Rome/Carthage)

2. The _____ was made up of rich and powerful Romans who helped run the city. (Pax Romana/Senate)

3. _____ were people who could take part in Rome's government. (Citizens/Aqueducts)

4. A _____ is a form of government that has the people vote for leaders to make the laws. (Senate/republic)

5. Under Octavian's leadership, Rome became a/an _____, a land that included many different peoples under one rule. (republic/empire)

6. In addition to roads and bridges, Roman engineers built

_____, channels used to carry water over long

distances. (aqueducts/Pax Romana)

7. The long period of peace and achievement that Rome experienced is called the

_____. (Pax Romana/Colosseum)

DIRECTIONS Choose five of the words from the word bank. On a separate sheet of paper, use these words to write a poem or short story that relates to the section.

MAIN IDEAS
1. The Christian church influenced nearly every aspect of society in the Middle Ages.
2. Complicated political and economic systems governed life in the Middle Ages.
3. The period after 1000 was a time of great changes in medieval society.

Key Terms and Places

Middle Ages a period of history between ancient and modern times that lasted from about 500 until about 1500

pope the head of the Christian church

Crusade a religious war

Holy Land the region in which Jesus had lived

Gothic architecture a style known for its high pointed ceilings, tall towers, and stained glass windows

feudal system a system of exchanging land for military service

manor a large estate owned by a noble or a knight

nation-state a country united under a single strong government

Section Summary

THE CHRISTIAN CHURCH AND SOCIETY

Europe broke into many small kingdoms. The period from about 500 until about 1500 is called the **Middle Ages**. During this time, no one leader could unify Europe. As a result, the Christian church gained influence, and church leaders became powerful.

The **pope** was the head of the Christian church. One pope started a religious war called a **Crusade**. He wanted Europeans to take over the **Holy Land**, where Jesus had lived. It was then ruled by Muslims. The Crusaders failed. However, they brought back new foods, goods, and ideas. Trade between Europe and Asia increased.

The church had a major influence on art and architecture. Many churches built during this period are examples of **Gothic architecture**. Most people's lives centered around their local church.

> Circle the dates when the Middle Ages took place.

> Who was the leader of the Christian church?
> _____

LIFE IN THE MIDDLE AGES

Religion was not the only influence on people's lives. Two other major influences were the **feudal system** and the **manor** system.

The feudal system was mainly a relationship between nobles and knights. The nobles gave land to knights. In turn, the knights promised to help defend their lands and the king.

The manor system was a relationship between manor, or large estate, owners and workers. The owners provided workers with a place to live and a piece of land where they could grow their own food. In exchange, most of the crops went to the owners.

> **Who participated in the feudal system? In the manor system?**
>
> _____
>
> _____

CHANGES IN MEDIEVAL SOCIETY

France's William the Conqueror invaded England in 1066. He became king, and built England's first strong government. In 1215, however, King John of England lost some of his power. A group of nobles insisted that the king should not be above the law. The nobles drew up a document called Magna Carta, which limited the monarch's power.

> **How did Magna Carta affect King John?**
>
> _____

In 1347 a disease called the Black Death swept through Europe. It killed about a third of the population. The plague caused a labor shortage. As a result, people could demand higher wages.

In 1348 the Hundred Years' War broke out between England and France. The French won, and kings began working to end the feudal system and gain more power. France became a **nation-state**, a country united under a single government. Other nation-states arose around Europe, and the Middle Ages came to an end.

> **What is one negative and one positive outcome of the Black Death?**
>
> _____
>
> _____

CHALLENGE ACTIVITY

Critical Thinking: Making Generalizations Draw up a document like Magna Carta that includes your ideas of the basic rights for common people as well as limits on the power of rulers.

Crusade	feudal system	Gothic architecture	Holy Land
Magna Carta	manor	Middle Ages	peasant
pope	serf	nation-state	

DIRECTIONS Read each sentence and fill in the blank with the word in the word pair that best completes the sentence.

1. The _____ is the time period between ancient and modern times, which lasted from about 500 to 1500. (Middle Ages/Magna Carta)

2. The head of the Christian church in the Middle Ages was called the _____. (manor/pope)

3. A religious war is called a _____. (Crusade/Holy Land)

4. The pope wanted Europeans to take over the _____, the region where Jesus had lived. (Crusade/Holy Land)

5. Many churches built in the Middle Ages are examples of _____, a style known for its high pointed ceilings, tall towers, and stained glass windows. (feudal system/Gothic architecture)

6. The system of trading land for military service was called the _____. (feudal system/serf)

7. A _____ was a large estate owned by a noble or knight. (peasant/manor)

8. A _____ was a country that was united under a single strong government. (Holy Land/nation-state)

DIRECTIONS What would your life be like if you lived in the Middle Ages? Write a letter to a friend and describe what it's like to live in the Middle Ages using five of the words in the word bank.

History of Early Modern Europe

MAIN IDEAS

1. The Renaissance was a period of new learning, new ideas, and new advances in art, literature, and science.
2. The Reformation changed the religious map of Europe.

Key Terms and Places

Renaissance period of creativity and new ideas that swept Europe from about 1350 through the 1500s

Florence Italian city that became rich through trade during and after the Crusades

Venice Italian city that became rich through trade during and after the Crusades

humanism new way of thinking and learning that emphasized the abilities and accomplishments of human beings

Reformation religious reform movement that began with complaints about problems within the Catholic Church

Protestants Christians who split from the Catholic Church over religious issues

Catholic Reformation series of reforms launched by Catholic Church officials

Section Summary

THE RENAISSANCE

The **Renaissance** started in Italy in such cities as **Florence** and **Venice**. These cities became rich through trade. As goods from Asia moved through these cities, Italians became curious about the larger world. At this same time, scholars from other parts of the world came to Italy, bringing books written by ancient Greeks and Romans. Interest in Greece and Rome grew. People studied subjects once taught in Greek and Roman schools such as history, poetry, and grammar. These subjects are known as the humanities. Increased study of the humanities led to **humanism**—an idea that people are capable of great achievements.

Renaissance artists developed new painting techniques such as perspective, which made their art

> Circle the name of the country where the Renaissance began.

> List three developments that led to the Renaissance.
>
> _____
> _____
> _____
> _____

look more realistic. The artists Michelangelo and Leonardo da Vinci showed their belief in humanism by making the people in their paintings look like unique individuals. William Shakespeare's plays looked closely at human nature and behavior.

Reading about Greek and Roman scientific advances inspired Europeans to study math, astronomy, and other sciences. Some used their new knowledge to create new inventions. Johannes Gutenberg's invention, the movable-type printing press, printed books quickly and cheaply. It spread Renaissance ideas to all parts of Europe.

> Circle the names of three Renaissance artists or writers.

> What effect did Gutenberg's printing press have on the Renaissance?
> _____
> _____

THE REFORMATION

The **Reformation**, a religious reform movement, began in Germany. Many people there felt priests and other Catholic Church officials cared more about power than their religious duties. Martin Luther, a German monk, was one of the first people to protest against the church. In 1517 he nailed a list of complaints on a church door in Wittenberg. Angry church officials expelled him from the church. Luther's followers became the first **Protestants**, splitting off from the Catholic Church. Other reformers created their own churches. By 1600 many Europeans had become Protestants.

In response, Catholic Church leaders began a series of reforms, called the **Catholic Reformation**. They asked churches to focus more on religious matters. They tried to make church teachings easier to understand. Priests and teachers went to Asia, Africa, and other lands to spread Catholic teachings. After the Reformation, religious wars broke out in Europe between Catholics and Protestants. These religious wars led to many changes in Europe.

> Underline the sentence that tells how Luther made his protest.

CHALLENGE ACTIVITY

Critical Thinking: Analyzing What events prompted Catholic leaders to begin the Catholic Reformation?

Catholic Reformation	Florence	humanism
perspective	Protestants	Reformation
Renaissance	Venice	Wittenberg

DIRECTIONS On the line provided before each statement, write **T** if a statement is true and **F** if a statement is false. If the statement is false, write the term from the word bank that would make the statement correct on the line after each sentence.

_____ 1. Lasting from about 1350 to 1500, the Reformation was a period of great creativity in Europe.

_____

_____ 2. People who followed Martin Luther in forming their own religion became the first Protestants.

_____

_____ 3. The technique of humanism enabled artists to show a realistic three-dimensional scene on a flat surface.

_____

_____ 4. Italian cities such as Florence and Wittenberg became rich through trade.

_____

_____ 5. Catholic Reformation emphasized the abilities and accomplishments of human beings.

_____

DIRECTIONS Choose five of the vocabulary words from the word bank. On a separate sheet of paper, use these words to write a story or poem that relates to the section.

Section 2

MAIN IDEAS

1. During the Scientific Revolution, discoveries and inventions expanded knowledge and changed life in Europe.

2. In the 1400s and 1500s, Europeans led voyages of discovery and exploration.

3. As Europeans discovered new lands, they created colonies and new empires all over the world.

Key Terms and Places

Scientific Revolution series of events that led to the birth of modern science

New World a term used by Europeans to describe the Americas after the voyages of Christopher Columbus

circumnavigate travel all the way around Earth

Section Summary

THE SCIENTIFIC REVOLUTION

Before the 1500s, most educated people depended on authorities such as ancient Greek writers and church officials for information. During the **Scientific Revolution**, people began to believe that what they observed was more important than what they were told. They developed logical explanations for how the world worked, based on what they observed. This focus on observation marked the start of modern science.

Many Europeans feared the spread of scientific ideas. Church officials opposed many ideas because they went against church teachings. For example, the church taught that the sun circled the Earth. From studying the skies, scientists now thought that the Earth circled the sun. In 1632 church officials arrested Italian scientist Galileo for publishing a book that supported this view. However, science still developed rapidly.

New discoveries occurred in astronomy, biology, physics, and other fields. New inventions included the telescope, microscope, and thermometer. Isaac

> Underline the sentence that explains how educated people learned about the world before the Scientific Revolution.

> Why did Church officials fear the spread of many scientific ideas?
>
> _____
>
> _____

Guided Reading Workbook

Newton made one of the most important discoveries—explaining how gravity works.

THE VOYAGES OF DISCOVERY

With improved devices such as the compass and astrolabe, and better ships, Europeans made longer, safer sea voyages. They found new routes to distant places. Europeans had many reasons for exploring. Some were curious about the world; some wanted riches, fame, adventure; and others hoped to spread Christianity. Prince Henry of Portugal sought new trade routes to Asia. After many other voyages, Portuguese explorer Vasco da Gama succeeded in finding a water route to Asia.

The voyages of Christopher Columbus, paid for by Queen Isabella of Spain, were the most significant. His explorations of the **New World** led other European countries to explore this new land, too. The crew of Ferdinand Magellan were the first people to **circumnavigate**, or sail completely around, the world. Others followed. Voyages of discovery added greatly to European wealth—and people's knowledge of the world.

> Circle the three advances that helped make the voyages of discovery possible.

> List three explorers and where they explored.
> _____
> _____
> _____

NEW EMPIRES

The Spanish were the first Europeans to build colonies in the Americas. They used metal weapons unknown to native peoples to conquer and destroy the Aztec and Inca Empires. Deadly diseases carried by the Spanish also helped them conquer new lands. The gold the Spanish found in the Americas made Spain the richest country in Europe. Britain, France, and other European nations also founded colonies in the Americas. In many places they forced out Native Americans. European nations grew rich from trade in wood, fur, and other natural resources.

> What effect did European explorers and colonists have on Native Americans?
> _____
> _____

CHALLENGE ACTIVITY

Critical Thinking: Drawing Conclusions What were three results of European explorations?

DIRECTIONS Read each sentence and fill in the blank with the word
in the word pair that best completes the sentence

1. In 1632 _____ was arrested for writing that Earth orbited the
   sun. (Sir Isaac Newton/Galileo)

2. The _____ led to the birth of modern science.
   (Scientific Revolution/astrolabe)

3. Without the support of _____, the voyage of Columbus might
   not have taken place. (Queen Isabella/Sir Isaac Newton)

4. In 1498 _____ sailed around the southern tip of Africa and on
   to India. (Chrisopher Columbus/Vasco da Gama)

5. _____ made important observations about the force of gravity.
   (Sir Isaac Newton/Galileo)

DIRECTIONS Write a word or phrase that has the same meaning as the
term given.

6. New World _____

7. circumnavigate _____

8. astrolabe _____

9. logical _____

10. gravity _____

History of Early Modern Europe

MAIN IDEAS
1. During the Enlightenment, new ideas about government took hold in Europe.
2. The 1600s and 1700s were an Age of Revolution in Europe.
3. Napoleon Bonaparte conquered much of Europe after the French Revolution.

Key Terms

Enlightenment period in the 1600s and 1700s when the use of reason shaped European ideas about society and politics, also known as the Age of Reason

English Bill of Rights 1689 document listing rights of Parliament and the English people

Declaration of Independence document signed in 1776 that declared the American colonies' independence from Britain

Declaration of the Rights of Man and of the Citizen French constitution that guaranteed some rights of French citizens and made taxes fairer

Reign of Terror period of great violence during the French Revolution

Section Summary

THE ENLIGHTENMENT

During the **Enlightenment** many people questioned common ideas about politics and government. However, most of Europe was ruled by kings and queens, also called monarchs. Most monarchs believed God gave them the right to rule as they chose. This belief was called rule by divine right.

Enlightenment thinkers disagreed. John Locke saw government as a contract, or binding legal agreement, between a ruler and the people. A ruler's job was to protect people's rights. If a ruler did not do this, people had the right to change rulers. Jean-Jacques Rousseau also felt government's purpose was to protect people's freedoms. Such ideas inspired revolutions and political change.

> Underline the sentence that explains what rule by divine right is.

> Circle the names of two Enlightenment thinkers who had new ideas about the rights of citizens and the role of government.

Guided Reading Workbook

THE AGE OF REVOLUTION

In the 1600s, England's rulers fought with Parliament for power. As a result, in 1689 Parliament passed the **English Bill of Rights** and made the king agree to honor the Magna Carta. These steps limited the monarch's power and gave more rights to Parliament and the English people.

Enlightenment ideas spread to Britain's North American colonies. There, colonial leaders claimed Britain had denied their rights—and started the American Revolution. In July of 1776 Americans signed the **Declaration of Independence**, declaring the American colonies' independence.

The American victory inspired the French people to fight for their rights. Members of the Third Estate, France's largest and poorest social class, demanded a part in government. They formed the National Assembly and demanded that the king limit his powers. When he refused, the French Revolution began. The National Assembly then issued the **Declaration of the Rights of Man and of the Citizen**, a new constitution for France.

France's revolutionary leaders ended the monarchy, but soon after the **Reign of Terror** began. It was a very violent time. After it ended, people longed for a strong leader to restore order.

> **How did the English Bill of Rights and the Magna Carta limit the monarch's power?**
>
> _____
>
> _____
>
> _____

> **Circle the names of two documents in addition to the English Bill of Rights that changed how rulers governed and that gave citizens more rights.**

NAPOLEON BONAPARTE

In 1799 Napoleon Bonaparte took control of France. He conquered most of Europe and built a French empire. Napoleon created a fair legal system, called the Napoleonic Code, but he was a harsh ruler. Napoleon's armies were defeated in 1814 and 1815. Soon after, European leaders met to decide how to divide up the former French empire.

> **List two of Napoleon's achievements.**
>
> _____
>
> _____

CHALLENGE ACTIVITY

Critical Thinking: Drawing Conclusions In the Age of Revolution, were ideas or armies more important? Give support for your answer.

Bastille	Declaration of Independence
English Bill of Rights	Enlightenment
Napoleon Bonaparte	Reign of Terror
Declaration of the Rights of Man and of the Citizen	

DIRECTIONS Answer each question by writing a sentence that contains at least one term from the word bank.

1. How did England's Parliament limit the monarchy's power?

_____

_____

2. What peaceful steps did France take to guarantee its people more freedoms?

_____

_____

_____

3. What effect did Enlightenment ideas have on the British colonies in North America?

_____

_____

_____

4. What period came right after the French Revolution? Why was it called this?

_____

_____

_____

5. Why did European leaders have to decide how to divide up the French Empire?

_____

_____

_____

MAIN IDEAS
1. Britain's large labor force, raw materials, and money to invest led to the start of the Industrial Revolution.
2. Industrial growth began in Great Britain and then spread to other parts of Europe.
3. The Industrial Revolution led to both positive and negative changes in society.

Key Terms

Industrial Revolution period of rapid growth in machine-made goods

textiles cloth products

capitalism an economic system in which individuals own most businesses and resources, and people invest money in hopes of making a profit

suffragettes women who campaigned for the right to vote

Section Summary

START OF THE INDUSTRIAL REVOLUTION

Changes in agriculture helped prepare Britain for industrial growth. Rich farmers bought land and created larger, more efficient farms. At the same time, Europe's population grew, creating a need for more food. To meet this need, farmers tried new farming methods and invented new machines.

> Underline the sentence that tells why farmers needed to grow more food.

These improved methods and inventions helped farmers grow more crops, but with fewer workers. As a result, many small farmers and farm workers lost their farms and jobs—and moved to the cities.

In Britain, all these changes sparked the **Industrial Revolution.** By the 1700s, Britain had labor, natural resources, and money to invest—all the resources needed for industry to grow. Demand for manufactured goods soon grew. People looked for ways to make these goods even faster.

> Circle three resources needed for industrial growth.

INDUSTRIAL GROWTH

The **textile** industry, makers of cloth products, developed first. In the early 1700s, cloth was still made by hand. This changed in 1769 when Richard Arkwright invented a waterpowered spinning machine. Other new machines enabled workers to make large amounts of cloth. As a result, the price of cloth fell. Soon workers were using machines to make other kinds of goods faster and cheaper.

Most early machines relied on water power. Factories, the buildings that housed the machines, had to be built near rivers. In the 1760s James Watt built the first modern steam engine. Factories could now be set up in cities. In 1856 Henry Bessemer invented a new way to make steel, and the steel industry grew. Transportation became faster as steam engines powered boats and trains.

Industrial growth changed how people worked. Many people—including children and young women—worked in unsafe factories. They worked long hours, usually for poor wages. However, by the late 1800s, the Industrial Revolution had spread. Industrial growth resulted in a new economic system—**capitalism**, in which individuals own most businesses and resources.

> Circle the industry that developed first. Then underline the invention that helped it grow first.

> Why do you think the price of cloth fell as workers made more cloth?
> _____
> _____

> Explain why you think the Industrial Revolution led to a new economic system.
> _____
> _____

CHANGES IN SOCIETY

The Industrial Revolution made life better for some, but worse for others. Manufactured goods became cheaper. New inventions made life easier. More people joined the middle class. Meanwhile, cities grew, becoming dirty, noisy, and crowded. Workers often remained poor, living in unsafe apartments where diseases spread. Some women, called **suffragettes**, pressed for the right to vote. Other reformers worked to improve society, too.

> Underline the sentences that explain how people's lives improved as a result of the Industrial Revolution.

CHALLENGE ACTIVITY

Critical Thinking: Drawing Conclusions Did the benefits of the Industrial Revolution outweigh the problems it caused? Explain.

DIRECTIONS Look at each set of four terms following each number. On the line provided, write the letter of the term that does not relate to the others.

_____ 1. a. voting   b. suffragette   c. guillotine   d. women

_____ 2. a. Jethro Tull   b. textiles   c. cloth   d. factories

_____ 3. a. capitalism   b. profit   c. investment   d. military

_____ 4. a. inventions   b. machines   c. literature   d. technology

_____ 5. a. steam power   b. iron   c. profit   d. steel

DIRECTIONS Write three words or phrases that describe each term.

6. capitalism _____

7. textiles _____

8. suffragette _____

9. Industrial Revolution _____

10. technology _____

MAIN IDEAS
1. Rivalries in Europe led to the outbreak of World War I.
2. After a long, devastating war, the Allies claimed victory.
3. The war's end brought great political and territorial changes to Europe.

Key Terms

nationalism devotion and loyalty to one's country

alliance an agreement between countries

trench warfare style of fighting in which each side fights from deep ditches, or trenches, dug into the ground

Treaty of Versailles final peace settlement of World War I

communism political system in which the government owns and controls all aspects of life in a country

Section Summary
THE OUTBREAK OF WAR

In the 1800s many people who were ruled by empires wanted to form their own nations. As **nationalism**—devotion and loyalty to one's country—became more common, tensions grew. In 1882 Italy, Germany, and Austria-Hungary formed the Triple Alliance. This **alliance** was an agreement to fight together if any of the three was attacked. Britain, Russia, and France also formed an alliance, the Triple Entente. By the 1900s many countries were preparing for war by building up their armies and stockpiling weapons. Germany and Great Britain built strong navies and powerful new battleships.

Underline the sentence that explains what an alliance is.

One source of tension was Bosnia and Herzegovina, a province of Austria-Hungary that Serbia wanted to control. On June 28, 1914, Archduke Francis Ferdinand of Austria-Hungary was killed by a Serbian gunman. Faced with war, Serbia turned to Russia for help. The alliance system split Europe into warring sides.

When was Archduke Francis Ferdinand killed? _____

WAR AND VICTORY

Germany attacked the Allies (France, Great Britain, Serbia, and Russia), sending its army into Belgium and France. Russia attacked the Central Powers (Germany and Austria-Hungary) from the east. The two sides quickly prepared for **trench warfare** by digging hundreds of miles of trenches, which were easy to defend but hard to attack. Millions of soldiers died in the trenches. New weapons, such as machine guns, poison gas, and tanks, were designed to break into the trenches.

In 1917 German U-boats attacked American ships that were helping Britain. The United States entered the war, strengthening the Allies. Around the same time, Russia pulled out of the war, and Germany attacked the Allies. This last effort failed, and the Central Powers surrendered in 1918.

> Circle the names of two countries that were part of the Central Powers.

> Why did the United States enter the war?
> _____
> _____

THE WAR'S END

World War I, in which over 8.5 million soldiers died, changed Europe forever. American president Woodrow Wilson wanted a just peace after the war, but the **Treaty of Versailles** blamed Germany alone for the war. The Germans were forced to slash the size of their army and pay billions of dollars. The German emperor was replaced with a fragile republic. A revolution had replaced the Russian czar (emperor) with a Communist leader, Vladimir Lenin. **Communism** is a political system in which the government owns and controls every aspect of life. In other government changes, Austria and Hungary became separate countries, Poland and Czechoslovakia gained independence, Yugoslavia was formed, and Finland, Latvia, Lithuania, and Estonia broke away from Russia.

> Where was the first communist government established?
> _____

CHALLENGE ACTIVITY

Critical Thinking: Drawing Inferences Write a sentence explaining why machine guns and trench warfare were such a deadly combination.

Guided Reading Workbook

| alliance | Allies | Central Powers | communism |
| nationalism | stalemate | Treaty of Versailles | trench warfare |

DIRECTIONS Answer each question by writing a sentence that contains at least one term from the word bank.

1. What led to the tension that sparked World War I?

_____

_____

2. What countries fought each other in World War I?

_____

_____

3. How did the new kind of fighting seen in World War I affect the soldiers?

_____

_____

4. What did the final peace settlement of World War I demand of Germany?

_____

_____

5. How did World War I change the way some European countries were governed?

_____

_____

DIRECTIONS Imagine that you are a newspaper reporter visiting Europe during the time that World War I is being fought. Write a short news article that explains what you have learned about the war and the fighting. Include at least five terms from the word bank in your article.

Section 2

> **MAIN IDEAS**
> 1. Economic and political problems troubled Europe in the years after World War I.
> 2. World War II broke out when Germany invaded Poland.
> 3. Nazi Germany targeted the Jews during the Holocaust.
> 4. Allied victories in Europe and Japan brought the end of World War II.

Key Terms

Great Depression a global economic crisis in the 1930s

dictator a ruler who has total control

Axis Powers an alliance among Germany, Italy, and Japan

Allies France, Great Britain, and other countries that opposed the Axis

Holocaust the attempt by the Nazi government during World War II to eliminate Europe's Jews

Section Summary
PROBLEMS TROUBLE EUROPE

With the economy booming after World War I, the United States provided loans to help Europe rebuild. But the U.S. stock market crashed in 1929, starting a global economic crisis, the **Great Depression**. Without United States funds, banks failed in Europe, and many people lost their jobs.

> What caused many Europeans to lose their jobs after 1929?
> _____
> _____

People blamed their leaders for the hard times. In some countries, **dictators** gained power by making false promises. In the 1920s, Benito Mussolini spoke of bringing back the glory of the Roman Empire to Italy but instead took away people's rights. In Russia in 1924, Joseph Stalin became dictator and oppressed the people, using secret police to spy on them. Promising to restore Germany's military and economic strength, Adolf Hitler rose to power in 1933. Once in power, he outlawed all political parties except the Nazi party. He also discriminated against Jews and other groups he believed to be inferior.

> Underline the sentence that tells Adolf Hitler's actions when he first took power.

WAR BREAKS OUT

No one moved to stop Mussolini when he invaded
Ethiopia in 1935. Meanwhile, Hitler added Austria
and Czechoslovakia to the German empire in 1938.
When Hitler invaded Poland in 1939, France and
Britain declared war on Germany, beginning World
War II. Germany, Italy, and Japan formed the **Axis
Powers**. They were opposed by the **Allies**—France,
Great Britain, and others. The Axis won most of the
early battles and soon defeated France. But Britain
withstood intense bombing and did not surrender.
The German army then turned toward Eastern
Europe and the Soviet Union, and Italy invaded
North Africa. In 1941 Japan attacked the United
States at Pearl Harbor, Hawaii.

> **Underline the countries that Mussolini and Hitler invaded.**

> **Who won most of the early battles in World War II?**
> _____

THE HOLOCAUST

The **Holocaust** was the Nazi party's plan to
eliminate people they believed were inferior,
especially the Jews. By 1942 the Nazis had put
millions of Jews in death camps, such as the one in
Auschwitz, Poland. Some Jews tried to hide,
escape, or fight back. In the end, however, the Nazis
killed about two-thirds of Europe's Jews and
several million non-Jews.

END OF THE WAR

In 1943 the Allies won some key battles. Then on
D-Day in 1944 they invaded Normandy, France,
and paved the way for an advance toward Germany.
The war ended in 1945 soon after the U.S. dropped
an atomic bomb on Japan. The war took the lives of
more than 50 million people and led to the
formation of the United Nations. It also made the
United States and the Soviet Union the world's
most powerful countries.

> **Circle the names of the most powerful countries in the world after World War II.**

CHALLENGE ACTIVITY

Critical Thinking: Sequence Make a time line
showing the main events leading up to Germany's
invasion of Poland in 1939.

| Allies | Axis Powers | dictator |
| Great Depression | Holocaust | Nazi |

DIRECTIONS On the line provided before each statement, write **T** if the statement is true and **F** if the statement is false. If the statement is false, write the term that makes the sentence a true statement on the line after each sentence.

_____ 1. The two alliances fighting in World War II were the Allies and the <u>Nazi Powers</u>.

_____

_____ 2. The <u>Great Depression</u> was triggered by the stock market crash in 1929.

_____

_____ 3. Benito Mussolini was Italy's first <u>communist</u>.

_____

_____ 4. During the Holocaust, the <u>Nazi</u> government tried to wipe out Europe's Jews.

_____

_____ 5. Vladimir Lenin and <u>Joseph Stalin</u> were both communist leaders of the Soviet Union.

_____

_____ 6. A major victory for the <u>Axis Powers</u> occurred in the D-Day invasion on the beaches of Normandy, France.

_____

DIRECTIONS Look up three of the vocabulary terms in the word bank. On a separate sheet of paper, write the dictionary definition of the word that is closest to the definition used in your textbook.

Modern European History

MAIN IDEAS
1. The Cold War divided Europe between democratic and Communist nations.
2. Many Eastern European countries changed boundaries and forms of government at the end of the Cold War.
3. European cooperation has brought economic and political change to Europe.

Key Terms

superpowers strong and influential countries

Cold War period of tense rivalry between the United States and the Soviet Union

arms race competition between countries to build superior weapons

common market group of nations that cooperates to make trade among members easier

European Union (EU) organization that promotes political and economic cooperation in Europe

Section Summary
THE COLD WAR

After World War II, the two **superpowers**—the United States and the Soviet Union—distrusted each other. This led to the **Cold War**, a period of tense rivalry between these two countries. The Soviet Union stood for communism, and the United States stood for democracy and free enterprise.

> Underline the sentence that defines the Cold War.

The United States and several Western nations formed an alliance called the North Atlantic Treaty Organization (NATO). The Soviet Union and most Eastern European countries were allies under the Warsaw Pact. The two sides used the threat of nuclear war to defend themselves.

> Which alliance did most Eastern European countries join after World War II?
> _____

Germany was split into East Germany and West Germany. Communist leaders built the Berlin Wall to prevent East Germans from fleeing to the West. Western countries were more successful economically than Communist Eastern Europe. People in the East suffered from shortages of money, food, clothing, and cars.

THE END OF THE COLD WAR

By the 1980s, the **arms race**—a competition to build superior weapons—between the Soviet Union and the U.S. was damaging the Soviet economy. To solve the problem, Soviet leader Mikhail Gorbachev made changes. He reduced government control of the economy and held democratic elections.

These policies helped inspire change throughout the East. Poland and Czechoslovakia threw off Communist rule. The Berlin wall came down in 1989. East and West Germany reunited to form a single country again in 1990. In December 1991 the Soviet Union broke up.

Ukraine, Lithuania, and Belarus became independent countries. In 1993 Czechoslovakia split peacefully into the Czech Republic and Slovakia. However, ethnic conflict in Yugoslavia caused much violence. By 1994 Yugoslavia had split into five countries—Bosnia and Herzogovina, Croatia, Macedonia, Slovenia, and Serbia and Montenegro.

> In what year did the Soviet Union break up?
> _____

> Underline the five countries that were created when Yugoslavia split.

EUROPEAN COOPERATION

After two deadly wars, many Europeans thought a sense of community would make more wars less likely. In the 1950s West Germany, Luxembourg, Italy, Belgium, France, and the Netherlands moved toward unity with a **common market**, a single economic unit to improve trade between members. Today 27 countries have joined to make up the **European Union (EU)**, and many use a common currency, the euro. The European Union deals with issues such as environment, trade, and migration. Their governing body has executive, legislative, and judicial branches. Representatives are selected from all member nations. The EU has helped unify Europe, and other countries hope to join in the future.

> Circle the issues that concern the European Union.

Critical Thinking: Cause and Effect How might the establishment of the European Union make wars in Europe less likely in the future?

arms race	Berlin Wall	Cold War
common market	ethnic tensions	European Union (EU)
reunification	superpowers	

DIRECTIONS Read each sentence and fill in the blank with the word in the word pair that best completes the sentence.

1. The United States and the Soviet Union were rivals in the

   _____. (Cold War/European Union)

2. The _____ of East and West Germany came in 1989 when the Berlin Wall was torn down. (common market/reunification)

3. After the Cold War, _____ led to the breakup of Czechoslovakia and Yugoslavia. (superpowers/ethnic tensions)

4. Belgium, France, Italy, Luxembourg, the Netherlands, and West Germany were

   the first countries to form a common market, which is now known as the

   _____. (superpowers/European Union)

5. The high costs of the _____ hurt the Soviet Union. (arms race/Berlin Wall)

DIRECTIONS Choose five of the vocabulary words from the word bank. On a separate sheet of paper, write a summary of what you learned in the section using these terms.

Southern Europe

MAIN IDEAS
1. Southern Europe's physical features include rugged mountains and narrow coastal plains.
2. The region's climate and resources support such industries as agriculture, fishing, and tourism.

Key Terms and Places

Mediterranean Sea sea that borders Southern Europe

Pyrenees mountain range separating Spain and France

Apennines mountain range running along the whole Italian Peninsula

Alps Europe's highest mountains, some of which are located in northern Italy

Mediterranean climate type of climate found across Southern Europe, with warm, sunny days and mild nights for most of the year

Section Summary

PHYSICAL FEATURES

Southern Europe is composed of three peninsulas—the Iberian, the Italian, and the Balkan—and some large islands. All of the peninsulas have coastlines on the **Mediterranean Sea**.

These peninsulas are largely covered with rugged mountains. The **Pyrenees** form a boundary between Spain and France. The **Apennines** run along the Italian Peninsula. The **Alps**—Europe's highest mountains—are in northern Italy. The Pindus Mountains cover much of Greece. The region also has coastal plains and river valleys, where most of the farming is done and where most of the people live. Crete, which is south of Greece, and Sicily, at the southern tip of Italy, are two of the larger islands in the region. Many of the region's islands are the peaks of undersea mountains.

In addition to the Mediterranean Sea, the Adriatic, Aegean, and Ionian seas are important to Southern Europe. They give the people food and an

> **What are the three peninsulas of Southern Europe?**
>
> _____
> _____
> _____

> **Circle the four mountain ranges in Southern Europe.**

easy way to travel around the region. The Po and
the Tagus are two important rivers in Southern
Europe. The Po flows across northern Italy. The
Tagus, the region's longest river, flows across the
Iberian Peninsula.

CLIMATE AND RESOURCES

The climate in Southern Europe is called a
Mediterranean climate. The climate is warm and
sunny in the summer and mild and rainy in the
winter. Southern Europe's climate is one of its most
valuable resources. It supports the growing of many
crops, and it attracts tourists.

The seas are another important resource in
Southern Europe. Many of the region's cities are
ports, shipping goods all over the world. In
addition, the seas support profitable fishing
industries.

> **What are the
> characteristics of a
> Mediterranean climate?**
>
> _____
> _____

CHALLENGE ACTIVITY

Critical Thinking: Analyzing Explain how
Southern Europe's climate supports the region's
economy.

Mediterranean Sea	Pyrenees	Apennines
Alps	Mediterranean climate	plains
undersea mountains		

DIRECTIONS On the line provided before each statement, write **T** if a statement is true and **F** if a statement is false. If the statement is false, write the term from the word bank that would make the statement true on the line after each sentence.

_____ 1. The <u>Alps</u> form a boundary between Spain and France.

_____

_____ 2. Islands and <u>peninsulas</u> form the region of Southern Europe.

_____

_____ 3. The <u>Apennines</u> are Europe's highest mountain range.

_____

_____ 4. The countries of Southern Europe all share a common location on the <u>Adriatic Sea</u>.

_____

_____ 5. The <u>Pyrenees</u> run along the Italian Peninsula.

_____

DIRECTIONS Read each sentence and fill in the blank with the word in the word pair that best completes the sentence.

6. Many of Southern Europe's islands are formed by _____.
   (undersea mountains/plains)

7. The _____ is ideal for growing a variety of crops.
   (Mediterranean Sea/Mediterranean climate)

MAIN IDEAS

1. Early in its history, Greece was the home of a great civilization, but it was later ruled by foreign powers.

2. The Greek language, the Orthodox Church, and varied customs have helped shape Greece's culture.

3. In Greece today, many people are looking for new economic opportunities.

Key Terms and Places

Orthodox Church a branch of Christianity that dates to the Byzantine Empire

Athens Greece's capital and largest city

Section Summary

HISTORY

Greece has been called the birthplace of Western culture. Ancient Greeks created statues and paintings that inspired later artists. They invented new forms of history and drama. They made advances in geometry. They developed a system of reason that is the basis for modern science, and they created democracy.

> **Name two achievements of ancient Greece.**
> _____
> _____

In the 300s BC, Greece was conquered by Alexander the Great. Later, it was ruled by the Romans, the Byzantines, and the Ottoman Turks. Many Greeks were not happy with Turkish rule. In the 1800s they rebelled against the Turks and drove them out. Greece then became a monarchy.

> **Circle the groups who ruled Greece before it became a monarchy.**

Greece experienced instability for much of the 1900s. A military dictatorship ruled from 1967 to 1974. More recently Greece has become democratic again.

CULTURE

The Greek people today speak a form of the same language as their ancient ancestors, but their ancient religions have disappeared. Nearly everyone in Greece is a member of the **Orthodox Church**, a

> **To what church do most people in Greece belong?**
> _____

branch of Christianity that dates to the Byzantine Empire. Religion is important to the Greek people and religious holidays are popular times for celebration and family gatherings.

The customs of the Greeks have been influenced by the country's geography and by past foreign rulers. Their customs rely on food native to Greece, and they have borrowed ideas for ingredients and food preparation from the groups who have ruled them. For centuries, the family has been central to Greek culture, and today it remains the cornerstone of Greek society.

> **What is the cornerstone of Greek society?**
> _____

GREECE TODAY

About three-fifths of all people in Greece live in cities. **Athens** is the largest city in Greece and its capital. Athens has both modern skyscrapers and ancient ruins. It is a major center of industry, and as a result, suffers from air pollution.

People in rural areas live much like they did in the past. Many live in isolated mountain villages. They grow crops, raise sheep and goats, and socialize in the village square.

Today, Greece's economy is growing but still lags behind other European nations. Greece has few mineral resources, and only one-fifth of the land is suitable for growing crops. However, Greece is a leading country in the shipping industry, with one of the largest shipping fleets in the world.

Another profitable industry is tourism. Many people from around the world are attracted to the ancient ruins of Athens and to the sandy beaches of Greece's islands.

> **Underline two important industries in Greece.**

CHALLENGE ACTIVITY

Critical Thinking: Synthesizing Explain how religion and family work together to form a central part of Greek culture.

Athens	Alexander the Great	Byzantine Empire
Roman Empire	Orthodox Church	monarchy
philosophy	democracy	

DIRECTIONS Write three words or phrases that describe the term.

1. democracy _____

2. monarchy _____

3. philosophy _____

DIRECTIONS Look at each set of vocabulary terms. On the line provided, write the letter of the term that does not relate to the others.

_____ 4. a. theater

   b. philosophy

   c. democracy

   d. population

_____ 5. a. Orthodox Church

   b. Parthenon

   c. Byzantine Empire

   d. Christianity

DIRECTIONS Choose five of the words from the word bank. Use the words to write a summary of what you learned in the section.

_____

_____

_____

_____

_____

_____

_____

_____

_____

Section 3

MAIN IDEAS

1. Italian history can be divided into three periods: ancient Rome, the Renaissance, and unified Italy.
2. Religion and local traditions have helped shape Italy's culture.
3. Italy today has two distinct economic regions—northern Italy and southern Italy.

Key Terms and Places

pope the spiritual head of the Roman Catholic Church

Vatican City an independent state within the city of Rome

Sicily an island at Italy's southern tip

Naples largest city in southern Italy and an important port

Milan major industrial city in northern Italy and a fashion center

Rome the capital of Italy

Section Summary
HISTORY

Ancient Rome grew from a tiny village in 700 BC to an empire that stretched from Britain in the northwest to the Persian Gulf. Ancient Rome's achievements in art, architecture, literature, law, and government still influence the world today. When the Roman Empire collapsed in the AD 400s, cities in Italy formed their own states. Later they became centers of trade. Merchants became rich and started supporting artists. The merchants' support of the arts helped lead to a period of great creativity in Europe called the Renaissance. During this time, artists and writers created some of the greatest works of art and literature in the world.

Italy remained divided until the mid-1800s when a rise in nationalism, or strong patriotic feelings for a country, led to a fight for unification. Italy was officially unified in 1861. In the 1920s Italy became a dictatorship under Benito Mussolini. This lasted

> Underline five areas in which the achievements of ancient Rome still influence the world today.

> What helped lead to the Renaissance?
> _____
> _____
> _____

until Italy's defeat in World War II, after which
Italy became a democracy.

CULTURE

The Roman Catholic Church has historically been
the strongest influence on Italian culture. The **pope**,
who is the spiritual head of the Roman Catholic
Church, lives in **Vatican City**, which is an
independent state located within Rome. Religious
holidays and festivals are major events.

Local traditions and regional geography have also
influenced Italian culture. For example, Italian food
varies widely from region to region. Those
variations are based on local preferences and
products. Other traditions reflect Italy's past.
Italians have long been trendsetters in contemporary
art forms, including painting, composing, fashion,
and film.

> Underline three influences
> on Italian culture.

ITALY TODAY

Southern Italy is poorer than northern Italy. It has
less industry and relies on agriculture and tourism
for its survival. Farming is especially important in
Sicily, an island at the southern tip of Italy. **Naples**
is the largest city in southern Italy and a busy port.

Northern Italy has a strong economy, including
major industrial centers, the most productive
farmland, and the most popular tourist destinations.
Milan is a major industrial center and a worldwide
center for fashion design. Turin and Genoa are also
industrial centers. Florence, Pisa, and Venice are
popular tourist destinations. **Rome**, Italy's capital,
is located between northern Italy and southern Italy.

> Why is the economy of
> northern Italy strong?
>
> _____
>
> _____

CHALLENGE ACTIVITY

Critical Thinking: Analyzing and Evaluating

Identify three important periods in Italy's history,
and explain why each one is important to Italy
today.

Rome	Renaissance	nationalism	dictatorship
pope	Vatican City	Sicily	Naples
Milan			

DIRECTIONS Read each sentence and fill in the blank with the word
in the word pair that best completes the sentence.

1. _____, or strong patriotic feelings for a country, led people
   across Italy to fight for unification. (Nationalism/ Renaissance)

2. The _____ is the head of the Roman Catholic church.
   (pope/prime minister)

3. _____ is an independent state located within the city of
   Rome. (Venice/Vatican City)

4. _____, Italy's capital, has ties to both northern and southern
   Italy. (Rome/Naples)

5. The island of _____ at Italy's southern tip depends on
   agriculture for its survival. (Milan/Sicily)

6. _____ is a center for industry and fashion design.
   (Naples/Milan)

DIRECTIONS Choose five of the words from the word bank. On a
separate piece of paper use these words to write a poem, story, or letter
that relates to the section.

Southern Europe

 MAIN IDEAS

1. Over the centuries, Spain and Portugal have been part of many large and powerful empires.

2. The cultures of Spain and Portugal reflect their long histories.

3. Having been both rich and poor in the past, Spain and Portugal today have growing economies.

Key Terms and Places

Iberia westernmost peninsula in Europe

parliamentary monarchy form of government in which a king rules with the help of an elected parliament

Madrid capital of Spain

Barcelona center of industry, culture, and tourism in Spain

Lisbon large city in Portugal and important industrial center

Section Summary
HISTORY

Spain and Portugal lie on the Iberian Peninsula, or **Iberia**. Both countries have been part of large, powerful empires. Coastal areas of what is now Spain were first ruled by Phoenicians from the eastern Mediterranean. Later the Greeks established colonies there. A few centuries later, Iberia became part of the Roman Empire. After the fall of Rome, they were conquered by the Moors—Muslims from north Africa. For about 600 years, much of the Iberian Peninsula was under Muslim rule.

Eventually the Christian kingdoms of Spain and Portugal banded together to drive out the Muslims. Both countries went on to establish empires of their own in the Americas, Africa, and Asia. Both countries became rich and powerful until the 1800s, when most of their colonies broke away and became independent.

> **What foreign powers have ruled Spain and Portugal?**
> _____
> _____

> **Where did Spain and Portugal establish colonies?**
> _____
> _____

CULTURE

Many dialects of Spanish and Portuguese are spoken in various parts of Iberia. In addition, Catalan, which is similar to Spanish, is spoken in eastern Spain. Galician, which is more closely related to Portuguese, is spoken in northwest Spain. The Basques of the Pyrenees have their own language and customs. In both Spain and Portugal the people are mainly Roman Catholic.

Music is important to both countries. The Portuguese are famous for sad folk songs called fados. The Spanish are famous for a style of song and dance called flamenco. Much of the peninsula's art and architecture reflect its Muslim past. The round arches and elaborate tilework on many buildings were influenced by Muslim design.

> **Circle the group in Spain that has its own language and customs.**

> **What Muslim influences can be seen on buildings in Iberia?**
> _____
> _____

SPAIN AND PORTUGAL TODAY

With the gold and silver found in their colonies, Spain and Portugal were once the richest countries in Europe. When other countries started building industrial economies, Spain and Portugal continued to rely on their colonies. When their colonies broke away, the income they had depended on was lost. Today the economies of Spain and Portugal are growing rapidly.

Spain is governed by a **parliamentary monarchy**—a king rules with the help of an elected parliament. **Madrid**—the capital—and **Barcelona** are centers of industry, culture, and tourism.

Portugal is a republic whose leaders are elected. The economy is based on industries in **Lisbon** and other large cities. In rural areas farmers grow many crops but are most famous for grapes and cork.

> **Underline the definition of a parliamentary monarchy.**

CHALLENGE ACTIVITY

Critical Thinking: Comparing and Contrasting

Compare and contrast Spain and Portugal. Then explain which country you would prefer to visit.

Lisbon	republic	Madrid
fado	flamenco	parliamentary monarchy
Barcelona	Iberia	

DIRECTIONS Answer each question by writing a sentence that contains at least one word from the word bank.

1. Describe one cultural contribution of Spain or Portugal in the area of music or art.

_____

_____

2. How are Spain and Portugal governed today?

_____

_____

3. Where are the centers of industry, tourism, and culture in Spain?

_____

_____

4. Where are the industries of Portugal based?

_____

_____

DIRECTIONS Look at each set of terms. On the line provided, write the letter of the term that does not relate to the others.

_____ 5. a. Basque   b. Catalan   c. Galician   d. Lisbon

_____ 6. a. Muslim   b. Greek   c. Roman   d. Portuguese

MAIN IDEAS
1. The physical features of West-Central Europe include plains, uplands, mountains, rivers, and seas.
2. West-Central Europe's mild climate and resources support agriculture, energy production, and tourism.

Key Terms and Places

Northern European Plain broad coastal plain that stretches from the Atlantic coast into Eastern Europe

North Sea large body of water to the north of the region

English Channel narrow waterway to the north of the region that separates West-Central Europe from the United Kingdom

Danube River one of the major rivers of the region

Rhine River one of the major rivers of the region

navigable river river that is deep and wide enough for ships to use

Section Summary
PHYSICAL FEATURES

West-Central Europe has three major types of landforms: plains, uplands, and mountains. Most of the **Northern European Plain** is flat or rolling, but in the Netherlands the plains drop below sea level. The plain has the region's best farmland and largest cities. The Central Uplands are in the middle of the region. This area has many rounded hills, small plateaus, and valleys. In France, the uplands include the Massif Central, a plateau region, and the Jura Mountains, a low mountain range on the French-Swiss border. Coal fields in the Central Uplands have helped to make it a major mining and industrial area. The area has some fertile soil, but is mostly too rocky for farming.

The region has two high mountain ranges. The Alps and Pyrenees form the alpine mountain system. The Alps are the highest mountains in Europe.

> Circle the three major landform types in West-Central Europe.

> Underline the names of three mountain ranges in West-Central Europe.

Water is an important part of the region's physical geography. The Mediterranean Sea borders France to the south. The Atlantic Ocean lies to the west and the **North Sea** and the **English Channel** lie to the north. The **Danube** and the **Rhine** rivers are important waterways for trade and travel. Several of the region's rivers are **navigable**. These rivers and a system of canals link the region's interior to the seas. People and goods travel on these waterways, and cities, farms, and industrial areas line their banks.

> Circle the names of two important rivers in the region.

CLIMATE AND RESOURCES

Most of West-Central Europe has a marine west coast climate. This is a mild climate with colder winters. In the Alps and other higher elevation areas, the climate is colder and wetter. In contrast, southern France has a warm Mediterranean climate with dry, hot summers and mild, wet winters.

The mild climate is a valuable resource. Mild temperatures and ample rainfall, along with rich soil, have made the region's farmlands very productive. Farmers grow grapes, grains, and vegetables. In the Alps and the uplands, farmers raise livestock.

> Why is a mild climate a valuable resource for the region?
> _____
> _____

Energy resources are not evenly divided. France has iron ore and coal. Germany has coal, and the Netherlands has natural gas. Fast-flowing alpine rivers provide hydroelectric power. Even so, many countries have to import fuel.

> Circle the energy resources of France. Underline the energy resources of Germany and the Netherlands.

The Alps are another important resource. Tourists come to the mountains for the scenery and to ski and hike.

> In what way are the Alps an important resource for the region?
> _____

CHALLENGE ACTIVITY

Critical Thinking: Evaluating Information How have landforms and bodies of water affected activities in the region? Give support for your answer.

Massif Central	Northern European Plain	Danube River
Rhine River	Jura Mountains	English Channel
North Sea	navigable river	

DIRECTIONS On the line provided before each statement, write **T** if a statement is true and **F** if a statement is false. If the statement is false, write the correct term or terms on the line after each sentence that makes the sentence a true statement.

_____ 1. The vast plain that stretches from the Atlantic coast into Eastern Europe is called the <u>Northern European Plain</u>.

_____

_____ 2. The two most important rivers in West-Central Europe are the <u>Nile</u> and the <u>Mississippi</u>. Many cities and industrial areas line their banks.

_____

_____ 3. A <u>navigable river</u> is one that is deep and wide enough for ships to use.

_____

_____ 4. The <u>Atlantic Ocean</u> is north of Belgium and the Netherlands.

_____

_____ 5. The <u>Danube</u> is the body of water between the North Sea and the Atlantic Ocean.

_____

DIRECTIONS Choose four of the vocabulary terms from the word bank. On a separate sheet of paper, use these terms to write directions for how to travel (by boat, car, train, or air) across West-Central Europe from the United Kingdom to Italy.

MAIN IDEAS

1. During its history France has been a kingdom, empire, colonial power, and republic.
2. The culture of France has contributed to the world's arts and ideas.
3. France today is a farming and manufacturing center.
4. The Benelux Countries have strong economies and high standards of living.

Key Terms and Places

Paris capital and largest city in France

Amsterdam capital of the Netherlands

The Hague seat of government in the Netherlands

Brussels capital of Belgium, headquarters of many international organizations

cosmopolitan characterized by many foreign influences

Section Summary

HISTORY OF FRANCE

France has a history as a major European power. Early in its history, the Romans and Franks conquered lands that became France. The Franks' ruler, Charlemagne, built a large empire. Later the Normans claimed northwestern France. They extended their rule to England, becoming kings of England and ruling part of France as well. English rule in France ended in 1453 after the Hundred Years' War. In the 1500s France became a colonial power with colonies in Asia, Africa, and the Americas.

In 1789 the French Revolution led to greater equality and more rights for the French. In 1799 Napoleon Bonaparte took power. He conquered most of Europe, creating a vast empire, which ended in 1815 when European powers defeated his armies. In the 1900s during World Wars I and II, Germany invaded France. In the 1950s and 1960s, many French colonies declared independence. France is now a democratic republic.

> Circle the names of three groups that ruled France during its early history.

> Underline the sentence that tells how Napoleon Bonaparte affected French history.

THE CULTURE OF FRANCE

The French share a common heritage. Most speak French and are Catholic. Recently France has become more diverse due to immigrants. The French share a love of good food and company. The French have made major contributions to the arts and ideas—including impressionism, Gothic cathedrals, and Enlightenment ideas about government.

> Underline the sentences that describe the ways the French are alike.

FRANCE TODAY

France is a European and world leader. **Paris** is a center of business, finance, learning, and culture. France has a strong economy and it is the EU's top agricultural producer. Its economy also relies on tourism and the export of goods such as perfumes and wines.

THE BENELUX COUNTRIES

Belgium, the Netherlands, and Luxembourg are the Benelux Countries. Their location has led to invasions but has also promoted trade. All are densely populated, lie at low elevations between larger, stronger countries, and have strong economies and democratic governments. North Sea harbors have made the Netherlands a center for trade. Major cities include Rotterdam, **Amsterdam**, and **The Hague**. In Belgium, **Brussels** is a **cosmopolitan** city with many international organizations. Luxembourg's economy is based on banking and steel and chemical production.

> Circle the names of the three Benelux Countries.

> Underline the sentence that tells how the Benelux Countries are alike.

CHALLENGE ACTIVITY

Critical Thinking: Drawing Conclusions How has the location of the Benelux Countries both helped and hurt them?

DIRECTIONS Read each sentence and fill in the blank with the word
in the word pair that best completes the sentence.

1. _____ is a style of painting developed by French artists that
uses rippling light to create an impression of a scene.
(Impressionism/Abstract expressionism)

2. _____ is the capital of France. (London/Paris)

3. The Dutch use _____, or earthen walls, in addition to dams
and pumps to hold back the sea. (dikes/trenches)

4. Brussels, the capital of Belgium, is considered a _____ city
because of its many foreign influences. (cosmopolitan/sprawling)

5. _____ is the capital of the Netherlands.
(Amsterdam/The Hague)

DIRECTIONS Write a word or short phrase that has the same meaning
as the term given.

6. *joie de vivre* _____

7. Marseille _____

8. The Hague _____

9. Brussels _____

10. Benelux _____

West-Central Europe

MAIN IDEAS

1. After a history of division and two world wars, Germany is now a unified country.
2. German culture, known for its contributions to music, literature, and science, is growing more diverse.
3. Germany today has Europe's largest economy, but eastern Germany faces challenges.
4. The Alpine Countries reflect German culture and have strong economies based on tourism and services.

Key Terms and Places

Berlin capital of Germany

chancellor prime minister elected by Parliament who runs the government

Vienna Austria's capital and largest city

cantons districts of Switzerland's federal republic

Bern capital of Switzerland

Section Summary

HISTORY OF GERMANY

The land that is now Germany was a loose association of small states for hundreds of years. In 1871 Prussia united them to create Germany, which grew into a world power. In the 1900s Germany lost two world wars. After its defeat in World War II, Germany was divided into West Germany and East Germany. West Germany kept control of western **Berlin** and Communists took eastern Berlin. They built the Berlin Wall to stop East Germans from escaping. In 1989 democracy movements swept Eastern Europe and communism collapsed. In 1990 East and West Germany were reunited.

> **Why did Communist leaders build the Berlin Wall?**
> _____
> _____

> **What events helped East and West Germany reunite?**
> _____
> _____

CULTURE OF GERMANY

Most people in Germany are ethnic Germans who speak German. Germany also has immigrants from Turkey, Italy, and Eastern Europe. Most people are either Protestant or Catholic. Germans have made important contributions to classical music, literature, chemistry, engineering, and medicine.

Most Germans belong to one or the other of which two religious groups?
_____
_____

GERMANY TODAY

Today Germany is a leading European power. A parliament with a **chancellor** governs the nation. Berlin is the largest city. Germany is Europe's largest economy, exporting many products, including cars. Its economy is based mainly on industries such as chemicals, engineering, and steel, but agriculture is also still important. The reuniting of East and West Germany slowed economic growth.

What economic activities have made Germany Europe's strongest economy?
_____
_____

THE ALPINE COUNTRIES

Austria and Switzerland are the Alpine Countries. Both were once part of the Holy Roman Empire, are landlocked, influenced by German culture, and prosperous. Austria once led the powerful Habsburg Empire that ruled much of Europe. After World War I the empire collapsed. Today Austria is a modern, industrialized nation. **Vienna** is a center of music and fine arts. Austria has a strong economy with little unemployment. Service industries and tourism are important.

Underline the sentence that explains what the Alpine Countries have in common.

Switzerland has been independent since the 1600s. It is a federal republic made up of 26 **cantons**. It is neutral and not a member of the EU or NATO. The Swiss speak several languages, including German and French. Its capital is **Bern**. Like Austria, Switzerland is a modern, industrialized nation. It is known for tourism and for its banks, watches, chocolate, and cheese.

List two important industries in the Alpine Countries.
_____
_____

CHALLENGE ACTIVITY

Critical Thinking: Drawing Inferences What are some factors that have contributed to the Alpine Countries' prosperity?

| Berlin | chancellor | cantons | purpose |
| Vienna | neutral | Bern | |

DIRECTIONS Read each sentence and fill in the blank with the word in the word pair that best completes the sentence.

1. _____ is the capital of Germany. (Vienna/Berlin)

2. In Germany, a parliament elects a _____, or prime minister, who runs the government. (canton/chancellor)

3. Switzerland is made up of 26 districts called _____. (cantons/Bern)

4. _____ is the capital of Austria and also its largest city. (Berlin/Vienna)

5. The capital of Switzerland, _____, is centrally located between the country's German- and French-speaking regions. (Bern/Vienna)

DIRECTIONS Choose five terms from the word bank. Use these terms to write a summary of what you learned in this section.

_____

_____

_____

_____

_____

_____

_____

_____

MAIN IDEAS

1. The physical features of Northern Europe include low mountain ranges and jagged coastlines.
2. Northern Europe's natural resources include energy sources, soils, and seas.
3. The climates of Northern Europe range from a mild coastal climate to a freezing ice cap climate.

Key Terms and Places

British Isles a group of islands located across the English Channel from the rest of Europe

Scandinavia a region of islands and peninsulas in far northern Europe

fjord a narrow inlet of the sea set between high, rocky cliffs

geothermal energy energy from the heat of Earth's interior

North Atlantic Drift an ocean current that brings warm, moist air across the Atlantic Ocean

Section Summary

PHYSICAL FEATURES

Northern Europe consists of two regions. The **British Isles** are a group of islands located across the English Channel from the rest of Europe. **Scandinavia** is a region of islands and peninsulas in far northern Europe. Iceland, to the west, is often considered part of Scandinavia.

Fewer people live in the northern portion of the region, which is covered by rocky hills and low mountains. Farmland and plains stretch across the southern part of the region.

Slow moving sheets of ice called glaciers once covered the region. They carved lakes and **fjords**, narrow inlets between high, rocky cliffs. The fjords make the coast of Norway irregular and jagged.

> Underline the sentence that describes the land in the northern portion of the region.

> What two features were created by glaciers?
>
> _____
>
> _____

NATURAL RESOURCES

Northern Europe has many natural resources that have helped make it one of the world's wealthiest regions. Energy resources include oil and natural gas in areas of the North Sea controlled by the United Kingdom and Norway. Hydroelectric energy is created by machines that are turned by flowing water channeled from lakes and rivers. Iceland's hot springs produce **geothermal energy**, or energy from the heat of the Earth's interior.

Forests in Norway, Sweden, and Finland provide timber. Fertile farmland in southern areas provides crops such as wheat and potatoes. The seas and oceans that surround the region have provided fish to the people of Northern Europe for centuries.

> Underline the sentences that describe energy resources located in the North Sea.

CLIMATES

Although much of the region is very far north and close to the Arctic Circle, the climates in Northern Europe are surprisingly mild. The **North Atlantic Drift** is a warm ocean current that brings warm, moist air across the Atlantic Ocean to Northern Europe. It creates warmer temperatures than other areas located as far north.

Much of the region has a marine west coast climate with mild summers and frequent rainfall. Central Norway, Sweden, and southern Finland have a humid continental climate with four seasons. Farther north are subarctic regions, with long, cold winters and short summers. Tundra and ice cap climates produce extremely cold temperatures year-round.

> How does the North Atlantic Drift affect the climate?
> _____
> _____

CHALLENGE ACTIVITY

Critical Thinking: Making Inferences Fewer people live in the northern portion of the region than in the southern portion. List all of the factors that you can think of which might help explain this pattern.

DIRECTIONS Read each sentence and fill in the blank with the word in the word pair that best completes each sentence.

1. Many lakes in the British Isles were carved by _____ millions of years ago. (volcanoes/glaciers)

2. Northern Europe is made up of the British Isles and _____. (Scandinavia/the Artic Circle)

3. A _____ is a narrow inlet of the sea set between high, rocky cliffs. (fjord/peninsula)

4. Energy produced from the heat of Earth's interior is called

_____. (geothermal energy/hydroelectric energy)

5. Northern Europe experiences a mild climate due to the

_____. (Arctic Circle/North Atlantic Drift)

DIRECTIONS Look at each set of four vocabulary terms or places. On the line provided, write the letter of the term that does not relate to the others.

_____ 6. a. glacier
      b. rainfall
      c. fjord
      d. cliff

_____ 7. a. tundra
      b. soil
      c. forest
      d. ocean

_____ 8. a. Northern Europe
      b. British Isles
      c. Scandinavia
      d. Antarctic Circle

_____ 9. a. North Atlantic Drift
      b. mild climate
      c. ocean current
      d. subarctic climate

MAIN IDEAS

1. Invaders and a global empire have shaped the history of the British Isles.
2. British culture, such as government and music, has influenced much of the world.
3. Efforts to bring peace to Northern Ireland and maintain strong economies are important issues in the British Isles today.

Key Terms and Places

constitutional monarchy a type of democracy in which a king or queen serves as head of state, but a legislature makes the laws

Magna Carta a document that limited the powers of kings and required everyone to obey the law

disarm give up all weapons

London the capital of the United Kingdom

Dublin the capital of Ireland

Section Summary

HISTORY

The Republic of Ireland and the United Kingdom make up the British Isles. The United Kingdom consists of England, Scotland, Wales, and Northern Ireland.

The Celts were early settlers of the British Isles. Later, Romans, Angles, Saxons, Vikings, and Normans invaded Britain. Over time England grew in strength, and by the 1500s it had become a world power. England eventually formed the United Kingdom with Wales, Scotland, and Ireland. It then developed a strong economy thanks to the Industrial Revolution and its colonies abroad.

The British Empire stretched around the world by 1900, but later declined. The Republic of Ireland won its independence in 1921. By the mid-1900s Britain had given up most of its colonies.

> **What two countries make up the British Isles?**
> _____

> **Underline the sentence that lists the countries that formed the United Kingdom.**

CULTURE

The United Kingdom is a **constitutional monarchy**, a type of democracy in which a monarch serves as head of state, but a legislature makes the laws. England first limited the power of monarchs during the Middle Ages in a document called **Magna Carta**. Ireland has a president that serves as head of state and a prime minister who runs the government along with Parliament.

The people of the British Isles share many culture traits, but each culture is also unique. The people of Ireland and Scotland keep many traditions alive, and immigrants from all over the world add new traits to the culture of the British Isles.

British popular culture has influenced people around the world. British literature and music are well known and the English language is used in many countries.

In what ways are the governments of the United Kingdom and Ireland similar and different?

_____

_____

_____

Underline the sentence that describes how British popular culture has influenced other people.

BRITISH ISLES TODAY

Efforts to bring a long-lasting peace to Northern Ireland remain an important issue. Many Catholics there feel they have not been treated fairly by Protestants. Some hope to unite with the Republic of Ireland. In the late 1990s peace talks led to the creation of a national assembly in Northern Ireland. However, some groups refused to **disarm**, or give up all weapons.

Maintaining powerful economies in the British Isles is a key issue today. **London**, the capital of the United Kingdom, is a center for world trade, and the country has reserves of oil and natural gas in the North Sea. **Dublin**, the capital of Ireland, has attracted new industries like computers and electronics.

What is one economic issue facing the British Isles today?

_____

_____

CHALLENGE ACTIVITY

Critical Thinking: Identify Cause and Effect

Explain the factors that caused the development of a strong economy in the United Kingdom following its formation. Then explain two effects of the decline of the British Empire.

Guided Reading Workbook

DIRECTIONS Read each sentence and fill in the blank with the word
in the word pair that best completes the sentence.

1. The _____ was characterized by the growth of industries like
   textiles, iron, and steel. (Industrial Revolution/Magna Carta)

2. An _____ led to the creation of a national assembly and a
   cease fire in Northern Ireland in the late 1990s.
   (agreement/Industrial Revolution)

3. _____ is an ancient monument in the British Isles that was
   built 5,000 years ago. (Dublin/Stonehenge)

4. A _____ is a government that has a monarch, but a
   legislative body that makes the laws. (Magna Carta/constitutional monarchy)

5. Peace talks in Northern Ireland were stalled when some groups refused to
   _____. (disarm/agreement)

DIRECTIONS Write three words or phrases that describe the term.

6. London _____

7. Dublin _____

8. Magna Carta _____

Northern Europe

MAIN IDEAS
1. The history of Scandinavia dates back to the time of the Vikings.
2. Scandinavia today is known for its peaceful and prosperous countries.

Key Terms and Places

Vikings Scandinavian warriors who raided Europe in the early Middle Ages

Stockholm Sweden's capital and largest city

neutral not taking sides in an international conflict

uninhabitable not able to support human settlement

Oslo the capital of Norway

Helsinki Finland's capital and largest city

geyser a spring that shoots hot water and steam into the air

Section Summary

HISTORY

Vikings were Scandinavian warriors who raided Europe during the Middle Ages. They were greatly feared and conquered the British Isles, Finland, and parts of France, Germany, and Russia.

Vikings were excellent sailors. They were the first Europeans with settlements in Iceland and Greenland and the first Europeans to reach North America. They stopped raiding in the 1100s and focused on strengthening their kingdoms. Norway, Sweden, and Denmark competed for control of the region, and by the late 1300s Denmark ruled all the Scandinavian Kingdoms and territories. Sweden eventually broke away, taking Finland, and later Norway, with it. Norway, Finland, and Iceland became independent countries during the 1900s. Greenland remains part of Denmark as a self-ruling territory.

> Underline the sentence that tells areas that Vikings explored.

> What three countries did not become independent until the 1900s?
>
> _____
> _____

SCANDINAVIA TODAY

Scandinavians share many things, including culture traits like similar political views, languages, and religions. They enjoy high standards of living, are well-educated, and get free health care. The countries have strong economies and large cities.

Each country is unique as well. Sweden has the largest area and population. Most people live in the south in large towns and cities. **Stockholm** is Sweden's capital and largest city. For about 200 years, Sweden has been **neutral**, choosing not to take sides in international conflicts.

Denmark is the smallest country and the most densely populated. Its economy relies on excellent farmland and modern industries. Greenland is a territory of Denmark but most of it is covered with ice and is **uninhabitable**, or not able to support human settlement.

Norway has one of the longest coastlines in the world. **Oslo** is Norway's capital, a leading seaport and industrial center. Important industries include timber, shipping, and fishing. Oil and natural gas provide Scandinavia with the highest per capita GDP in the region; however, oil fields in the North Sea are expected to run out during the next century.

Finland relies on trade and exports paper and other forest products. Shipbuilding and electronics are also important. **Helsinki** is its capital and largest city.

Iceland has fertile farmland and rich fishing grounds. Tourists come to see its volcanoes, glaciers, and **geysers**, springs that shoot hot water and steam into the air. Geothermal energy heats many buildings.

> Underline the sentence that lists culture traits Scandinavians share.

> What is the largest country in area? What is the smallest?
> _____
> _____

> Why are tourists attracted to Iceland?
> _____
> _____

CHALLENGE ACTIVITY

Critical Thinking: Making Inferences How do you think the Scandinavian countries might change if oil fields run out during the next century?

domination	geysers	Helsinki
hot springs	neutral	Oslo
Stockholm	uninhabitable	Vikings

DIRECTIONS Answer each question by writing a sentence that
contains at least one word from the word bank.

1. How were longboats used by Scandinavian warriors?

   _____

   _____

2. Why do most people in Greenland live on the southwest coast?

   _____

   _____

3. What role did Sweden play in World War I and World War II?

   _____

   _____

4. How are many homes in Iceland heated?

   _____

   _____

5. What city in Scandinavia is often called a floating city and why?

   _____

   _____

Eastern Europe

MAIN IDEAS

1. The physical features of Eastern Europe include wide open plains, rugged mountain ranges, and many rivers.
2. The climate and vegetation of Eastern Europe differ widely in the north and the south.

Key Places

Carpathians a low mountain range stretching from the Alps to the Black Sea area

Balkan Peninsula one of the largest peninsulas in Europe, extends into the Mediterranean

Danube longest river in the region, begins in Germany and flows east across the Great Hungarian Plain

Chernobyl a nuclear power plant in Ukraine

Section Summary

PHYSICAL FEATURES

The landforms of Eastern Europe stretch across the region in broad bands of plains and mountains. The Northern European Plain covers most of northern Europe. The **Carpathians** are south of the plains. These mountains extend from the Alps to the Black Sea area. South of the Carpathians is another large plain, the Great Hungarian Plain, located mostly in Hungary. South of this plain are the Dinaric Alps and Balkan Mountains. These mountain ranges cover most of the **Balkan Peninsula**. The peninsula extends into the Mediterranean.

Eastern Europe has many water bodies that are important routes for transportation and trade. The Adriatic Sea lies to the southwest. The Black Sea is east of the region. The Baltic Sea is in the far north. It remains frozen some part of the year, reducing its usefulness.

The rivers that flow through Eastern Europe are also important for trade and transportation, especially the **Danube**. The Danube crosses nine

> Circle three mountain ranges in Eastern Europe.

> Why are rivers important to the economy of Eastern Europe?
> _____

Guided Reading Workbook

countries before it empties into the Black Sea. This river is very important to Eastern Europe's economy. Many of the region's largest cities are along its banks. Dams on the river provide electricity for the region. This busy river has become very polluted from heavy use.

> **Why is the Danube so polluted?**
> _____

CLIMATE AND VEGETATION

Types of climates and vegetation in Eastern Europe vary widely. The shores of the Baltic Sea in the far north have the coldest climate. The area does not get much rain, but is sometimes foggy. Its cold, damp climate allows huge forests to grow.

The interior plains have a much milder climate than the Baltic Region. Winters can be very cold, but summers are mild. The western parts of the interior plains get more rain than the eastern parts. Because of its varied climate, the forests cover much of the north and open grassy plains lie in the south. In 1986 Eastern Europe's forests were damaged by a major nuclear accident at **Chernobyl**. An explosion released huge amounts of radiation into the air that poisoned forests and ruined soil across the region.

The Balkan coast has a Mediterranean climate with warm summers and mild winters. Some of its beaches attract tourists. The area does not get much rain so there are not many forests. The land is covered by shrubs and trees that do not need much water.

> **Circle the type of climate found along the Balkan coast.**

> **Why is the vegetation along the Balkan coast different from the vegetation of the Baltic Region?**
> _____
> _____

CHALLENGE ACTIVITY

Critical Thinking: Analyzing Information How has climate affected the vegetation in Eastern Europe? Explain your answer in a brief paragraph.

| Adriatic Sea | Balkan Mountains | Balkan Peninsula | Carpathians |
| Chernobyl | Danube | function | radiation |

DIRECTIONS On the line provided before each statement, write **T** if a statement is true and **F** if a statement is false. If the statement is false, write the correct term from the word bank on the line after each sentence that makes the sentence a true statement.

_____ 1. The <u>Balkan Mountains</u> are a low mountain range that stretch in a long arc from the Alps to the Black Sea area.

_____

_____ 2. The Black Sea serves the same function as the <u>Carpathians</u>; they are both important trade routes.

_____

_____ 3. A nuclear explosion at the <u>Chernobyl</u> power plant released huge amounts of radiation into the air.

_____

_____ 4. The <u>Danube</u> begins in Germany and flows through nine countries before emptying into the Black Sea.

_____

_____ 5. One of the largest landforms in Europe, the <u>Chernobyl</u> extends south into the Mediterranean Sea.

_____

Eastern Europe

MAIN IDEAS

1. History ties Poland and the Baltic Republics together.
2. The cultures of Poland and the Baltic Republics differ in language and religion but share common customs.
3. Economic growth is a major issue in the region today.

Key Terms and Places

infrastructure the set of resources—like roads, airports, and factories—that a country needs in order to support economic activities

Warsaw capital of Poland

Section Summary

HISTORY

The groups who settled around the Baltic Sea in ancient times developed into the Estonians, Latvians, Lithuanians, and Polish. Each group had its own language and culture, but in time they became connected by a shared history. By the Middle Ages, each had formed an independent kingdom. Lithuania and Poland were the largest and strongest. They ruled large parts of Eastern and Northern Europe. Latvia and Estonia were smaller, weaker, and often invaded.

In the 1900s two world wars greatly damaged the Baltic region. In World War I millions died in Poland, and thousands more were killed in the Baltic countries. The region also suffered greatly during World War II. This war began with the invasion of Poland by Germany. While fighting the Germans, troops from the Soviet Union invaded Poland and occupied Estonia, Latvia, and Lithuania.

After World War II ended, the Soviet Union took over much of Eastern Europe, making Estonia, Latvia, and Lithuania part of the Soviet Union. The Soviets also forced Poland to accept a Communist government. In 1989 Poland rejected communism

How did the Baltic Republics lose their independence after World War II?

_____

and elected new leaders. In 1991 the Baltic Republics broke away from the Soviet Union. They became independent countries again.

Underline the sentences that tell how the governments of the Baltic countries changed after 1989.

CULTURE

The Baltic countries differ from each other in languages and religion, but are alike in other ways. The Latvian and Lithuanian languages are alike, but Estonian is like Finnish, the language spoken in Finland. Polish is more like languages of countries farther south. Most Polish people and Lithuanians are Roman Catholics because their trading partners were from Catholic countries. Latvians and Estonians are Lutherans, because these countries were once ruled by Sweden, where most people are Lutherans.

These countries share many customs and practices. They eat similar foods, practice crafts such as ceramics, painting, and embroidery, and enjoy music and dance.

THE REGION TODAY

The economies of Baltic countries grew more slowly than those of Western European nations because the Soviets did not build a decent **infrastructure**. Poland and the Baltic Republics are working hard to rebuild their economies. As a result, cities like **Warsaw** have become major industrial centers. To help their economies grow, many Baltic countries are trying to attract more tourists. Since the Soviet Union collapsed in 1991, the rich cultures, historic sites, and cool summer climates attract visitors.

What economic problems did Soviet rule cause for Poland and the Baltic Republics?
_____
_____
_____

What new source of income have the Baltic countries found?
_____
_____

CHALLENGE ACTIVITY

Critical Thinking: Understanding Effects

Imagine that you are a newly elected leader of a Baltic country. Write a speech that tells what you will do to improve the country's economy.

| Baltic Republics | embroidery | infrastructure |
| Krakow | Poland | Warsaw |

DIRECTIONS Read each sentence and fill in the blank with the word in the word pair that best completes the sentence.

1. The Soviets failed to build a strong _____, which has weakened the economies of the Baltic states. (embroidery/infrastructure)

2. By the Middle Ages, the kingdoms of Lithuania and _____ were large and strong. (Poland/Warsaw)

3. _____ is the capital of Poland. (Warsaw/Krakow)

4. The _____ include(s) Latvia, Estonia, and Lithuania. (infrastructure/Baltic Republics)

5. _____ is a type of decorative sewing that is popular among people in the Baltic region. (Krakow/Embroidery)

DIRECTIONS Choose four of the terms from the word bank. On a separate sheet of paper, use these words to write a short story that relates to the section.

Eastern Europe

Section 3

MAIN IDEAS
1. The histories and cultures of inland Eastern Europe vary from country to country.
2. Most of inland Eastern Europe today has stable governments, strong economies, and influential cities.

Key Terms and Places

Prague capital of the Czech Republic

Kiev present-day city where the Rus built a settlement

Commonwealth of Independent States CIS, an international alliance that meets to discuss issues such as trade and immigration that affect former Soviet republics

Budapest capital of Hungary

Section Summary

HISTORY AND CULTURE

Inland Eastern Europe consists of the Czech Republic, Slovakia, Hungary, Ukraine, Belarus, and Moldova. The region is located on the Northern European and Hungarian plains. The area of the Czech Republic and Slovakia was settled by Slavs, people from Asia who moved into Europe by 1000 BC. In time more powerful countries like Austria conquered these Slavic kingdoms. After World War I, land was taken away from Austria to create the nation of Czechoslovakia. In 1993 Czechoslovakia split into the Czech Republic and Slovakia.

Because the Czech Republic and Slovakia are located in Central Europe, they have long had ties to Western Europe. Many people are Roman Catholic. The architecture of **Prague** and other cities shows Western influences.

In the 900s Magyar people invaded what is now Hungary. The Magyars influenced Hungarian culture, especially the Hungarian language. It developed from the Magyar language.

> **What group of people settled the area of the Czech Republic and Slovakia?**
>
> _____

> **Circle the country that land was taken from to create Czechoslovakia.**

> **When was Czechoslovakia created and when did it split?**
>
> _____
>
> _____

Guided Reading Workbook

Ukraine, Belarus, and Moldova are more closely tied to Russia than to the West. The Rus people built the settlement that is now **Kiev**. The rulers of Kiev created a huge empire that became part of Russia in the late 1700s. In 1922 Russia became the Soviet Union. Ukraine, Belarus, and Moldova became Soviet republics. After the breakup of the Soviet Union in 1991, these countries became independent. Russia has strongly influenced their cultures. Most people are Orthodox Christians, and the Ukrainian and Belarusian languages are written in the Cyrillic, or Russian, alphabet.

> Underline two ways the cultures of Ukraine, Belarus, and Moldova have been influenced by Russia.

INLAND EASTERN EUROPE TODAY

All inland Eastern European countries were once either part of the Soviet Union or run by Soviet-influenced Communist governments. People had few freedoms. The Soviets did a poor job of managing these economies. Since the collapse of the Soviet Union, Hungary, Slovakia, the Czech Republic, Ukraine, and Moldova have become republics. Although Belarus also claims to be a republic, it is really a dictatorship.

> How have the governments and the economies of the region changed since the collapse of the Soviet Union?
>
> _____
> _____
> _____
> _____

Countries of the region belong to international unions. Belarus, Ukraine, and Moldova belong to the **Commonwealth of Independent States**. Its members meet to talk about such issues as trade and immigration. The Czech Republic, Slovakia, and Hungary seek closer ties to the West and belong to the EU. Slovakia, Hungary, and Ukraine have become prosperous industrial centers.

The capital cities of the region are also economic and cultural centers. Prague, Kiev, and **Budapest** are especially important. They are the most prosperous cities in the region. Many tourists visit these cities.

CHALLENGE ACTIVITY

Critical Thinking: Evaluating Write a brief essay that explains how the location of inland Eastern Europe has affected its culture and history.

Budapest	Kiev	Magyars
Prague	Slavs	
Commonwealth of Independent States		

DIRECTIONS Read each sentence and choose the correct term from the word bank to replace the underlined phrase. Write the term in the space provided and then define the term in your own words.

1. Members of <u>this alliance</u> meet in Minsk to discuss issues such as trade and

   immigration. _____

   Your definition: _____

   _____

2. This <u>group of fierce invaders</u> swept into Hungary and established a strong culture

   there. _____

   Your definition: _____

   _____

3. <u>This</u> is the capital city of the Czech Republic. _____

   Your definition: _____

   _____

4. The Rus established <u>this city</u> in the 800s, which still stands in Ukraine today.

   _____

   Your definition: _____

   _____

5. Ukraine, Belarus, and Moldavia were settled by <u>this group of people</u>.

   _____

   Your definition: _____

   _____

Section 4

MAIN IDEAS
1. The history of the Balkan countries is one of conquest and conflict.
2. The cultures of the Balkan countries are shaped by the many ethnic groups who live there.
3. Civil War and weak economies are major challenges to the region today.

Key Terms

ethnic cleansing effort to remove all members of a group from a country or region

Section Summary

HISTORY

The Balkan Peninsula has been ruled by many different groups. In ancient times, the Greeks founded colonies near the Black Sea. This area is now Bulgaria and Romania. Next the Romans conquered most of the area between the Adriatic Sea and the Danube River. When the Roman Empire divided into west and east in AD 300s, the Balkan Peninsula became part of the Byzantine Empire. Under Byzantine rule many people became Orthodox Christians.

Over a thousand years later, Muslim Ottoman Turks conquered the Byzantine Empire. Many people in the Balkans became Muslims. Ottoman rule lasted until the 1800s, when the people of the Balkans drove the Ottomans out. They then created their own kingdoms. In the late 1800s, the Austria-Hungarian Empire took over part of the peninsula. To protest the takeover, a man from Serbia shot the heir to the Austro-Hungarian throne. This event led to World War I. After the war Europe's leaders combined many formerly independent countries into Yugoslavia. In the 1990s this country broke apart. Ethnic and religious conflict led to its collapse.

> Underline the names of groups or empires that ruled the Balkan Peninsula until the 1800s.

Guided Reading Workbook

CULTURE

The Balkans are Europe's most diverse region. People practice different religions and speak many different languages. Most people are Christians. They are either Orthodox, Roman Catholic, or Protestant. Islam is also practiced. Most people speak Slavic languages that are related to Russian. People in Romania speak Germanic languages or a language that comes from Latin.

> **What makes the Balkans Europe's most diverse region?**
> _____
> _____
> _____

THE BALKANS TODAY

Balkan countries were once run by Communist governments. Poor economic planning has hurt the economies of the region. It is still the poorest region in Europe today. After the breakup of Yugoslavia, many of the countries that had been a part of this country faced violent ethnic and religious conflicts. These conflicts led to **ethnic cleansing** in some areas. In 1995 troops from all over the world came to Bosnia and Herzegovina to help end the fighting.

> **What caused the violence in the Balkans after Yugoslavia broke apart? What stopped the fighting?**
> _____
> _____
> _____

Seven of the Balkan countries were once part of the former Yugoslavia. Macedonia and Slovenia were the first to break away. When Croatia broke away, fighting started between ethnic Croats and Serbs. Peace did not return until many Serbs left Croatia. Bosnia and Herzegovina also had terrible ethnic fighting. Serbia, the largest country to emerge from the former Yugoslavia, also saw terrible fighting. Both Montenegro and Kosovo separated from Serbia.

The Balkans includes three other countries. Albania and Romania are poor and have serious economic and political problems. Bulgaria has a strong economy based on industry and tourism.

CHALLENGE ACTIVITY

Critical Thinking: Predicting Write a paragraph that explains how ethnic diversity could be an advantage for the Balkan countries in the future.

Balkans	ethnic cleansing	implications
Mostar	Orthodox	Roma
Slavic	Soviet Union	Yugoslavia

DIRECTIONS Look at each set of terms following each number. On the line provided, write the letter of the term that does not relate to the others.

_____ 1. a. Protestant   b. Orthodox   c. Catholic   d. Slavic

_____ 2. a. World War I   b. Serbia   c. Germanic   d. Austro-Hungarians

_____ 3. a. Albania   b. Hungary   c. Croatia   d. Slovenia

_____ 4. a. Macedonia   b. Yugoslavia   c. violence   d. ethnic cleansing

_____ 5. a. Roma   b. Greeks   c. Romans   d. Ottomans

DIRECTIONS Choose at least three of the terms from the word bank. On a separate sheet of paper, use these words to write a summary of what you learned in Section 4.

Name _____ Class _____ Date _____

Russia and the Caucasus

 MAIN IDEAS

1. The physical features of Russia and the Caucasus include plains, mountains, and rivers.
2. Climate and plant life change from north to south in Russia and vary in the Caucasus.
3. Russia and the Caucasus have a wealth of resources, but many are hard to access.

Key Terms and Places

Ural Mountains mountain range where Europe and Asia meet

Caspian Sea the world's largest inland sea, borders the Caucasus Mountains

Caucasus Mountains mountain range which forms the Caucasus region's northern border with Russia

Moscow Russia's capital

Siberia a vast region in Russia, stretching from the Urals to the Pacific Ocean

Volga River the longest river in Europe, located in western Russia

taiga a forest of mainly evergreen trees covering much of Russia

Section Summary

PHYSICAL FEATURES

The continents of Asia and Europe meet in Russia's **Ural Mountains**. Together, Asia and Europe form the large landmass of Eurasia. A large part of Eurasia is Russia, the world's largest country in area.

Three much smaller countries, Georgia, Armenia, and Azerbaijan, lie to the south in an area called the Caucasus. This area, which lies between the Black Sea and the **Caspian Sea**, is named for the **Caucasus Mountains**.

Plains and mountains cover much of Russia and the Caucasus. The fertile Northern European Plain, Russia's heartland, extends across western Russia. Here lies **Moscow**, Russia's capital.

> **Which two continents meet in the Ural Mountains?**
> _____
> _____

> **What three countries make up the Caucasus?**
> _____
> _____
> _____

> **What is the capital of Russia?**
> _____

Beyond this plain, the vast region of **Siberia** stretches from the Ural Mountains to the Pacific Ocean. The West Siberian Plain is a huge, flat, marshy area. East of this plain lies the Central Siberian Plateau. High mountain ranges run through southern and eastern Siberia. Eastern Siberia is called the Russian Far East, which includes the Kamchatka Peninsula and several islands. This area is part of the Ring of Fire, known for its earthquakes and active volcanoes.

The Caucasus countries consist mainly of rugged uplands. The Caucasus Mountains contain Europe's highest peak, Mount Elbrus.

Rivers in Russia include the Ob, Yenisey, Lena, and **Volga**, the longest river in Europe. Russia also has some 200,000 lakes, including Lake Baikal, the world's deepest lake. The Black Sea connects to the Mediterranean Sea and is important for trade. The Caspian Sea is the world's largest inland sea.

> **What is the Ring of Fire?**
> _____
> _____

> **What is the longest river in Europe?**
> _____

CLIMATE AND PLANT LIFE

Russia is mainly cold, with short summers and long, snowy winters. Plant life includes small plants in the north and the vast **taiga**, a forest of mainly evergreen trees. Climate in the Caucasus ranges from cooler in the uplands to warm and wet along the Black Sea to mainly hot and dry in Azerbaijan.

NATURAL RESOURCES

Russia and the Caucasus have a wealth of natural resources, including rich soils, timber, metals, precious gems, and energy resources. These resources have been poorly managed, however, and many remaining resources lie in remote Siberia.

> **What are the region's natural resources?**
> _____
> _____

CHALLENGE ACTIVITY

Critical Thinking: Making Generalizations Based on what you've read so far, write a short essay about what it might be like to live in Russia.

Caspian Sea	Caucasus Mountains	Moscow
Siberia	taiga	Ural Mountains
Volga River	steppe	

DIRECTIONS Read each sentence and fill in the blank with the word in the word pair that best completes the sentence.

1. The _____ form the northern border between the Causcasus region and Russia. (Caucasus Mountains/Ural Mountains)

2. It is in the _____ that the continents of Europe and Asia meet. (Caucasus Mountains/Ural Mountains)

3. The _____ provides an important transportation route through Russia. (Caspian Sea/Volga River)

4. The _____'s rich, black soil has made it Russia's main farming area. (steppe/taiga)

5. _____ is a cold, empty land of barren plains and endless forests. (Siberia/Moscow)

DIRECTIONS Choose four of the terms from the word bank. On a separate sheet of paper, use these words to write a story or poem that relates to the section.

Russia and the Caucasus

MAIN IDEAS
1. The Russian empire grew under powerful leaders, but unrest and war led to its end.
2. The Soviet Union emerged as a Communist superpower with rigid government control.
3. Russia's history and diversity have influenced its culture.

Key Terms and Places

Kiev early center of Russia, now the capital of Ukraine

Cyrillic a form of the Greek alphabet

czar emperor

Bolsheviks Communist group that seized power during the Russian Revolution

gulags Soviet labor camps

Section Summary

THE RUSSIAN EMPIRE

In the AD 800s, Viking traders from Scandinavia helped create the first Russian state of Kievan among the Slavs. Kievan was centered around the city of **Kiev**, now the capital of Ukraine.

Over time, missionaries introduced Orthodox Christianity and **Cyrillic**, a form of the Greek alphabet which Russians still use today.

In the 1200s, Mongol invaders called Tatars conquered Kiev. Local Russian princes ruled several states under the Mongols. Muscovy became the strongest state, with Moscow its main city. After about 200 years Muscovy's prince, Ivan III, seized control from the Mongols. Then in the 1540s, his grandson Ivan IV crowned himself **czar**, or emperor. He became known as Ivan the Terrible for being a cruel and savage ruler.

Muscovy developed into the country of Russia. Peter the Great and then Catherine the Great ruled as czars, building a huge empire and world power.

> **What is Cyrillic?**
> _____
> _____

> **What name was Ivan IV given for being such a cruel and savage ruler?**
> _____
> _____

Section 2, *continued*

Unrest, war, and other problems weakened the Russian empire. In 1917, the czar lost support and was forced to give up the throne. The **Bolsheviks**, a Russian Communist group, seized power in the Russian Revolution. Bolshevik leaders formed the Soviet Union in 1922.

What was the name of the Russian Communist group that seized power during the Russian Revolution?
_____
_____

THE SOVIET UNION

The Soviet Union became a Communist country, led by Vladimir Lenin. In this political system, the government controls all aspects of life and owns all property. After Lenin's death in 1924, Joseph Stalin ruled as a brutal dictator. He set up a command economy. The government made all economic decisions, took over all industries and farms, and strictly controlled its people. Anyone who spoke out against the government was sent to **gulags**, harsh Soviet labor camps often located in Siberia.

Who was the first leader of the Soviet Union when it became a Communist country?
_____
_____

After suffering many losses in World War II, Stalin worked to create a protective buffer around the Soviet Union. He set up Communist governments in Eastern Europe. As a result, the Cold War, a period of tense rivalry and arms race between the United States and the Soviet Union, developed. The Soviet Union grew weak in the 1980s, and then it fell apart in 1991.

What was the Cold War?
_____
_____

CULTURE

More than 140 million people live in Russia. Most are ethnic Russians, or Slavs, but Russia also has many other ethnic groups. The main faith is Russian Orthodox Christian. Russia has made many contributions to the arts and sciences, including ballet and space research.

How many people live in Russia today?
_____
_____

CHALLENGE ACTIVITY

Critical Thinking: Drawing Inferences What do you think Russia would be like today if the Soviet Union had not collapsed? Give support for your answer.

Guided Reading Workbook

Bolsheviks	Cold War	communism
Cyrillic	czar	gulags
Kiev	propaganda	reaction

DIRECTIONS Look at each set of four terms. On the line provided,
write the letter of the term that does not relate to the others.

_____ 1. a. Cyrillic   b. Stalin   c. communism   d. gulags

_____ 2. a. Cold War   b. weapons   c. Bolsheviks   d. arms race

_____ 3. a. communism   b. propaganda   c. Soviet Union   d. czar

_____ 4. a. Vikings   b. Bolsheviks   c. Kiev   d. Rus

_____ 5. a. Ivan IV   b. czar   c. Catherine the Great   d. Kiev

DIRECTIONS Choose five of the terms from the word bank. Use these
words to write a summary of what you learned in the section.

_____

_____

_____

_____

_____

_____

_____

_____

_____

_____

_____

Section 3

 MAIN IDEAS

1. The Russian Federation is working to develop democracy and a market economy.
2. Russia's physical geography, cities, and economy define its many culture regions.
3. Russia faces a number of serious challenges.

Key Terms and Places

dachas Russian country houses

St. Petersburg city founded by Peter the Great and styled after those of Western Europe

smelters factories that produce metal ores

Trans-Siberian Railroad the longest single rail line in the world, running from Moscow to Vladivostok on the east coast

Chechnya a Russian republic in the Caucasus Mountains, an area of ethnic conflict

Section Summary

THE RUSSIAN FEDERATION

The Russian Federation is governed by an elected president, an appointed prime minister, and a legislature called the Federal Assembly. Since 1991, Russia has been changing from communism to a democracy with a market economy based on free trade and competition. These changes have led to economic growth that is most visible today in Russia's cities. A wide range of goods and services can be found here. Most Russians live in large apartment buildings in cities, but they still enjoy nature. Cities often have large parks and many richer Russians own **dachas**, or country houses.

> **What is the Russian legislature called?**
>
> _____

CULTURE REGIONS

Four western culture regions—the Moscow, St. Petersburg, Volga, and Urals regions—make up Russia's heartland. These regions are home to the vast majority of Russia's people.

> **What are the four culture regions of Russia's heartland?**
>
> _____

Guided Reading Workbook

Moscow is Russia's capital and largest city. The Kremlin holds Russia's government offices, beautiful palaces, and gold-domed churches. Moscow is a huge industrial region.

Founded by Peter the Great, **St. Petersburg** was styled after cities of Western Europe and served as Russia's capital for some 200 years. Its location on the Gulf of Finland has made the city an important trade center.

Where is St. Petersburg located?
_____

The Volga River of the Volga region is a major shipping route and source of hydroelectric power. Factories here process oil and gas. The Caspian Sea provides black caviar.

Which river is a major shipping route in the Volga region?
_____

The Urals region is an important mining region. **Smelters**, or factories that process metal ores, process copper and iron.

Siberia, another of Russia's culture regions, is east of the Urals. Winters there are long and severe. Siberia has many natural resources, but accessing them is difficult. Lumber, mining, and oil production are the most important industries. Most towns follow the route of the **Trans-Siberian Railroad**, the longest single rail line in the world.

What are winters like in Siberia?
_____

What is notable about the Trans-Siberian Railroad?
_____
_____

Siberia's coastal areas and islands are known as the Russian Far East. This culture region's resources include timber, rich soils, oil, minerals, and fishing. Vladivostock is the region's main seaport.

RUSSIA'S CHALLENGES

Russia faces economic, employment, health, population, environmental, and ethnic challenges. A major ethnic conflict is in the Russian republic of Chechnya, where some people desire independence.

CHALLENGE ACTIVITY

Critical Thinking: Drawing Inferences Based on what you've learned about each region, which area do you think holds the most potential economically for Russia? Why?

| Chechnya | smelters | dachas |
| St. Petersburg | Sea of Okhotsk | Trans-Siberian Railroad |

DIRECTIONS Read each sentence and fill in the blank with the word in the word pair that best completes the sentence.

1. Located on the Gulf of Finland, _____ has been called the Venice of the North for its many canals. (Chechnya/St. Petersburg)

2. In the Ural Mountains, factories called _____ process the copper and iron that is mined in the region. (dachas/smelters)

DIRECTIONS On the line provided before each statement, write **T** if a statement is true and **F** if a statement is false. If the statement is false, write the correct term from the word bank on the line after each sentence that makes the sentence a true statement.

_____ 3. Cities and towns in Siberia are mostly located near the <u>Sea of Okhotsk</u>.

_____

_____ 4. Wealthy Russians go to their <u>dachas</u> to enjoy outdoor activities.

_____

_____ 5. Ethnic conflict is responsible for fighting in <u>St. Petersburg</u>.

_____

Russia and the Caucasus

MAIN IDEAS

1. Many groups have ruled and influenced the Caucasus during its long history.
2. Today the Caucasus republics are working to improve their economies but struggle with ethnic unrest and conflict.

Key Places

Tbilisi the capital of Georgia

Yerevan the capital of Armenia

Baku the capital of Azerbaijan, center of a large oil-refining industry

Section Summary

HISTORY

The Caucasus lies in the Caucasus Mountains between the Black and Caspian seas. The region reflects a range of cultural influences and at one time or another has been ruled or invaded by Persians, Greeks, Romans, Arabs, Turks, Mongols, and Russians.

In the early 1800s, Russia took over much of the Caucasus, but the Ottoman Turks held western Armenia. Before and during World War I, hundreds of thousands of Armenians were killed by the Turks. After the war, Armenia, Azerbaijan, and Georgia were independent, but became part of the Soviet Union in 1922. They regained independence when the Soviet Union fell in 1991.

> Which groups have ruled or invaded the Caucasus?
>
> _____
>
> _____

THE CAUCASUS TODAY

Although the region has a long history, the Caucasus countries have had to create new governments and economies. Progress has been slowed by ethnic unrest and conflicts. Each country's government has an elected president, an appointed prime minister, and an elected parliament, or legislature.

Georgia is located between the Caucasus Mountains and the Black Sea. **Tbilisi** is the capital. About 70 percent of the people are ethnic Georgians and belong to the Georgian Orthodox Church. Georgian is the official language.

Georgia has struggled with unrest and civil war. Georgians forced out their president in 2003.

Georgia's economy is based on services and farming. Other industries include steel, mining, wine, and tourism.

Armenia is a small, landlocked country south of Georgia. **Yerevan** is the capital. Most of the people are Armenian and belong to the Armenian Orthodox Church.

Armenia fought a war with Azerbaijan in the early 1990s. The war involved an ethnic Armenian area of Azerbaijan that is still controlled by Armenian forces today. This conflict has hurt Armenia's economy, but international aid is helping.

Azerbaijan is east of Armenia and borders the Caspian Sea. The Azeri make up 90 percent of the population and are mostly Muslim. Oil is the most important part of the economy. **Baku**, the capital, is the center of this industry. Problems include corruption, poverty, and refugees as a result of the conflict with Armenia.

What are Georgia's main industries?   _____   _____

What country was Armenia at war with in the early 1990s?   _____

What is the most important part of Azerbaijan's economy?   _____

CHALLENGE ACTIVITY
Critical Thinking: Compare and Contrast
Describe the similarities and differences between the Caucasus countries.

Guided Reading Workbook

| agrarian | Armenia | Azerbaijan | Baku |
| Black Sea | Caspian Sea | Tbilisi | Yerevan |

DIRECTIONS Write three words or phrases that describe each term.

1. agrarian _____

2. Baku _____

DIRECTIONS Read each sentence and fill in the blank with the word in the word pair that best completes the sentence.

3. The capital of Armenia is _____. (Baku/Yerevan)

4. _____ is the capital of Georgia. (Yerevan/Tbilisi)

5. Oil is the most important part of _____'s economy. (Armenia/Azerbaijan)

6. After World War I, _____, Azerbaijan, and Georgia became part of the Soviet Union. (Chechnya/Armenia)

7. The _____ draws tourists to Georgia each year. (Caspian Sea/Black Sea)

DIRECTIONS On a separate sheet of paper, write two or three paragraphs describing what a person who is about to visit the Caucasus might see. Include at least five terms from the word bank in your paragraphs.

CURRICULUM MATERIALS
BALDWIN WALLACE UNIVERSITY